T0130516

THE PERILS OF ONE FROM ROCK COCAINE IN AMERICA

RONALD BACY

authorHOUSE®

AuthorHouse™
1663 Liberty Drive
Bloomington, IN 47403
www.authorhouse.com
Phone: 1 (800) 839-8640

Published by AuthorHouse 11/21/2015

ISBN: 978-1-5049-6350-3 (sc)
ISBN: 978-1-5049-6349-7 (hc)
ISBN: 978-1-5049-6348-0 (e)

Library of Congress Control Number: 2015919112

Print information available on the last page.

This book is printed on acid-free paper.

INTRODUCTION

The story of this book reveals the explicit escapades of a Black American male enduring the hardships of life caused by his excessive indulgence in rock cocaine.

From an ambitious pursuit of success, and a good life after graduating from high school; to the introduction through an associate of cocaine in powder form, from there on into selling it in powder, and finally ending up both selling, and using it in rock form.

His unusual confrontations from drug dealers, encounters with the law, the frivolous contacts with stray people for the purpose of acquiring more currency to support his addiction, the manipulation of vulnerable prospects, the hustling, the stealing, and lying; all of the attributes that would eventually either bring an end to his life, or land him in prison.

In this story there are also other related analogies of persons directly, or indirectly involved with the main character of this book, all of which give a vivid description of the fallible missions conjured up by his consumption, and involvement with rock cocaine.

The names of the people in this book are ficticious so as to prevent any form of incrimination against any one person, or persons; however, some of the locations and places are actually real.

I hope my audience will be able to extrapulate the realities of how significant this drug can completely devour a human being morals, self esteem, ethics, and finally their life.

The incidents in this story are actual tribulations to the testimony of the events that led up to the main characters imprisonment, eventual understanding of the perils caused by rock cocaine, a revelation of the power structure in America and their will-full endorsement of rock cocaine to be administered into the black communities in this Country as a tool to impoverish the people with.

This rock cocaine is a devilish substance and I hope that the impact of the message in this book will serve to deter any, and everyone away from ever thinking of trying this drug.

I also hope that the readers of my book will find it's contents beneficial to them in one way or another, furthermore, I hope that the material in this book will either prevent any would be curiosity seekers from ever trying this substance, and/or help any current users to reconsider their destiny if they continue using this wicked substance.

The book is dedicated to the many Black American men and women in the United States, and abroad whom have become victims to the rock cocaine plague in the Black communities across the Country.

This plague was designed and placed at the disposal of Black people Nationally, as a tool of destruction to African American's in an attempt to aide the Nations ruling class, and their counterparts; the authorities in their conspiratorial impingement of the Black male in America, and as a means of stifling the reproduction of the Black family from becoming a reconcilable race of people in this Country.

Rock cocaine is a drug of modern times, my overall feelings is that the Nations ruling class(power structure), behind cabal conferences, engendered a destructive ingredient (by product), unified this product through experimental procedures with cocaine, which in effect debilitates one after using the substance.

Then in turn administered the distribution of this product into the main stream of Black communities to confound the existence of Blacks in America.

The end product of powder cocaine is rock cocaine, which consist of precarious unknown additives; it's lure after using it one time is both addictive and pernicious.

It is my belief that this substance is a result of covert experiments by our Government, and was intentionally designed as a catalyst to human impoverishment; to restrict, inhibit, and keep stagnant a race of people who's inherent nature is to be progressive in all facets of life by leading and exceeding excellence.

Strategically, the Black American is in an imposition as a consequence if this nefarious instrument of the devils, in all actuality the real sacrificial lamb, so to speak is the many Black Americans whom are addicted in the ghettos around the Nation.

We are slowly being subjugated, primarily by the captivating force of this rock cocaine,nontheless, by the local, state, and federal authorities as well.

Unless the Black American people open their eyes and discover the hidden element of modern day enslavement that has been thrust upon them through their use, abuse, and affiliation with this rock cocaine, the Black American as a free human being in society will come to an end.

Through the Black on Black homicides, imprisonment, separation from our women and children; we(the Black male) will no longer be a prominent role model for our younger Black males; which will inevitably began the process of extinction of the Black American race.

To the Black people of this Country of America, the time was yesterday for you to become aware of the futile consequences of this rock cocaine that has been set out there for you.

As long as you have your freedom, and sanity, it's never to late for one to refrain from using this substance that renders you vulnerable to the many injustices that prey upon your vulnerabilities while your under the influence of that drug.

Break free from this modern day tool of enslavement while there's still time for you to do so.

MAY GOD BE WITH YOU

PROLOGUE

I can personally attest to this fall from grace behind rock cocaine addiction, the behavior I exhibited once I began smoking rock cocaine was way out of character for me.

My personality dramatically changed; where I was a good hearted and humane individual normally, after my rock cocaine addiction took hold of me I became cunning, irresponsible, and inconsiderate to the feelings of loved ones and people in general.

I emphasize this differentiation of character of myself to exemplify the anomalous transformation I underwent as a rock cocaine addict that was brought about by this substance.

The rock cocaine plague in America has taken a heavy toll on Black Americans to date, it is my belief that the substance is the culprit for the advent of young Black female prostitution, Black male homosexuality, unprecedented Black on Black homocides, an increased rate of both loss of employment, loss of trust within the family circle, the rise of hideous crimes committed by Blacks, the imposition of both unjust, and lengthy incarcerations from the judicial system, deaths, caused by overdosing of the substance, and I could go on, but you get my point.

My synopsis of what's taken place is that the power structure in America mechanized this outcome, beginning with the conspiratorial eliminations of our Countries opened minded, and strong leaders; both of the president Kennedy brothers, Dr. Martin Luther King jr., and Malcolm X.

I truly feel that the power structure in this Country were directly involved with the elimination of those prominent men, with the intent being to pave the way for continued white male dominance in America.

The martyr's mentioned above were all advocates of peace, and equality for everyone, and the demise of these men left Black people, and other minorities stagnant and leaderless with no sense of hope; and more vulnerable to the unjust wraths of the white male dictatorship in America.

It is a methodical process known as kill the head and the body will follow, now what we have in this Country is Black official tokenism; or Jim Crows' if you will, where by as long as them and their families are out of harms way, and prospering, they'll be in accord with, and/ or condone the mistreatment and destruction of their own race of people.

What I see happening in America is silent hardcore racism, and prejudice almost in the realm of the slave era, but more in a modern day clandestine mode of operation.

Any act of criminal activity should be punished by the laws, but there should not be a stigma that targets Blacks, as opposed to any other ethnicity, everyone should receive their due punishment for their crimes.

However, rock cocaine trafficking of any kind has prompted the judicial system in America to run rampant with unjust sentencing guidelines, and imprisonment of Blacks into what I call modern day slave plantations.(prisons), in this Country.

What disturbs me most behind all of this is that the justice system is imprisoning otherwise decent minded law abiding Black people as a result of their rock cocaine addiction.

The Blacks, or any ethnicity whom commit serious criminal offenses such as drive by shootings, strong arming vehicles, rapes, murders, etc, should be imprisoned, but for being caught with a couple of pieces of rock cocaine for personal use and be sentenced to prison time, this is a travesty.

Rock cocaine trafficking by blacks in America has led the power structure in this Country to suspect, and disrepect Black people as a whole, regardless of their status.

There's evidence of this everywhere, police automatically suspect the Black man when a crime has been committed, we are discriminated against in employment, housing, financial loans, and in nearly all facets of life.

Through this outright blatant disrespect that the system has embarked upon towards the Black race, I'd like to elaborate further in detail of where, and how one may see evidence of this in America.

There was a young woman whom was in the media light early to mid 1990's debating an issue with then President Bill Clinton.

The issue under discussion was relative to Blacks in America, her street name was sister soldier, and she called the plight of Black people in this Country the way she saw it, and was right on many of her views.

One insight of hers was that the White man fears and dispises the Black man, yet, mimics, and tries to emulate his every move, all the while lusting after the Black woman.

This is quite true, and evident as it is depicted on Television, in movies, soap operas, commercials, cartoons, and any means they can use to project this.

The television is in many ways a tool of deception, one of the popular uses that the T.V. syndication relies heavily on is the art of delusion, and the main intention of this is to program it's viewers into believing that what their seeing is reality, and in most cases it is not.

The White mans vision of creating this union of himself and the Black woman on T.V. programs is sublimely having an impact upon it's viewers, counting on this as a reality that will eventually plant itself, and come to pass.

Singer Bobby Brown was upset at the making, and filming of his wife Whitney Houston's movie the body guard because of the depiction, and message it was sending out to the public, Black woman, white man.

If one reads between the lines, the title of the movie itself is significant not as a guarding of her body from anything in particular, but rather, a guarding of her from her own natural counterpart; the Black man.

Unbeknownst to the public, that was the subliminal message that was being sent out to the viewers.

The subtleness of that message is displayed yet again in another movie that was released, waiting to exhale, but this was with a diffirent twist to it; kind of like a showing of where the Black woman is tired of the Black man, and is holding her breath waiting on him to improve himself, or she'll start considering on dating other ethnics.

I saw that movie as a bashing, and critiquing of the Black man in relationships with the Black woman, and goes on to prompt the Black woman to contemplate her union with the Black man in the future.

These kind of scenes being played out on National T.V. puts the thought in the Black woman's mind that they no longer need the Black man, and in turn opens the door for the White man to cater to her needs, this is called, divide and conquer.

It's questionable as to whether the intent behind this scheme is to stifle the reproduction of the Black family, the Black man and Black woman union, or to coax the Black woman into fulfilling their plan of miscegenation.

In conclusion to this Introductory chapter I'd like to go back to the sister soldier debate with the President in office then Bill Clinton.

She had discovered and recognized the White mans genocidal conspiracy against Blacks in America and was speaking out about it on National T.V., mysteriously though, she was somehow silenced after that airing because you've never heard anything from her after that.

This calls one to speculate on the possibility that the power structure in America is in fact conspiring against the Black race of people, and this is where rock cocaine play's it's role in all of the scheme of things.

Trafficking in, and/or using rock cocaine will, one, dull your senses, and keep you out of focus of what's going on around you; secondly, you subject yourself to the authorities which could ultimately take away your freedom by sending you to one of their modern day slave plantations(prisons).

I remember reading an article in some newspaper a few years back where the authorities of all branches around the Country met annually in secret, this club was for White cops only; no Black cops were allowed.

Their main topic of discussion was applicable ways to bring down Black people, if I'm not mistaken the name of their organization was called the good ol boys round up club.

Their mode of operation was to shoot first and ask questions later when it came to dealing with Blacks on the streets of this Country of America.

I appeal to the readers of this book in hopes that you'll come to understand that the purpose of this book is to reveal the underhandedness of this Countries power structure towards Blacks, and minorities, and to reveal to the masses that drugs in their life should be a thing of the past, because that's the means by which this system in America is going to destroy you by.

So people of this Country just stay on guard against what the power structue in America is capable of orchestrating right in front of your eyes, and you'll have the upper hand in your future, in this Country.

GOD BLESS YOU ALL

THE GRACE PERIOD

Cocaine once signified the glamorous life in the way that it attracted power, wealth, and prestige, some would think however, to the contrary, that in it's neo form rock cocaine, it brings about impoverishment, weakness, subjugation to the authorities and homicidal tendencies.

The cocoa plant, a natural resource created by our GOD for humanitarian purposes, has ended up in the hands of some of the devils disciples(cynic men) here on earth, and have caused havoc on African Americans in astronomical proportions.

Most of the chaos that has developed over the past couple of decades among black Americans are attributes of the negative influence that the rock cocaine has had in their life.

Rock cocaine causes such a disastrous influence of bad behavior that it encompasses' a host of consequential misdeeds as a result of it's influence.

My name is Siege Black, I am a California born black American and I'm about to reveal to you the many painful, judicial injustices, and the unfortunate hardships that befell me due to this rock cocaine plague.

By nature I'm a kind hearted, compassionate, and humanly considerate type of an individual, always ready to extend a helping hand whenever I could to a stranger.

I displayed a divine good will towards human beings, never entertaining the idea or intent of ill will, or malicious behavior in my heart towards anyone or anything.

For the record, I was a classy character with good morals; I was also energetic and out going, a quality that made me susceptible of being liked by many, as was I socially active in the community.

Being this type of an individual brought me into contact with many different kinds of temptations that the devil puts before one, and there was one that was to great for me to ignore: it was rock cocaine.

Once I was exposed to it there would be no immediate recourse of action for a solution to the hardships, anguish, and injustices that I would encounter.

Being in control of my life's destiny was relatively easy for me up until that point in my life, I didn't feel that I had an addictive personality, and most everything that would present itself as a detriment to me, I would conquer it.

Rock cocaine proved to overpower this innate will of mine, and, at the onset of it, and for more than two decades following, it would lead me on a merry-go-round of hardships, and daring missions where unpredictable endings lurked.

I wasn't aware of rock cocaines obscured element of destruction that using the substance entailed, what started out as recreational use, escalated into a monstrous long term nightmare of living hell for me.

Before I would begin to take notice of my state of being, it would be hard of breaking free from the abyss of rock cocaine use; tough experience was going to become my best mentor.

From one phase to the next, in what would be a snowball effect, I'd learn that I was challenging the devil with his own powerful weapon, the rock cocaine, and I could never win, not on his terms anyway.

I would however, continue to sometimes outwit the snares that the devil had set for me when I smoked the substance until my will to outwit him finally left me and I became destitute.

Mr. and Mrs. Black. together did a swell job of raising me and my other siblings, this was reflective in our mannerisms, however, my parents separated just before I was to graduate from high school.

Mr. Blacks' nerves worsened as he got older, coupled with an alcohol addiction, made it unbearable for my mother to continue living around him.

My father still oversaw family matters, came around on holidays, his kids birthdays, and other special gatherings to show that he was still the man of our family.

His austere personality still held weight among us kids and mother alike, although it was remote, nevertheless, he was proud of the way most of his kids turned out in life.

Me especially because I, of all of the sons was the one whom not only resembled him, but also had his ingenuity on matters in life, but my dad begin to lose hope in me after my addiction to the rock cocaine got hold of me; he felt I was on a capricious and destructive course.

I was a relatively charming young man, brought up in a middle class neighborhood of Sacramento, Ca., I was reared by a caring and nurturing mother; but at the same time by a no-nonesense and demanding father.

I was a popular kind of person with a lot of acquaintances, was a fairly educated and inteligent individual always in pursuit of greater feats to accomplish; all the while striving for perfection in everything that I did.

I participated in sports, particularly basketball; I loved the one on one challenges propositioned me almost every day after school in the gym by another school mate, a white guy, and friend named A.J., he played a good game of ball, and loved the rivalry between us on the court, we shared back and forth victories at a game called 21.

I was in my senior year at Luther Burbank high school, it was March of 75, and the class of that year was preparing themselves for their entrance into society with what all of the younger years of academics had trained them for, I'd decided that college was an ideal plan for me to enhance my knowledge for the greater things that this life had to offer.

Graduation ceremony came and left, giving me my certificate of diplomacy.

I had a V.W. that I'd bought with money saved from working in Luther Burbanks cafeteria as a stock and store worker while attending school, summertime was fun, but it came and went fast.

In the Fall of 75 I enrolled at Consumer River college and majored in Sociology, my underlining classes were English 1A, African American history, and a boxing class to keep fit.

While attending Consumer River college I would occaisionally stop by the bulletin board there in the financial aide office to see what jobs they had listed on the board.

One day I noticed that the campus mail room had a position open for a printing press operator, duties consisted of sorting mail and assisting staff at the over the counter service booth, while of course running the press.

I went through the appropriate channels of staff to find out about the qualifications required, and filled out an application for the position.

A few weeks went by before I was called into the mail room and interviewed, I had no experience with operating a printing press, however,

I must have been convincing at selling myself to the interviewer because the next week I had the job.

I thanked GOD, everything was going good for me, my grades were decent, I was working, and at the same time obtaining the knowledge I needed for a better life for my future. One night I decided I would go out partying, so I dressed myself in trendy clothing and went to a gathering for students from local colleges around the greater Sacramento area.

I was solo, yet I knew a small percentage of the people there; I drank a little, but mostly satyed to myself.

Looking around, I noticed a young lady that throuhout the evening at that gathering seemed to be by herself.

She was looking nice, and after a while I gradually built up the nerves to approach her and introduce myself, she retorted," I'm Mary."

I then asked her if she'd like to dance and we went to the dance floor, after the music ended, we sat, conversed a little and got better acquainted.

I felt comfortable talking with her, and learned a little later that we both had some things in common; we were both single, and working while going to college.

As we casually drank some wine, Mary told me that she had to leave, so I escorted her to her vehicle, afterwards I went back inside and stayed a little while longer, but meeting her made me realize that I'd accomplished what I set out to do, it being done, I left the scene.

It was Monday which meant the start of the weekly routine of my academic itinerary, I'd been performing my duties as a printing press operator proficiently with regular praises from my supervisor, moreover, I began to enjoy that profession and had decided that this field of work was something that I could really become content with doing as a life long career.

In addition to running the presses, I ran errands around the campus grounds, answered phones, and assisted staff with over the counter printing job orders; I loved the job. After school one day I got the urge to stop by the unemployment office to see what they had posted on the bulletin board in the printing press field. I was scanning the job listings and came across a couple of jobs in that field of work, so I wrote down the pertinent info and stood in line to inquire about them.

I was called out by an employment counselor, we sat down and discussed the job sites, and the qualifications for those positions; I became anxious.

She then called those companies and set up interviews, I went to them, and after each interview I thought that I had sold myself well, and was satisfied.

I waited a couple of weeks, but heard nothing from either of the companies, so I called them; one position had been filled, and the reply from the other one was that I wasn't experiencd enough for the position.

The week following from that discouraging let down, I went back to the unemployment office, this time I didn't see any jobs in that field, but I did see something else that interested me; it was a meter reading position for the prestigious Sacramento Electric Company;(S.E.C.).

The requirements for the position were contingent upon one being enrolled in college, and to work hours around their class schedules, and of course work full time in the summer; the prerequisite for the job was to stay enrolled, and attend college while working for the Co. part time.

I aced the interview, and while driving home I begin thinking back to when I was a kid and would ride by that colorful utility building off of I-50 and the 65th street expressway in the car with my parents; I'd say to myself that one day Im going to work there.

GOD is such a gracious provider, because he was making my vision from the past become a reality in my future, and I thanked him for it. I got home, tired from the days events, laid down to take a nap and ended up falling fast asleep.

The next few days I studied hard at school, went to my boxing class, sparred a little with some of my class mates, and didn't give much thought about the meter reading interview. The weekend came; on weekends I passed the time by washing my car and socializing with friends to wind down from the previous week, however another week was to begin, and I would follow my normal itinerary of classes, and tending to the mail room duties.

As that day came to an end I walked to my car in the campus parking lot, got in, and headed home, when I got home my mother mentioned that a Mr. Juan from the Sacramento Electric Co.'s meter reading Dept. called for me, left his phone#, and wanted me to return his call, she happily said.

I was expecting a disappointment, but at the same time a feeling of exultation was running through me at having received the call.

I picked up the phone and begin dialing the number my mother had written down for me, after three rings a voice came on the other end of the line revealing his name and Dept.

"Siege, I have some good news for you, human resources have selected you for the position, and we'd like for you to come into the Dept. for further details of preparing you to start work next week, congratulations Mr. Black". Mr. Juan and I finalized all of the other necessary arrangements over the phone and ended the conversation, elated that I had just landed a prestigious position at a prominent Co. in Sacramento, it was time to celebrate.

I called Mary, "hey guess what?"

"What?"

"You remember I told you I applied for that job at S.E.C."

"Yes."

"Well they hired me, Listen I'm excited about it and was hoping you'd like to share my exhilaration with me over a drink somewhere," I asked excitedly.

"Of course, I'd be honored," she responded in a delightful voice.

We went to Browns Paradise lounge and happy hour, conversed on plans of how we could enjoy a good life together, then toasted to a new beginning with one another. I went over to the utility Co. on Tuesday, went through the orientation for new employees', was given several uniforms, and told to start work on Monday.

On Wednesday I had to work in the mail room on the college campus after my class, that was when I gave notice to my present supervisor. She was a little indignant at the news of my leaving the mail room because I was a model worker there, but at the same time was happy for me of beginning work with such a big company.

My life was excelling in all directions, I was nearing the end of the semester; with good grades, a lucrative place of employment, and feeling like the whole world was within my grasp. I envisioned myself purchasing a brand new luxury automobile, and over the course of the next three months, the for sale sign I'd had on my Voltswagon bug,brought me in a sum of $1,500.00 when I sold it. I used that money as a down payment on a new 1978 Dodge Diplomat coupe.

I was enjoying life, traveling to other cities in California on weekends, buying clothes, meeting good people and giving the Lord his time on Sundays; the farthest thing from my mind was drugs. I was the epitome of my peers, life couldn't have been any better to me at that point and time.

As I financially progressed Mary brought up the idea of us living together, I really wanted to live by the laws of GOD and wait until I was ready for marriage; which I wasn't. Reluctantly, I decided for it, and we moved together; we worked endlessly at renovating her deceased mothers place which hadn't been occupied in over a year, it needed plumbing repairs in the toilet, plus lots of rubble needed to be hauled away.

As time passed on, Mary became pregnant, I was happy at the prospect of becoming a father, but was not in the market for becoming a husband, which was what she wanted. We quarreled about this on a regular basis, I had began to suspect that Mary was pushing the idea of marriage onto me as a result of her being pregnant, and my having employment with such a reputable utility Co. in Sacramento.

This caused problems in our relationship, which eventually would lead to a separation between us, when the separation finally came to pass I moved back home to my mothers, but in doing so felt as though I had deserted my obligations as a mate.

But on the other hand, me, unlike many other men whom would marry under pressure, decided I wasn't ready to take on such a commitment.

Feeling the anxiety setting in from the guilt of my actions, I begin to drink more than usual,and drinking, a high percentage of the time leads to the enticement of drug use and/or other ill fated endeavors brought about by peers.

One night I was hanging out with some friends in front of a liquor store called T.N.T., located in south Sacramento on florin rd. It was a place where the fellows congregated and passed the time talking and drinking, I knew everyone whom mostly frequented this hangout, as well as the store's owner.

There was an Asian employee working in there that evening as I went in to buy some alcohol; while standing at the refrigerated beer doors, the Asian came up to me and alleged that I had taken something, of which I had not.

An argument between us followed which prompted the Asian to strike me in the jaw, startled by this action I momentarily froze; seconds afterwards though I jumped into action and commenced to finishing up what he'd started. The fight was broken up by other employee's, I left the store, went home, and got set to go back up there and settle things up with this kid for his having struck me like that on the assumption that he felt I had stole something.

Telling my mother of what had just happened to me, and all the while preparing to go back up there, she gave me a good bit of advice.

"Son you need not to go back up there and add fuel to that fire, but rather call our family Attorney and get his input on whether or not if you can file a lawsuit against the stores owners", she advised.

The next day I went to our attorney, explained the incident to him and discovered that I had a solid lawsuit in the making.

After continuous pain in my jaw, I went to my Dr. and learned that my jaw had been broken during the fight, and had to get my mouth wired shut for the next three and a half months, mums became my way of communicating.

This was when cocaine started to become interesting to me, my associates and I begin to recreationally indulge in powder cocaine, it wasn't excessive use though, however, it gradually increased with each encounter.

Mary and I had reconciled and moved into an apartment together, I was a responsible parent, spending time with my son in an exemplary fashion.

I showered Siege II with lots of love, buying him toys, but my growing desire for cocaine kept me on the go, and I spent little time around the apartment, which caused Mary to start complaining about it.

With the addition of another mouth to feed I pondered with the idea of selling powder cocaine to generate more money for my new family.

I had become acquainted with the main supplier through a friend, and after careful consideration of all of the obstacles that I could be fronted with, I decided to put my plan into action. To start I bought a half of an ounce of powder cocaine and began packaging quarter grams that sold for $25.00.

I wasn't splurging with friends at this point, nor was I indulging myself, this side occupation that I undertook was strictly for increasing my currency for the prosperity of my family. My side business of selling cocaine began to expand in the way of clientele, as I was introduced to influential people whom were already into the fast lane of that lifestyle.

I was fulfilling my quest for extra income, but during my ascension to financial freedom, I felt myself vulnerable to the lower echelon of cocaine users, which were in the practice of freebasing cocaine. I wasn't familiar with this aspect of cocaine ingestion, nor had I even heard of it, this was all new to me.

One night I was called by an acquaintance and asked if I could deliver a half of a gram to him, I came to his aide, I'd known him since middle school days, but we'd never really socialized; his name was Gaines.

I would always deliver to him there after, primarily because he would purchase no less than $50.00. This went on for several months, one night I took him a package of cocaine.

"Say Siege, do you freebase cocaine?" He asked.

"No I don't," was my response, "what is freebasing anyway?"

He explained the process, then proceeded to give me a demonstration of how the rock formed substance is inhaled, held in for a while, then exhaled.

"Siege you've got to try this stuff man, the brain experiences a euphoria out of this world," he said exhaling the combustion of smoke, "would you like to try some of it?"

"I'm really not interested in that substance like that," I replied as I prepared to leave his place.

I went back home and thought about how unusual an encounter that was, I was witnessing first hand the creative way in which cocaine was now being consumed.

It was in the month of June and school was nearing it's end, I needed 5 semester units to complete my prerequisites required to receive my AA degree from a Jr. college, then transfer to Sac Cal State University where I could start out on a bachelors degree.

I worked through the summer at S.E.C. reading meters, and sold cocaine on the side in my free time.

September came and it was time to enroll back into college to finish up my semester units, but being caught up and involved in selling the cocaine, I did not enroll in school. I was emerged into the life of glamour, the money, women, and all that comes with it, and found that I had little time left now to enroll in college, moreover, to even have the time to study the class material.

As it was I still went to work, and that in itself left just enough time for me to be available to tend to my cocaine clientele. Nevertheless, the stipulations of my employment with S.E.C. was that I remain a student while working at the Co. I felt though, that because I had an excellent attendance record, coupled with an outstanding job performance status that I'd be an acception to the company policies and be assigned as a permanent employee. At work that next day, my boss, upon discovering that I no longer was enrolled and attending college that fall semester at C.R.C. called me into his office, closing the door behind us.

"Siege the conditions of your employment with us was that you stay enrolled in College, and I regret having to be the one to inform you that you are being terminated from the Co., my hands are tied on this matter."

"You're a superb worker; you could take the meter reading exam, and be put on a priority status of re-instatement rights in our Dept. when a permanent position comes open, if you'd like."

I was allowed to work for the rest of that week, that Friday was my last day, the exam test for that position wasn't due to be posted until the following summer.

I was now out of work, Mary was already complaining, now she would surely have a solid defense for her bickering at me.

My dealing cocaine was bad enough, losing my job just added fuel to the fire so to speak, feeling depressed and acting on impulse, I packed up all of my things around the apartment and moved back to my mother's house.

I assiduously stayed active in distributing my cocaine after losing my job.

My one client, Gaine's, that was a free-baser had increased his request to have packages delivered.

As freebasing began it's rampage upon and into the U.S. communities of blacks, the standard price of cocaine was $25.00 a quarter gram, this radically decreased, making the substance more easily available.

Now the dealers were selling pieces of cocaine rock for 5, 10 and 15 dollars to the users, I didn't pay much attention to this discrepancy at first, because it was all money, but later I would discern this to be the way that would lead to the demise of the black people in this Country of ours.

I did notice that Gaines was becoming more frequently short on his purchases when I delivered to him, I began to think that he was beginning to become more of a liability to me than an asset, and felt that the time was approaching when I would have to cut him off as a client.

One day I was deceived by him into bringing over a gram, which went for a hundred dollars, when I got to his place he only had $50.00 on him, I ended up selling him half of that package.

"Hey man why don't you have a sit down and try some of this rock with me!", feeling down behind the events that were unfolding in my life, I went along with his offer and watched closely as he prepared to mix the cocaine with baking soda, and a little water in a glass vile, after the mixing, then holding it over a flame that would solidify it into a solid rock form.

After finishing the task he chipped off a piece of the rock with a razor blade, put it on a glass pipe, took a lighter and began to melt the substance on the pipe.

He put his mouth up to the pipe with the flame burning at the other end of it, inhaled a stream of smoke flowing through the stem pipe, held in the combustion of smoke in his lungs as long as he could, then exhaled; I then noticed a change in his demeanor as something of desperation for more.

He then passed the pipe to me, chipped off another piece of the solid cocaine substance and placed it into the pipes bowl area.

He instructed me to inhale as soon as he begin to light and melt the rock in the pipes bowl.

He put the flame to the pipes bowl and I began to inhale, I took in as much of the combustible smoke as I could, held it in for a moment, then exhaled.

I did not feel, or notice any change in my natural being, but then, I didn't know what to expect because I had never smoked rock cocaine before.

I commented that I felt nothing and said that I had to leave, my not knowing what kind of a feeling to expect from the high created in me a lose of interest of ever trying the stuff again.

A few hours later I delivered another package to him, and again I was coerced into trying another hit, this made me realize the relentless tactics the devil uses to tempt mankind hear on this earth.

This time I watched his process of solidifying the powder into a rock form, he repeated the procedure exactly the same way he'd done earlier, and I stored that process into my brain. When he finished, he put a piece of the rock into the pipes bowl and passed it to me, once again I did exactly as I had before, still not anticipating anything extraordinary, but this time, to my surprise, after exhaling the smoke I felt sentient, as though I was floating on air. This supernatural kind of a feeling captivated me, I wasn't sure how to react to it, and indulged myself a second time.

After letting the effects of the intense head rush settle down, I regained my composure and left his place. I went home, and remembering the process by which he had earlier cooked the powder cocaine, I gathered the necessary tools and begin to mix the ingredients together to make the rock.

I was an amateur at this task but my mental recording of watching Gaines' method of making the rock form served me well in my attempt to solidify the powder into a rock form, because I successfully rocked a gram of the powder. I, however, after accomplishing this feat realized that I had no utensils with which to smoke the substance in, this in effect prompted me to have to make a run to the neighborhood drug paraphernalia store where they sold items for such practices.

I purchased a glass freebase pipe for $5.00 and returned home.

Inside my mothers garage I had all of the equipment needed for me to recapture that intense feeling of euphoria that I had experienced earlier at Gaines' apartment. Putting a piece of the cooked cocaine base unto the pipe and melting it, I inhaled an excessive amount of smoke, held it in for a moment, then exhaled, all the while anticipating that previous feeling of heightened awareness that I had gotten before.

Repeating this process over and over again I was unaware of how much time had lapsed by, moreover, of how much of the substance I had consumed. Reluctantly, I felt a compelling urge to reconviene on this mission once more to satisfy my senses all over again, and I did so.

After letting time put some distance between the act, and my desire for more, I settled back and fell fast asleep.

MY DESCEND FROM GRACE

This would be the beginning of the declination of my character, self esteem, morals, and the principles that I was accustomed to portraying in my life, and soon I would become my own best customer.

Occasionally I ran packages to Gaines, and would relish the pleasure of smoking rock cocaine with him, at times even splurging myself.

My profits from selling powder cocaine began to recess, and I was finding myself at times hustling, I mentioned to Gaines about the prospect of employment, because he was a construction worker at the State Capital's renovation project at that time.

"Man show up at the site in the morning and I'll give a good reference of you to the local Lathers union boss," was his reply. I needed to pay off my cars balance and become the owner of that vehicle, in addition to that I had a son to provide for, and was responsible for paying certain bills at my mothers house.

I reported to the work site that next morning, spoke with the union boss, and was given a chance to prove my worth as a viable asset working under the Lathers union. I had to buy my own tools, and was told that I would start out as an apprentice on the following Monday.

I was appreciative of Gaines for opening up the door of employment opportunity for me, and thanked him by stopping by his place after work and smoking a gram of my supply with him, I was truly grateful of him for what he had done for me.

Every day after work I would encapsulate myself off from the rest of the world, and would smoke base cocaine, and although I wasn't in debt to anyone yet, I was etching a course on that path for myself. My money wasn't plentiful anymore and I needed it to be, I thought about my lawsuit and called my attorney the next day.

He answered, "Hello Mr. Black, I have some good news for you."

"The liquor store owner wants to settle out of court, but it may still be awhile before we'll arrive at a sufficient cash amount to accommodate you for the anguish, and suffering inflicted upon you."

"I'll be in touch with you when we've reached an agreement on mutual terms," he concluded.

I felt a sense of relief and retribution upon hearing this news of my being compensated for the injury that I sustained from the Liquor store attack.

This gave me a renewed feeling of hope, and insurance that I was going to be receiving money in the near future this was the pass that led me to smoke even more. I continued to smoke base cocaine in excessive amounts, each encounter exceeding the former amount, but smoking cocaine base, I saw as a recreation for me, I felt relaxed, content, and I was fast becoming superfluruous with the use of the substance, without any kinds of calamities, discomforts, or ill feelings from it, other than the chronic depletion of my funds in doing so.

This infusion of base cocaine smoking was a new era of drug use, there was a time when cocaine itself was a drug used by the elite class of people, but now it had been allowed to funnel down to the lower channels of society and into the hands of the less auspicious ones. Through my involvement with cocaine I met quite a few blacks of whom were becoming involved with this drug as well, and I sometimes wondered why it was so. It appeared to me that this particular kind of drug ingestion was both a covert plan by our U.S. power structure, and specifically pre-empted for blacks in this Country.

I pondered the posibility of this action around in my head because it seemed such an uncanny arrival of this cocaine base use into the mainstream of black communities in the United States. It was fast becoming the norm of every black person that I came into contact with was affiliated with cocaine in some way or another. I groped over the thought that this surge of cocaine base was a planned U.S. conspiracy.

As my cocaine base smoking habit increased I was introduced to another way of solidifying the powder and smoking it through what was called ether-base, which is a mixture of cocaine and ether.

Ether itself is a drug, and the combination of both drugs together intensifies the height of ones high, this mixture could also become lethal as well.

An example of just how life threatening and lethal this combination could become was the incident involving comedian/actor Richard Pryor, in which he was severely burned in his attempt to light the above mentioned mixture while trying to inhale it.

I tried this method of cocaine smoking, but realized that it was to dangerous and refrained from smoking it that way.

I would regularly freebase cocaine though, and in my doing so it created some ill feelings from Mary when it came to me visiting my son, and I was disgruntled about this, so it brought more distance between us.

The huge appetite I had for smoking cocaine kept luring me in, I had quit selling the substance and was at a point where my supply was just enough to support my habit.

In the summer of 1980, I was laid off at the job site on the State Capital restoration project because the local Lathers union had completed their contract of the renovation. I was forced to sign up for unemployment benefits, this in effect allowed me more idle time, and with that, I dug myself deeper and deeper into a financial crisis.

My main supplier knew that I had once been successful at selling cocaine, and also knew of the impending lawsuit that I was about to receive.

Unemployment benefits were not enough to accommodate both my bills and my cocaine habit; and finding work with the kind of wages I had been used to enjoying was a tedious task, so I contemplated on enrolling at Sacramento city college that Fall.

September was weeks away, I enrolled for that Fall semester and applied for both the student loan and the Government financial aide, I was granted both.

This additional currency supplemented my unemployment benefits and sufficed my needs for the time being. I attended college classes and maintained a moderate level of academic achievement in them, all the while my cocaine habit seemed to demand more than I was bringing in, this unsettling persistency required me to embark upon a consignment plan with my cocaine supplier.

My final car note balance was due, and after I paid that bill off, I would own the vehicle, I finalized that debt and could now enjoy other desirable expenses, which was my habit. I had a little more money to give towards the wellfare of my son now, but the ill feelings I had towards Mary for denying me visiting rights to my son ended any hope of us ever reconciliating with each other in the future.

I would only provide for my son, Mary and I were through, lamenting over what was happening to me in life at that time, I needed an uplifting, and that would come in the form of a rock cocaine high.

I called my supplier and made preparations to pick up a package, my debt to him was increasing, but because of the numming effects caused from using cocaine, I gave little thought to how soon I would be able to start paying him back.

My addiction was so great until at times I would settle for less in either the quantity, or quality just to satisfy my cravings.

My supplier kept feeding my habit because he knew that one day he would be reimbursed for the credit he gave me on his product.

This arrangement between him, and I held a steady course for several months, the Christmas holiday of 1980 was upon me and my credit line was extended even more, increasing my debt.

After the holidays it was time to make an assessment of how much I was into my supplier, I was at the apex of my line of credit with him, I owed him $4,000.00 and he was starting to drop little subtle pressure statements on me about my giving back instead of constantly receiving from him.

I was not the kind of a guy to renege on a promise, especially on a debt of that magnitude, so I told him that I would make some kind of a retribution on my balance soon.

What I started doing was everytime I had money I would go to him, make a purchase with the majority of that money, and with what was left I would put it towards my debt. This smoothed him over for the moment but it did not greatly reduce my debt, so there were still some ill feelings that remained against me. He began to put more pressure on me by sending messages through his family members, saying that I needed to pay up or something could happen to me.

Acknowledging the seriousness of my situation, and not really knowing for sure of when my settlement was going to be awarded to me, I decided that the only way out of this hole I had dug for myself was to sell my vehicle, and the idea of that really hit me hard. I had purchased that automobile right off of the showroom floor, and it was the first, and only new car that I had ever owned. I prided that automobile, putting in an expensive stereo system, had true spoke wire wheels put on it, the paint job was a gray/black metalic color, with red kid skin leather interior; it was an awesome vehicle.

Nevertheless, I had to make an effort to repay this man, and this was the only means of worth for me with which to do that.

I put a for sale sign in the rear window with a price quote of $3,000.00, It would be advertised whenever I drove it around town.

One day a young lady flagged me down, I pulled over, got out and we started talking about my car.

She said her father wanted a second car, so she took down my phone #and said she would give me a call about it. I could not discern her sinserity about buying my car, so I didn't expect a any call from her.

That next day she called, and asked if I could drive the car over, I said I would and she gave me the address.

When I found the house her father was outside as I pulled up, he was a Chrysler automobile man, and knew good quality when he saw it.

He admired the vehicle, so I let him test drive the car, when he returned he complemented me on the over-all appearance of it, and said he wanted it.

The next day he went to his bank and withdrew the $3,000.00, called me up and told me to drive the car over, I took him the pink slip, we talked for a while, and finalized the transaction.

His daughter whom had orchestrated the deal drove me back to my place; and all the while I reminisced back on all the good times I had enjoyed in that car. When I first bought the car Mary and I drove the California coastline Interstate 1 to Los Angelos to visit her Grandparents.

One other time my sisters, Mary, and I drove to Portland,Ore to visit my relatives on my mother's side of our family.

Coming back to reality though, brought with it the fact that I no longer owned that vehicle that I'd bought brand new off the show room floor. The daughter Sharon, and I began conversing, we talked and laughed and became attracted to one another, she was single,as was I.

As I was stepping out of her car she passed me her phone#, I assured her that I would be in touch. Standing outside on the sidewalk I watched as she drove the car away, I stood there for a moment then turned and went inside to call the guy that I owed all that money to, to make arrangements to pay as much as I could on what I owed.

He picked up the phone after a couple of rings.

"Hey man I just sold my vehicle so you can come pick up some of the cash that I owe you."

"Really! Well that's something, I wasn't expecting it this soon, I'll be right over."

I wasn't going to hand over all of the money I had just got, I would keep a thousand of it for myself, the balance owed to him would be paid later when I got my settlement. Within a half an hour he was knocking at my door, I thought to myself of how funny a thing it is that money will always dictate the pace of the things.

I let him in, we sat down and I counted out $2,000.00 for him, he was very greatful to receive this money from me and said nothing as to when I needed to pay the rest.

Before he left though, I eased any remaining tension between us by stating,

"Yeah man the rest of the cash would follow as soon as I received my settlement, and that shouldn't be too much longer."

"O.K. man I'm good with that, and hears a little something for you for the payment you made today", he left with me a half a gram, I then asked if he could sell me a $500.00 package.

"Yeah, you'll have to follow me back to the house, I didn't bring anymore along." I was relieved that the bulk of my debt was paid, and for the first time in a long time I was beginning to see some light through all of the darkness I had fell into behind my rock cocaine habit.

My idea now was to make the cocaine I was buying work for me by bringing in a profit through selling again. Through hindsight of my having to sell my car, and the subsequent cocaine missions I went on which put me in debt, I could now began to turn a negative into a positive. I went and picked up the package of powder cocaine and went to work putting them into $25.00 packages, however, my plan backfired on me when I'd made up the last package, and decided to reward myself by cooking up the last loose powder into a rock.

I took a hit of the rock substance, failing to realize that I was a victim of this candy of the devils, and that I could not just take a hit and quit; the effects of this substance was designed to conquer it's challenger.

I was not able to refrain from the continuous smoking of that package and eventually consumed the rest of the other packages I'd made up to sell.

I called him again and went over to spend the rest of the cash I had left, and consequentially consumed that package as well.

I wasn't conscientious of the pernicious outcome of smoking rock yet, and because of this I could not ascertain how critical it would become for me if I continued on with this fiasco.

I was in the premature stages of my addiction, and for me, experience was going to be my best mentor, at this period in my life I was unconcerned with the trials and tribulations which I had already been through, and un-beknownest to me, was going to continue to go through.

All I knew was that I enjoyed smoking rock cocaine and that I derived pleasure from it doing so.

That Monday came around and it was time to resume my perfunctory schedule, my resilance level was 80% that day, considering how late I'd stayed up smoking the rock, and how much I had consumed.

I was a young man though, and in good health, it would be a while before my continuous abuse from smoking this substance would take it's toll on me in the way of lackadaisicalness.

At present my vehemence was ingratiating with many whom I came into contact with, particularly one young lady I'd met on the campus at Sacramento city college named Angie.

Angie was a student at the college, she was academically inclined, and saw something in me that I couldn't see myself.

Meeting her was a welcomed delight for me primarily because I was single, even moreso because I needed that void of a female companionship filled.

Here was now a woman in my life that I could be with and/or converse with through this crisis I had created for myself, I felt reborn again so to speak, in her presence.

she was young, pretty, and had left the city of Chicago, ILL with her infant child in hopes of obtaining a fresh new lease on life in Ca.

Her baby daughters name was amber and she was only a month old, Angie resided in the G parkway area off of franklin blvd.

We would talk on the telephone quite often, I would catch the Regional transit bus over to visit her at her place, however, I was still trapped in the world of smoking cocaine, and would stray away from her on ocaissions.

Angie was attracted to me though, as I was to her, and she wanted to be with me, but when I disappeared sometimes without calling her for days she'd become distressed and would start calling asking my mother where I was, and to have me call her as soon as I got home.

I returned her call and came to realize from our conversation that she could be the woman that could fill the emptyness in my life.

From that point on we became very close with one another, she would monitor my whereabouts as if she was my guardian angel; I admired this about her and began to spend more quality time with her.

As time passed we discussed the feasibility of living together, and within the next few days I moved into her apartment.

I respected Angie and provided for her and her infant as best I could, not having transportation available, the three of us would ride the Sacramento's R.T. system to city college throughout the week.

I loved her divine affection towards me and in return I acted as a fatherly figure to her daughter, and only indulged in smoking the rock when I wasn't in their presents.

This would backfire on me as my appetite for the rock cocaine increased.

We strove together as a team, I helped furnish her apartment through applying my hustling skills, we kept food in the refrigerator, we'd put aside money for weekend recreations, and did almost everything together.

I did not go off on drug escapades and stay gone for days,I relished being in her company more than I did smoking the rock cocaine, I believed that our relationship would aide me in my attempt to escape the clutches, that that substance had on me.

We went on like this for months, only at times when I had a little extra cash would I indulge myself in freebasing, and even then I wouldn't expose my habit to her.

After close to a year into our relationship Angie discovered my involvement in cocaine use through other acquaintances of ours, but by this time she was in love with me and stayed by my side.

I had never disrespected her in any way, and always did my freebasing outside of our residence, furthermore, I loved her too, and did not want to expose her to that.

G parkway was, and still is an area known for drug trafficking, and gang activity, so my next concern for us was to relocate to another area as soon as possible. It was becoming difficult for me to shy away from the constant tempting of the drugs evolving in and around that community, because it had become so rampantly pervasive. Just about everyone that was black had in one way or another fallen victim to it, it was as though the enception of this drug started out as a black peoples thing, making it seem to me as though it was contrived for blacks people.

I became conscientious to this because everyone I came into contact with whom freebased cocaine was a black person, yet we weren't aware of the ramifications that rock cocaine years later would entail.

It opened the doors to the decline of self morals, police injustices that would lead to imprisonment, the rise in female prostitution, male homosexuality, and the escalation of black on black homicides across the Country.

We both searched for a place in a better community of Sacramento and found one that was suitable, it was a fairly quiet neighborhood and was a few blocks from Sacramento city college. We had a couple of weeks left on the lease at the place in G parkway, so we went on and signed the other rental lease and was set up to move in on the 1rst of April 1982.

Later that month I got a letter from my attorney telling me to come into his office so I could sign papers for a settlement sum of $15,000.00.

My consternation was shared with Angie as we both anticipated the things that kind of money could buy for our little family.

After receiving the check I went straight to the First Interstate bank and deposited it into a new savings account and was issued a versateller card to go along with it.

We were without a car, so I thought of the type of a car I could buy, as well as furniture, and other appliances for our new residence.

As for the vehicle I had an attraction for the Cadillac Sevile model, and waited patiently until I found one that was reasonably priced, I finally did and purchased it for $6,000.00.

I gave my mother, father, sisters and brothers each a sizable amount of cash, then bought clothes, and other neccessities for Angie and her daughter, and finally finished my buying spree on my son for the things he needed and wanted.

I then called my supplier and made arrangements to pay off the remaining debt with him, after which, I no longer had any dealing with; but to my dismay I acquired another source for buying cocaine after leaving his place.

There happened to be an old acquaintance of mine at the 7/11 mini mart on amherst way, and meadowview rd when I stopped in to buy some cigarettes.

As we talked he told me that he had some good cocaine, and that he just lived right around the corner from the store, it's uncanny how Satan can manifest himself in ones dealings with other people.

I was excited, and capricious all at the same time when he told me this, because I yearned to smoke some cocaine, but was trying hard to refrain from doing so, nevertheless, I succumbed to the invitation and followed him to his house.

Once inside the house, there were other people sitting around smoking rock cocaine, some dude in the kitchen was leaning over the stove range cooking powder cocaine into a rock form. I was not comfortable being in this type of an enviorment, so I bought a $50.00 package and left.

This fresh encounter with another dealer was like a bad omen for me, in light of my just having paid off an outstanding cocaine debt,and now to turn around and come into contact with another dealer was just unreal to me.

I took the bought cocaine over to Gaines' place and we got high, this was the beginning to an all night mission of freebasing.

Angie was at the house content with everything she desired for her and Amber, so there was I felt no reason for me to have to rush home to her.

Being over exorbitant with this mission I was on, I ended up spending $500.00 on freebasing with Gaines.

After having bought a car, providing for Angie with her wants and needs, giving money to family members, seeing to my sons needs, and paying off my debts, I had $5,000.00 left in the bank.

When I returned home after freebasing for hours with Gaines, it was 2:00a.m., Angie was asleep but was awakened as I got into bed, she was obviously disturbed about my being gone all the day and half the morning, but did not push the issue with me.

I did not hear anything more from her on that incident in the days following. Summertime was approaching, and from that time of my last binge on, Id spend quality time with her, but I also made time to get away and freebase, leaving her at home, or over a friends visiting.

On one of my freebasing escapades I met a Pac Bell worker whom was a freebaser, we both had money to spend and shared a common cause, so a short term association developed.

Travis was a financially sound individual whom was buying his home in the south area of Sacramento; he was doing well for himself all except for his ever increasing habit of smoking rock cocaine.

At times I would go make the purchases for us both, on some occaisions we'd go together, with the frequency that we were both freebasing, my weightloss was becoming noticeable.

This in turn caused Angie to suspect me of smoking the rock cocaine pretty regularly, and the long overdue question was popped.

"Are you still smoking on that rock she asked?"

"No, why do you asked?," I hated lying to her like that.

"I am getting mixed indicators that's telling me otherwise, that's why I asked."

"No, I've just been busy with friends hustling here and there, I'm alright."

My cash was slowly disappearing, it wouldn't be long before I would be broke again.

My relationship with the new connection was business, and I was starting to become a regular with him as well, but I would not fall into debt this time. Dealing with this new source subjected me to a lot of undesirable events at his place, on one account when I went to make a purchase I was caught in the middle of an attempted drug robbery of his house.

The occupants of the dwelling submitted to the assailants while being robbed until one of them was able to stealthily retrieve his gun nearby, and a gun fight erupted in the house as the robbers were fleeing.

The assailants escaped with one being shot in the arm, and one of the household members received a bullet in his leg.

After that incident I was always precautious whenever entering into a drug house. This type of impetuous activity was to later in time become common ground activity in the escalation of violence pertinent of drug houses, and drug sales in America's Black communities.

There was a big surge in the escalation of rock cocaine clientele around the years end of 1982, and this was due to the luring effect that the rock cocaine had procured on blacks at it's inception.

I witnessed an influx of blacks just in Sacramento alone fall victim to this drug; either through personal experiences, the news media, or from hearing someone telling a story about an unusual incident that had happened behind rock cocaine. This plague was digging it's tenacles into Americas' black neighborhoods, more, and more, I would notice increases of traffic in drug houses, freebasing was becoming a favored passtime for many blacks.

Some would exercise this habit many times a day, including myself on some occasions.

This rock cocaine trafficking also opened up the doors for the enterprise of trading valuable possessions, such things as T.V. sets, other household appliances, new clothing, jewelry, and even food stamps.

As the clientele for rock cocaine grew, so did the establishment of new drug houses in, and around the Sacramento area, freebasing was a common thing now.

This made access to obtain rock cocaine very easy and convenient, the consistant availability of the drug was not limited anymore as it once was.

This in effect gave me more fluidity in acquiring the rock, if one supplier was sold out, I could go to another.

THE REVELATION

B oth Travis and I were freebasing in excess of $500.00 or better a day, I had evaporated the funds in my account, and travis was starting to sell items around his house to support his habit.

I had not enrolled in college that fall semester of 82, this gave me unlimited time to indulge in whatever I fancied while riding around in my Cadillac Seville. By this time however, I was broke and was relying on my hustling skills to support my drug use.

Angie had become a co-dependant because she loved me, and didn't really understand the seriousness of this addiction of mine, so she tolerated me for the time being, I would contribute to the household in between my periods of using.

The holidays of the years end; Christmas, and New Years came and left; the month of January 83, I learned Angie was pregnant.

My not having an income, in addition to spending most of the money I'd hustle on freebasing made matters even worse.

We needed a family vehicle now more than ever, not a flashy Cadillac, now that she was expecting, I weighed out our situation and came to the conclusion that I did not need a Cadillac Seville anymore.

Trying to be a family man, I thought it best to just sell the vehicle, once again, I put a for sale sign in the cars rear window with an asking price of $7,000.00 or best offer.

I was satisfied at having owned it for almost a year, and would be grateful at the prospect of getting back my asking price of what I had paid for it.

Within a couple of weeks I had a prominent buyer for the seville, they were an Iranian couple, whom, as soon as they saw the car said they would take it.

It was a nice looking automobile, money green was the color of it, but it ran on deisel fuel, which had been alright, but I hadn't been ecstatic over it.

I had come out a winner though with the sale of the car because I not only enjoyed the privilage of owning, and driving the vehicle for a year, but I also gained a profit of a thousand dollars on the sale.

The couple bought the car with cash, mostly one hundred dollar bills and with that money I was able to go straight to the bank and opened another savings account.

I put $6,000.00 dollars into the bank, and kept out a thousand so that Angie and I could buy some kind of a get around car.

The next day we went out to fulton ave where there were a lot of used car dealers with prices that suited the public and their budgets.

We scouted out cars together, Angie suddenly noticed a nice 1976 Toyota Corolla, we test drove it, and ended up buying it for $900.00.

I had splurged off my previous lump sum of money that I'd received from my settlement, and became dubious about how I was going to handle the money I now had.

Nevertheless, freebasing cocaine had it's hold on me, and once I would start smoking the substance it would be almost impossible to stop.

When we got home I sat around the house, and my stomach kept alarming me to the call of the cocaine, I wasn't sure what prompted this feeling, but knew that whenever I had money on me I would begin to experience that anticipitory state of anxiously wanting to indulge myself.

That feeling of anticipation was what usually led me to the act of freebasing, and after the first inhalation of the rock cocaine smoke I would feel better. I thought this condition to be anomalous, because it seemed to only happen when I had cash on me; when I had no cash on hand I wasn't subjected to that feeling.

I told Angie I was going for a drive in the car and left the house, only to end up at a drug house buying cocaine.

After the buy I went to Travis' house, I wasn't sure how long travis had been freebasing prior to our meeting one another, but it appeared as though each encounter that he and I had when smoking the rock, his state of being was becoming more precarious. I overlooked his ill looking state of being and felt that I would not fall into his footsteps, and thought no more on it.

We sat and freebased until it was gone, I then had travis take me to pick up another package of cocaine. Prior to that purchase I'd spent $50.00; I repeated the earlier buy again, this time emptying my pocket of spending money. When we finished smoking that package, travis started thinking of ways with which to come up with more cocaine to smoke.

When we met, he had the cash to spend on cocaine, but now it seemed that he was resorting to trading in valuable items around his house to get the substance he craved in between his paychecks.

As far as I new he was still working at Pac Bell telephone Co., and was going to work regularly. On his payday's he would call me, and say," Man come over here and try out some of this good rock I just picked up,"

I'd oblidge him and we'd smoke cocaine until early in the morning.

When I would arrive home at daybreak Angie would be furious, and waiting for me, after some harsh exchange of words I would sooth her with sweet talk and she would calm down.

I wouldn't realize what a good woman I'd had until years later, and by then it would be way too late for us with regard to any reconciliation.

That next day when I finally awoke, she and amber had left for school, so I cooked myself some breakfast and tried to eat, but trying to swallow the bites of food became agonizing to my throat.

I had been freebasing quite frequently over the past few days, and hadn't been eating or drinking anything while doing so, which brought about a raw and inflamed throat.

In effect, my throat had become dry and parched from the heat of the flame while inhaling the combustion from the rock cocaine pipe, this, in turn is just one of the many health threatening consequences one subjects their body to when smoking rock cocaine.

I wasn't aware of the side effects caused by smoking cocaine at that time and thought maybe I was experiencing symptoms of an oncoming cold.

The soreness of my throat eventually subsided between intervals of my excessive freebasing missions, periodically my sore throat syndrome reoccured when I used heavily, I then, at that time realized what had caused this condition with my throat.

The fact that I craved to freebase whenever possible created in me a sense of immunity to the throat pains I would feel afterwards, because regardless of how unpleasant the ailment became afterwards, I still indulged myself in smoking the substance.

The following day came, and boredom, and the idleness of time led me to take a walk to William Land Park on freeport blvd, which was just a few blocks from our house. William Land Park, the biggest park in the Sacramento area is a very huge place of which host a variety of different kinds of gatherings for people, it has a public golf course and at it's center is the Sacramento Zoo.

My quess is that it encompasse's an area of about 75 acres, anyway, when I got there, there were many people standing around talking, drinking alcohol, smoking marijuana, and socializing; there wasn't anyone around with which I was familiar with so I sauntered over to the picnic benches and sat down.

After hanging at the park for little over an hour a guy came up to me drinking a can of beer and introduced himself, "I'm Dale my brother, what's going on with you today"?

"Just hanging bra, I'm Siege." "Hey Siege would you like a beer"? he asked?

"Yeah man that sounds like just what I need right now!, thanks."

As we talked the subject of freebasing cocaine came up, we discussed the events that the drug caused to happen to people by and through it's use, neither of us knew the other well enough to get on a personal level about our own involvement with the substance.

However, as we talked further Dale became comfortable enough, perhaps by the influence of the beer to inquire, "Hey Siege do you know where I can buy a $20.00 package of cocaine."

"Yeah there is a place I know of not to far from here."

"Why don't we finish off our beers and I'll drive us there" he plainly stated, we talked some more until the beers were gone and then left the park.

Silently in my mind I thought that freebasing was becoming so pervasive among the black people that everyone I would come into contact with was either selling or using this substance. At this time I did not have an inkling as to why this uncanny attraction of blacks to freebasing cocaine was so prevalent, nevertheless, I continued to indulge myself in it.

We went to the source, and bought the package, but we needed a place to smoke it at; and I had never smoked in my place before, not even by myself.

Angie was at school, and the urge to smoke cocaine over-rode my better judgement of not smoking in the house.

I said that we could smoke at my place, but that it would have to be quick, this rash decision of mine would be the start of a pattern that would go on as long as Angie and I would live there, when she was away of course.

We got started and ended up smoking until just before 4:00 p.m., a total of 5 hours, un-beknownst to me, Dale had had a pocket full of money which enabled us to make many more purchases of cocaine.

Angie came home from school, and wasn't feeling to well; she was two months from having our child, I was still under the influence of the rock, but had come down some, so I catered to her needs as necessary.

My cocaine use was starting to become the topic of our discussions lately, I knew I had a good woman and desparately wanted to quit smoking the stuff, not solely to satisfy her, but for my self as well.

I had started to notice what freebasing had began to deduce travis down to, in addition to how it was taking it's toll on my life force as well.

I agreed with Angie that I would make a sincere attempt to exclude myself from such people whom were involved with it, however, this truce of mine would always fall through whenever my rock cocaine smoking partners would show up at our house asking me where they could buy some cocaine.

I was weak in this regard, drugs was not in my upbringing, and I could not fathom how I, or anyone else could fall prey to such a substance, and find it almost impossible to break free of it's clutches.

Trying to conceal my participation in cocaine use from Angie always seemed to work because the indicators of my use were always visible within an hour after smoking it, so staying away from her during that period of time would resolve the issue of my appearing to be under the influence.

Tranquility was somewhat restored in our household, Angie was more at ease with my effort of not using cocaine, and being near her in the last stages of her pragnancy, sometimes though I would slip away in the evenings and visit my mother and family.

One night while at my mothers house, to my surprise, both my youngest brother, and sister were in the garage freebasing cocaine.

Shocked was an understatement upon seeing this, both because they were younger siblings, and because I was the one whom was the example setter.

Smoking cocaine is such a mind altering drug until it wouldn't have benefited any of us had I acted in a rash manner, instead, being enticed myself by their activity I joined in with them figuring that sooner or later they would be exposed to it anyway from someone else.

We all finished what little was left,by my taking a little hit with them, this in effect incited my interest to continue on with freebasing.

My sister Holly was a beautiful girl with a sharp mind and a very independent energy about her, she was an employee for the State of California at the Dept. of transportation. Drugs were never a part of her lifestyle, however, she had fallen victim as well as myself and many other African Americans to this drug called rock cocaine.

My Bank card had come in the mail a few days earlier, I had it in my possession, after finishing the hit I got up said I would be back and left.

An hour later I returned with $50.00 worth of cocaine and the three of us sat in the garage and freebased cocaine.

Smoking rock cocaine in the early 80's was a high that one could enjoy the effects of it, in contrast, later to come as it would be, this substance weighed heavily on it's consumers mental, and physical faculties.

When the three of us had finished that package of cocaine, I left and headed towards home, driving there I felt a sense of disappointment at what had just taken place with my siblings and I, because I, at that point could not reverse that seed of destruction that had already been planted by someone else.

I got home and into bed, cuddling up next to Angie whom was asleep, after thinking about the magnitude of this rock cocaine epidemic,and it's impact on black people I drifted off to sleep myself.

I awoke the next morning to a knock at the door, Angie had gone on to school, I got up, and answered the door only to find travis standing there looking like he had been up smoking rock all night, so I waved him in.

He had with him a small black tote bag, he sat down, unzipped it and brought out a razor, mirror, some cocaine, and a glass freebase pipe.

He had in fact been smoking all morning long, and became bored smoking by himself, so decided to show up at my place and smoke with me. "Aren't you supposed to be at work I asked him?"

"Well I'm supposed to be, but I called in early this morning and told them I wasn't feeling well enough to come today, and that's that."

The incessant freebasing he was doing was taking a toll on him, because he looked malnutritioned, smelt badly, and was very unkempt.

Travis had not divulged any information regarding his attendance on his job to me, but by accident I caught him up in his story when he had mentioned to me that he'd been freebasing at his house for the past three days straight with other associates, so apparently he was not going to work.

This is a characteristic of freebase addiction, in that it renders a person helpless in their ability to prioritize their life's day to day functions.

Their welfare, and immediate responsibilities always become secondary to that addiction.

He cooked the powder cocaine into a rock form, and we both commenced to smoking the rock, we smoked until noon, he than got up to leave saying, "I have to get out there to hustle up my next package, Ill see you later."

Having a lot of idle time on my hands, I would sometimes go up to the college and visit Angie, or William Land park and drink beer, I was starting to drink beer more frequently now.

Perhaps my drinking more was due to the fact that freebasing causes dehydration, in addition to making you hyperactive all at the same time; beer seemed to satisfy the effects of those discomforts.

MY AWAKENING

My perfunctory routine worsened as days passed, I was relapsing on the agreement Angie, and I had made, because, although I would call often while I was out, I still ran the streets and freebased more.

At times when I would smoke rock I would make a withdraw from the A.T.M. machine just before midnight, then wait there until after midnight, and draw out the maximum amount of cash allowed on a daily basis from an A.T.M. machine, which was $200.00.

I would deplete my whole savings account this way in just under two months time, in addition to, during the day, going straight into my bank and making withdrawals of hundreds of dollars, eventually my account was closed with that bank.

Angie went into labor on the morning of Sept. 25th 1983 and later that day gave birth to our baby boy; I named him Counsel.

That morning I had driven her to the hospital, but my having been so engrossed with smoking rock prior to her labor pains that at the hospital I waited there until she was admitted then left the hospital, missing the birth of our son.

She was furious about my being absent for the birth of our son, even more so of my going back to freebasing again, but the agony of child birth calmed her anger towards me for the time being.

She also knew of the potential within me to become a reputable citizen of the community and a responsible man if I could only quit using the stuff.

Because of this she became dubious as to our future, and of us being viable mates for one another, she lay in her hospital bed and cried, partly because she did not know how to intervene and thwart this destructive drug Iwas so addicted to.

Even further, she did not understand how smoking rock cocaine could seize a person, and render them unfunctionable in life's everyday simple duties.

A couple of days later I went to pick Angie and our son up from the hospital, on the way home we talked about my drug problem.

Although I listened, I was unattentive to her because of the after effects of the drug which caused me to be both lethargic and sleepy.

With no income once again I was dependant upon her for my livelihood, not in the way to support my drug habbit because I hustled for that, but in the way of a place to lay my head at night, eating, and for minute expenses.

A months time had lapsed since the birth of our son, my freebasing had escalated again, and by this time she had had enough and wanted to get away.

She called her mother in Chicago, Ill and asked her if she could send round trip fares for her and the kids.

After hanging up the phone we argued about her untimely call and get away plan to her mothers.

I chided her for wanting to go to her mothers in Chicago, and went on to say that she sure wasn't taking our son Counsel to that cold weather of Chicago's, she was bent on going though and went into the room to began packing.

Later that night her mother called her, and said she had reservations set up for them to board a United Airlines jet at 7:30 p.m. the next day.

The following night she was loaded up and ready to take the kids with her, and waiting on a friend of hers to arrive and take them to the airport.

I held my ground about our son not going on that trip, so Angie, being the weaker half of us submitted to me and stormed out of the door without Counsel in her arms, heading to the airport.

I had gambled on her as bluffing me about really leaving Counsel behind with me on account of his early stage of infancy, and his need of her breast fed milk, however, the night passed and she did not return.

That next morning she phoned and said she was in fact in chicago, I was shocked that she had actually followed through with her departure, now I was faced with the ultimate challenge of fatherhood in front of me, coupled with battling with my addiction.

Paternal instinct was the perogative that took presidence in the matter, as I would provide and care for my son to the fullest; temporarily abandoning the urges to freebase.

Angie, feeling guilty about having left her son as she did, called several times a day giving me advice on what, and what not to do while caring for our child, and all the while threatening me on what she'd do to me if anything were to happen to her son.

Travis came by the house every other day to either freebase, or inquire as to wether I wanted to or not; it's funny how misery loves company isn't it.

Talking with him one day I finally learned that he'd been fired from Pac Bell Telephone Co., he was looking very disheveled, smelled badly, and it appeared that all that mattered to him was the freebasing missions, and his relentless quest to obtain more when that was finished.

I, on the other hand, had become all of a sudden very responsible with the fatherly duties to my son, and very seldom smoked any rock during this period, unless someone I knew stopped by the house, and Counsel was asleep; otherwise I would decline an offer to smoke it.

Sometimes dale would pop up, and smoke a quarter of a gram with me, drink a couple of beers and leave, I learned later that dale was one of the few people that didn't seem to exceed his limit when freebasing, their was also a mutual respect between us regarding family life, because he had a family himself.

He would keep his visits both short and rare, I never seen dale again after when Angie came back home a month later and told him to never come by her house again to smoke any rock when she wasn't there or else. After that order was given to him, he and I lost contact with one another and never crossed paths again.

Angie was happy to see that I had kept house well, and had nurtured our son successfully while she was away, and for that she showered me with love and affection.

She showed remorse about having left us, and went on to say, "I was on the verge of having a nervous breakdown was the reason I left so abruptly," "that short get away from things did me a world of good."

We both started feeling as though there was a divine entervention from GOD, and that we were given a new lease on life; this could be the fresh start that we both deserved.

Happy that she was back home, and the prospect of maybe losing her to my drug habit, I made an attempt to rectify our union by conforming to the previous plans of refraining from using rock.

I stayed in accordance with that agreement for a brief period of a couple of months, but was constantly tempted with the untimely run-ins of travis.

He was unemployed now, and his unexpected pop ups at our house either with cocaine, or the plan of wanting to go buy some was hard for me.

Consistantly being challenged by travis to freebase with him, one day I lost my will, and gave in to taking a hit of some rock, that hit just sparked my hidden urge to start freebasing again.

After finishing the rock we both got into his Datson 280 ZX and drove off on a mission to hustle up some cash for the next package of cocaine.

We first stopped by his house which no longer adorned the lavish look as it once did, inside, he looked for anything that a drug dealer might be interested in trading cocaine for.

He found a short waist length leather jacket, we got back into his car and made the trip to the dealers house, he went inside and came back without the jacket which meant that he had scored.

We finished off that package quickly, by now it was nearing the time for Angie to be coming home from school, so I needed a period of time with which to recoup before she got there.

"Travis it's about that time for you to clear out man, Angie will be hear soon."

"O.k. siege I'm out, but give me a call a little latter because I have something you might be interested in," and he was gone.

She came in 30 minutes later and suspected that I might have broken my truce with her because of certain signals she was receiving, but rather than act prematurely on assumptions she disregarded the thought and busied herself with household chores around the place.

Travis' obsession with freebasing steadily increased his state of poverty to where he was literally almost living on the streets, he had bartered away all of his most prized possessions to the dealers for cocaine.

I would accompany him sometimes on these uncertain quest of his to get more cocaine, and I would end up in trouble with Angie because these quest would keep me out well into the early morning hours.

This type of activity enticed my already present, yet dormant desire to freebase more, and I would sometimes after parting from him, go out on my own search for more rock cocaine.

One night after a lengthy period of smoking rock, and drinking alcohol while driving home around 4:00a.m., my hyperactiveness from having smoked too much cocaine caused me to misjudge the distance of an oncoming car.

Closely trailing behind the car ahead of me I made a futile attempt to pass it, realizing my error to late to react and pull back into my lane I ran head on into the oncoming vehicle.

Fortunately we were both not traveling more than 35 miles an hour, and neither of us were seriously injured, just minor cuts and bruises.

The front left grill and corner ends of both cars were mangled and twisted beyond repair.

Luckily for me, when the paramedics arrived at the scene shortly after the accident, and found me on the roadside from where I had been thrown from my car, they weren't suspicious as to my being under the influence of any drugs, or alcohol and I wasn't cited as such when the police arrived there.

The police observed the incident and stated to each of us to notify our own Insurance Co's regarding this accident, and neither of us was cited as to whom was at fault.

This incident was certainly a reality check, and a wake up call form GOD as a reminder to me of the kind of lifestyle I was living at the time.

A taking a heed to this should have been the right thing for me to have done. Nevertheless, I was in a state of delusion and denial, and acting out a mode of defiance, which resisted any call to reform the life I was living.

The car was towed to my residence, when Angie looked upon my cuts and bruises she thought for sure they were as a result of my affiliations from the drug world.

When I informed her as to what really had happened she ran outside and saw for herself that I was telling the truth, came back inside, looked at me with a look that felt like it could have burned right through me, and then hysterically started hittings me; crying loudly as she did so.

All I could do was stand there and take what she was dishing out to me and told myself of what a mentally strong woman she was to go through what all I was putting her through, yet, still love and stick with me.

I grabbed and hugged her, and tried to console her by saying "baby I will make everything right again soon," and in midstatement began crying myself telling her that I didn't know how to refrain from using the stuff.

The tension eased as we kissed and held each other tight and just stood in silence for a while, and again I thought to myself of how blessed and lucky I was to have her by my side, now I would have to show her that I was the man that she believed me to be.

It was November of 83, Thanksgiving was a couple of weeks away and we were without transportation.

I remembered from a while back that there was a Toyota wrecking yard out in east Sacramento, in the community of Rancho Cordova near Mather Air Force base where I'd either buy, or exchange parts on our wrecked Toyota.

I had come to know the owner well because of my being a regular patron of his establishment, and when I would be in the yard looking for parts I would see a bunch of Toyota bodies lined up next to each other.

I never thought that I would have to use any of them, so I never paid that much attention to them other than seeing them all lined together in a row.

That next day I called my little brother Chance, and asked if he could run me out there to take a look around, he came to my rescue.

When we got there I began explaining to the owner of what had happened and what I was looking for, he told me got out and examine all of the Toyota bodies and see if I could use any one of them.

After a thorough look over all, I selected one that was in almost perfect condition; even in better shape than the one I had totaled out.

The Toyota hull consisted of just the body and tires, which was all I really needed, since the engine in our vehicle had been spared in the accident.

This was perfect, I located Joe the owner and had him to appraise it's worth.

"You know young man you've been coming out here buying Toyota parts for some time now, and because of that I'm going to let you have that hull for only $75.00."

I left a $5.00 retainer as a claim to that body and told him, "Well now Mr. Joe it's a deal, I'll be back to pick it up next week."

In the mean-time Angie, the children, and I adjusted to not having a vehicle by enjoying the homelife, onThanksgiving day my family invited us over for dinner.

Despite our inability to travel anywhere when we needed to, my family was always there to cater to our needs, but on the contrary, our being bound to the house in the evenings, and on weekends brought us more in touch with each others needs and feelings.

We would catch Regional Transit's bus lines together going shopping, and enjoy the time we spent together doing it.

Angie enjoyed the quality time we spent with one another, and would go into a rage when Travis would show up and disrupt those moments.

"Travis if you weren't such a rock monster you'd have a life, and wouldn't be coming around here so much tempting my man to destroy his life any further," she would say.

"And Siege if you think you're going anywhere with him you better think again on it you understand me," were her exact words.

In all actuality I was under surveilance around the clock by her because of my careless approach, and out of control demeanor whenever smoking rock cocaine, so when I was put in check by her in that manner, "yes my woman," was my only reply.

In light of my car accident, and her obnoxiousness towards anything associated with rock cocaine, I warned Travis not to come by anymore and eventually our association faded away.

All the better that it did because I would learn at a short time later that Travis had sold his 280ZX for cocaine, and had ended up at the Salvation Army shelter for the homeless people.

Nearing the end of November I began removing parts from our wrecked Toyota that I could salvage towards the other hull.

Busying myself with that project of rebuilding another vehicle took my mind off smoking rock, and this gave me a sense of self worth.

Working diligently everyday renewed my spirit, it gave me satisfaction to see Angie and the kids come home from school everyday, and praise me on what I had accomplished thus far.

I kept at this task until the wrecked vehicle was totally stripped inside and out, the last thing left was to lift out the engine, but that would wait until I had the other car body present so I could transfer the engine right into it.

On December 1rst 1983 I bought the Toyota hull from the wrecking yard, and had Chance tow me in it back to our house.

we rented a hoist, and had earlier lifted the engine out of the wrecked car, so when we got to the house we just put it directly into the hull of the Toyota bought from the wrecking yard.

We towed off the other wrecked hull to the metal recycling center where they gave me $40.00 for it.

After the engine was placed in to the salvaged hull, bolted down, and all of the pertinent wires connected, all that remained was the moment of hearing the motor roar to life.

I put the key into the ignition and turned it, but nothing happened, puzzled by this I got out, and looked at the engine, then soon realized that the battery had not been put in, and hooked up.

I set the battery on a prop designed for it and put each terminal where they belonged, wretch through the window, turned the key and the engine roared to life.

Feeling triumphant that I had prevailed against the odds of successfully restoring another vehicle, I sent Chance to the store to buy a 6 pack of Miller draft beer to celebrate the occasion.

I was able to take every part from the wrecked vehicle, and put them right into the other salvaged body before Angie got home from school that day.

After I finished, a test drive was in order to see if all was well with the suspension. axles, and etc.

I took it for a test drive down a busy street, and upon returning was very satisfied that the Toyota I'd built from scratch was in better overall condition then it's predecessor.

Angie was ecstatic when she came home and saw that I'd rebuilt a better vehicle than the one I had wrecked, and all peace was restored to our relationship.

We were able to go Christmas shopping, and prepare for the Holidays to come, Christmas of 83 was very peaceful, I did not indulge in any rock smoking excursions, none that led to anything anyway.

The New Year of 1984 arrived, along with it came a more profound prevalence of blacks using rock cocaine.

Prior to this time the only derivative to getting a solid rock from powder cocaine was to go through the process of mixing the powder with either baking soda, or ether, then adding a little water, where one would slowly cook the mixture over a flame until a solid rock formed.

By this method for the most part you knew what you had, or what you were smoking, most often the powder cocaine would be 65% pure with no other additives in it. But now with the advent of the ready made rock hitting the streets at the beginning of 1984 it became uncertain as to what other additives there would be in this ready rock coming unto the streets.

Everywhere one went to buy cocaine, where as before only powder was available, now you would be sold a solid piece of cooked up cocaine.

I was relieved in one sense that I now no longer needed to stand over a stove and play like a chemist anymore because at times it was a painstaking task to cook powder into a rock.

However, at the same time I was indignant at what I was beginning to buy on the streets, because I began to notice when I would smoke the ready rock I got a different feeling from the high in relation to the rock I would cook myself from the powder.

It appeared to be a more intense rush to the brain, in addition to that enigma, this ready rock seemed to have a more alluring, and addictive catch to it. I couldn't fathom this unusual feeling, it was almost sinister, nevertheless, I, like a fool, continued to be a patron to this rock cocaine.

At the same time my sister Holly was beginning to patronize this drug on a more pronounced level.

She worked for the State of California, the Dept. of Motor vehicles and loved her job, had an impeccable attendance record prior to this rock cocaine plague. But I started seeing lately when I would go by and visit my mother, Holly would be there still in bed on a work week day after having called in earlier to say that she wasn't feeling well, and that she wouldn't be in for that day.

She'd also been sparring frequently with this rock cocaine I'd learned, but all I could admonish on to her was how my former associate Travis had hit rock bottom behind his freebasing missions.

"I'll be alright" she'd say, and I wouldn't say anything more to her about it after that, after all, who was I to chide her, in light of how I was living my life.

I wasn't driving our car as much anymore, I would ride with my little brother, or friends of mine when I wanted to get around.

With rock cocaine came the incorporation of youngsters setting up rock houses, and the selling of rock out in front of houses on street corners, or apartment housing complexes, this caused the competition for that market to escalate.

This type of street marketing really opened the doors for the addict to be able to bring goods of all sorts, aside from money, because the young drug dealers would stay out on the streets, and sell their rock all night, and morning long, and would exchange their product for alcohol of any kind, cartons of cigarettes, etc.

One night my little brother, and I were out riding around, we both had just bought a rock, and had smoked it, didn't have the money to buy anymore, so I told him to go to a store where I could get a case of beer to take to the youngsters.

We came upon a Circle K mini mart store on Freeport blvd, I went in and there was a young white boy working the counter by his self that night.

"Hey man I'm looking for a certain brand of beer called Red Tap," I asked, as he went into the back of the freezer to look for it, I grabbed two cases of the Miller draft beer, and ran out of the store.

We'd gotten away at the time, as fate would have though, we thought we did anyway, a few hours later at another quick stop store on Florin rd, I'd gotten into an argument with the cashier there whom called the police on us after we'd left the store.

Minutes later we were stopped down the street by the police, and over the loud speaker, and with their guns drawn came the order of, "driver and passenger exit the vehicle, and lay unto the pavement with your arms extended outward".

We complied with their demands, were handcuffed and placed into the back of the squad car, we were charged with strong armed robbery.

Both Chance, and I had went into that Circle K store, but the car had been parked around the corner and out of sight, so the car was not what had incriminated us, but rather, our clothing.

That store clerk had called out the police and had given a description of how we looked, and what we were wearing, and had probably used the ploy of strong armed robbery to the cops to cover his own ass for the loss.

As a result of his lie we were taken to jail and booked under the charge of strong arm robbery.

At 27 years of age this was my first time behind bars, and to make matters worse, on a trumped up charge; and all behind an attempt to get some alcohol that I could use to present to the youngsters for some more of their ready rock Cocaine.

At my arraignment I accepted full responsibility for our actions, and the court let Chance off with a slap on the hand, he received time served for the 4 days he'd stayed in jail and was released.

I felt that the charge of strong arm robbery was both bogus, and unjust, and was prepared to take this charge all the way to trial, I contacted my mother and told her to get into contact with our family attorney.

I was disappointed when I learned later that our attorney handled only civil, not criminal cases, so I was stuck with a public pretender,(public defender).

I stayed in jail through-out the whole trial, after being locked up for a little more than two months, the trial came to an end.

The facts of the case as to how it all actually happened which would've supported a lesser charge of petty theft were in my favor, or so I thought anyway, however, the jurors; whom were mostly all white males, found me guilty of strong arm robbery.

Because of it being my first time in trouble with the law though, the presiding judge sentenced me to only 6 months County jail time, with 3 years probation to follow when released from custody.

The conviction I received made me ponder over how unfair, and biased Americas' judicial system really is when it comes to the sentencing of black men in this Country.

I was sent to the Sacramento County branch jail to complete the remaining 2 months I had left on my sentence, while there at the branch I met several guys that were incarcerated for possession of rock cocaine; one guy in particular I became very close with, his name was Coolie.

Coolie wasn't the kind of person whom stayed in trouble around the clock with the law, furthermore, he was just a misled individual due to his rock cocaine habit, and ended up like me, and the countless other black people in jail behind either direct, or indirect involvement of some kind with rock cocaine.

We'd both grown up in the south area of Sacramento but at the opposite ends of the community, went to the same high school, but hung in different crowds of each other; neither of which were trouble making crowds.

Coolie was released a couple of weeks before I was, and was found shortly after his release shot multiple times in the body, and dumped in a garbage dumpster at an apartment complex somewhere in the Oak Park area of Sacramento.

The story was that he had consigned to sell rock for some dealer in the Oak Park area, but instead of selling the product, he smoked it all up and couldn't pay the dude, and had to pay with his life.

This type of black on black homicide would eventually become common practice in America in the years to come.

The reality of it all would at that time affirm my inner notions that rock cocaine was truly an instrument of the devils that was being promoted by his advocates; the wicked men of power in America.

While in jail I kept in contact with my family, my mother was in constant anguish over my sister Holly's calling in to work with some kind of a story of why she wouldn't be in to work that day.

It had progressed into a two or three day a week thing now, and the culprit was the real long nights, and early mornings with the rock of course.

I sympathized with my mother, and hoped and prayed that everything would work itself out for the best.

Unfortunately Holly would become a victim to this plague like myself, and the hundreds of thousands of other blacks that would fall prey to rock cocaine in the years to come.

I was released after serving the two remaining months; being on probation meant that I would have to by mindful of whom I associated with, being under this type of scrutiny by the probation Dept. led me to straighten up my act, and start looking for employment.

I went to the unemployment office every other day while Angie was at school, she was happy that I was back home, and encouraged me to turn my life around, and work hard at doing the right thing.

The period of incarceration had cleaned me up and dwindled my urge to smoke the rock, now I needed to concentrate on improving my quality of life, so I kept on looking for employment everywhere.

Two months passed, then one day while at the unemployment office I noticed a printing position that was posted on the bulletin board, I inquired of it and was scheduled an interview.

When I was given the slip of paper for the interview and glanced at the name of the Co. on it, I was shocked to see that it was with S.E.C.(Sacramento's Electric co).

The irony to this was that I had previously worked for the Co. but had lost my job there due to failing to comply with the Co.'s policy of remaining in college while working there, and now I was possibly knocking at their door for another opportunity to work there again.

Holly, on the other hand, kept on her destructive course of calling in to work with either an excuse of not showing up for the day, or she'd be in late; and she was eventually reprimanded by her supervisor, and was suspended from work for a few days.

This should have brought her attention to the seriousness of her drug addiction, however, it just gave her more time to dig a deeper hole for herself.

In April of 85 I was hired on with S.E.C. for the second time, although the position was a temporary one upon being hired; it gave me the opportunity to once again get ahead in life.

My prior supervisors both from Consumers River College's mail room, and from S.E.C.'S meter reading dept. had given their seal of approval on my work ethics.

I started work on April 1rst, I had also started to hit, and miss again with the rock cocaine as well, but kept my indulgences in it to a bare minimum because I was randomly drug testing with the probation dept. and didn't want to be violated for a dirty test which would jeopardize my job at S.E.C.

In March of 86 the testing notification for the printing position at S.E.C. was sent to my address, the date was set for April of 86.

On the day of the test I did an excellent job of acing every question, and demonstration applicable to the performances required of the position.

A few weeks later I received the results congratulating me of passing the test with a score of 92%.

Days later I was sent an interview notification letter; at the interview I was re-instated back with the Co on a permanent basis.

I was happy about finally attaining permanent employment at S.E.C. with a good salary; I would start out at $9.00 an hour which was good money at that time.

Angie was intrigued when she heard the news, and a celebration was in order, we took the kids out with us to dinner that night, and enjoyed some good food at Red Lobster Sea food restaurant.

I started work on a fulltime permanent basis with the Co. on June 1rst 1986, I was already familiar with the duties of the job and loved every minute of it.

Both Angie and I were unhappy with the antics of our current landlord so we began looking for another place to live, after a couple of weeks of searching we found a nice tri-level duplex on 29th street off of florin rd.

We contacted, and met with the owner of the property, and surprisingly were able to get into the place, within a month we moved into that dwelling, and gave all the praise to GOD for making things happen for us.

Everything was going smoothly until engine trouble developed with the Toyota, having transportation was a must now that I was working,

So rather than put money into repair cost, we both decided to just start looking for a newer model vehicle.

My having just starting working at S.EC., I hadn't the funds to buy a new car, in addition to that neither of our credit ratings would have worked for a loan, so Angie sought the aide of her mother for a $2,000.00 loan.

We found an 81 Olds Omega sedan in grand condition for $2,000.00, her mother wired us the money to purchase the car with, and at the same time I sold the Toyota to a friend of mine for $400.00.

On the other side of things, Holly, aside from missing days of work had began putting her life in jeopardy on a regular basis by turning dates with strangers, hitching rides from strangers, and by hanging in, and around drug houses on her quests for more of the rock.

Holly had become so engrossed with the rock that her livelihood was secondary to it, and she simply quit going to work altogether; the Motor Vehicles dept. of transportation terminated her employment with them in November of 1985.

She was not phased by this detachment, and continued on with her daily, and endless quest to smoke rock cocaine.

I had gotten a small dose of act right about myself by being sent to jail, and because of that I was discretely indulging in the smoking of rock.

I knew the consequences that it offered if I was to get careless with the stuff again while using it.

I didn't inform the probation dept. of my employment with S.E.C., which was a condition of my probation, had I done so, they would have been the instrument of my demise with the Co. by showing up there unannounced, and portraying me as a criminal.

The termination of my probation with the County had finally arrived, I had completed it without getting any violations, so the County discharged me.

With the threat of being put back in jail for a violation out of the picture, I could move about more freely now without having to report to anyone.

1985 was an especially good year for me in a variety of ways, but on the contrary, it was a bad year for African Americans with regard to the rock cocaine epidemic.

Rock cocaine was exacting it's toll in catastrophic proportions that were a ridicule to black people, not only were there a rise in black on black homicides, but overdoses from this pernicious substance was abundant as well.

Superstar NFL draftee Donald Rodgers met an untimely death from his first encounter with the rock.

I myself was seeing firsthand the misfortunes of Blacks brought about by patronizing this drug, and I didn't want to fall into that category.

The examples of people I had witnessed was enough to make me as cautious as possible whenever I did smoke the rock.

In 1986 another devastating event shook the black populace, the culprit was again rock cocaine, I was grieved to learn of the news that superstar Len Bias, NBA's top draft pick had overdosed on rock cocaine and had died.

There was becoming too many casualties among Blacks as a result of patronizing this rock cocaine, and I began to feel uneasy about the stuff, but what could I possibly do to counter this epidemic.

As rock continued it's course of devastation across America, it's lure prompted women, primarily black women, to commit degrading sex acts, I thought this to be a disgraceful misfortune and was unhappy about it.

One night Angie, and I were sleeping when the phone ringing woke us up, I picked it up, and my mother was on the other end crying hysterically.

"Siege your sister Holly has just been hit by a drunken driver while she was walking home from one of her rock smoking binges, she's in the hospital in critical condition."

"Can you meet me at the U.C.D. Med Center and I'll fill you in on the severity of her injuries."

"Sure mom I'm on my way I assured her," hysterically I jumped out of bed and begin dressing myself, telling Angie of the news all at the same time.

I left for the hospital, when I arrived at the emergency room I was greeted by my mother, and several family members whom were all crying.

Through all of the commotion I learned that Holly had been struck while walking at 2:00 A.M. by a drunken driver whom had fled the scene, but returned back to the scene later to take responsibility for his actions.

Holly's condition was critical, her injuries consisted of a broken right femur bone, blood hemorrhage of the brain, multiple cuts, scrapes, and bruises, and she was in a coma.

This was a heartbreaking incident for the family because of the uncertainty of her pulling through this tragedy, for days members of our family would alternate on the shifts of staying at the hospital, all the while trying to discern the likelihood of her recovering from this traumatic accident.

All of the residing Doctors were specialist in their field of work, one of them mentioned that a comatose status usually takes a turn for the better, or worse within 9 days of the time that the incident occurred.

By that he meant that on the 9th day a patient can start coming out of the comatose state, if not, and after that time it would be undeterminable as to when or if she would actually ever come out of if or not.

On the ninth day with everybody present watching and praying that GOD'S grace would shine down on her, I noticed her index finger begin to twitch.

With all of us at her bedside speaking to her in the comatose state she was in, it was a miraculous revelation as she began to slowly open her eyelids.

This was the major hurdle of her recovery, but there was still yet another life threatening obstacle for her to get past, this being the bleeding and hemorrhaging on her brain which was a result of the trauma to her head.

This required a special surgical operation on the brain to relieve the pressure, and stop the blood-clotting there, a team of doctors performed the surgery, and successfully drained all of the excess blood from her brain.

The operation took 9 hours, after which her Dr. told the family that she would never retrieve her voice back again because the area of the brain that enables one to speak was damaged.

In addition to this, because her femur bone was broken in half we were told that she would never be able to walk again, aside from that information given to us, happiness was in the air that she was revived and recovering well, but there was also a feeling of despair about the suspected permanent physical impairments.

Holly was mentally aware of what had happened, and she would nod her head in response to our questions, her healing process was remarkable, after a week they removed her from the critical ward and placed her in the intensive care unit.

She stayed hospitalized for 2 months, when she was released they gave her a quad-cane, and a wheelchair, a few of the specialist whom had worked on her through the crisis were in awe of her survival, and speedy recovery, and hated to see her leave.

Holly could barely utter words, or speak, Angie and I had that tri-level duplex with a lot of room, so she stayed with us.

Working with her daily, she gradually started putting words together, and spoke, shortly following that, she began to make sentences.

I hated seeing my sister in this state, it was almost as if she was a child again learning to walk, and talk all over, eventually she got her speech back, and regained the level of common sense that she had had, however, her voice would remain hoarse sounding for the rest of her life.

One day at our place I saw Holly walking on her quad-cane, this was 7 months after the accident, I asked, "can you stand by yourself?"

"I don't know brother I can try, and see if I can, catch me if I began to fall!" was her reply.

She removed her hands from the walker, and stood for a few seconds, impressed with her effort, I knew then that I could teach her to walk again.

Despite the Dr.'s having put a steal rod in her femur bone she was still able to use her leg, day by day I worked with her in my spare time, I would hold her out in front of me with my arms extended to catch her if she were to fall, and tell her to take small steps at a time, she'd comply, and everyday would become stronger in doing this.

The next phase of her therapy which she would do on her own, was to leave from one area that was within a few steps to another area, this was done to teach her balance, and give her the needed confidence to learn how to walk again.

This proved to be constructive for her, in December of 86, she began to walk all by herself, and had defied the prediction of her Dr. of never being able to walk again; surely GOD was with her throughout this whole ordeal.

The Christmas holidays were joyous, GOD had spared her life and had restored her from the life threatening injuries she'd received from that accident.

The physical impairments that she sustained from it all was a hardly noticeable limp in her walk, and a raspy sounding voice box.

My oldest son Siege II was now 7 years old and I was keeping him on the weekends, much to Mary's disdain.

I had both of my sons together for the Christmas Holiday, as all of our family gathered together around the dining table and I gave grace to our Lord before we ate our supper.

The man whom was at fault for Holly's injuries we'd learned later, was very wealthy, was sued, and agreed to settle out of court for a sum of $300,000.00., Holly would receive her settlement in Feb of 87.

The year of 1987 was for me the beginning to the end of my prosperity, I would began to indulge in rock cocaine like it was no tomorrow, and as a result of it I would bring upon myself many unpleasant consequences.

I was still smoking rock when I could, but it wasn't, or I wasn't letting it interfere with my job or home life, up till that time I'd maintained a good attendance record with S.E.C.

I would take my paychecks, and give Angie half of it for bills, her, and the kids expenses, give Mary money for Siege II, then treat myself by indulging in some rock cocaine smoking..

The aftermath of smoking the rock would be in the way I'd come home in the early morning hours, where sometimes the kids would be up watching cartoons, I would hug them both and head to the bed and sleep until 2:00 p.m.

I was slowly digging myself an unpleasant hole that would subject me to a dire fate that would haunt me for the rest of my life.

My addiction was becoming capricious for me in the way of after my cash was gone I would resort to renting out the family vehicle to young rock dealers, most of which were either affiliated with street gangs known as the bloods or crips, depending on what neighborhood I was in at the time.

Neither the misfortunes that befell other victims of this plague, nor my own previous personal hardships with the drug was enough to deter, or prevent me from smoking the substance.

Fortunately for me when I rented the car out it was never wrecked, in light of how those youngsters drink their alcohol, and smoke their refer, the lots of them just don't give a damn about tearing up a vehicle that was rented to them by a rock smoker.

At times, I would be out there waiting on the streets long after the rock I'd gotten from them was gone, waiting and hoping that nothing had happened to the car until almost dawn, then they'd finally show up with the car; it would be trash, and beer bottles everywhere in it.

Then on a couple of occasions the youngsters would not come back, and I would have to track them down, and threaten them, they would then release the car.

My addiction had began to take a turn for the worse after a little while, and I had started to call in to work sick every other Friday, the day after my payday, which was on Thursdays.

I was repeating my sisters scenario at the workplace, but on a less dramatic level.

Had I not been so deluded mentally from my excessive use of the substance, and had been focused enough to discern where I was headed by continuing to use the substance, I could have prevented myself from falling into that same trick bag as my younger sister had.

But that's the trickery that the devil puts in front of one, and you don't see it coming until it's too late.

Although my no-shows to work after paydays wasn't immediately addressed by my supervisor, my weight loss was noticed by co-workers, and they'd asked, "hey is your absentness related to any illness because your looking very frail."

"No, I've just been over exerting myself around the house, and haven't been eating right is the reason to my lose of weight", that inquiry should have served as a wake up call for me, but I didn't take a heed to it, and dismissed it off as a personal intrusion into my life.

In February of 87 Holly received her settlement, our eldest sibling was assigned by the family as Holly's care provider, and manager of her finances, since Holly was not able to efficiently oversee her own money management; Holly gave each family member $5,000.00.

I gave Angie a few hundred dollars, and went off to spend the rest of it on rock, it was on a Saturday, I had the whole weekend left before I'd need to get prepared for work on Monday.

I went off, did my do, and didn't return home until Sunday night, and was completely broke.

I loved Angie with all my heart, but it seemed that the rock was reaching a stage where it was having a profound effect, on both my behavior, and my relationship with her.

Under normal circumstances I would cater to her every whim, but I was beginning to disregard the important things to her, not intentionally of course, but because of the powerful control that the rock had over me.

There were instances when I was to pick the kids up from somewhere, but being under the influence of the rock I would not pick them up, and later we would argue about it.

I could not discern the type of behavior I was now exhibiting, because when I was freebasing cooked up powder cocaine, it never had that kind of control over me like this ready rock now on the market did.

This ready rock was disrupting every faucet of my life, I was powerless to it, always in submission to it, yet not able to walk away from it.

I began to experience feelings of paranoia whenever I smoked this ready rock, in addition to that, I discovered that it also aroused my libido, which in effect led me to lust after stray women every-time I would smoke the ready rock, it created a ruthlessness in me that I could not control.

I thought these effects to be strange, because it all began happening when I started smoking the ready rock that was now on the streets for the consumer.

I thought of the possibility that perhaps the additives put into the ready rock was what caused these ill minded, and odd behaviors, I had never cheated on Angie, but now my fidelity was always being challenged whenever I smoked the ready rock.

I than reflected back to when in rock houses, I would see men, and women exiting bedrooms, and/or bathrooms partially nude, but it hadn't dawned on me then.

Now, all of those incidents were coming back to light in my mind, and I was understanding the reasons why those events were taking place.

I pondered with all of this in my mind, and concluded that there must be some type of an aphrodisiacal, and/or paranoia enhancing ingredient that is compounded into the cocaine paste before it even hit's the streets that's causing this ill state of mind.

Angie satisfied me sexually, there was no apparent reason for me to be promiscuous on her, furthermore, with the prevalence of aids in the American society, that type of a lifestyle could quickly become life threatening, or even fatal. I would occasionally cross paths with an attractive woman whom smoked rock, and although the temptation was at my disposal to engage in a one night affair, I never committed myself to one.

Being a man whom appreciates the beauty of the female anatomy, besides just a pretty face, she must have all of the credentials that come with it; brains, body, and personality for me to even be enticed by her.

There were a few rock smoking woman whom fell into that category though at the current time, but with the escalation of rock smokers hitting the streets, there would be many more to come.

I continued to rent out the car without any hardships behind it, and kept calling in to work with an excuse after paydays which was now be looked into by my supervisor.

One weekend I drove to Stockton, Ca to get away, while there I met a fellow whom stated that he needed a ride to go and pick up his T.V. and V.C.R. from where he was living because he was moving out, it was 2:00 a.m., being a nice guy I offered my assistance, so we drove to his place.

"Hey my brother can you park right hear on the streets, and turn off your lights?", he ask.

"Yeah, how long is this going to take you?"

"I'll be back out in about 10 minutes, so please don't take off on me!"

10 minutes later he comes running back with a T.V., puts it in the back of my car.

"I have one more thing to get out," he stated, and took off to go back.

I waited another 5 minutes, but started getting suspicious of his actions so I started up my car and left.

just as I was leaving a car was pulling up to the house, I immediately got unto the I-5 freeway, and came straight back to Sacramento.

I never really knew what that guy was actually up to, but had my suspicions.

I never saw the guy anymore, or anywhere after that, and wouldn't recognize him if I did, but by putting together the pieces of what was unfolding, I suspected that he was probably burglarizing some-ones place to support his drug habit.

I brought the T.V. home,plugged it in, it worked good, since I hadn't yet bought a T.V. set for our house I decided to just keep it.

That was a scenario which could have, without my knowing anything about it, turned bad for me in many ways.

Another evening while I was out washing our vehicle in front of the house a pretty young lady that I'd never seen before walked up to me.

"Excuse me brother do you smoke rock cocaine?"

"Yeah I smoke it, why do you asked?"

"I have some of it, but I'm new to Sacramento, I've only been here a week and don't know many people, I need a place where I could smoke some at", "would you like to smoke some of it with me she asked?"

However, Angie and the kids were home with friends over, so I retorted, "yeah just walk on up the street, and I'll be along to pick you up shortly."

Minutes later she was in the car with me, and Introduced herself, "I'm Angela, this dude I was with left me in this area, and I'm a good ways from my studio, when I saw you I figured maybe that you could help me out."

"I'm new to California from the Washington D.C. area, and I'm trying to get high."

We drove to her studio apartment, and smoked the rock that she had, and as usual, the rock enhanced my already present libido.

This would be the first incident in which I would cheat on Angie, as Angela, and I enjoyed some real good sex together that moment.

We developed a relationship after that, one that would last for a few more months, she learned of my family, but still wanted to get together with me in discretion, and it was kept confidential.

However, I did not know that she was also turning dates to support her rock habit.

Angela was an outgoing type of a person, and frequented the Oak Park area in pursuit of rock cocaine, it had been a couple of months since we'd met.

I hadn't seen her in almost a week so I went by her place to see her, her aunt was there, and told me that she had not seen her in over a week as well.

A couple of days went by, and I went back over to her place to see if she was there, when I got there her aunt shot a question my way that startled me.

"Hey dude where were you when they discovered Angela's body in the backyard of a vacant house in Oak Park?"

"What, When, and how did she die?", was my reaction to her inquiry.

Angela's aunt knew that she was with me a lot of times, and so not knowing much about me, she suspected that I was in some way responsible for Angela's death.

But Angela had, we all would learn sometime later, become one of the many females that was killed by a psychopathic killer of prostitutes in Oak Park.

Near the end of 1987 a handy man named Morris Solomon went on a killing spree of young black prostitutes in the Oak Park community whom would perform sexual acts in exchange for his giving them rock cocaine.

Angela had become one of his nine victims, which were all discovered either hung by the neck with extension cords inside of a closet in a vacant house that he was doing work on, or buried in the back yards of those houses.

I was heartbroken when I learned of her fate, because despite her having been a lady of the evening, and a rock smoker, she had a good heart, and didn't deserve to die in that manner.

Nevertheless, the consequences that come along with smoking rock are sometimes not revealed to one until it's too late.

Around this time in 1987 another form of cocaine hit the streets known as crack, I noticed distinctions between rock, and crack right away, because a few times I had bought the crack version of cocaine not knowing that it was crack.

I noticed that the color of the crack was like that of butter; an off yellow, also, in addition to this, if one held crack in their hands on a hot day for longer than 10 minutes, the substance would begin to turn mushy like dough, and when smoked, it left vile after taste in ones mouth.

Young rock dealers were trying to pass this synthetic crack onto the smokers relentlessly, sometimes giving double the amounts for their money, this is where the term crack originated from; it's after effects were critical to the smokers, leaving them sick to their stomach, sending some into convulsions, and sending others to the hospital.

Cracks crusade was short lived though after clientele wouldn't buy the stuff anymore, it eventually faded out, it was never really discerned whether this crack was another one of the systems attempts to filter in an unknown substance into the black communities as a means of destroying a race of people, as the rock cocaine had already begun doing.

THE CONSPITATORS TRAPS

The summer of 87 brought an explosion of violence into the State of California, and perhaps Nationally as well by the hands of the street gangs known as the bloods and the crips.

The debut of the movie colors was the means through which this Country's power structure depicted how these gangs portrayed themselves in society. Which was in fact, and in many ways a misrepresentation of those gangs, which in turn, by and through the movies debut caused a lot of bloodshed between the two gangs, and innocent bystanders were in the crossfire.

The movie colors brought death to young black men across California because of the medias misrepresentation of the information about the gangs.

This inaccurate portrayal of these gangs led to shoot-outs at theatre dwellings, sometimes claiming the lives of innocent people.

The blood and crip gangs were ignorant in coming to the realization that they'd been played by the media system of California as a result of releasing the movie colors, which in effect caused the two gangs to start riffs with each other when, and wherever possible, sometimes leading to fatalities.

I could not ascertain why these young black men could kill one another over some colors, colors that in part represent the American flag.

Further on this, the gangs other activities included the packaging and distribution of the lucrative rock cocaine, through which prompted them to disrespect their clientele, exploit the black woman sexually, and became the culprit of many black on black homicides, so for this I considered them to be a travesty of gangsters.

I had met and knew some of the blood and crips gang members of the Sacramento area through my dealings with them in the rock trade business, and some, not all, were morally conscience to the codes of human ethics.

However, I thought most of these gang-bangers to be as a fictitious entity, as the rock cocaine is a plague in America.

Shortly after I saw the movie colors I was in the G parkway area where Angie, and I had lived for a few years back then, it had become a drug haven, and killing grounds for young black gang-bangers.

I had stopped by to buy some rock, it was typical for dozens of gang members to stand about, and compete with one another for the sales of their rock cocaine.

I went to the first guy to see what he had to offer, didn't want it, so I moved on to the next guy, well the first guy got upset behind this, and stated to me "hey man your going to buy my product because I showed it to you."

I replied, "I'm not buying your shit," and started walking away, the dude came up in my face, and begin arguing with me; the next thing I knew his partners had jumped me, and commenced to striking me with a small club like weapon.

I managed to get up and escape the attack, but while running away I realized that my right eye's orbital socket had been shattered from a blow I'd received during the attack, and my eye was dangling out of it's socket.

It was early morning hours, I scrambled to my car, got in and raced to my mothers house where a family member rushed me to the Mercy General hospitals emergency room.

I was hospitalized, and had to under-go reconstructive eye orbital surgery, the operation was a success, and I recovered in a weeks time, my supervisor, and co-workers came to the hospital after they'd heard what had happened.

I had had to deviate from the truth to my co-workers of what really had happened to me in order to prevent any kind of follow up actions from my place of employment, and told them that I'd been in an accident.

I was off from work for a week, when I returned I was wearing dark prescription sun glasses, one of the inner dept. upstairs staff whom I saw every other day, ironically enough, asked me if I was on drugs because of my wearing of the glasses.

I told her of the accident, and the type of injury I sustained from it, but thought to myself, if she really only knew.

My work ethics remained in tact, and I was proficient on the job, it was only my attendance that had been the problem, after the incident I showed up to work for two months straight after paydays, and this was primarily due to my un-involvement with the rock cocaine because of the injury to my eye.

I had to take it easy, plus, being disabled I wasn't eager to have another misdeed happen to me in the condition I was in, so I stayed on the course of going to work after every other pay period.

Sometimes fate has a way of causing things to happen that one has no control over; while performing my duties at work one evening I was handling a box cutting knife cutting the plastic band off from around a box of paper, and on accident I cut through the band and on into my hand that was holding the band.

It was a very deep gash, and such incidents have to be reported as a policy of the company, so I phoned my supervisor at home whom came to the office and took me over to the Co.'s medical dept. to have it sewn up.

I was also advised by him that when accidents occurred to an employee while on duty, that employee would have to submit to a drug test to determine if that person was under the influence of drugs at the time of the injury.

That next day when I went to work my supervisor had the drug test bottle, and paper work all ready for me, I knew I had cocaine in my system, but there was nothing I could do, and had to go through with the test.

Three days later the test came back positive for cocaine, this in turn prompted an indeterminate period of random drug testing for me.

After several months of not using due to the eye injury, I had started back to hitting and missing, then onto smoking at will, I had become once again, out of control; the incident with my eye hadn't taught me a lesson of the perils of rock cocaine.

I knew that S.E.C. might test me at any time while at work, so I had my youngest son to urinate into a few small bottles, and I took them to work, and stored them in my locker.

Whenever I was requested to test I would retrieve from my locker one bottle of urine, and take it with me to the nurses station, go into the restroom, run the water until it got hot, add a little of the hot water into my son's urine, then pour that contents into their sample container; from that point on I never gave another positive test to them again.

In October my addiction was at it's peak, I went back to missing days after payday, one day I was on a smoking binge, and when it came time for me to punch in at 3:00 p.m. for the swing shift, I neither called in, nor went in to work that day.

The next day I called my supervisor, and finally came forth with the truth that I had a cocaine problem, and for help with it.

"Why yes Siege our Company has many substance abuse programs to choose from, we'll have to take a look at the type of medical Insurance that you selected to see which one will cover your treatment."

"Tomorrow before you begin your shift stop into my office, we'll sit down and go over your coverage and get you into the right treatment facility."

That next day I told my supervisor and his superior whom had now come into the picture, about my cocaine addiction and that I was really wanting help with getting myself clean and staying off of the substance.

My medical insurance covered only one rehab agency, that one was Starting Point, they called the place, and scheduled an appointment for the next day.

I went out to the appointment, was registered, and admitted all at the same time for a 30 day program.

Detoxification for 3 days meant that I wasn't allowed contact with anyone for those days, after that process I was relocated to the mainstream of the program where I began group sessions with other addicts, assigned a counselor, and given study assignments, and information pertinent to my drug of choice.

Ironically, there were drugs on the compound of the facility, it was a co-ed rehab which enticed the patients to engage in sexual activity among each other upon mutual consent, even further, some patients left the premises at night, and went to a liquor store a block away and brought back alcohol.

I was dubious on the theory that rehabs helped addicts anyway, personally I felt that it was all a political money making scheme, I mean they have good information in those programs, but it's all really up to the individual to turn his/her life around.

Nevertheless, I had to go through with it regardless of how I felt, because my job was now on the line.

One night a party was given to celebrate the graduation of a few of the patients, one guy slipped away to the liquor store and came back with some vodka, the staff learned of this, questioned everyone, and in the end I was the one whom was blamed for slipping alcohol into the place.

Certain staff members were racist there, and one in particular had me on their shit list, so she requested that I be removed from the program.

I had had 27 days in and was nearing my graduation, because of this incident, in which GOD was my witness, I had nothing to do with, I was in effect taken out of the program.

While I was in the program I kept receiving pay from my job, plus disability, and sick leave payments, all together, I had a total of $2,500.00 coming to me when I left the program.

I collected all of my back pay from my supervisor, that weekend Angie and I went Christmas shopping, where I gave her a thousand dollars for her and the kids.

It was December of 87 when I started back to work, I worked steadily until that week of Christmas, than I relapsed and went on a smoking binge.

The whole weekend I smoked rock, when it came the time for me to go to work on Monday afternoon, I was so engrossed with the rock until instead of preparing for work, I went out looking for more rock.

Starting Point had made one good point on addicts and their addictions, it being, that starting back on a drug after weeks, months, or even years of sobriety, that first encounter, and it's intensity sends one right over the edge and into never-land.

If I didn't learn anything from them, this was one of their teachings that was true, and was coming to past because I was living it a that time.

I went on a rock searching mission that Monday on up until it was time to punch in for work, I did the one thing that would cost me my employment with S.E.C.; I called in and said that I wasn't feeling well and wouldn't be in for the day.

Never once did I show up at work under the influence for fear of exposing myself to my co-workers, this is why I would always call in, nevertheless, this was to be my last time of calling in.

"Hello Robert I'm not feeling to good today, can I come in to work tomorrow?"

"Sure Siege, we'll see you tomorrow afternoon", was his reply!

The next day when I showed up to work my Sup. came up to me.

"How are you feeling today Siege?"

"Better than yesterday Robert!"

"Good, we have a meeting with my superior and the Co.'s district attorney in his office."

At that moment a strange feeling ran through me that my tenure with S.E.C. was about to come to an end.

At the meeting all the cards were put on the table so to speak, and I was offered the chance to resign, or face suspension, pending an imminent termination.

In order of sparing myself all of the humiliation and embarrassment, I simply signed the pertinent documents that finalized my resignation with the company

In that affidavit my term with the company would expire on 12-31-87, this contract allowed me to sulk in my defeat for a couple more weeks.

I showed up to work everyday for those two weeks, and displayed no bitterness towards my supervisor or the Co., I couldn't blame anyone but myself, the devil, and his candy, the rock cocaine for my demise.

Over the Christmas holidays Angie's mother called, and wanted to visit us and the kids, she gave Angie her arrival time and asked if we could pick her up at the airport.

Angie was furious at me for having lost my job and acted cool towards me for it, despite all the money I'd given to her, my employment was our livelihood, and she was mad.

Carol, Angie's mother was happy to see her Grandchildren, and had plenty of gifts for them, she embraced me and commented, "you guys are doing so good for yourselves, keep it up", but she hadn't learned of the news yet.

Angie was hesitant on telling her mother of this because it was the holidays, and because Carol had leant us the money to buy our car with, so she decided to just let things work themselves out for the time being.

On Christmas day both of our families were there at our place, we were all watching videos, eating, drinking, and socializing; everybody was joyous and celebrating the Christmas holiday.

My sister Holly was now both walking and talking since the accident, she hadn't went back to smoking rock again, I, was I whom continued on with the destructive course of chasing the glass phallic.

Later that evening when everyone had departed Carol wanted to buy some beer from the liquor store, and was going to walk there which was only a few blocks away from our house.

She grabbed her purse and took out her wallet where she had $60.00 put away, she looked for her money over and over but could not seam to find it.

Her purse had been laying in the corner of our room all that day, earlier in the day I had seen her purse there, had opened it up, got out her wallet and taken out the $60.00.

I had been craving the rock and was broke, this was my ticket to the next hit of rock.

Carol, after diligently searching through her purse blurted out, "where is my damn money?"

Angie and her mother didn't accuse me of taking the money, because I'd never stolen anything from Angie, let alone money, however, during the holidays I had had one of my friends over, and suggested that he could have went upstairs to use the bathroom, and perhaps slipped into our room when no-one was looking and took Carols money.

After the discussion I left for a while, when I returned it was 2:00 a.m., I had been smoking rock and wanted some more.

Carol was up sitting in the living room listening to music, the T.V. that I'd brought back from Stockton, Ca was plugged into the living room wall, I began unplugging it.

"What do you think your doing with that television set Siege?", she asked,

"I' m selling it because it was stolen from someone in another town, I'll be buying a new one soon to replace it", grabbed it up and left the house.

When I came back a few hours later, Carol and Angie were up talking, Angie had told her mother everything about my losing my job, my drug habit, and the probability that I was the culprit in her money coming up missing; all this was brought about by my taking off with the T.V. set.

Angie started out, "where do you get off taking appliances out of our home while I'm asleep?"

"Your probably the one who took my mothers money, after all she's done to help us!," this allegation put me on the defense, and I struck back.

"I didn't take Carol's money, but I should be able to take this T.V. set that was stolen anyway, without any repercussions from anyone."

Carol came to her daughter's defense.

"Siege you are really out of line on this, I believe that you did take my money."

All of the arguing and commotion woke up the children, and they were standing in the hallway crying.

Angie grabbed some clothes; Carol gathered up all of her belongings and they all left the house, it would be almost a week before I'd see or hear anything from Angie, and the kids.

They had went to Carols sisters house whom also lived in the Sacramento area, that incident was the beginning to the end of our relationship.

Carol had her sisters husband take her back to the San Fransisco International Airport after she'd rescheduled an earlier flight back to Chicago.

Angie, although still in love with me, was now distancing herself from me. she was at a point now where I had forced her hand and she wasn't sure of what to do next to resolve this problem.

After careful thought she decided it was time for us to separate, maybe this would open my eyes as to what I was doing to myself and to the people who loved me.

She started searching for a smaller two bedroom apartment without any plans of me being in the picture.

I was hurt by her decision and realized that I was nearing the end of my rope with her as well, sadly though as that may have been, I was in such a state of delusion by my excessive rock smoking that her decision to leave me didn't really sink into until the reality of it hit when she and the kids were really gone.

I was at a point in my life where the things that mattered most to me, like family, employment, and spousal love weren't as important to me as they once were, the only thing that mattered to me was that next hit of rock, I had fallen victim to this substance like I had witnessed other people do.

Still not taking a heed to all that had be-fallen me, one night I was driving around on a search for some more rock, I came to a stop at a red light. When the light turned green for me to advance on to make my left turn, as I was turning, a car ran it's red light; I saw it coming upon me and tried to speed up, but wasn't fast enough and was broadsided on the passengers side.

The oncoming vehicle struck the right rear side of my car spinning it around and throwing me from within the vehicle upon impact.

I was taken to the U.C.D. Med center where I was treated for an injury to my neck and released.

The impact to our car totaled it, but more than that, GOD was throwing me warning signals about the way I was living my life.

Rock cocaine was a man made instrument of the devils which was deployed and used to destroy people, and I needed to become aware of this revelation.

I had been blessed and lucky thus far, but my time was running out, however, I would still go through more trials, and tribulations before I would finally see rock as an evil plague that was designed to destroy black people in this Country.

The loss of another car, one that we still owed Angie's mother for just added fuel to the fire when I told Angie of what had happened, she lit into me with both hands, I could do nothing but just stand there and take the wrath that she was throwing at me, because I had really let her down with this incident.

Now she was without transportation, and this compounded the situation even more, she wouldn't be able to facilitate her business everyday, this was distressing, and there was no immediate solution to this crisis I'd put us in.

Angie resorted to living with her aunt until she was able to locate a decent two bedroom apartment for her and the children.

After she moved out of the duplex we shared together, I still kept my key, I went into that empty dwelling and stripped the windows of all it's curtains, took them to a rock dealer and got rock for them.

This malicious deed would later fall back on Angie when the landlord charged her for the missing curtains, and didn't refund her the deposit even though the place was left clean.

I hadn't intentionally done that to her, it was the demonic influence of the rock that governed my actions.

I moved in with my sister Deneice whom didn't use drugs, her and Angie had been good friends every since we'd started out together as a couple. I'd realize how badly I'd screwed up whenever Angie and the kids would come by and visit deneice and her children.

I wouldn't be at my sisters long enough to get comfortable there though after her household items started coming up missing in action by me.

A month after I was there I took her cordless telephone and traded it for rock, and she gave me the boot for it.

Around March of 88 the woman's insurance Co. whom had totaled out our car settled with us on a sum of $3,200.00 for the cost of our car, which I gave straight to Angie, and for my personal injuries I was awarded $3,900.00.

Angie used her money as a down payment towards a 1987 Hyundai hatchback, I went to a used car lot and paid $2,000.00 for a 1982 Buick skylark.

We were both back into the swing of things again, the tension and ill feelings that had come between us had somewhat eased now, we were communicating with each other.

I was homeless and would sleep at my mothers place sometimes, or I would crash out in my vehicle, on occasions I would hang around in drug areas all night searching for some rock.

I had bought some clothes with some of my settlement money, and basically smoked the remainder of it away.

Being homeless now I gave thought to retrieving the currency that was paid into S.E.C. for my retirement, which was called P.E.R.S.,(personnel early retirement system), but as I thought more on it, I abandoned the idea.

However, one day while in a department store I ran into a co-worker and learned from him that I was entitled to a severance pay.

That next day I contacted the S.E.C. personnel dept. and found out that they did in fact owe me severance money in the amount of $7,000.00.

It was appearing to seem that GOD was still watching over me despite my wrecklessness of habit, even though all money I got went up in smoke.

After receiving that money a couple a days later I eventually went through it on wild spurges with the rock, alcohol, and women.

Being single I had begun participating in promiscuous sex with unknown woman occasionally, at that time Aides was indeed an epidemic to be concerned about when I had these encounters with stray woman.

The virus was previously limited to the gay population, but was just being discovered that it could be transmitted by the heterosexual population as well.

This recent finding, led me to believe that the media was still uncertain about the transmission of the virus onto other promiscuous groups.

This, coupled with my state of delusion when I was under the influence of rock gave me little cause for concern about aides when I did ravish these woman I would have just met.

It doesn't take long to spend up a few thousand dollars when one is smoking the rock, because no matter how much you smoke you'll never get enough to satisfy your cravings, and you'll always want more.

By the summer of 88 I was down on my luck with no cash on hand, I started hanging around in the Oak Park area hustling; I would drive the rock smokers to get their poison, in addition to renting out my vehicle.

In Oak Park I met an old man named Rob that owned his house, he was allowing a youngster to sell rock out of his place so long as the youngster kept him supplied with the rock.

My luck was changing in that I now had a place to lay my head at night, the old man had no means of transportation, so I would take him on his errands.

His living quarters was a little precarious for me because at that time the authorities were just starting to kick in the doors of drug houses.

By staying there I was putting my freedom in jeopardy by tending the doors when all of the customers came to buy rock, so I kept a watchful eye out for the cops.

At the end of my shift I was given some rock for my services, this arrangement went on for several months, and un-knowingly, all the while the police had had the place under surveilance.

One day while away from the house, it got raided, the police found a few pounds of cocaine, arrested the occupants of the premises and shut the place down, the LORD had took me out of the line of fire at that particular moment, and I thanked him for it.

With no place to go I began hanging out on the streets of Oak Park again and taking addicts to buy their rock, in return they'd either smoke with me or break me off a piece of what they'd bought.

In this ungodly business of rock cocaine trafficking, one is subjected to meet and have dealings with scandalous people at least once or more a day.

I met a fellow in Oak Park one night whom had to bags of clothing he said to be brand new, he asked, "hey my brother can you take me somewhere to trade these bags of clothes to a rock dealer, I'll take care of you," he asked me.

"Well yeah I don't see why I can't, get in the car", I replied.

We left the area and went to the Glen Elders community, another predominately black area of Sacramento where there was a lot of the rock.

We ran into a dealer, and the guy gave him one bag of the clothes where there was new items only on the top, underneath were used clothing, so the dealer took the bag and gave us a rock.

After we smoked that, the dude suggested, "hey man I got that other bag of clothes back there," when we showed up, the dealer ran up to the car, and said "hey dudes you got some more clothes for me huh?, wait right here, I'll be back."

When he returned he had a .44 magnum in his hand, he went around to the guy in the passenger seat of my car.

"Sucker, only half of those clothes were new, are you trying to work me?" I had had no idea that the dude was running a sham.

"Get out of the fucking car dude," he hollered, I was in a bad fix, because I had parked into a stall facing a fence with the motor running, there was no way I could stealthily take off without him blasting out my windows as I did so. He then came around to my side and at gun point, demanded me out.

We both stood there looking down the barrel of his .44 magnum, other youngsters, both male and female looked on laughing about the situation.

"I don't like the idea of being worked the way you just did with them used clothes."

"So now both of you dudes strip down butt as naked, if you want to live!" Standing there in the nude, and not knowing what was to come next.

He said, "Now you assholes leave your belongings right there, and go get and bring back my money, and when you come back you'll get all of your stuff back."

I was furious at this because I didn't know that some of the clothes were used, however, we left to hustle up that 20 dollars we owed him, with no luck, I had to drive naked over to my oldest sisters house and enter her house with a newspaper wrapped around my waist.

"Hey sis can you please help me out of this mess I'm in, and I explained it to her."

"Damn Siege, we've all told you of what can happen when your involved in that lifestyle, I'll do it this time, but you'd better straighten yourself out because I might not be around for you a next time!"

She gave me the money and we drove back over there, our clothes were still laying in the streets where we'd left them, we paid the dealer, collected all our things and left.

That incident was humiliating, and could have turned fatal for me, and it was one of the many precarious situations that I would subject myself to while dealing in the rock cocaine game.

Gun play among young black men in gangs had become notorious in California, most every gang member/rock dealer carries a gun; dealing in the rock trade necessitates having one to protect himself, and his product.

The black on black homicides were rapidly increasing in California, as well as the Country as a result of this rock cocaine plague.

THE TRAPS OF THE TRADE

In November of 88, Cadillac T, an acquaintance of mine, whom was a crip, was shot in the chest at point blank range by a blood member for no other reason other than his challenging the blood about selling rock on his turf.

It was believed by everyone whom witnessed the incident, that T. had had a 50/50 chance of surviving the gun shot wound had the paramedics turned on the siren and rushed him to the U.C.D. Med centers emergency room.

Nevertheless, they drove to the hospital casually, not warranting it as a rush situation, and he died on the way there.

Another rock related killing took place shortly after T's death in the Del Paso Heights area where a young high roller(rock dealer) was found dead in his house with several gun shots to his head.

This was a micro percentage of the National statistics of rock related black on black homicides, nevertheless it was happening.

I would take notice of several more deaths, most all of which were attributes of either the rock cocaine, or gang retaliation killings.

In hindsight of all of these killings, I began to associate both the rock and gangs as instruments of death and destruction for many black American young men.

The rock cocaine plague didn't just limit itself to the poverty stricken black communities in America, it was also playing host to many of America's elite blacks as well.

To name a few, there was singer Natalie Cole, singer Chaka Kan, acter Todd Bridges, N.B.A. star Irving Magic Johnson; even the

Mayor of our Nations capital, Marion Barry was caught up in this rock cocaine business to everyone's surprise.

Why this rock cocaine was so luring, attractive, and forthcoming only to blacks mystified me, it's almost as if the ingredients, and/or formula in this rock were somehow an arcane concoction designed specifically for the black people.

The pernicious and luring characteristics of the rock are demonic in the sense of how vulnerable and disoriented it renders one while under the influence of it.

I pondered this all around in my head, thinking of all I'd brought upon myself behind the rock, and it made me re-evaluate my self worth in life.

I had come to realize through the searching of my sole that one has to put GOD in his life, plus want badly to give up smoking rock in order to successfully quit it.

Rock is an evil omen of the devil, designed by his earthly followers, cynic men of power, and distributed out into the world to destroy people.

I, would later, have to hit the very bottom, or be given an ultimatum of either sincerely quitting, or be forever bound in that vicious and precariousness triggered by and through using rock cocaine.

I would go by and visit my mother whenever I could manage the time to do so, it would be times when I would need to escape the rock scene and relax. When this period of rest and relaxation would occur, I'd sit around the house talking with family, and watching T.V.

One evening while watching the tube an educational program was on, during a commercial break, a cocaine abuse commercial came on the air.

It was a depiction of a scene from the T.V. movie roots, with the showing of the actor Levar Burton in shackles around his waist, neck, and ankles; behind him were a line of other blacks linked together by chains, and shackled together in the same manner.

At the bottom of this scene there were several white pieces of rock cocaine along with a statement saying if you use this, you'll end up like this; the message being, by using rock one would be falling into the trap of the chains of modern day slavery.

It was a perfect illustrative message to black Americans as to the realities and the implications that that small white piece of rock cocaine carried.

The irony of this depiction was that back in the slave era black people were subjugated by the white man, but now some 200 plus years later, blacks are again under subjugation, but this time by a small white substance known as rock cocaine.

After that airing, I never again saw that commercial in circulation on any National T.V. networks.

The American power structure knew that there was a message in that commercial that would serve to wake Black Americans up to the reality of the systems true intentions behind this rock cocaine plague, so they pulled it from the T.V. networks.

By my seeing that true to life depiction behind the rock cocaine's purpose for black Americans, I gradually began to associate every injustice, and misfortune caused by rock cocaine as a means of debilitating black people in this Country.

This also made me see rock cocaine in a different light now, although I still continued to smoke the stuff, I became more conscientious to the impositions on Blacks utilized by the authorities, and the unjust laws beginning to govern the judicial system regarding rock cocaine charges.

Although my feelings about the rock was now a negative one, and very opinionated, I still found it a difficult task of breaking free form it's evil hold, and what complicated it more was the ever growing enticement of the women that were beginning to surface in large numbers in and around rock trafficking areas.

Rock had a depraved effect on woman in the way that it rendered them vulnerable to the whims of men's sexual acts in exchange for the high, 90% of the time the ladies I'd come into contact with would accept my invitation to smoke with me regardless of what the proposition to them was.

I was single now and did meet a few lovely looking women when I was smoking the stuff, and the girls that I would encounter while smoking rock were always eager to provide some type of sexual pleasure in exchange for a rock high.

I was a kind hearted guy with a soft spot for women, simply because they are the weaker of our species, and I would never disrespect a woman just because she was susceptible to me during her times of vulnerability due to her rock addiction.

Some of the ladies I would meet were not only nice looking, but intelligent as well, I met one who's name was lea, she was quiet and easy going, so I took a lighting to her, and we ended up spending a lot of time together. Because she too was homeless; I took her under my wing and tried to get her off of the rock along with myself.

We adhered to this plan only while in each others company though, when we were separated, each would return to smoking rock behind the others back, then at times I would catch her in the presence of others guys, and assume that she was trading sex for rock, which turned out to be true.

I realized then that a man would never be able to rehabilitate a prospective woman that smoked rock unless she set it in her heart to really want to quit.

I had to dismiss Lea, and in doing so thought to myself of what a waste of a wonderful person.

I missed Angie and the kids desperately, but knew in my mind that she was a lot better off without me, and that she was not about to reconcile with me now, if ever at all.

While on my rock smoking binges I sought companionship, as a replacement of Angie through some of the women I would encounter out there in traffic.

It wasn't my nature to just enjoy the sexual aspect of it at all, if I liked the girl I would try to get her to reconsider her lifestyle with regards to her abuse of the rock, and what it brought back to them;

the promiscuous sex they engaged in, and hoped that they would try to turn their life around.

I had witnessed an inhuman sex act on a woman one time at the hands of one of the sick minded gang members whom just didn't give a shit about a rock smoking women, one way or the other.

The atrocity of this act disgusted me as I looked on in disbelief, I was there in the rock house with another guy whom was buying a large amount of rock, I wanted to break up this travesty, but didn't want to cause any form of retaliation upon myself from other gang members.

However, the girl was on all fours and beginning to look terrified, and that was when I intervened and told the youngsters to get the dog off of the girl.

Surprisingly though, while all laughing at the exhibition, they pulled the pit off the girl, she got up, got dressed, got her rock and left.

I would either eyewitness myself, or hear from other people all of the wicked absurdities of sexual depravities that woman would encounter on their quest to smoke more rock cocaine, and it sickened me.

Holly was now living with my mother, I would periodically drop in and visit from time to time and stay over if I was drained from running the streets and smoking too much rock.

As the Christmas of 88 was approaching I started going over to mothers house more frequently, at times when I was there I'd see indicators from the past in Holly's character of when she was smoking the rock, I thought that maybe I was mistaken by this.

But when I asked my mother if she suspected that Holly was smoking rock again, her reply was, "yes she is on it again Siege."

"Son," she would start out with, "she goes out, buys the stuff, comes back home, locks herself in her room, and smokes until it's all gone."

I couldn't believe what I was hearing after her near death encounter, that she would give the devil another chance at her by indulging herself in his candy again.

My conviction to the belief that this rock plague is truly a tool of the devils was now affirmed.

At first, our eldest sister Dee, Holly's power of attorney, would at her request go to the bank and draw money out for her, and Holly would buy expensive clothes, gold jewelry, diamond earrings, and the remainder of her cash she would buy some rock with.

Holly had thousands in her account from the settlement and it was her money, so Dee would always accommodate her with her withdrawal request. This went on through the Christmas holidays, on into the New Year of 89, and there after, then Dee, at our mothers demand would either limit, or deny funds to Holly in large amounts.

She would only be issued enough money for personal things and/or periodical shopping sprees, this prompted Holly to start trading her expensive jewelry to the rock dealers, and later come up with an excuse that she'd lost her jewelry and wanted to buy some more, and those items were always replaced.

Holly repeated this process endlessly and was always compensated for them in the end, until one day all of the family got together and agreed that Holly had traded thousands of dollars worth of jewelry to the rock dealers for less than 1/4th of their worth, and she was not able to buy anymore jewelry unless she'd gotten off of the rock.

All she was allowed to buy was clothes, perfumes and personal items, she became upset about it because it was her money, but the family just couldn't see her being taken advantage of by those rock dealers.

Because of this defeat she eventually started staying around the house more often.

In February of 89 I got back into renting out my car for rock, I had always bought rock from this one house in Oak Park, one of the guys and I were fairly close, so I rented out my car to one of his friends.

The dudes offer to me was a quarter of a ounce of rock for the use of my vehicle for a straight week.

I had never sold rock myself, but now I began entertaining the idea of it, so I accepted the offer and turned over the keys to the guy.

The opportunity I'd been given to sell rock for myself sounded good, but once I'd taken that first hit of the stuff, my plan to sell it never got off the ground.

By the next day all of the rock was gone, I was broke and all I could do was see my car rolling around in traffic for the next six days.

I was not one to renege on an oath by calling it in as stolen, or try and take it back as some rock smokers would be inclined to do after their dope was gone.

So I hung around Oak Parks pebble beach as it was called because of it's easy access of getting rocks, and hustled, by leading buyers to get their stuff, or by being the middle man in a deal which insured me a piece of some of the rock.

Pebble beach was a block park where everybody went to buy their rock, drink, hustle, or just plain party with other people there.

At night I'd roam the streets, or hang around rock houses in the vicinity and be given some rock to pose as a lookout for the cops to the dealers.

When the week was up on the rental of my car, I went to get it back, the dude had installed some boom speakers in the back, and had put another tape deck in the dash, and said to me.

"Man this car belongs to me now, I bought it from you when I gave you all of that dope, don't you remember?"

"No, I didn't sell you my car for the amount that you gave me, If I'd have sold it to you it would have been for more than what you'd given to me."

I had a problem on my hands now, because the dude always had a few of his homies with him wherever he went.

I wasn't a snitch, and wasn't going to involve the cops, for by doing that things would surely escalate into some kind of trouble for me, so I had to bide my time and wait for a sneak surprise opportunity to get it back.

I would retrieve my vehicle even if it meant going into some kind of a battle with the dude and his crew, so I devised a plan of how to get back my car.

I took record of all the places that the guy visited and kept the list with me at all times.

Some of those so called gang-bangers are cowards and hide behind a gun, or their posse, a characteristic that's akin to the tactics of the police.

Biding time for the right moment presented itself when I caught the dude by his self one morning at a house in the south area of Sacramento.

Having boxed for three years while at Consumers River College I had no fears, and was physically, quite capable of handling myself.

He came out of one of the houses where I'd kept a record of, I had had an extra set of keys that I had picked up from my mother's house, and was already in the vehicle removing all of his belongings from my car as he approached the car.

He walked up to me talking big shit.

"Hey mother fucker what do you think your doing in my car?"

I replied, "You better face the facts dude cause neither you, or anybody else is going to just take nothing from me like what your trying to do, so make your next move, but I'm driving my car away from here."

"Just because I smoke rock isn't reason enough for you to think me as being a sucker," and as I said that to him he sucker punched me in the jaw from outside of the open window.

I shook off the blow like it was nothing and looked at the dude as if to imply was that all that you have for me.

I wasn't sure if there were any of his partners in the house, so I didn't get out and mix it up with him, but rather, started up my car and slowly drove off.

My mission with this guy was to get back what was mine, not to get into a scrape with him unless it was absolutely unavoidable.

I quit hanging around the Oak Park area for a little while after that, in part because I didn't want to deal with any kind of retaliation from his comrades, but also because the guy still had my other set of keys to the car.

I had been a step ahead of him by not having gave to him the key that unlocked the door at the time of the deal.

Nevertheless, as ruthless as he was if he'd come across the car out there somewhere he probably would have busted out one of the windows to gain access, and I wanted to avoid that.

Locating to a new area wasn't complicated now that I was back in motion though, the rock was prolific in just about every black community of Sacramento.

I didn't have far to go from the Oak Park area, I stationed up over in the area of fruitridge, and Martin Luther King Jr. blvd.

It was about 3 miles outside of Oak Park, and full of condominium housing units where rock cocaine was around in abundance.

The prospect of hustling was even better there, I ran into several people that I hadn't seen in years which made me more comfortable being in the area.

There was a quick stop convenience store in the area that stayed open 24 hours, this is where the start to my patterns of petty thievery would began.

I would go into the store with big clothing on and take bottles of 40 ounce alcohol and trade it to the youngsters for their rock cocaine, I would only do this on certain shifts at that store, and relied on my intuition of things when I stole.

Committing these acts of petty thievery served to heighten my participation in more criminal activity, mostly small stuff, but still crimes none the less.

I have a trust worthy demeanor about myself, but being under the influence of the rock, I would take advantage of some peoples kindness at times; good people whom I would have just met, and whom were not drug users.

I was raised with good morals, but smoking that rock made me just put aside those morals and become somewhat scandalous at times, something like a Dr. good and Mr. bad.

One afternoon I was over an acquaintances house, his neighbor from across the street had a little drink in him, was feeling good and came over to socialize briefly, upon leaving he invited me over to his house for another beer.

While inside, my demeanor, or personality must have led him to confide in me enough to show me an envelope full of $50.00 bills, perhaps his being tipsy prompted him to flash his money as he did.

After putting the money back where he'd gotten it, he went to his bathroom to relieve himself, remembering where he'd put the envelope I went there, took half of it's contents and put it back.

When he returned, I sat and talked with him for a short while and then got up and left, I never heard anything mentioned about it from my friend.

Another incident of cunningness happened one night when I was with a female I'd just met, it was around 10:00 p.m. and we were stopping at people's houses pretending to have just run out of gas with our children in the car up the street.

We went to this one house and was invited in by an older couple, the man was a Christian and a very giving person, he gave us both sodas while listening to our story, after hearing our plight, being sympathetic he went into his wallet and came out with a $50.00 dollar bill for us, we thanked he and his wife, and left.

After an hour of rock smoking we were broke again, I felt that I could con the old guy a second time, and went back, this time saying that it turned out to be the fuel pump that was bad on the car.

I had, prior to going there the second time, written out a promissory note to repay the guy, and showed it to him along with my I.D.

I said that Auto Zone parts store on Fruitridge rd. had priced one for me at $60.00, the old guy sat there for a minute thinking about it then reluctantly gave in to us for the second time.

These kind of misdeeds were not characteristic of me, and the next day I felt bad about myself for having done something of that nature to such a GOD loving human being, and ask GOD for forgiveness.

But the rock has no conscience, as is typical with anyone affiliated with the devil and his demons, I felt that as long as I continued to use the devils candy I would be a disciple of his deceptive deeds.

Rock cocaine was so demonic that I began to wonder if when one inhales the combustion of smoke from the rock, are they in essence evoking the spirit of the devil into them, which in effect is what causes ones personality to change as it does.

Because I was in a sense becoming as ruthless as many of the rock addicts that I would cross paths with out there in that world.

Taking breaks from that sinister lifestyle, I would go by and visit my mother and sister Holly, upon some of those visits Holly would be smoking the rock, which meant that she had started back on it.

When she wasn't given money to get the stuff, she would panhandle in nearby shopping centers, and on her good days would raise up to $50.00.

This practice became so feasible for her until she would be gone all day as if it were her job, returning later with enough cash to buy a few $20.00 pieces of rocks.

When she'd come back I didn't pester her for hits of the stuff because I didn't even want to see her smoking the shit, even further, I loved my mother and knew that it was distressful for her knowing that we both used.

On occasions I'd take a hit if Holly offered me one, and our mother wasn't around when this happened, afterwards I'd go out with her, and join in with the panhandling to get the money for more of the rock.

This took place when I came around my mothers house, so I mainly stayed away, and over in the area where I had access to multiple hustles, and constant offers from rock smokers to take them somewhere to score.

One evening over in that area that I hung out in I ran into a young lady that I'd went to high school with named Sibil, she was one of those naïve type of girls that portrayed a divine quality of innocence about her.

We talked about the past and brought back old memories of how things were compared to how they are now.

She lived in the Oak Park area but came to the fruitridge Condo's to hustle and smoke rock every other day, when she mentioned this, I was surprised that up to that point I hadn't seen her around.

On this day we just drank beer, talked, then departed company of each other. I would soon learn just how stealthy, and cunning a person shed' become from her rock smoking, when we'd meet again.

Later that night I was in and around rock houses waiting for victims to approach wanting to buy some rock, I would intercept them if they appeared naïve to the game, get their money, and go and buy the rock for them. But before bringing it back to them I would break off a piece of it for myself.

This worked sometimes, but on some occasions it caused problems for me when a client wouldn't accept what I brought back because it was too small, I'd have to go back and put some of what I had taken out back with it and return to them.

Usually though I would apply some finesse at the outset of my operation and the client would be won over by my conversation and tactics and would accept what I'd give to them.

The one thing that I had become proficient at while trafficking in the rock cocaine trade was communication techniques, I had a mouth piece that could manipulate someone into trusting me of handling the transaction for them.

This was my way of hustling throughout the day that enabled me to have rock to smoke, and eliminated my having to resort to the acts of petty thefts.

Sometimes people would buy rock and need a pipe to smoke it in, I made sure that I had access to one of those when ever the time presented itself.

Early every morning I would retire to the car where I could get a little rest and be as fresh as possible for the next day.

The car was parked in a spot so that when I arose I would have a full view of what was going on in the area.

One morning I was sitting in my vehicle drinking a cup of coffee when an older man walked up to my window.

"Hey young fella you know of anyone who'd be interested in renting a Cadillac Coupe Deville for a little of some rock cocaine?"

Responding, "yeah I do as a matter of fact".

"You want to lock up your car, and come ride with me to that place?,"

"Yeah give me a minute here" was my retort."

As we walked and talked the old guy said that he'd been smoking, ran out of money, and just wanted to rent the car out for a rock.

When we finally got to his Cadillac, I was awe struck as I glanced upon his 1984 baby blue coupe sitting there pretty as ever, it was only 5 years old and still in mint condition, I said to myself that this rock cocaine has one hell of an influence over it's victims, including myself.

I wondered if their wasn't anything that a rock smoker wouldn't do to get more of that stuff when they ran out of it.

We got in and drove to a rock house, even at 9:00 a.m. dealers stood out waiting for the clients to arrive, when we pulled up every dealer, in anticipation of big money being spent, ran up to the vehicles door.

I got out and went up to one of the guys I'd dealt with before on another occasion, explained the deal to him and, he jumped at the opportunity.

Two fat rocks were given to me which I took back to the old man, the dealer and I got into the Caddy with the old guy, and we drove back to the area where my car was, and was let out.

Three hours later the dealer pulls up on time, and says, "hey old man I'll give up an eighth of a gram more of rock if I could keep the car until the tomorrow morning, the old guy was sprung at this point, "that sounds good to me, lets do it," he says, and the Cadillac left for a second time.

We smoked pretty big all that day, and even had a couple of females join us on our smoking spree, the old guy loved the company of women while he was smoking, and was able to get real loose with them.

Around 1:00 a.m. after the partying was over, the rock was gone, and the girls too, the two of us just sat in my car pondering over what the next day would bring in.

Much to my surprise the old man blurted out, "young man do you think those guys would be willing to trade a lot of rock straight across for my Cadillac, I have other newer vehicles at my house."

Curious, I asked, "how much rock were you looking to get for your car?"

After some silent thought to himself, he replied, "two ounces."

That was a bargain deal for someone if the man was indeed serious about this transaction, and from the way things were unfolding, it appeared that he was.

I wanted the automobile for myself, but knew I could in no way raise that kind of money, at best I would be able to orchestrate the deal with the dealer and come out of it with quite a bit of rock for myself.

I took control by instructing the old guy to let me handle the business which would insure that he'd get a lot of rock for his vehicle, he agreed with that idea, now all we had to do was wait for the dealer with the car to show up.

We waited all day for the right prospect to come around, but to no avail, and the dealer whom had the car hadn't shown up yet, so we could present that deal to him also, the old man was beginning to worry.

I said, "lets give him another hour, and if he's not hear by then, we'll go looking for him", I knew all of the dealer's selling locations.

It was 11:00 p.m., we were about to make our move to start looking for this dude when we spotted the Caddy.

The youngster kept on going though, I knew the tricks played by these youngsters, acting quickly on behalf of the old guy I said, "hop into my car quick", we took off and caught up with the youngster, and flagged him down.

The car was full of youngsters, and they didn't stop so I followed them to the rock house, this evasion angered me, and when they finally came to a stop, I yelled out, "exit the fucking car fast, you evaded us", they all complied.

Revealing our idea to the dealer he became interested and asked, "where is the pink slip for the car?", so I went back to ask the old man.

Apparently he'd planned on trading the car off anyway because he produced the pink slip.

I got the slip and went inside the house, and explained that I was going to be handling the deal because the old man was my uncle.

Most rock houses were shabby dwellings, bare of furniture, dishes everywhere, and just plain filthy; as was the case with this one.

The youngster left the living quarters and returned with two plastic bags; each with chunks of rock in them about the size of bars of soap.

I then went into phase two of the operation and told the youngster, "I'm taking out my issue of the dope ahead of time, but don't worry about it because my uncle is definitely going through with the deal."

I went into each bag and broke off a third of the rock then sealed them back up, the dealer then followed me out to the car where the old man was and I presented the product to him.

The old man either didn't know the true quantity of an ounce, or the youngster had unusually big ounces because he was very satisfied with what he was receiving, even though I had broke off of each ounce.

The deal was sealed, the old man went all throughout the automobile gathering up what belonged to him, and then signed the slip over to the young dealer.

The old man and I hopped into my car and we drove back to the area where we'd first met.

There was an apartment building there where the landlord was a rock smoker, and would rent out apartment dwellings for days at a time when they were vacant in exchange for rock cocaine.

There were several available units to rent out, but the complex, once a decent residential apartment complex had become a haven for drug, and gang activity, prostitution was practiced there also, and at least once a week the sheriffs were raiding the grounds.

I gave the slumlord 1/16 of an ounce of rock which bought the old man and I three days of residence there.

We went in and started some serious smoking, I led on like I hadn't gotten much for my services rendered throughout the whole ordeal, and asked the old man, "hey O.G, can you break me off a good size piece for myself?".

He broke me off an eighth of an ounce of his stash as gratitude for my having made the whole thing happen.

After we smoked about a gram of the stuff the old man asked,

"can you run me back out to my house in the Rancho Cordova community of east Sacramento?"

His mission in coming to that area where we'd met was probably to trade that vehicle for rock from the start anyway.

"Yeah I can do that for you O.G", we left, and drove for about 30 minutes, then, following his directions pulled up in front of his place, which was pretty nice, there were two other vehicles parked in the driveway; one was a brand new big body Mercedes Benz, and the other was a Lincoln Town car; also new.

I couldn't discern all that I was taking into my brain at that instant, the adobe ranch style home set back off of the streets with two big cars sitting in front of it; yet this old guy was out in drug areas risking his life trying to trade one of his cars for rock cocaine.

I had began to realize that rock cocaine addiction made people do irrational things in their life, as the old man was doing, I just hoped that this wasn't the beginning of a down hill spiral for the old man.

I thanked the old guy and said, "I'm always in that area if you need my services in the future", and started out on my way back to the drug, and poverty stricken area from where I had come.

Back at the complex I spotted a female in the mist of the congregation of complex dwellers, and gestured for her to come over to me.

She was cute, but was a rock smoker and would serve the purpose I had intended for her once I re-convened to smoking my rock.

We went into the apartment and got acquainted with each other.

"Hi I'm Gina", she stated.

"I'm Siege.", I then put a hit on the pipe for her, after taking the hit she blew out the smoke and immediately began to undress herself.

I was delighted at the sight of her nude body, it was voluptuous in every way, and once again I gave thought to the power that this rock wielded over people.

I thou that she was probably used to exchanging sex for rock and didn't need to be coached on at deriving at what was expected of her next.

I didn't want her to feel isolated in her nudity, so I joined her and we both sat nude together, and smoked some more of the rock.

After we had smoked a gram or so, I put the rest away and said to her "you can get comfortable if you'd like because I'm exhausted, and am going to relax", she must have been up for a couple of days herself, because she curled up next to me and fell fast asleep.

When we awoke it was night outside, she turned my way, kissed me and said, "your different than most other guys whom always demanded me to perform oral sex on them," having said that she climbed on top of me and slid my phallic into her.

Gina had won my heart by that sweet and crafty maneuver, and we enjoyed some real good sex together that night.

When we finished I asked.

"Are you hungry?"

"Yes I'm starving", was her reply.

So we got dressed and walked to the little market down the street where I spent the last few dollars I had left on some cold cut sandwiches, and drinks for us.

Having rock meant having money, so there was no problem there, all I had to do was to intercept a client of one of the dealers approaching,and sell him/her what they wanted, being that I still had quite a bit of the rock left.

When we returned to the apartment I gave her a piece of rock and stated, "get us a couple of blankets from someone for the night will you," just about everyone in that complex smoked, so I didn't think it would be a problem getting them.

She was witty, as I was learning, she returned with not only the blankets, but with toiletries as well, Gina was homeless as a result of her involvement and abuse of the rock; she'd lost all of the trust that her family had for her by stealing, and lying to them in order to obtain her poison, the rock.

Like most addicts she was pleasant to be around when she wasn't smoking, however, once a rock addict takes that first hit they transform into a cunning and conniving individual.

Our union lasted for the three days that I had the apartment, at times when hunger pains came on I would sit out front and sell some rock, the money helped me to buy food, and gas for the car.

A rock addict has no conscience, on the last day of our tenure in the place, Gina's interest shifted from me to whom ever else around that had a sack of the rock that she could smoke on, since mine was now gone.

Our union was initiated by the rock of course, but during that time we shared some closeness, and both displayed goodwill towards one another, yet in the end I felt that it was all very superficial.

I was lonely, and tired of this rock business, plus I missed Angie and the children, I would go by and visit always feeling a sense of nostalgia, and I would reminisce to myself of what once was, and if it could be again, but then I wasn't making any effort to clean up my act.

My thought and action process would always be altered by the enticement of the rock while I was in the mainstream of things, and the intent to turn my life around would always be put on the waiting list of itineraries.

Angie still loved me, and was kept informed of my doings by my sister deniese, but Angie couldn't rescue me from the destructive course I was on, I would have to be the one to make that decision to take back control of my life, then and only then would she come back to me.

Leaving that complex I asked one of the dealers if they were interested in renting my car, but none of them needed any transportation for anything at that time.

Hanging around there for another hour seemed fruitless so, I left and headed back over to an area adjacent to the fruitridge community ctr, I would find some youngster in that area to rent out the car to.

In the meantime I had a taste for a beer, there was enough change in my pocket, so with that I bought myself a 40 once bottle of Miller high life, a pack of Benson&Hedges cigarettes and hung out a little.

It was October of 88, the weather was fairly nice and it was a pleasant morning, having had the leisure to stretch out and get some amount of sleep or rest if you will from that apartment that I'd had refreshed me.

Now it was time to get things rolling again, it was 10:30a.m., and the non-working class of people were just waking up from their deeds of the night before.

I noticed a bunch of dudes standing out in an alley way by one of the condo buildings, I approached them all slowly, when I reached them I realized that they were all a clan of rock smokers cleaning the residue from their rock pipes by repeating the process of pushing the wire mesh screen inside of the pipe back and forth with a thin long stick or metal rod.

After doing this they would put the screen back in place at one end of the pipe, light it with a lighter and they would in effect be inhaling all of the accumulated built up rock cocaine residue that had been smoked in the pipe over a period of time.

This practice was equivalent to smoking a rock, or in most instances even more intense.

Walking up with the beer in my hand, I was invited to join in, provided I share my beer, that was all I needed to get me into the mode of operation that morning.

Taking a hit of rock always instigates one into the hustling mode, lots of these hustling missions are usually futile in some manner, but it did not have such an effect on me this morning, but rather got me to thinking on who might be wanting to rent a car.

We all finished smoking the residue pipes and as the morning passed so did the necessity to seek more rock from somewhere, the one good aspect of smoking rock is that it evokes a nature for the potential of one to craftily exert themselves to the fullest of their ability to hustle; be it stealing, cunning, or working, etc.

If one was naturally inclined to exhibit this type of a disposition on a regular basis, there would be no limit to what they could achieve in a day on a normal schedule.

The fact that smoking rock excells one into overdrive, both mentally and physically does not justify patronizing this substance though, aside from that one and only attribute of the substance, everything else that derives from it is negative.

The unexplained loss of time is a factor in smoking rock as well, while indulging oneself in this substance the essence of time goes unnoticed, and when the reality of time lapsed dawns on one there at a loss to account for it's disappearance.

This was the scenario this morning before I'd begun smoking rock, it appeared that time was dragging along, but after I'd finished smoking it was well into the afternoon time.

The busy lunch hour made me conscious of how engrossed I had been into taking those hits of the residue pipes, and how I placed little importance on the element of time.

I left the guys and began walking throughout the condo's seeing what there was to see in hopes that an opportunity would lead to my being able to smoke some more rock.

People were out now so it was open market so to speak, in the midst of people I spotted sibil standing outside of a condo unit and I went over to her.

As we talked she asked.

"Siege can you give me a ride over to 47th and Martin Luther King blvd to pick up some cash from my sister?"

"Yeah, lets go", I took her there to pick up the money, I knew that my patience of hanging around the condo's would pay off and it had, in the form of sibil.

We got the money and went straight to the rock house, arriving there, there were a few youngsters standing outside selling their product, one of them popped the question of giving some rock to rent my car later on that evening, at that time we had money so we bought our poison and left.

It didn't take long before we were back buying some more, sibil had been given $60.00, and this was the second trip back to the rock spot, after smoking that piece we went back for the third and last time, after which the money would be gone.

It was now 5:00p.m., after that last purchase I told the youngster that I would be back to rent him the car.

At 6:30p.m. I took the car over there, but the young dealer didn't want to miss any money by having to drive us back to our area, instead he sealed the deal by giving me a couple of rocks and told me to bring the car back around 8:00 that night and he'd give me another rock and drive me back.

I accepted this consignment deal and left, sibil and I remained together until that time.

Between 6:30 and 8:00 p.m., I had manipulated a naïve rock smoker who'd been hanging around the condo's out of $50.00 through a drug deal I had orchestrated myself.

Sibil and I had been smoking rock in an empty condo that had been broken into, and left unlocked, at 8:00 I instructed her to take the vehicle over to the youngsters house and give it to him.

It was a foolish idea for me to have trusted her to take the car to the youngster, but being caught up in the moment of smoking rock I didn't want to leave just then, so I told her to do it.

I'd known her from high school as a naïve girl which was in part why I entrusted her to deliver the car.

I told her to bring back the other rock the dealer had promised me when he drove her back to the condo's, being under the influence of the rock causes one to become irresponsible, negligent, and display a tendency to make bad judgements of situations.

Being desultory about anything of importance, I continued to smoke my rock, time was passing without my taking notice of it, as the rock gradually diminished it dawned on me that sibil should have been back long ago.

It had been two hours since she'd left, feeling that she'd show up at any time I went back to smoking what rock was left.

I sat around on old torn up furniture, the former tenants must have been evicted,and couldn't manage to take everything before they could get out, because their was clothes laying around, dirty dishes, and things of little value everywhere.

In addition to the former tenants filth, there was trash from rock smokers visits; burnt matches, beer bottles, condoms, and all other types of debris, attributes of the rock cocaine clientele.

Finishing my last piece of rock, my thoughts were now centering more on where sibil was, coming down off of a rock rush, which last only a few minutes after exhalation was bringing me back to the reality of things.

I got up and went to the window in hopes that she would be coming up at any time, the after affects of the rock high left me tense and anxious, I paced the floor of the vacant condo, trying to come down from the ill feelings of hypertension, and the anxiety I was experiencing.

The filth and stench of something rotten that I was insentient to while I was smoking the rock was now making it's presents known, this discomfort, along with needing to track down sibil made it all the more reason for me to go outside and feel the air, I collected myself and stepped out.

Stepping out into the air brought with it a sense of comfort to me, the burden of not knowing what went wrong was still there though, I knew she was known in the area, but also that she was homeless, so there was no way for me to get a lead as to her whereabouts.

I had misjudged her character, and it would cost me dearly, not only now, but in the long run as well.

There was no immediate way for me to get around to look for my automobile, or to go over to the youngsters house because she had my car, so I was stuck like chuck. Time continued to pass but still no sibil, it was 2:00a.m. and a little chilly outside, I was reluctantly forced to go back inside the vacant building and just sit it out, she knew where I was at.

All throughout the morning rock smokers would quietly slip in and out of the condo to prevent the neighbors from calling out the law and revealing their little retreat, I was in one of the other bedrooms and could hear everything that went on out there.

I heard the unjust plights of women whom were shortchanged of rock for their sex, the bickering about whom gets the bigger piece of the rock, who hit's the pipe first, the searching of the floors for the fallen rock crumbs, the looking out of the windows, and all of the other characteristics that are played out when one smokes that rock.

Having come down from my high, I could discern clearly now the demeaning effects of smoking rock, then to compound the situation more I was faced with the uncertainty of what had happened to my vehicle, this rock cocaine business was really starting to take it's toll on my life in more ways than one.

All I could do was lay still on the carpet floor and hope that everything was alright and that she would at any minute show up.

My mind raced from this thought to that, I wondered whether she was carjacked, or if she'd delivered the car as planned and kept the other rock for herself, or if she was in an accident or something, I could only speculate.

When dawn came, not having been able to sleep I got up and immediately went outside in search of my car, I would be able to get around now.

Asking any and everyone who knew her if they'd seen her, all answers were a no, something had definitely happened, but I was still at a lost as to what.

I walked to the Regional Transit bus stop and waited until a bus came along, I boarded one and went straight over to the young dealers spot, it was early, but I didn't care I wanted to know where the car was.

The youngster answered the door, and to my surprise he yelled out,

"Where is the fucking car dude, I paid you half on it already, he then said, wait a minute!", and went into another room, when he came back he had a double barrel sawed off shotgun in his hand.

I froze in my stance, not showing any fear I told the youngster, "I gave the car to sibil last night at 7:30p.m. and told her to drop it off to you, I came this morning to pick it up, but apparently the bitch had never shown up with the car for you."

The shotgun was pointblank range from my face, the youngster went on to say.

"I haven't seen the bitch, or the car yet, but I feel like your trying to play me like I'm a sucker or something."

"Youngster I'm sincere about everything I'm saying to you right now, it's no game, so if your going to shoot me, do it now or get the gun out my face."

He must have detected some margin of truth in what I was telling him because he lowered the gun out of my face, saying,

"You owe me O.G., bring me my money for the rock you were given, or bring back your car and we'll square up this debt."

The youngster stepped back into his place and closed the door, I gave a sigh of relief, turned and walked away.

I had smoothly prevailed in that untimely encounter with death, getting over that hurdle was truly the workings of the lord, I guess GOD wasn't ready for my at that time, because a lot of the young gangster drug dealers are gun crazy and would kill someone at the hint of disrespect or game playing that was directed towards them.

Now my concern was shifted towards what had happened to sibil and my car, or where they were, I knew her last name so I called the U.C.D. Med center to see if she'd been involved in an accident.

They told me no one by that name had been brought in to the emergency last night, I then phoned the Sacramento City police dept. to see if she had been arrested, or if their was an accident report filed, that was a no.

I couldn't fathom what was transpiring before me, so my only recourse of action was to ask around and hope that somebody had seen that bitch somewhere.

I started out asking people in Oak Park, an area that she also frequented, after a few inquiries I finally got some solid information that was pertinent to the whereabouts of my car.

I was told that she was driving around the Oak Park area trying to rent out the car, and that after a few unsuccessful attempts at it she drove out to the Del Paso Heights community.

I was finally breaking ground in the search for my car, so I hopped onto the bus line going out to the Heights, once I got there I still didn't have a clue as to where to start looking.

Once again I started asking questions to anyone whom I felt might be into the rock smoking business that could direct me to a prospective lead.

I came up with nothing, frustrated I went around to as many rock cocaine areas as I could manage, giving a description of my vehicle and asking if they'd seen the car anywhere.

One guy in the background overheard my inquiry about the car and approached me with some unsettling news about what had happened to the car.

"Hey O.G. was that your car you were asking about?"

"Yes it is."

"Last night that car had been in an accident, and the whole passenger side had been wiped out."

"Who was driving the car, and how do you know this?"

"Some rock head bitch had rented it out to some youngsters I know who sell rock, they told me that they'd been speeding, lost control of the car, ran into two parked cars, hopped out after impact, and ran off to avoid getting caught by the police."

I was distraught upon hearing this information, at that point it was fruitless and irrelevant to ask the names of the youngsters, they weren't the direct culprits to blame, and the fellow that gave me that info probably wouldn't have given me their names anyway, it was sibil whom was to blame for my loss.

Now I had to find the towing yard that had towed away the car that night, which wouldn't be hard to locate once I had the police report.

I went to a phone booth and called the police dept., when a female officer came on the line I gave her the make, model, and year of my car and ask if it had been in an accident last night.

She came back to the phone with a confirmation that my car had in fact been wrecked, and that when the police arrived the vehicle was abandoned, she gave me the name and address of the towing Co., after hearing this information my heart sank.

That damn rock had brought another hardship upon me.

At that instant I cleared myself of any future repercussions by stating to the officer that I had given the young lady Sibil Grace permission to go to the store and back, but that she did not return right away, and that I had waited a little too long to report it stolen, but that she had in fact stolen the car and had rented it out to some young dudes, and upon learning of this accident I'm reporting it as stolen and placing full responsibility on her in the police report.

The police dept. filed the report as such, relieving me of any responsibilities as a result of the accident.

I hung up the phone and stood in silence for a while thinking of what type of action I could exact upon sibil, because she had taken away both my wheels and my residence.

Coming back to myself, I was wanting to go the tow yard to assess the damage done to the car, I would deal with sibil in my own way and when the right opportunity presented itself.

The Capital city tow yard was located on Del Paso blvd which was a few blocks away, so I started my walk over to that location..

Upon approaching the yard I tried to locate my vehicle visually, hoping that there wasn't extensive damage done to it.

I didn't have a good view of the yard though because of the thin strips of wood slated between the fencing.

I entered the building, identified myself and inquired about the Buick Skylark, the yard attendant remembered the car alright and took me right to it.

Once inside the yard I scoped my car instantly, but by the way it was parked, as I closed in on it, it didn't look damaged at all, the front grill had not been touched, and I prayed silently that the other damage was minimal, the car still looked good from that angle.

This notion all changed as soon as I got up close and saw the other side of it, it looked twisted as it sat there, finally without anymore delays I went around to the passengers side.

When I glanced at that side of the car, sheer madness engulfed me as I flashed on how to kill that bitch sibil for what she had brought upon me, and those youngsters for acting so careless and irresponsible.

As it was described to me by the tow yard man, the whole front right quarter panel, both front and rear doors, and half of the rear quarter panel was ripped, gashed, and pushed about a foot in from it's original state of being. There was a combination of two different colors present in the mixture of paints, which confirmed it having struck two other vehicles.

The tires were free of the twisted wreckage which meant that it was still drivable, the yard attendant confirmed this by saying that the body wasn't scraping the tires anywhere, but that it wouldn't start up, that something was probably jarred loose by the impact.

The body frame was still good I found out, and it could be repaired, but at what cost to me?.

I wasn't financially able to have it repaired, I could have it towed to my mothers house, or a repair shop somewhere to find out why it wouldn't start up, but first I needed to find out what the towing, and storage charges were.

When I got to the service counter the total cost of towing and storage came to $40.00, I left there on my way back to the other side of town to start hustling up the money to get the car out of the tow yard before another day lapsed on the bill.

I decided it would be best to just ask my mother for the money since time was crucial, I was reluctant to ask her since she was on a set income, but I desperately needed to get the car then or I would lose it.

I couldn't ask any of my sisters, because they would suspect I was fabricating up a story just to get some rock, this was what my credibility was deduced to with my family as a result of my using the rock cocaine over the years, all except my mother, a mother usually never gives up on her kids regardless of the circumstances.

My mother was a good Christian woman, and I was one of her favorite children, despite my addiction to the rock, to her, I could do no wrong.

She knew the way I was before I began using the substance, so in a sense, she sympathized with me on my unfortunate loss.

Mrs. Black was a small and petite woman of African and Indian decent, she had a dark chocolate hue to her complexion, with long salt and pepper hair.

She was sensitive to her children's needs, and over all was a good spirited kind of a person, she was aware that this rock cocaine was a plague set in motion by the Countries power structure, for it to have hooked 3 of her children, whom otherwise would have been successful citizens of society.

She gave me the $40.00 in good faith, and said me to, "let your conscience be my guide son".

I took the money, thanked her, and gave her the assurance that it was in deed for the purpose of getting my wrecked car out of the tow yard.

I rushed back to the tow yard, paid the bill, and had to push the car out of the yard and onto the streets, I then had to find someone to tow me to a repair shop I knew of on the south side of town.

Hanging around outside of the tow yard with my wrecked vehicle trying to get it towed to a repair shop on the south side was a task to contend with. For one thing I was way on the north side of Sacramento trying to get to the south side, secondly, I had no money with which to pay someone to tow me there.

I kept asking people anyway, finally a young Hispanic fellow offered to help me, he had a thick chain which could pull me, he hooked the chains up to each cars bumper, and we began our trek.

It was a risky mission because of the traffic at that time of the day, plus it was illegal.

Taking the back roads, and being careful as we moved, arriving to our destination was almost fulfilled, I had to time taking off from a stop sign, or a red light with his pressing on the gas pedal to keep from snapping the chain or pulling away either bumpers of the cars, I also had to ride the brakes to keep the chain tight between stops.

Through the whole traveling distance only twice did the chain pop loose, when we got to the shop I opened my trunk to see what was in there that I could give the man for his troubles, because he was GOD sent.

After searching in the trunk, I came up with two matching Sanyo car speakers that were not damaged, I gave the guy those, thanked him, shook hands and we departed company.

The owner of the auto repair shop was there, it was a small two man business in a residential area off of Franklin blvd.

I had done business with this guy when I owned my V.W. bug back in the 70's era when I was in high school, Kristo was the owner, and a do it all person, very good at whatever he did.

Kristo was of Mexican decent, he worked on cars at a reasonable price, his clientele was small which meant that he had time to devote on each automobile that he repaired.

I explained to him what had happened, he told me he'd check everything out and for me to stop back by later that day.

I left the shop and went back over to the Fruitridge condo's, in hopes of running across sibil, after a few hours of waiting to catch her, with no luck, I went back to Kristo's auto repair shop.

He told me, "hey, the starter had somehow come disconnected from the impact of the accident, but that it was now starting up with the key after I tightened it up."

"That's great, but I'm broke at the time, can the car sit here at the shop until I come up with the $29.00 to pay you for your services?"

"O.K., but it Can't be for too long, I get kind of busy sometimes."

I left the shop a second time and went back over to the condo's looking for sibil, I felt the bitch was indebted to me for causing this misfortune, and for that, anytime I seen her and she had money I was taking it from her.

At the condo's I still had no luck in my search for her, but while there I ran into some old comrades of mine and ended up talking about old news, and what was currently happening.

In the conversation I learned that my old acquaintance Gaines, whom had gotten me started on the freebasing, had gotten caught up with doing a string of armed robberies, and was sentenced to a term of 8 years in California's State prison system.

Reflecting back, I remembered when Gaines and another high school friend of ours named Carlos were riding around in Carlos' car on a rock smoking mission.

That night I ask Carlos if I could join them, Carlos being naïve went along with me being a 3rd passenger in his car.

Gaines was a domineering type of an individual and more or less took over the car, and I remembered that Gaines was looking bad and was broke, but what caught my attention was that he had Carlos taking him to lots of different gas stations where he said he knew the cashiers.

He would go inside to talk to the clerks, they'd both leave the counter and go somewhere in the back of the store, a few minutes later Gaines would walk back to the car with money, and say lets go.

Once in the car he would pull out some bills and start counting them, I thought that it was all to coincidental for him to be able to just go to all of these gas stations and get money like that, his story was that he was collecting old debts.

He'd become so obsessed with the smoking of rock, and didn't like sharing it, that I became intolerant of his behavior and told Carlos to put him out of his car.

Thinking back though Gaines was actually robbing those gas stations, and had jeopardized our freedom in the process without even telling us what he was doing, I wasn't surprised of hearing that news about him.

FROM BAD TO WORSE

It was getting late now and I was without a place to lay my head, I was tired from all of the running around I'd done for the car, the only option I had left was to go back up to Kristo's auto shop and hope that my car was left outside in the front so I could sleep in it.

I walked up there and to my amaze it had been left out over night, I got in it and went right to sleep, when I woke up the next morning Kristo was there working on a car.

He didn't say anything to me about being on the property sleeping in the car because we'd developed a good friendship over the years, but stated to me.

"Siege your vehicle is taking up space at the shop, could you please hustle up the repair money A.S.A.P. please, I'll give you a couple more days for this."

"I'm going to work on it today Kristo, you have my word on that."

"Good, because I'm going to be needing that space very soon", was his reply, so I got up and began my day thinking on how I was going to raise that money.

I walked around aimlessly, until on a mishap I ran into a Mexican dude whom propositioned me with cashing a hot unassigned payroll check from an Allstate Insurance Co.

The checks were blank where the payee's name went, but all six checks he had were for a sum of four hundred and sixty dallors and 0 cents.

The guy and his girl must have been on heroin, they appeared to be anyway, and had already cashed a few themselves, but wanted to take the heat off of them by propositioning anybody whom seemed a good prospect.

He began by saying, "Hey man all you have to do is print your name on the check, cash it, and give me back half of the money."

"Meet me back here at this spot at 3:00 p.m., right now it's 11:00 a.m."

"Alright, that seems like a fair enough deal, I'm going to get started now." I told him.

The guy must have either had a bunch of people doing the same thing because he trusted me enough to return in good faith later, or doubted that I'd be able to cash anymore of the checks, or maybe was doing this to take some of the heat off of him and his girl, whatever the reason, for me it was like Manna dropping out of heaven.

I agreed with their plan and left in search of someone with a typewriter.

Walking around the area, I was spotted by an associate I'd went to high school with.

Kevin grew up in another area, but attended the same school as I, he was driving a white Ford pinto automobile, and said that he recognized me, and thought he'd stop to speak.

I'd remembered him too, he too had fell victim to the rock cocaine plague.

After high school he'd landed a good paying custodial position with the City of Sacramento, had married a good woman from my neighborhood, they had had a child, bought a home, had two nice new cars, but the vicious rock cocaine had ruined him too.

We spoke briefly on our bad and untimely misfortunes, then I brought up my plan.

"Kevin I need a typewriter so I can type my name on this Insurance check."

"My sister has one a few blocks from here."

The plan was coming together, and hopefully soon I'll have a few hundred dollars.

We went there and typed all of the necessary information onto the blank check, and drove over to a privately owned quick check cashing place on 24th and Florin rd.

I had a check cashing card made up while I tried to cash the check, by the check appearing as a legitimate payroll check it shouldn't be a problem cashing it.

That wasn't what bothered me though, it was the fact that if ever it was traced down by the authorities, it wouldn't he hard for them to track me down.

My needing money to get my car out of the shop, and the prospect of being able to buy some more rock after all was said and done, over-rode my better conscience, and the possible consequences behind cashing the check, and I went through with it.

I went up to the window outlet acting normal, plus I knew the owners well so they didn't suspect any fraudulent activity was in the making from me.

They didn't even run a check on it, the cashier cordially assisted me by handing over the dead presidential denominations in the amount of four hundred and sixty nine dollars to me and I grabbed the money and left.

Getting back to the car, Kevin asked, "did it work," I flashed a small roll of bills, peeling him off a $20.00 bill for his assistance in making it all happen.

Kevin was soft spoken, in appearance he had the physique of a basketball player, he was dark skinned with lean pointed features.

He wasn't from what I remembered of him very much of a talker, but on this day it was as if he'd just hit the lotto, because he wouldn't stop talking.

He mentioned to me that he knew of a couple of girls that he and I could ravish, once we'd got some rock, that didn't seem like a bad idea I thought.

But my mind was on paying the cars bill, so I told Kevin to stop by a quick stop store so I could buy some alcohol for us, and then on to Kristo's auto repair shop.

He stopped at the market, this particular market is frequented by rock dealers, rock stars(smokers), gang bangers, and prostitutes.

I went in to make my purchase as Kevin was at work outside buying the rock, I was unaware of this though.

When I got back in the car, Kevin had things already in motion for us, not only did he hand me the rock pipe with a hit melted down on it, but also had a very cute and sexy looking woman sitting in the back seat with a look on her face of come and get me.,

I took a hit of the pipe, when I finished exhaling the smoke, the head rush magnified the woman's beauty, as I turned around she gave me a flash of her goods.

Kevin must have mentioned to her that I was buying more rock because her bid to secure her involvement on this rock smoking mission was secured even more when she again spread her legs while in the back seat revealing nothing underneath her skirt but pure pussy.

As we sat there and smoked, time flew by, I'd ended up buying one hundred dollars more of the rock, before long, while smoking, drinking, and touching on the prostitute in the back, 5:00 p.m. had passed and Kristo's had closed for the day, I told myself that tomorrow's another day.

The prostitute introduced herself, "hi, I'm Dawn,", her name was well fitting, she was tall,and stacked in all the right places, her skin color was coffee cream brown, she had dreamy eyes, small lips, with a short neck cut hair style.

She had earlier climbed through the middle of the front of the console and sat in my lap, seducing me more as she moved on top of me.

The three of us left that spot and went to get a motel room somewhere, we checked into one and smoked some more rock, Kevin, feeling kind of left out decided to leave the room in search of another female.

While he was away Dawn and I had some sexual fun, when he returned with another beautiful woman, we coupled off, when all of that rock was gone I sent Kevin out with a hundred dollars to get some more, when he came back we all smoked until that was gone.

The next purchase we all left together, on the way we stopped at a convenient store and picked up some more alcohol and cigarettes along with some snacks.

We went back to the room and partied all morning long, making several more trips to buy more rock, we watched the sun come up, around 8:30 a.m., when I assessed my money I found that that I had only fifty dollars left.

Being sprung, and in the mix of things from continuous smoking, I decided to go all the way and sent Kevin out to buy one last rock for us all, he took his lady friend along with him for the ride and never came back.

Dawn and I were stuck there broke, we stayed there until noon, she gave me a phone number where I could reach her and left after we checked out of the motel.

Rock cocaine had done it to me again, now I wasn't able to pay for the repair charge to get my car out of the shop, in addition to that I was seeing first hand how the rock was converting, otherwise good people, into ruthless inconsiderate manipulators.

That day I went by Kristo's to let him know that it would be a little while before I could come up with the money, he said he'd give me another week to come up with it.

The shop was small but with cars coming in everyday for repairs he needed the space I was taking up with my car.

Rock cocaine in it's pursuit of destroying peoples lives had such a grasp on me and my life until I had become unable to discern my immediate priorities.

As the days passed, every little bit of money that I either hustled or acquired some kind of a way, I spent it on rock and alcohol.

Disgruntled over my state of being, and not having the funds to get my car out of the shop, I chalked it up as a loss, and never did go back to pick up the car.

I suspect that he probably sold it for what-ever he could get out of it.

It was April of 89, I was on the streets now sleeping wherever I could lay my head, hanging around drug houses, and stealing alcohol for youngsters in exchange for their rock.

During my carefree and out of control behavior I'd learned from two different sources that two of my friends had been shot and killed, gang style in G parkway, both behind the rock cocaine epidemic.

One was a person I'd grown up with, it was said that he sold a small rock to someone and when the person complained, and wanted their money back, it wasn't given back, the person left, came back with a .45 colt pistol, fired a single round that took the back of my friends head off.

The other friend, bowie, was a cousin to a girl that I'd dated when Angie and I lived in the G parkway area in the early 80's.

Bowie ran off with a dealers bag of rocks, and was being sought out by them, one night they caught up with him in the G parkway area and emptied their whole 9 mm hand gun clip on him, he died sitting up right, riddled full of bullets.

Rock was the culprit in the deadly misfortunes of black American young men in more real life ways than just it's toxic form.

I was almost at the lowest point in my life now, I'd lost a good paying job, my family, my automobile, and now every little bit of cash I'd obtain I'd lose to the rock cocaine, life was becoming a self made bitch for me.

I hadn't lost my life, my sanity, or my freedom yet though, but soon as I continued on this course, the latter one would be compromised.

Being broke, busted, and disgusted prompted me to lead a transient type of a lifestyle, I might at any given time end up in any given area of Sacramento's rock plagued communities.

Oak Park was the closest area to midtown which was where I would hang out, many of the young rock dealers would put in their orders for the type of booze they would give a rock for.

When I desperately wanted to smoke some rock I would go into Safeway grocery store and steal 2 bottles of Royal Crown liquor.

On one occasion a youngster drove me there, he went into the store with me at 3:00a.m., it looked like it was going to be an easy target because their were only a couple of clerks working, and very few customers, so I stashed away a couple of bottles and headed towards the exit doors.

As I neared the exit doors two other clerks came from out of nowhere zeroed in on me asking if they could look inside of my jacket.

I couldn't run because their was another clerk standing in front of the entrance door, so I just handed over the two bottles to them, they called out the police whom came, arrested and charged me with petty theft.

The next morning in court I pled guilty and was sentenced to 14 days in the county jail, in any institution in California an inmate does two thirds of their sentence which meant I'd serve 10 days and be released.

It was then April the 14th, I'd be back on the streets before the end of the month; that was a bad mentality to have about what was going to become a norm in my life over the next 10 years.

I subjected myself to the mercy of the California's penal code system behind my necessity to smoke some rock cocaine.

The demonic and delusional state that the rock would keep me in would lead to a vicious cycle of periodical incarcerations for years to come.

On April 24th I was given my freedom again, in a sense at the time of my arrest I was rescued from myself, simply because after doing that time I looked refreshed, healthier from eating 3 meals a day, and I got a lot of rest and relaxation.

After my release however, not having a source of income with which to live and sustain myself, I fell back into the petty thievery again, this time I was caught stealing liquor out of Jumbo's market on Florin rd, and I was to go before the judge again.

The Courts sentence was a little stiffer this time, I was sentenced to 3 weeks which I served at the County branch jail, I was in custody for 2 weeks was released, and went back to doing the same thing all over again.

Apparently those little short periods of confinement weren't significant enough to deter my unlawful misdeeds, or was it the rocks subliminal lies dictating to me subconsciously that in turn led me on those futile stealing missions.

By nature I was not a thief, nor a criminal, which was why I wasn't crafty enough to evade being caught when I shop lifted.

I began sharpening up my tools of the trade and became craftier, I was then able to outsmart the stores securities, and staff which made getting caught less of a worry for me.

But fate, especially when someone is doing wrong, has a way of catching up with one, as it gradually did to me, I was arrested again for shoplifting in Thrifty's Drug store for trying to take 4 cartons of Newport cigarettes.

The same Municipal Court Judge that resided over all of my other cases resided over this one, this time I was sentenced to 40 days in the County jail.

Each period of incarceration became a collective process of learning about the injustices of the American judicial system for me.

Either I would be exposed to the injustices of California's judicial court system through hearing of other cases by black inmates while I was in custody, or I would see how racist and dogmatic the law enforcement officials really were in these institutions.

In August I was set free again, this time, shoplifting wasn't on my itinerary, but having a roof over my head was.

I had been talking with my mother and sister Holly while in custody, they felt it was time for me to straighten up my act, and get off of the streets, so I moved in with the two of them.

Holly was still smoking rock though, and when she wasn't panhandling she was acting out another scheme she'd devised where she would stop at houses at random with a gas can in hand and say she'd run out of gas and could the people spare a few bucks to her.

With this hustle she generated more funds then from her efforts of panhandling, sometimes she'd be out until early in the morning.

I, along with my mother would worry for her safety out there like that at night, a few times I went along to watch over her since she was defiant about refraining from it.

I would not smoke the stuff in my mothers house, and even though I now resided there, I would still leave early in the morning, and stay gone all day, sometimes days at a time, and come back only to catch up on my sleep.

Angie and I had communicated also while I was in jail, she was curious about how I'd been and was interested as to just how I was fairing along.

She'd asked me to come by and see the kids, it had been a while since I'd last seen or talked to them, the rock scene had taken control of me, even over my own livelihood, let alone my interest in seeing my children.

As far as I knew she was still single, which delighted me, I would eventually get around to going by and seeing them.

All of these events were happening at the same time, and my having went back to chasing the rock myself, I only found time to run the streets and hustle a rock to smoke on.

August 1rst 1989 was when I found the time to go by and visit Angie and the kids, she was cordial and respondent to me, it had almost been a couple of years since we shared this kind of a resolve with one another.

She had changed a little though, when we'd met she was new to California from Chicago and displayed the good morals of divine womanhood, but since our separation she'd been influenced by the negative attitudes of typical California women of spontaneous sex, partying, and street running.

Although she was still a good and decent mother to the children, I didn't respect her the way I once did because of the way she was living her life.

She had met a fast paced slut named Mishell after we split up, one evening the both of them came by to drop off the kids to my sister's house Deniese.

I happened to be there at the time of the drop off, when they came inside, Angie was dressed like Mishell that night, wearing skirts cut just below their asses.

This was out of character for Angie, and as far as I was concerned mishell was bad company for her, I had once heard the slut telling Angie that she changed men like she changed her underwear.

Nevertheless, I couldn't convince Angie to see the light, she was grown, furthermore, I wasn't the best example setter myself in light of all I'd been mixed up in, because a good woman follows the path of her man in many ways, so I couldn't say much else.

I was happy to be in Angie's company at that time though because I still loved her and although she was hurt by my atrocious behavior when we were together, I felt that she still loved me too, but just couldn't trust getting back with me at that time.

However, despite how long we'd been apart, and how much I missed my family, I was indignant towards her with regards to the company she kept, and her new found type of free spirited lifestyle.

I had ill feelings towards her and a sense of resentment as to what she'd become, I could no longer control her and this bothered me tremendously.

I played with the kids and watched her as she moved about my sisters apartment.

One day while I was visiting her and the kids some guy called the house, she talked on the phone a minute, then hung up, I questioned her about it, she stated that they were just friends; the usual line all women use, but went on to say that he was a big baller(drug dealer) she'd met at a club, and that she kind of liked him.

This puzzled me, I couldn't fathom how she could want to have anything to do with anyone involved with drugs, since she'd left me, despite my being at the other end of that trade.

I looked at her crazily, but didn't say anything more, but now I began thinking vindictively towards her, to me it didn't matter if one was a supplier, or a user, both affiliates of that rock cocaine business will eventually bring about some kind of a crisis within a family.

Feeling traded in by her, I wanted to do something about it, but I didn't have a clue as to what, so I ask if I could use her car, the Audi she'd bought with her insurance settlement money.

She gave me the keys without hesitation, she had never come to know that I had a history of renting out my cars to rock dealers, otherwise she'd have probably not given me the keys so quickly.

I kissed the kids and left, my plan was to go shoplifting, by having transportation now I could move around to different stores and stack up as much merchandise as possible.

My destination at the outset was the Oak Park area, there I would be among comrades of the rock business. Arriving to my location I immediately recognized an old acquaintance so I pulled over to park the car and got out.

I walked up to Crazo and asked, "hey man you smoking today?"

"Yo man," he pulled out a hit for me and we walked over to avacant lot where we could smoke undetected.

After that hit I was sprung and ready to embark on another ruthless mission to obtain some more of the rock.

The wickedness of the unnatural effects that the rock high gives you makes one transform after taking that first hit of the day, one becomes ill minded in their thinking process and it causes unplanned activities to start to occur.

I had not intended to keep Angie's car for a few days, because I knew it was imperative that she have transportation for the kids, however, at that time, the rock had taken control of my mental faculties which impaired my ability to generalize on a priority.

I invited Crazo to accompany me on a shoplifting spree and we both hopped into the vehicle and left.

The first place we hit was Luckys supermarket, I went in and 10 minutes later came out with two 5ths of Royal Crown liquor, we traded those for some rock, a couple hours later we went back to the same store, and Crazo got the job done.

This went on all that day and into the night, his girl was also a good shoplifter, so he suggested that we pick her up too.

The two were an equally matched pair, he was short and dark skinned with big eyes, she was likewise, not only were they a benefit to have with me while we did our thefts, but they were comedians at best and kept me in a good state of mind by laughing at their comments and jokes.

Each of us would take turns at going into different stores, in the end we had enough liquor and cartons of Newport cigarettes to enable us to smoke rock throughout all of the night and morning.

Day one passed, and I refrained from taking the car back to Angie, not because I didn't want to, but because smoking the rock had me stuck like chuck and not giving a fuck.

The second day came in as the three of us saw the sunrise, it marked another beginning to a day of unproductiveness in the sense that all we three were doing was shoplifting and smoking rock.

Angie, as a result of my keeping her vehicle from her, had become unable to move about, not only did I create a hardship for her, but for myself as well because I'd learned from my sister that she had called the police on me.

So now there was an A.P.B. out on the automobile, later that afternoon the three of us had cashed in on all of the hot commodities that we had from that morning, and split up the rock that we'd received in exchange for it.

I parted company with them, and had run across a lovely dark skinned female and invited her to join me with smoking some rock, she accepted my offer and got into the car.

I drove to the Oak Park community center off of Martin Luther King Jr. blvd, it was a good place to sit in the car and smoke rock without to much detection from passersby's or the authorities.

She introduced herself as Jackie, I'd picked her up not for the purpose of sex, but rather, for mere companionship as I got high to relieve some of the anguish I was feeling for Angie's decision to start consorting with a drug dealer.

Jackie was in part receptive to my disdain regarding Angie's attraction to a drug dealer, because she'd been dropped by a drug boy and felt that money was all that mattered to them.

But being under the influence of rock and trying to be diplomatic is as impossible as trying to swim and smoke.

Her attentiveness to my plight was a consolation nevertheless, she seemed to sympathize with me as she listened.

It was nearing noon on the second day of my having the vehicle, finishing off what rock I had had, she said we could pick up some more rock from her X boyfriend if I could take her to his place.

I started the car and we left going over to her X's, Angie must have gotten word from someone that I was in the Oak Park vicinity, because as we drove down Franklin blvd, I drove right past her sitting in the passenger seat of my sister's car.

They swung a u-turn and got behind us, and almost at the same time a police car swooped on me from out of nowhere, so I just pulled over to the curb, and both the police and my sister's car came to a stop right behind me.

Angie got out of my sisters car arguing and yelling at me, she advanced to hit the female riding with me, but my sister stopped her.

The police searched the car and asked Angie if she wanted to press charges, at that time she yelled out yes, they handcuffed me and took me off to jail.

After a few days of letting her cool off from the whole ordeal, I called her to see if she was actually going to go through with pressing the charges.

"No I'm not pressing charges on you, I just wanted to teach you a lesson for what you did by having you sit in jail for a few days", was her reply.

I apologized to her for the inconvenience that I had brought to her and thanked her for not pressing any charges against me, while talking, I revealed to her my disdain towards her for consorting with a rock dealer, and went on to say that that was why I had kept her car.

I, in my heart, knew that she wasn't going through with this case in court, so I got ready to take it to trial, ironically enough though my public defender came on as a diligent advocate in my defense, but later towards the end, and before going on to trial deceived me by saying that she'd spoke to Angie, and that she was going all the way with the prosecution against me.

The public defender went on to say that I would be better off taking a 16 month state prison deal than to take it to trial and lose.

I'd known better from talking to Angie myself, so I cussed that public defender out got up and walked out of the courts counsel/inmate conference chamber.

Sure enough when I entered the courtroom in that orange jumpsuit, Angie was sitting there with the kids, and the judge ordered the charges dismissed because the plantiff in the case was backing out.

I wondered was this the kind of deceptive tactics that the D.A'S public counsel, and the judicial system uses to convict otherwise innocent people in these courtrooms of America.

I stayed in jail for three weeks too long going through the motions of unnecessary court appearances before the judge, when they ascertained that Angie wasn't pressing any charges, dismissed the case.

What they'd wanted was for me to accept a bogus conviction by using deception to get it.

California's judicial, and penal system would still yet worsen with their unjust sentencing practices particularly with regards to the rock cocaine cases where a black male is involved.

This type of blatant recourse of action directed at a defendant is just an out right travesty of justice, and needs to be looked at by America's media system so the courts can be exposed.

Upon my release from the jail house, I ran into a young lady named Kenya, whom I'd known for some years, she was being released from jail as well on a possession charge.

She had held dear our first encounter together as friends and upon running into me wanted to rekindle that friendship by taking it a little further than that, but had not known how to get into contact with me.

She mentioned that her and her son were moving, and that if I wanted to help her move I could also reside with them.

Kenya was an older woman, fairly nice looking, she was bronze colored, short in stature, had a shapely body with features of a black queen, her personality was amicable, and she was interested in me.

The only discrepancy that she had was that she smoked rock, which was how we'd met in the first place.

The narcotics squad had raided a rock house and had busted her there with some rock in her possession.

Me being a grown man I didn't relish the idea of living with my mother and sister to well, so I took Kenya up on her offer, and we both left the jailhouse together via the bus to where her young son and property was, so she could start packing things up.

When we reached the south Sacramento neighborhood of Meadowview, her son happily greeted her and shook my hand, her son Todd was a well raised and mannerable young kid at the age of 10, he and I took a liking to one another from the start.

I could try to be a positive type of a role model for the kid, and at the same time be a help to Kenya around her new place.

She had stated to me that morning we got released that she wanted to stop smoking rock, not only for herself, but because of her son as well, since she'd already put him through enough hardship behind the rock.

I was in the same mode she was in with regard to the rock scene, I was now beginning to discern it's worth as something of a devilish plague that was imposed on Blacks by the power structure in this Country and I wanted to quit.

She had apparently been orchestrating her move while she was in custody, and had a family member pay the rent for her new apartment, the place she was moving into was in Oak Park on 10th Ave.

When we arrived there the apartment was old looking, but cute, we all liked it and began unpacking things.

Kenya didn't have much furniture, just a floor mattress, her sons bed, and a sofa, she'd have to add on as she went along.

We got all settled in after a few hours, it was still afternoon, so I asked Todd, "hey young man would you like to take a walk with me to the store," which was around the corner, while Kenya made lunch for all of us, "yes, mom can I go please"?, was his reply.

Walking to the neighborhood market gave me a feel of that location and familiarized me with the area, everything appeared to be normal in the daytime, I didn't suspect any rock cocaine trafficking in the immediate area.

It was the month of August, the nice weather brings people out of their houses, there were kids out playing, which Todd met earlier that day, and older people were sitting on porches talking, everything was pleasant about the new place, that was until night time fell.

I discovered an abundance of night traffic across the street from our apartment complex, there was a combination of two rock houses, in a sense I was upset, but on the other hand I was glad, because that meant that when I wanted to buy some rock, it was right there.

Both Kenya and I were serious about refraining from smoking rock, and although access to it was seconds away, we both vowed together to stand firm on our word.

Neither one of us, nor many of the other millions of blacks in this Country whom are now victims of the rock, know what other extra additives there are in that rock cocaine that makes it so luring to black people, but unless one is truly tired of being tired of smoking the rock, their not going to quit smoking it.

As was the case with Kenya and I, we gradually succumbed to the pressure, got weak and made a trip across the street to one of the rock houses and bought a twenty dollar rock.

The trips across the street rapidly increased, although we both smoked the rock in another room away from her son, he still knew what was going on, and I didn't feel comfortable about it.

I had never enticed, nor condoned a child getting any knowledge about rock cocaine, it's an obstructive force, and our children are the future of black America.

Some blacks whom smoke the rock are contrary to this principle, which was in part why the rock has excelled as a drug patronized by blacks; as our trips increased to the rock house, so did the amount of traffic in and out of her place.

Sometimes I would notice that she would have people smoking in all compartments of the house when Todd was outside playing, when he came home there would be burnt matches laying around the house and the smell of sulfur was in the air.

Todd was an intelligent young boy, academically inclined, he was smart and always talked of becoming a teacher, it was unfortunate that he didn't have the right encouragement from inspirational sources to aide him in pursuing his goal.

I did my best when I spent quality time with him, however, how influential was I when the boy knew I smoked rock right along with his mother.

Kenya was becoming more and more obsessed with the smoking of rock, to the point that she wasn't preparing meals for Todd and I at times, she would rather smoke rock, or hustle money to secure buying some more of it.

This aggravated me, so I took it upon myself to start cooking some of the meals so that Todd could go to sleep on a full stomach.

I was developing doubts about my living arrangements with her and was uncertain as to how much longer I could stand up under all of it, but for the time being I acted as a mentor to Kenya, whom was steadily becoming obnoxious, adamant, and selfish with the rock.

I was calling to her attention everything that she was in violation of around the house, but she wasn't going to hear of it', it all came to an end one afternoon in late August though.

I resented all that was going on in her place, and had stayed out all night long, I'd stolen a 10 speed bike in the south area early that morning and was out riding around in Oak Park, come dawn I stopped at a rock house to trade the bike for some rock and walk back to Kenya's.

I'd had no idea that the rock house I was at was under surveillance, when I completed the trade, I didn't notice that the police had just pulled up and was walking up on the side of the house.

One officer was questioning people out front of the house, another was making his way to the back of the garage where the rock was being sold out of.

The dealer had just given me a hand full of crumbs which I placed in my front pants pocket, just as I turned to leave, one cop was approaching the garage as I was leaving.

Startled, I eased my hand in my pocket, took out, and emptied as much of the crumbs as I could unto the pavement and started walking away, that officer didn't stop me, he was concerned with getting the dealer, but when I got out to the sidewalk the other officer stopped me and ask, "what are you doing back there?"

I replied, "I'm here to do some work on a car out front".

He went on to say, "this is a drug house, who do you know here?"

I said, "I stopped by to do some work on the guys car who lives here, but he's not here so I was on my way to leave.

I prepared to leave but the cop grabbed me and told me to remain put, so I could be searched, I shook free and took on a defensive posture, by this time the other cop comes up from behind me and they both wrestle me down to the pavement.

After cuffing me they searched my pockets and discovered some remaining crumbs, they placed those in a plastic baggie and arrested me for possession of a controlled substance, the amount they'd gotten off of me appeared to be less than 0.05 grams, which was later confirmed to be 0.03 grams of rock.

I despised the law where officers policed neighborhoods because of the rock and felt disdain towards them, mainly because of the abuse of the power they perpetrate when it comes to the black communities where they unnecessarily harass black people behind the suspicion that there involved in the rock cocaine business.

It's almost as if, if you're a Black American in a black neighborhood, your automatically a suspect for either rock cocaine usage, or selling, which in turn subjects one to be harassed by them.

I was unaware of the legalities surrounding the types of search and seizures that can be done on people by cops, and was also ignorant to their technical and formal procedures of testing controlled substances.

I didn't know that I could have beaten the case by requesting to the courts that I wanted a full lab testing of those crumbs, by doing that they would have exhausted the 0.03 grams of rock on test performed on it and in effect there would have been no evidence left to be brought to a trial.

I'd discovered that the law prescribes that a sufficient testing of any controlled substance requires a thorough testing of a minimum of 0.15 grams for the test to be conclusive, and for an amount to be left for evidence in case of a court trial.

Not knowing this prior to my arrest, I took a deal of 90 days in the County jail, and 5 years probation, and this would be for me the start of periodical incarcerations in the Sacramento County Jailhouse.

I wasn't able to discern at that time that rock cocaine was a means of not only self destruction for black Americans, but also a form of subjugation to the authorities as well.

I would stay confined in jail for the next 60 days, while in there I learned of many other black men whom were arrested for small amounts of rock cocaine.

OUR SYSTEMS CONQUEST OF DIVISION AND CONQUER

The sentencing discrepancies between rock, and crank possession arrestee's were noticed and compared when some of the white boys in jail would speak on their sentences for being caught with an ounce of crank, as opposed to blacks being caught with a gram or less of rock, blacks received lengthier sentences.

In October of 89 I was released from the County jail, Kenya and I had fallen out of contact with each other while I was incarcerated, so I went by her place to check on her and Todd.

When I got there the place was vacant and unoccupied, I asked the neighbors if they knew where she' moved to, and to my surprise was told that the police had raided her place, taken her to jail for rock possession, and took Todd to a County receiving home.

I was hurt behind hearing that news, Todd didn't deserve such a fate in his early life, at a later time I learned the boy was completely taken from Kenya and was adopted by some foster parents, which was good for him.

I hoped that the kid would be treated right, and that he would be encouraged to pursue his goal of becoming a teacher while residing at his foster home.

For me, I was once again on the streets without a solid hint of what path to take on improving my life, I was becoming tired of the consequences that befell me because of the rock, yet, I still craved to smoke the stuff, it was a bad omen.

In mid September I went on a rock smoking binge that led me back into the shoplifting mode, as a result of it I was arrested for stealing 6 expensive leather wallets from Weinstocks dept. store in downtown Sacramento's K st mall.

The judge was lenient in his sentencing of me this time, and I was given 30 days in the County jail.

While in jail I corresponded with Angie whom was finding out the hard way that a lot of the guys out there were perpetrators pretending to fit the bill with her and the kids, but that after they got into her pants things changed.

She stated "Yeah I realized that after the fact, if you could leave the rock alone I would come back to you".

So this sounded like a start in the right direction for me, and I replied, "I'll give it my best effort possible".

I'd also found out while in jail that sibil whom was responsible for the lost of my car was in jail as well on a possession charge.

I wrote to her through the inner jail correspondence mail and warned her that she'd better try to make some kind of a compensatory effort to me for the trouble she caused me, but I never heard anything back from her.

The first of November I was released, I went to my mothers place and called Angie.

"Hey Siege I see you've made it out once again huh, I hope that this time it's for good and that you've learned a lesson about that wicked ass rock cocaine shit."

"I'll be by your mothers place in a little while to pick you up, bring you home with me and the kids, and fix you a nice expensive home cooked meal of your choice."

This was the break I'd been waiting for, the chance to get back with my family.

She arrived a short while later with the kids, we left, went and rented some videos, bought some groceries, and headed back to her place.

Angie and I hadn't been intimate with each other in over 3 years, I'd almost forgotten how she felt inside when we were together.

I played with Amber and Counsil while she diligently prepared dinner, I occasionally went into the kitchen to assist her in what ever she needed done, but she'd wave me out saying, "this is your day, just kick back relax, and save your energy for bigger things to come later".

That little subtle hint gave me an idea as to what she was referring to and I smiled and rejoined the kids in the living room.

My mind wasn't on rock cocaine this time which was good, and GOD had given me back what I had allowed the devil to take away from me by catering to his demonic rock cocaine.

I was grateful to the Lord for restoring my family back to me, and I was going to sincerely try to refrain from having anything to do with rock cocaine from that point on since I'd gotten back what was important to me.

When dinner was set, I said grace for all and we began to eat.

The meal Angie had fixed was great, there was marinated jumbo shrimp, bar-b-qued steak slabs, shrimp salad, and for desert we had cheese cake.

The reunion was pleasant as we all ate and talked, when we all finished I helped Angie clean the kitchen and put things away.

Then we all gathered around the television set to watch the movie the Terminator, Angie and I cuddled up next to each other while the kids lay on the warmth of the floor with their head perched on their balled up hands.

She'd bought some Remy Martin Brandy for us to sip on, which enhanced our ever growing mood for each other, the kids were serene about our getting back together as they commented on us staying together and my not ever leaving again.

I had wanted to spend some time with my oldest son Siege II also, but Mary had married, and moved off somewhere, and I had no clue as to where to locate them.

He had called my mothers place while I was in jail, she asked him for his phone number, when he ask Mary if he could give it to her, she said no.

Mary had become somewhat spiteful towards me for not having stayed with her, and for this she was trying to keep my oldest son from around me.

This hurt me tremendously because I hadn't seen him in over four years due to the kind of a lifestyle I was living, but for the moment I was content to have gotten the family back that I'd recently lost.

I would take the kids to school in the morning, come back and drive Angie to work, she was a beautician, years ago I had driven her down to San Francisco, Ca to take her State board exam, where she passed, and was given her license to do hair.

I'd drop her off to work and ride around some mornings, on one occasion I'd ran into a sexy girl whom ask me to transport her to buy some rock, and that she'd pay me to do so, and invited me to get high with her.

The devil is relentless at tricking people up especially when their not idolizing what ever it was that had them doing his work.

I reluctantly joined the girl, but not going over-board by any means because I didn't want to raise any suspicions from Angie.

But the devils advocates comes in many other forms than just rock, as was the case with michell, Angie's friend, whom happened to be in a rock house when I took that girl to buy some rock.

She made it her business to relay that information about my being in a rock house with another woman back to Angie, not sparing her the anguish from hearing this news in light of what she'd been through with me, even further, knowing that Angie was trying to reconcile her relationship with me.

Her informing Angie of this did nothing but cause unnecessary added problems to our relationship, I told Angie that I knew the girl, saw her walking, stopped to ask her where she was going, and accepted some cash from her to take her to get some rock.

The half of a tank of gas was proof that I'd been given some money from somebody, because that morning the tank was low and Angie didn't have the money to get anymore gas.

She was reluctant to believe my story and went on to question what I was doing in a drug area, well this upset me and I questioned her association with that bitch Mitchell whom frequents drug houses.

She became obnoxious and stood to defend michell, but really not having any grounds for a defense of the bitch because she hadn't known her that long, plus did not know for a fact that she wasn't a rock smoker.

I remembered a while back when Angie, Michell and some other women were all socializing, Mitchell mentioned that she had smoked rock before but had stopped, but whose to say that she hadn't fallen back into it again. I know for a fact that one will struggle with that temptation for the rest of their life, she could still be a hit and miss patron of the substance.

As a result of this untimely news Angie scrutinized my every move, she would sometimes fabricate allegations, I'd always known that the second time around in a relationship the spouse in question would always be suspected of misdeeds.

But when some outside informer interferes it complicates the situation more, I suspected from the beginning that Mitchell was a conniving and two faced bitch, as time would actually proved her to really be.

With the constant encouragement from Mitchell for her to get out, keep partying, and meeting other guys, Angie began to resume the role of going out to the night clubs.

Disputes about this arose between us, her being adamant with regards to this issue brought discord to our relationship, moreover, the kids were being effected by these events as well.

Where I was feeling complacent at the outset, and really putting some earnest effort into our reconciliation, now my contentment and regard for Angie's best interest were displaced.

I didn't like how she'd become so easily influenced and misled by her acquaintances, especially the types of Mitchell's caliber.

Angie was experiencing financial hardship, she was several months behind on the payments of her hatchback vehicle, she'd told me that, but I'd also learned from my sister that she had quit spending time with the big baller (drug dealer) because he wouldn't help her with her car payments.

This prompted me to feel that our reunion was based more on a financial note rather than the propensity of love and/or feelings, nevertheless, my intentions to ameliorate the relationship was serious, but now I was seeing a new light.

Everyday something seemed to add fuel to the blaze, after few weeks of enduring this mistreatment, I decided in my mind that it just wasn't going to ever return to the way it had been with her in the beginning.

She'd become to liberated and misled by the association with the care-free, get all you can get from a man types of women, and she wasn't going to change back.

After finishing the routines of the morning rituals, one day I went off on a rock smoking binge in her car, I'd been receiving subliminal messages from the rock telling me that I was overdue on my next hit of rock.

I started out taking someone to get some rock, and I took a hit, once one takes that first hit, especially after it's been a long while since indulging themselves, well everything else of importance gets put on the shelf.

When it came time to pick up Angie and the kids, I couldn't be held accountable for not showing up because I was stuck like chuck and not giving a fuck behind smoking the rock.

The evening passed, I wasn't even concerned enough to call and find out how they'd made it home, the main concern for me at that time was to keep on chasing the glass phallic.

I stayed out on that mission all morning long, the next day some of the rock dealers in Oak Park, had noticed my having the car again and propositioned me with some rock to rent it.

I was kind of reluctant to follow through on this, but the calling of the rock got the best of me and I reasoned that the car was going to eventually be up for repossession anyway, so I rented it out.

Luckily, that rental arrangement went well for a couple of days because the dealers knew me personally and always came back on time, and I was always supplied with rock as they continued to rent it.

On the third day I rented it out to a female rock dealer; females selling the rock was becoming a big thing, sort of a new trend for them since a lot of the males were getting busted, they figured they might as well make the money.

I didn't know her name, but had been in contact with her a few times and knew that she was from the area.

I'd let her use it early that morning, by mid afternoon, and by her not showing back up I was starting to worry, an hour later she shows up in some other vehicle.

She charged up to me.

"Hey man the fucking police stopped me, along with a tow truck and they pulled me out of the car, said it was a repossession vehicle and towed it away."

All I could say was, "my x- girl was behind on her notes and that was probably why it was seized."

There was no animosity between us two behind what had happened, and she got back in that other car and took off.

I felt bad that things had ended for Angie the way that they had, but after living with her for those few weeks I'd come to realize that there wasn't much there for us anymore, because of the way she'd become while I was away from her over those few years.

Although I stilled loved her, I wasn't in love with her anymore and the sexual gratification with her was gone as well, it was not fulfilling.

The incident of her car being repossessed while in my care put us back on bad terms again.

But then by her using me as a rebound tool in hopes that she could save her car left me feeling unsympathetic towards her.

My sister Deniese however, was there supporting Angie to the fullest, by giving her a ride to work and the kids to school until Angie became able to purchase another used car.

Me, on the other hand, after that repossession incident, sought refuge in the downtown area of Sacramento, I had never hung out in that locality, but knew that there were places to receive three meals a day, and shelters where I could lay my head at night.

When I got downtown I was new to the scene, it appeared that everyone on location was in the same predicament as I myself was, homelessness as a result of their families losing trust in them behind some kind of a drug addiction, and ultimately throwing them out of their lives.

In that regard I didn't feel out of place, as I did in some of the other locations, where I was out on the streets all the morning long.

Years back when I'd worked for S.E.C the first time as a meter reader, my general duties were to travel around the greater Sacramento area to read customers meters.

On several occasions I had to get readings from the Salvation Army, and the surrounding adjacent areas of the homeless people.

I was cordial to all of the homeless people, sometimes giving them money if they'd ask me for it, back then, which was in the late 70's, homelessness was prevalent among wino's and human beings whom had lost hope and had just given up.

Today though, homelessness as I was seeing all over the town was a hard faced reality for young people, women with children, and rock cocaine or Meth addicted people.

I figured the reason for the big influx of homeless people in society today were attributed to rock cocaine abuse, in retrospect, I never imagined that years later, and after having seen those people at Sally's shelter while reading meters, I'd become one of those homeless individuals myself.

Rock had placed me in a dire situation, to my own chagrin, but I hadn't quite hit rock bottom yet, which meant there were still more trials and tribulations for me to have to endure.

On the streets in the downtown area I immediately ran into an old high school acquaintance, his name was smooth, he had arrived to the homeless scene a year prior behind his family ousting him out because of his rock cocaine involvement.

Smooth had turned real scandalous I'd heard, I would have to stay watchful of him and his deeds, although it was good to see him though.

We talked of another high school friend of ours named C.D., and elaborated on how insidious C.D. had gotten in his quest for the rock cocaine.

Smooth said that C.D. had rented out a brand new Pontiac Trans Am that his wife was making car payments on, and that he'd left his 2 year old son in the car with the person to whom he had rented it to, with whom he was not even acquainted with, to insure the safe return of the vehicle.

Upon hearing that, and of how such a precarious and uncertain an action that that was for anyone to have done, I thought to myself that, I've heard it all.

A new decade was ready to emerge, 1990, the 90's would well substantiate the dissonance displayed demography in America, due to the rock trade.

The prevailing decadence among Black Americans was more wide spread and abroad, in the way of the ruthlessness of crimes, homelessness, homosexuality, prostitution, child abandoning, and homicides.

The ever increasing addiction to the rock cocaine was the culprit to the above mentioned deeds, my arrival to the downtown area was a testimony to this pervasive decadence.

The luring effect of the rock cocaine generated among blacks I thought to be mysterious, I was seeing more clearly now the true nature of rock as an impediment, this was clearly visible in the downtown locality.

I'd guessed that the reasons for this influx were the easy access to finding food and shelter, and the easiness of their getting around.

As I roamed around the area I met more homeless people, and familiarized myself with all of the different hangouts; and two spots that I would come to frequent a lot, the Camelia, and the Caravan motels, I would coexist with them both.

Both places were located on 16th street, between Capital and L streets, and both spots were heavy in rock cocaine trafficking, prostitution, and just about any other type of illegal activities.

Right away I was led to a room in the Caravan motel where an older white man was smoking rock, the discomforting thing about seeing this man smoking rock though was that he was a paraplegic.

He had seen me approach the building and had sent someone out to me, bring me up because he'd thought I was a rock dealer.

The dealers came and left the spot on and off all day and night long, I wasn't a dealer, but this gave me a chance to establish some credentials with the guy.

His name was Auto, we acquainted ourselves with the exchange of names and handshakes.

Auto lived there by himself, but the rock dealers, smokers and prostitutes frequented his place often, he would entrust many different individuals with his money to buy rock.

Some he trusted to come back, never would return, others would, but with little of his product, so he had quit trusting people.

I had that honest looking face, and was fairly articulate and intelligent which won me over with him, or perhaps, my timing was right because there was nobody around he could trust at that time.

Auto wanted to spend thirty dollars on some rock, I took a gamble and called his bluff by telling him that I'd just left a dealer around the corner at Compton's market.

I told him that I'd go and buy the rock but that I'd have to take the money with me, and finished by saying that I wouldn't feel right taking advantage of someone disabled, and left my wallet with him in good faith.

He sat pensively for a moment then went into his wallet and pulled out a ten and a twenty dollar bill.

I took the money and left, at that time, just having got downtown, I knew of no one whom was selling, but I went to the market up the street.

There were a few youngsters standing about talking, I approached them with the question of where the rock was, sure enough, they all said what do you need.

I was broke, so I said a twenty and they all came out of their pockets with a dub(rock cocaine), I chose the biggest one and went back to Auto's.

I pocketed the ten bill, Compton's market was on 17th and Capital, I was only a block away, I contemplated on cutting out and following that vicious cycle of everyone else that Auto had trusted, but something told me not to do it.

Since I'd only spent twenty dollars, I split the dub, giving him two thirds and I kept a third for myself, when I got to the rooms door, which was all the way open, Auto was sitting in his wheel chair a few feet from the door.

I stepped in, closed the door, and brought out the dub, he was delighted, not just because I had returned with the rock, but at the size of it.

What I gathered from that was that the people he'd trusted with his money would bring him back very little pieces of rock,

He took the rock from my hand and said that it was big, offered me a good sized hit which I accepted, and stated.

"Hey man could you always make yourself accessible to me by staying within close proximity to my room so you can make my purchases for me?"

"I can do that for you Auto", was my retort.

Auto was a character of sorts, he resembled a Boris Karloff, the horror films actor, in appearance, but he was amicable in character.

His demeanor bordered the sinister type, his fancy was to smoke rock and drink beer when ever possible.

He'd been ripped off so many times before he wasn't sure if he could trust anyone anymore, but he deserved a break and I was the one who gave it to him, which was in part why I didn't run off with his money.

He also needed a good friend, so I befriended, and accommodated him with those needs, we both sat, drank beer, and smoked on the rock.

While we conversed different individuals stopped by to see what they could work him out of, Auto gave me the power of authority to turn around at the door anyone whom he didn't want in his place.

I was gaining his approval on every measure of power within his domain, earlier in our conversation I'd mentioned to him that I was homeless and new to the downtown area.

He replied to that by saying, "my door will always be open to you if you need a place to crash out at", his room was a little filthy, and although he couldn't help that, it would be a place for me to lay my head some nights, and would indeed prove valuable.

He was also a Veteran whom was injured in the Vietnam war, he received a hefty monthly income from the Government for his injuries, he had no children, was made bitter behind the partial paralysis of his lower body, and was content with just existing from day to day.

A rock cocaine prostitute had introduced him to the rock cocaine a few years back, and he'd never stopped smoking it.

He figured that he might as well enjoy the remaining life he had left doing what he liked, which was living in a motel room, smoking rock and entertaining people whom he liked to be around, I felt sorry for him, but it was his pleasure.

His room was in bad shape so after we'd finished smoking the rock I straightened up the place for him.

After cleaning his room, which was small, approximately 10 feet by 10 feet, I felt that I could perhaps crash out on the floor when I needed to.

He kept an abundance of blankets around for people who needed to sleep over.

A week had passed, I'd stayed over at his room only a few times out of that week, the other days I stayed at the Salvation Armies shelter for the homeless.

The Caravan motel was a haven for insidious characters, and staying amongst those types of people for too long would incite trouble, so I kept my sleep over's to a minimum.

Both motels stayed full of rock traffic twenty four hours a day, between them both, I could at any time hustle myself up on a hit of the rock.

There was always someone either wanting to buy some rock, or already had it and needed a pipe or a place to smoke it at.

The rock cocaine business in the downtown area in a sense was easily accessible, which made coming to that location all the more feasible for me.

I gradually developed a sense of belonging down there, and soon discovered other rock trafficking locations abroad, in addition to becoming acquainted with most any and everyone affiliated with the business.

It was December of 89, with Christmas and New Years approaching, I wanted to have a little money in my pocket.

I'd heard from other homeless people about G.A.(general assistance), but I had never applied for it, so I pondered with the idea that maybe now was the time for it.

The Sacramento County Welfare office was located downtown on twenty eighth and R streets, the next day I would go there and apply for assistance.

Staying out of jail was a pleasant feeling; for a little while there it had almost become like a second home for me.

I was still on probation with the County for the possession of a controlled substance I'd gotten earlier that year, part of the stipulations of probation was that I was subject to search and seizure at random, in addition to a bi-weekly drug testing.

I, up to that point had been crafty enough in avoiding a dirty test by drinking vinegar and a lot of water a few days before the test date.

That thwarting of the test usually worked, but I was surprised by a rude awakening from my P.O.(probation officer) that next day after I'd left the Welfare office and stopped by the probation office on fifth and E streets.

He mentioned that I'd given him a dirty test that was positive for cocaine use, but said that he wasn't going to remand me back into custody on this one, but that there better not be another one in the future.

Drug testing for either the State or County custodial agencies was much different than testing done for Civilian workers, in that when you tested for a custodial agency they stood there and watched you urinate so that one couldn't thwart a test.

I felt as though this was an infringement upon my person, in which it was, but that were the consequences I'd have to accept as a result of my rock cocaine addiction, and getting caught up in the penal system.

I began putting the pieces of the puzzle together that heightened my awareness to America's conspiracy of subjugating Blacks by and through rock cocaine.

I left the probation office feeling compromised, with not much I was able to do about it, in my mind, it was as if you'd better conform boy or we'll take away your freedom.

I was in defiance of this and headed back towards Auto's place to find a way to smoke some more rock, I somewhat felt that I was reaping the long term effects of my cocaine use.

Rock cocaine had deprived, depraved, and humiliated me, and although I was beginning to see it as a pernicious substance, yet I still found it hard to refrain from it.

The time would come when I would have to rely on the spiritual strength through GOD to say that I was done with that shit, but that time wasn't now, furthermore, simply because of my P.O. put an ultimatum before me, it increased my urge to go there even more.

Getting back to Auto's room was quick, but being able to readily smoke some rock wasn't, bored I walked the block and sat in the State Capitals park pensively going over why this rock cocaine was so designed to attract Black Americans.

It wasn't just limited to the impoverished Blacks, but the elite as well, I pondered with the fates of Singer Natalie Cole, Actor Todd Bridges, and the likes; this all seamed so uncanny.

I sat there thinking a while longer, trying to discern what it all meant, not being able to decipher any concrete conclusion on this issue, I got up and started aimlessly on a walk.

After wandering around I ended up at the Greyhound bus terminal, standing there observing pedestrians I ran into my X brother- in-law.

Jeffry was married to Mary's sister, and at one time Mary, our son Siege II, and myself had stayed with them for a few months in between our moving.

Jeffry, and I had become pretty close back then drinking beer and watching sports together, he said he had long ago divorced Mary's sister, and went on to say that his health had deteriorated due to excessive use and abuse of rock cocaine and alcohol.

It had been over 10 years since I'd last seen him, and to learn of this was shocking to say the least.

He continued on saying, "yeah Siege my kidneys have failed me behind smoking rock, drinking alcohol, and not drinking enough water; in effect causing my body to dehydrate, which ultimately shut down my kidneys, and thus making me have to be put on a dialysis machine 3 times a week to have my blood purified in order to stay alive."

"I'm living at the Verry motel next to Greyhounds bus station and have been there for over a year now,."

"I'll be praying for you Jeff," was all I could say, he was still smoking the rock despite his life now threatened because of his abuse of the rock, I couldn't fathom this.

I was at odds with how a person could continue to jeopardize their existence hear on earth by patronizing the very substance that had impaired them.

I had also just learned of another piece of discomforting information of the perils of rock cocaine, aside from all of the other consequential effects of the rock, I had no idea that rock cocaine exacts it's toll by physically destroying organs in one's body.

This was another form of a life threatening reality for one to be aware of when smoking the rock, and it heightened my conscience to the other unknown dangers of smoking rock cocaine.

My sister Holly had gotten worse with smoking rock which I found out when I called to check on her and my Mother, she had embarked on the mission of dating men for money to get her rock, when I went back out there I'd have to talk to her.

The benevolence was always there in me when it came to my family and relatives, even close associates, despite the destructive course I was on in my own life.

The next morning I took a leave from my location and went to my mothers house, when I arrived, around late morning Holly had not to long ago came in herself.

I looked at my beautiful black sister, grabbed and hugged her tight, all the while conveying my disapproval to her about what our mother had told me she was now doing with men.

I emphasized to her the fact that she wasn't brought up to even entertain the idea of selling sex, furthermore, I stressed the possibility of her contracting the aides virus from one of those tricks, and that it would serve her well to stop doing that.

We were close growing up as siblings, I'd always looked out for her, not because she was naïve, because she was far from that, but because she was one of my favorite sisters.

I stated to her, "I Do not want to hear that you are back out there selling yourself again from our mother or anyone else, or I'll be back out here and whip that urge from your butt."

To summarize the chastisement of her I mentioned the incident about Solomon the serial killer in Oak Park when he'd killed those 8 young black women, one of whom we'd both grown up with, and was a good friend of hers.

"Do you want to end up like that?" I went on to ask her.

"Hell no I don't". She responded back to me in a pretty high spirited mode from having been out all morning long, and went on to talk about one weirdo that she had encountered last night.

"Hey brother last night an older white male pulled up to me in a van and invited me inside, I got in and he drove off."

"While driving he propositioned me with the most obscene and perverted sexual act I'd ever heard of, he ask me if I'd like to be paid $80.00 to just squat over his head and shit in his mouth?'

Continuing on with her story, I couldn't hold myself any longer and burst out laughing.

"I'm serious", she went on to say, "I took off one pants leg, and I squatted over him while he lay flat on his back."

"I had just used the toilet and wasn't able to let anything out, yet, he was just laying there waiting for me to release."

"Finally, after several attempts of serious grunting, two small peanut sized droplets of shit oozed out and into his mouth, and he just chewed them up." "After I finished releasing he went into his wallet and handed me four 20 dollar bills, ask how often I was in the area, because he'd like to do it again sometime, and we parted company."

I was still laughing, couldn't believe what I'd heard, and ask her, "put it on the Bible," she was a GOD fearing person and when she said, "go get the Bible," I said, "never mind," because I knew that it must have been true.

I couldn't conceive that sick minded people like that even existed in the world, but then the world is a big place full of wicked and despicable human beings.

We laughed quite a while at that, then, feeling a sense of nostalgia, I thought I'd make myself useful and started making lunch for my mother and sister.

I reiterated to her the seriousness of the kind of lifestyle she was involved in, and went on to say that rock cocaine creates a state of delusion to it's consumer, making them feel invincible to the dangers that lurk around, and causes one to act out of their normal character.

Finishing, I said, "I hope that you'll soon see it for what it really is, an instrument of the devils, and refrain from using it."

She concluded by saying, "I will because I'm getting tired of this shit," and with that, we went on to discuss other things of importance.

I stayed there with them throughout the rest of the Years end Holidays to make sure that Holly didn't renege on her promise of not selling herself.

The first week of January 90, I received my G.A. funds from the County.

I had been using my mothers address for my mail, leaving them to go back downtown, I kissed them both, said I'd stay in touch and left.

I got on the Regional Transit bus and rode to the midtown check cashing outlet on 19th and Broadway, and cashed my G.A. check.

At that time the Counties G.A. program was giving it's recipients two hundred and eighty six dollars in cash, and one hundred and eleven dollars in food stamps.

It wasn't a lot of money, but it was better than being broke, I was that much richer.

After I received my money the burdening urge to smoke some rock came upon me, I had money now, and the devil had his candy(the rock) calling to me.

For a rock addict, the devil always calls out to you when you have money on your possession, it's a non-stop kind of call.

The Cievie circle projects on 5th and Broadway wasn't that far away, located just at the west end of Broadway near a Detox facility for the wino's.

I went there to buy a half of a gram of rock cocaine, while there I ran into a young lady whom I'd had a crush on back in high school.

I was shocked to see Jane there in that element, because she had been such a high & mighty girl back in the day, but in the here and now she'd become an avid rock smoker.

Reflecting back, I remembered when we were in the same math class together, she sat in the next row over from me, but a couple of chairs back, I can remember when I would purposely drop my pencil on the floor and while picking it up I would get a look up under her dress, which made me want her.

Jane was a pretty girl, she had a coffee cream hue to her complexion, long brown hair, nice small nose and lips, and green eyes with long lashes, she was also nicely built with small breast and a nice round butt.

I'd had a crush on her, but was kind of shy, young and inexperienced with the girls, I doubted if she ever became aware that I was admirer of hers.

She was a scholar student, and a cheerleader for the schools football team, she more or less catered to the jocks, or so I felt.

Back then I would have relished the possibility to have gotten the chance to kiss her on the lips, but now I speculated on the idea of finally, with some rock, getting her into bed.

She was still pretty, older looking and grown up though, talking to her I told her, "I'm surprised to see you down in this area, but even further, I'm disturbed to see that you too have become a victim to this rock cocaine plague too."

She replied, "my 6 year old daughters father started me out using rock back in 1985, and I left him because he'd lost himself in it, I'm now a single parent, and occasionally get high on rock."

Continuing on to say, "smoking this rock cocaine caused me to loose my employment with the State, and now I'm on County welfare."

I extended my sympathy to her, and said, "Jane I had a crush on you back in junior high school," hoping to cheer her up a little in light of how life had turned out for.

It brought a smile to her face, and she replied, "I thought that you were cute back then, but I wasn't aware that you had felt that way about me, had I known it than maybe we could have gotten something going back then," with that, that brought a smile to my face.

I had earlier bought a half a gram of rock prior to running into Jane and asked, "hey Jane I have a half of a gram of rock do you feel like smoking some?"

"Really, man I've been craving for a hit of some rock all morning," and led me into her apartment.

"My daughter is in school, so we have the place to ourselves for a few hours."

We smoked half of the package and I said, "I have to head downtown to check on a friend," Jane, acting under the influence of the rock impetuously propositioned me with some sex in exchange for some more of the rock for herself.

My lament on this was short lived, and I accepted her offer, but before we engaged in the act of it, I expressed remorse towards her at how she'd come to be, and how the rock was dictating the lives, and actions of so many beautiful Black women in America prompting them to trade sex for rock.

I went on to say that the substance was destroying Black people and told her that I wasn't going to have sex with her simply on the pretense of the rock, but rather, enjoy making some good loving to her because I'd been fond of her.

She was in accordance with that and began to slip out of her skirt, and as she slowly undressed, I appreciated getting a full view of her lovely brown well developed figure, despite her age, she still displayed that girlish body I had remembered of her back in junior high.

I undressed and we got into her bed, kissed and enjoyed some small foreplay, then without further delay, I entered her and we performed together in unison until we both climaxed.

"Siege your really a good lover, I wished I'd had known the way you felt about me years earlier because I'm feeling like I've missed out on something that could have probably been good between us."

"Thank you Jane for that compliment."

After we were dressed I told her, "you should try hard at leaving the stuff alone Jane," and gave her a twenty dollar bill instead of the rock, as an incentive to divert her interest away from the rock, and said, "I hoped you use the money on yourself and your daughter."

I hugged and kissed her and turned to leave, but before I could make it through the door.

"Hey Siege maybe you can help me with this dilemma, by being a part of mine and my daughter's life, so please come by anytime."

"I'd like that, I'll be back," and I left.

Walking back to the downtown area I thought of how incredible a fate rock cocaine was handing out to many Blacks, whom like myself, were otherwise decent people with goals, aspirations, and a solid direction in life.

It was becoming more lucidly clear to me that the nature of rock was meant to disrupt and destroy people.

Getting back to midtown I glanced at some fashions in merchants store window, I hadn't treated myself to any new attire in quite some time.

I wasn't into the current trends, some casual wear would do, I bought a pair of blue 501 Levi jeans, a pair of leather penny loafer shoes, and a Polo shirt.

In all I spent $70.00, which wasn't a bad investment considering how it improved my personal appearance.

I went back over to Auto's place, it was near to 5:00 p.m. and the crowd around the motel was thick due to it being the 1rst of the new month.

The first of every month typically marks an increase in activity in cities around the Country for everyone, particularly Welfare, S.S.I., and G.A. recipients, in addition to State employee's and other Civil workers.

It also brings out the con artists, drug addicts, gang bangers, and prostitutes, in general anyone and everyone whom has a deep love for money and the things that it can buy.

As usual, Auto was into a session of rock smoking with a few would be associates, I stepped in and went into the bathroom to change into my new apparel.

I wasn't familiar with everyone in the room, there was Auto, two females, and three guys, the room was too small to comfortably accommodate everyone that was there.

I threw my old clothing into the closet and told Auto I was going over to Compton's market to buy some alcohol and would return at a later time.

Auto was so observed with the rock pipe, that he was un-comprehensive of my statement to him, as if he was in a trance and/or un-conscience to anything else around him while he inhaled the smoke from the rock pipe hit.

I left, I had learned that being in a dwelling with a crowd of people, either smoking rock, or selling it was a trap, and since the cops were heavily raiding rock houses now, I was careful not to be a part of that scenario again.

I bought a 40 ounce bottle of Millers genuine draft beer, lodged myself on a tree stump in an empty lot adjacent to Compton's market, opened my beer, and peacefully drink until it's contents were gone.

I sat there a moment enjoying the tranquility of peace, it was January, and although it was slightly breezy, the weather was nice with the absence of any rain.

An hour passed by, and it being the Winter season, it was dark outside at 6:00 p.m., with nothing else to do I rendezvoused back to Auto's place. when I arrived there the crowd had thickened, not only was the place congested, but the vestibule outside of his room was as well.

I'd still had a piece of rock on my person from earlier that day, and didn't want to chance being rode upon by the law for loitering around the motel.

Auto was still preoccupied with smoking his rock, drinking beer, and entertaining the perpetrators, this time he was a little more receptive of my appearance and offered me to make myself comfortable.

I had stepped in to tell him that I would either drop back by later that evening, or I would see him tomorrow, and that I was out of there.

Auto petitioned my leaving there by offering to run some of the people off, I declined the offer, and told him to watch himself around all those people.

I left walking, Jane was on my mind, she'd left some kind of an impression upon me in more ways than one, and a follow up visit to her was on my itinerary.

I'd met a few people downtown since I'd been in the area, and usually would meet someone new in the rock business everyday.

Normally, meeting people whom I would consider someone to associate with on a regular basis, by chance, and on a daily basis was rare, but being a recipient of the rock cocaine business instigates random association of anonymous individuals whom share a common quest.

I decided to put off going over to Jane's place for the moment, and headed back over to the market to buy another 40 ounce of Millers beer.

There were several people standing around in front of the market, I went in and got my beer, coming back out I was approached by a guy.

He mentioned that he had some straight shooters(a glass stem pipe) for sell for $5.00 a piece, I responded by saying to him that I could use one and that I would smoke some rock with him instead of buying one, and he jumped at that offer.

We moved around to the back of the market and into the alley way, and smoked the remaining piece that I had had left.

I still had a hundred and forty dollars left from my G.A. check.

The guy turned out to be quite a character, somewhat of a comedian, he introduced himself as Success, I kind of took a liking to the guy and ask him, "say man would you like to smoke on some more rock with me."

"Yeah man lets do it," was his reply.

I went back around to the front of the market and spotted the youngsters that I'd bought rock from earlier, I bought two more dubs.

Compton's market was a spot where rock dealers, smokers, prostitutes, hustlers, and most any and all other insidious types of people pass through twenty four hours a day.

We smoked a little more of my rock together, then Success asked.

"Hey man lets go down to the Greyhound bus station so I could sell some of this refer that I've got on me."

It was still early and being all hyped up from smoking the rock, I went along with him.

Although he was a funny type of a person to be around, after hanging with him for a few hours, and coming to learn that the alleged refer he was selling was imitation, plus watching how he was treating people, I knew that I couldn't continue associating with him.

It was near 10:00 p.m. now, I bid him a farewell, and started my walk over to Jane's apartment, on my way there, I passed through the New Hellviesha projects located near the end of Broadway and 5th streets.

I had on a light blue wind breaker jacket, my being an older guy I wasn't conscientious to the colors I had on, in relation to the area I was in, which was blood territory.

Half way through the projects two blood gang members came out of no where and made a statement of what's up blood, the statement was a taunting and provocative remark in view of the color jacket I was wearing.

I retorted back with the sky is what's up, they both seemed to be intoxicated and itching to make something happen.

I sensed trouble from these two, I had dealt with and knew members of both the bloods and crip gangs, and never had any problems from either, but it was something with these two that I knew something was about to happen.

One of them stepped to my left, the other stayed to my right, the one to the left asked.

"What you looking for blood a dub or something," I started to walk, all the while keeping my eyes shifting from one to the other.

At that instant out of the corner of my eye I saw the youngster to my left attempt a swing on me, I swiftly moved out of the blows path, but was grazed on the cheekbone from it.

Out of reflex I caught the kids swinging arm, pulling him into my own right fist and knocking him out cold, before the other youngster was able to react, I turned and caught him with a swift hard left knocking him down to the ground.

It was just the three of us there at that time, I wasn't sure whether either one of then had a gun on them or not, or if any more of their comrades would come to their aide, so I took off running before anything else could happen.

Jane's apartment was in Cievie circle, another different and huge set of projects several blocks away towards the end of Broadway, I ran all the way to her place.

Years back in G Parkway when those youngsters nearly cost me one of my eyes, I'd made a personal vow to never let, not only youngsters, but anyone, to ever get the jump on me.

I resent crip and blood gang members, because of the fratricidal tendencies they practice of killing their own race simply for wearing the wrong color.

They are in my eyes as bad as members of the klu klux klan, it was all bad enough that Black Americans live-li-hood had became precarious as a result of the rock cocaine plague, and then for the crips and bloods to compound the matter more behind colors that in actuality represent the colors of America, red for bloods, blue for crips, and the white is the rock cocaine, I found all this to be impetuous and desultory.

I got to Jane's place and knocked on the door for a good little while, then became disappointed when I realized that she wasn't there, I didn't want to remain in that area after what had just took place down the street, so I headed down to the end of Broadway to a place called detox.

Detox was an alcohol and substance abuse agency, It was similar to the Salvation Army and other missionary shelters in that it provided food and beds for it's recipients.

I'd never been their before and since it was only a few blocks away, decided to drop in and get some sleep as opposed to running the streets.

The agency was mainly for alcoholics, wino's and transients, I checked in and realized right away that the place wasn't anything like other shelters.

The variable distinctions were in the areas of cleanliness, sanitation, and clientele; most of the clients were chronic alcoholics whom the police brought in and were detained there for a 72 hour confinement.

The facility resembled that of a warehouse, there were bed roles lined up along the walls, and in the middle of the floor, it was infested with ticks, lice, and crabs and carried a fowl odor of filth from feet and butts.

I received a bed role, put it down and tried to dose off several rimes, but could not because of the type of environment I was in.

That morning breakfast was served, and as with the general condition of the place, breakfast too, was minimal and lacking in proper nutrients.

I left there and stopped back by Jane's apartment, she still hadn't come home from the night before, nor was there any sign that she'd been there.

I started on the walk over to Auto's room, on the way there I avoided going through the New Helvishia projects just to prevent any run in with those two youngsters again.

When I got to Auto's room he was still up smoking on some rock, the other occupants of his room had thinned out.

There was one female half nude, and a couple of dudes; they were all busy cleaning out the residue from inside of their pipes.

I sat down and pulled out my package of rock and gave Auto a piece, his company gathered around his side like they were leaches, apparently they'd all either smoked up his money or beat him out of it.

I stood up and said for everybody to clear out, the guys protested, so I asked Auto if he wanted them to stay, he gave me the authority to make that call, and with that I told the two dudes to get somewhere fast.

The girl stayed and I had her to clean up the room, when she finished I gave her a piece of rock to smoke for herself.

She paraded around the room half naked for a while thinking that I had a lot of rock, and that perhaps she could arouse me by looking at her half nude body and maybe proposition her for some sex.

But I didn't have anymore rock, but I did have some money though, and after all of that rock was gone, I went out and bought another half a gram.

When I came back we all started smoking on what I'd just got, the girl after taking a hit of the rock, started taking off her daisy duke skin tight shorts.

She propped herself right up on top of the bed butt ass naked, this kind of shocked me, but I'd noticed as of lately that rock was making people do unusual and impulsive things when they smoked it.

At that I began feeling a sexual heightening of my libido, the girl wasn't my type and she'd probably committed sexual acts that previous night with those two guys, so I withheld my urges on that.

In actuality I suspected that this was how the Aides virus was transmitted.

Putting two and two together, I concluded that smoking rock triggered one's sexual appetite, thus prompting one to participate in unprotected and random sex with strangers to appease their fancies for the moment.

I couldn't ascertain if there was some kind of an aphrodisiacal additive in the rock cocaine that made it become a substance that promotes promiscuities among it's users in America's black communities, but it all led me to ponder on whether these two plagues, rock cocaine and aides, were created for Black Americans by and through the power structure in America.

It just all seemed very preplanned and convenient that one, (the rock) plays host to the other,(sex), and the consummation of these two when practiced carelessly can open the window for and give birth to the virus of aides to it's participants.

I quit racking my brains for the moment with this mystery, but one day the truth in all of this would prevail, and I hoped that by that time, myself and all of the millions of other afflicted Black Americans would have long since refrained from smoking that poisonous substance.

The three of us sat in silence smoking more of the rock, I was becoming more agitated by her nudity, because the devil had been conjured up behind our smoking the rock, kept whispering to my subconscious mind telling me to indulge myself in this woman.

But the spirit of GOD in me rejected the temptation to proceed along with it, I was being swayed by both forces, soon one would succumb to the other.

I went with my spiritual nature and got up, told Auto I'd be back, and left the room.

The devil in all his craftiness with his temptations had almost lured me into that trap, had she been pretty, or my type of woman, I would have fell victim to her seduction, and put myself at risk by engaging myself with her and chancing the possibility of contracting the aides virus.

I walked to the market and bought a half a pint of Remy Martin brandy, as hyped up as I was, the brandy would bring me down a little.

I drank straight from the bottle, after a few good swigs I mellowed out some.

My money supply was shrinking, I had less than $50.00 left, when you're a rock smoker, place no value on money because it comes and goes in the blink of an eye.

RUINED AND CAUGHT UP

The devil must have had his mind set on capturing me that day though, because as I stood and drank my brandy, a beautiful girl showed up, stood at the corner momentarily, and then came way, she looked to be of Black and Mexican decent.

I asked her "what's on your agenda for the day?"

She asserted, "just seeing what's happening out here." I followed with, "do you smoke the rock?" "Yes, why do you have any,?" because I'll do just about anything to smoke on some right about now."

"Yeah I have some, but do you have a place where we could go to smoke at?"

"I have a studio apartment four blocks away, my name is Jasmine."

After the introduction, I offered her a sip of the brandy, and said, "shall we go there".

On the way to her place, I stopped a youngster on the streets and bought 30 more dollars of some rock, that purchase emptied my pockets, I was broke.

When we got to her studio, she went straight to a nightstand and produced a rock pipe, I broke off a piece of the rock and gave it to her.

She put it on the pipe and set a flame to it, inhaled all of the smoke, then exhaled, after the exhalation of smoke she began to undress herself; either she was a prostitute, or she new what to expect.

I conformed with her and we shared some wild sex, when we finished the sex act we laid together talking and smoking what rock was left, when that was gone we engaged ourselves once more in the act of sex.

I reflected on how rock cocaine brought about an awesome sexual revolution with it, it was both a splendid and a pernicious thing.

We completed our mission, got dressed and walked back down towards the market, apparently she'd been looking to turn a date, because she left me and went over to the corner and stood there soliciting.

I felt empty handed now being broke, when you have money or drugs, you have friends, but when your broke nobody knows you, I wasn't bothered by this though and went on about my business of wandering aimlessly.

It never crossed my mind to look for work, my line of work was printing, it was in demand, and I was good at it.

I'd gotten so caught up in the rock world until that was where my priorities lay.

As the day dwindled on into the night I became restful, I wanted to make my way over to Jane's, but feared the trip because she might not be there, so I went over to Auto's instead.

When I got to his place, I ran dead smack into sibil, the girl whom had taken my car and rented it out to some young rock dealers in Del Paso Heights.

I went straight to her and said, "bitch you can do one of two things, die right here and now, or be ready to break yourself every time that I see you."

She looked spooked, and had lost a lot of her weight, "I'll do what ever possible to make amends to you for the loss of your car," was her reply.

I told her that anything that she had of value when ever I saw her would be mine for the taking beginning now, and began searching her, unfortunately she didn't have anything worth taking.

I started to sock her in the mouth, but I wasn't the type of a guy to hit on women, I did tell her that if I needed some money or rock she'd better be ready to sell some sex for me, and she nobly accepted this consignment.

She had ruined her good standings with everyone that she knew, and was now homeless herself.

I learned after my arrival to the downtown area that the location was Ideal for the homeless because everything was close and convenient.

I ordered her to hang with me for a while, and when guys passed through the motel looking for a toss-up(girl who trades sex for rock) she was summoned by me to render her services.

She performed sex acts twice that night, and I was given the proceeds, once was cash, the other was rock which I gave her a hit of to motivate her.

I still had some morals left in me, I was against the using of a Black woman for my own personal gain, but because she'd crossed that line with me, I felt compelled with following through on forcing her to sell sex as a means of retribution to me.

The next day we got up from Auto's room, she dressed and said she was going to go try to hustle or sell sex to reimburse me for the lose she had brought to me.

I knew that I couldn't keep her around me 24/7, so I reiterated to her that she would always be subjected to a search and seizure, and I let her leave.

Later that afternoon I walked over to 20th,and H streets to a quick stop store in hopes of successfully shoplifting some liquor to both drink on, and to trade for some rock to the dealers.

I entered the store, with only one clerk it all looked to be easy, I stuffed two 5ths of Royal Crown brandy, and headed for the exit, but before I got to the door another clerk ran out from the small back room, came up behind me, grabbed me and pulled me back into the store.

The police were called, they came and took me off to the County jail.

In Court the Judge wasn't so light with me on the sentencing this time around, he gave me 4 months to be served at the County branch jail.

When I passed through the main jail downtown I met up with success, I'd wondered why I hadn't seen him and what had happened to him.

He told me the D.A was offering 18 years as a deal on a case of multiple charges consisting of kidnap, rape, sodomy, possession of a controlled substance, possession of a firearm, and grand theft auto.

He said he was going to trial with it, I couldn't believe what I was hearing from him, and thought that he was trying to trump up his charges to make himself look big-time, as some guys will do.

But later and through another source in the jail house I learned that all that he was saying was true.

He and another guy had stolen a vehicle, drove it to Oakland, Ca., ran into a white girl down there in Oakland while they were purchasing an once of cocaine, picked her up and brought her back to Sacramento against her will.

On the way back to Sac both success and the other guy took turns on the white girl with anal and regular sex acts, then upon returning to Sac they took her to an apartment downtown and continued those same sexual acts on her in the apartment, and then let her go free.

She returned later with the police and they both were arrested and fully charged on every account.

I'd figured success of being somewhat of a shyster, but I didn't think to that extent, but I knew for a fact that him, his girlfriend, and their 3 kids had come from Seattle, Wash., and that he would take her check that she was receiving from welfare every month and smoke it all up, leaving them all on the streets homeless.

I know that GOD doesn't like ugliness like that coming out of people, maybe GOD was punishing him for the way he treated that woman and those kids, karma can be a hell of a payback.

I left the main jail and went to the County branch, and loss contact with success, I wasn't able to know how his trial was going to turn out.

In April of 1990 I was released again, from the first arrest of petty theft, up to this one I was serving time for, I had accumulated almost a half of a dozen theft charges against me, all due to my rock cocaine smoking binges.

The laws were changing in California with regard to petty thefts, after one receives so many of the theft charges, they start turning into felonies, which meant that I would have to resort to doing something else to support my habit or become subject to doing prison time.

Once again back on the scene downtown felt good, that little period of incarceration had rejuvenated me, I was fresh mentally and physically.

Each time that I was taken from society and could not smoke any rock was a good thing, when released I was healthy, vibrant, and thus bringing me a step closer to realizing how very bad that rock is to your body.

However, the clutch of the rock is something to contend with, and to break free one has to pray to GOD, keep the faith in GOD, and really want to quit.

But as it appeared, more and more Blacks were becoming new patrons of the rock cocaine syndrome, Blacks whom would otherwise not be inclined to use hard drugs, were patronizing this one, and this was disturbing to me.

Back on the scene I ran into an old junior high school friend named T., he had went off to the air force straight out of high school.

He'd put in 11 years with the Government, exited with an honorable discharge, and was now employed with the U.S. postal service, his only fault was that he too was now smoking the rock.

A few years back shortly after T. had come home from the service, I saw him sporting around town in a brand new Chevrolet Corvette, he also had a Cadillac Seville.

After talking to him he told me that he'd sold the Corvette because of financial problems, and that the Seville was setting up in need of repairs that he couldn't afford.

He resided on the outskirts of downtown in an apartment away from the rock infested areas that I frequented.

After we both brought each other up to date on the current happenings he ask, "hey Siege where can I score an ounce of some cocaine."

I replied, "there's a dude just up the street from you that we can pick one up from."

As we walked, we talked of how things used to be with regards to being in relationships with women, the employment scene, loyalty of friends, comradeship among associates, and the concern of a citizens welfare by the authorities of the law.

But since the advent of the rock cocaine epidemic all that has dramatically changed.

He mentioned that despite his high income from the post office, he was barely surviving because of his involvement with rock cocaine, he was trapped too like the many other Black Americans whom got lured in by the rock.

He went on to say, "man I want desperately to refrain from using it, but it's lure is too overwhelming for me to overcome."

T. was a ladies man, of Creo decent, he was light skinned, nice keen features, with long hair, he mentioned that part of his enticement to the rock was that with it came an abundance of females, which he enjoyed every bit of.

I commented that that aspect of it was likewise for me as well, and that it was becoming a challenge for me to retreat from it as well.

We both walked the area around Compton's market, there was always rock in the vicinity.

"Hey man are there any females around that I could have some fun with?" he ask, I remembered Jasmine as being game for that kind of activity.

At that time our priority was locating and buying the ounce, which we continued in pursuit of, if in the pursuit of the ounce a female or females happened along, and was to our liking, they would be invited to join us.

T. lived about 10 blocks away from the market, so the walk back could quite possibly turn fruitful for us in the way of women along the way.

A block from the store there was a youngster on a mountain bike.

"Hey youngster where are the ounces of that rock at." I asked? T. was a laid back kind of person, so I did all of the talking.

"I got them, but I don't have that much on me right now, but if you'll wait here I'll go and pick up some more and shoot it right back to you," was his reply.

While waiting for the youngster to return a nice looking female walked by, T. being in the market for some women, intercepted her and put in his bid(propositioned her).

"Hey sweetie are you in the market for smoking on some rock, and having a little extra fun along with it," he asked?

"I'm all for that kind of excitement," she replied, and remained with us.

I still had in my mind to include Jasmine in on the activities as well, but first we had to buy the ounce of rock.

The girl T. had just met lived a block away in a studio, so we could make a short stop by there after this transaction was completed.

Twenty minutes later the youngster pulls back up on his bike, we all walked slowly while he shows us his product.

T. glanced at it and said, "I'll take it," at that time an ounce was selling for 6 hundred dollars, he forked over the money and we went on our way.

I thought of how at one time cocaine was considered a rich mans drug of choice, an ounce of powder would surely cost fifteen hundred dollars or more.

There was now a big disparity in the cost of cocaine from back then to now, I thought that perhaps this reduction in the price was a means through which the lower classes of people could afford the cost of the product.

T. tucked the ounce away in his groin area as we headed towards Jasmines place.

We got to her place, she answered the door and although it was early in the morning when I mentioned to her what was in order, she hurried herself to join us.

T.'s attention shifted from the female he'd met at the store to Jasmine, the attraction to Jasmine didn't bother me though, because he had the upper hand with the ounce and all.

Anyone with a sack(rock cocaine) always had the upper hand with regard to dictating the pace, or calling the shots if you will.

We all set out to his apartment, his place was lavishly furnished but upon entering it the drug paraphernalia laying about exposed his lifestyle.

We all got settled and sat in anticipation of smoking some rock, T. was one of the few Black men that I'd gotten high with that exhibited some class. After a couple of hits of rock, he got up and poured everyone a glass of Remy Martin Cognac brandy to accommodate us while smoking the rock.

As the smoking session progressed, T, gestured for Jasmine to accompany him in his room, "hey baby can I speak with you in privacy he asked?,"

she accepted, got up and followed him into his quarters.

He left the other young lady and I a nice piece of rock to smoke on, we sat there and started our smoking together.

"I'm Cherry, what's your name,?" she shot at me.

"Siege," I retorted.

A half an hour went by before T. opened his door and exited in his robe, went to the kitchen to retrieve some more brandy.

He refilled our two glasses and excused himself, but before he could get away, I ask, "hey T. if the situation presents itself could Cherry and I have some fun together in the living room.?"

"Go for it man, that's why were all here in the first place, isn't it, the couch lets out into a bed."

"Oh, by the way, in an hour or so I'll be out with Jasmine and we can switch females," and with that, he went back into his bedroom quarters.

I rejoined Cherry whom was busy smoking the rock, ten minutes passed before I propositioned her, "hey Cherry can we get into some nasty business while smoking?, if that's alright".

"Yes, if you don't mind undressing me while I'm standing up taking a hit on the rock", and with that reply I got busy taking off her clothing.

She had on a mini skirt that zipped up on the side, I unzipped it and the skirt fell to the floor, she had on a t-shirt which covered her loins after the skirt fell.

She sat back down on the couch and opened her legs for me to touch on the prize, and to my surprise she wasn't wearing any panties.

I calmly slipped out of my shoes and pants, got on my knees and positioned myself in front of her, I hadn't bothered to let out the couch, I pulled her up to me on the end of the couch, had her to recline herself back, and I went to work.

We both achieved our sexual satisfaction from that encounter, and went back to smoking on the rock, I liked this girl Cherry, she was a sweetheart.

I sat for a minute taking a break from hitting on the pipe, and watched her smoke, she was pretty too as I watched her take a hit of the rock.

I was a connoisseur of women, and had a keen eye for the beauty in them, although it's only skin deep, nevertheless, a woman's beauty always captured me.

T. opened his door, he and Jasmine came out together, Cherry and I motioned to cover ourselves, but relaxed when we saw Jasmine in a long T-shirt and T. in just boxers, they joined us in the living room.

After a moment, T. being the womanizer that he was gestured for Cherry to join him in his room, the switch commenced, and since I'd already been with Jasmine, we just sat together and smoked on some rock.

An hour later he and Cherry exited the room, it made me feel ashamed of the fact that so many women were sexually exploited behind the rock, many of them were good women too, but ended up turning bad behind their rock addiction.

There was no playing the role of a saint, or captain save a ho towards some of these women, because they were just as treacherous as many of the guys when it came to their character, but for the most part, it was just a mutual exchange of sex for the rock, yet, it was still a bad omen.

T. was a bachelor, and fancied ravishing woman after woman when smoking rock, he gave both ladies a piece of rock, and said they had to leave because he had other business to see after.

After they left he brought up the idea of going out and searching for some other females, he had the power of persuasion with his possession, the rock.

With that, he could sexually conquer many women, "I said lets do it," and we were on another quest for to find more females again.

Walking around downtown looking for rock smoking ladies was fruitless, as is the case usually when one is trying to make something happen, it never does.

While walking I mentioned to him the idea of the both of us selling rock as a team, he could be the source of the product, I would sell during the day and at night, and he could continue working on his regular job, he liked the idea and stated, "lets try it out."

I buttered up the plan by saying that by my selling rock I would always come into contact with pretty females and that I would bring them back to his place when I did.

Getting back to our business at hand, the thought popped into my head of going by Auto's room, I told T. about it and that there could be some girls at that spot.

When we got there another tenant had moved into Auto's room, I asked where Auto was and was told that he'd been forced to vacate the premises because of the traffic he'd kept 24/7, and that he'd relocated to West Sac's motel scene.

I'd never been to that locality before in all my life being there in Sacramento, and wasn't eager to start because of stories of how racist the cops were over there, I silently wished Auto well, and both T. and I, after not spotting any women left that spot.

"Siege lets just go back to my place and start breaking down what rock we have left into twenty dollar pieces to sell".

"Lets get it going," I said.

It was in the Month of April 1990, Easter was that next week, the present day was Saturday, and the weather was fairly pleasant.

After chipping the rock down to the right sizes, I counted out ten twenties, and put them in my pocket.

"T. I'm going out and try to off some of this rock."

"Take care of your business, I'll be hear at the house," he retorted.

"I'll keep my eyes open for any and all pretty ladies in the business, and with any luck I'll bring some back with me when I return."

Aside from the Compton's market location, I knew of another area where rock trafficking was abundant, that was over in the Alkali Flats community over on 15th and D streets.

Being familiar with the area made it easy to know where to go and who to deal with; this location, 17th and Capital streets was a rock haven district.

Even more so because the homeless shelters, and County clinic were all to within a block of each other, there was also a park called the C street park, located at 15th and C streets where all of the dealers and consumers of the rock hung out at all day long.

The Sacramento city light rail transit system operates a line 3 blocks from this park, by there being a train running that close every 15 minutes, drug trafficking at the park was usually always thick.

I walked around the park marketing my product, within an hour I'd made 60 dollars, the quantity of rock that I sold, varied from between 2 dollars to 20 dollars, depending on what the consumer wanted.

Cocaine, once being a drug that was limited to just the wealthy clientele was in a new era, and was being distributed on a superficial level now with provisions of easy access, and in abundance in the Black communities of America.

This mode of selling required me to have to breakdown a twenty dollar rock to accommodate the customers, most of which were homeless, but I was still able to build my Capital.

Hanging out a few more hours increased my currency to one hundred, there were a lot of transients hanging out drinking, smoking refer, and /or rock, but there was no decent looking ladies around that I could take back to T's with me.

After another twenty minutes of waiting around to see what might transpire in the park, I started my walk back towards 17th and Capital streets.

I'd made a little money there at the Caravan motel, but it was time to move on, the distance between the two areas back to T.'s place was about 8 blocks, along the way I quite possibly could generate some more money form sales, due to the decent weather, people were out and about.

The little walk from C street park was both profitable and brief, it took me only fifteen minutes, and while striding peacefully an older fellow discretely approached me.

"Hey young man do you know where I can pick up a couple of twenty dollar pieces of rock"?

I covertly went into my pocket and pulled out two of the dubs I had left, showed the fellow, and in return he slipped me two twenties and walked away.

I continued walking after the sale, I still had another twelve blocks to go before I got to T.'s place, I kept on course though and without making anymore sales, I was at his door.

Knocking on his door and waiting a few minutes, there was no answer, after a couple more attempts with no reply, I left I had two dubs left, another location came to my mind of where I might be able sell the remaining rock at was the Cievie circle projects of where Jane lived.

The one good thing about downtown Sacramento was that everything was within walking distance, it didn't take me very long to reach the projects.

As soon as I arrived to the projects, I sold the last two dubs instantly, next I thought I would stop by and pay Jane a visit.

I got to her place and something didn't set right in my mind with the appearance of it, she had had a few plants on the porch, they weren't there.

For some strange reason I got the feeling that the place was vacant, I knocked on the door several times before a lady next door came out and said she'd moved two weeks ago.

I asked, "do you know where she moved to"?

"I really don't have any idea as to her whereabouts young man, but I can tell you that she was evicted and had to get out of there in a hurry, and left some of her things in there."

Slightly broken down in spirit behind this news, I went to the nearest liquor store and bought some alcohol.

I drank on some E&J brandy until the effects of my losing contact with Jane were smoothed over, a few hours later I went back to T.'s place, this time he was there, as was three females I'd never seen before.

T., calling him to the side, I handed him two hundred dollars.

"Good working Siege, you are that hustler that I knew you to be, you keep fifty of this, now lets get ready for some kinkiness."

Seeing the ladies parading around half nude took some of my grief about losing contact with Jane away, and after a hit of rock my disposition was completely changed.

We all partied, drinking, smoking and getting kinky until that next day, I didn't bother mentioning to him that I'd been by earlier, he'd probably been out looking for females away.

There was no sleep all that night, that afternoon the ladies cleaned up the place and cooked some brunch for everyone.

He gave each of them a piece of rock and told them he had other business and that it was time to leave, but that they could drop back by anytime later.

During this period of time the renting out of vehicles was flourishing rapidly, it was the in thing to do if you didn't have a car, but had rock.

I was familiar with the business of renting out cars, but only with the renter aspect of it, now I was in the market of becoming the recipient of that.

T. had a 78 Cadillac Seville setting out back of his apartment building, but it needed work done on it, his being so engrossed with smoking rock and chasing women, he never had the money to put it in the shop.

The next package we'd rent a car and become mobile, this would provide a wider market range with which to sell our product, the rock, and also give us access to other locations with which to pick up on females.

He pulled out his money and began counting it, when he'd finished he gave me the cue that embarking on this rock selling business had kept him in the black, and that it was time to get another ounce.

Partying with the girls earlier had pretty much depleted the remainder of his supply, by me selling some of the rock it had kept him afloat financially.

We both took out together in search of that youngster we'd dealt with on the other ounce, it took a little longer this time around, but after diligently searching we spotted the dude, and another ounce was bought.

We cut up the ounce into twenty dollar pieces like before, he handed me a three hundred dollar count of rocks, which was fifteen dubs, their was a total of seventy rocks after breaking down the ounce, I knew what the remaining dubs would be for.

I took the package of rocks and tucked them away in my shoe, and we both sat down to try out the product.

T. was smoking too much, despite his polished appearance, and well dressing habit, his frailness showed, plus it appeared that his hair looked to be falling out, or thinning in places.

I knew the signs to look for in one who smoked incessantly, because I'd once been there, but I was working at putting less energy into smoking now.

Rock was bad for anyone in a multiple of ways, but during my binges on rock I took notice of my own hair and weight loss, which in effect was because cocaine robs the body of it's nutrients, in addition to, while smoking it most consumers don't bother to eat food, or drink water.

I understood his ignorance to this condition though, partly because being a rock addict over rides any natural or normal response to observe any defect of character in themselves, and also, because other people see you better than you see yourself.

He would have to catch himself before he took a fall, using rock, it's just a matter of time before it totally consumes one and takes them over the edge. There's no such a thing as being in control, or recreational use with the rock.

I made a comment to him about slowing down, but his reply was, "it won't take me to the curb" (destroy him), T. was no exception to the perils of rock cocaine, and with that I left the issue alone.

We smoked a dub together in silence, I was beginning to slowly back away from the smoking because of the way in which it makes one, like a zombie.

The intense head rush follows the exhalation of the smoke, but the stage afterwards is spooky.

Most people I'd seen smoke rock, including myself displayed abnormal behavior, like looking out of window curtains, picking at debris on the floor, being unable to communicate effectively, looking weird or crazy, and the list goes on.

I was about at my wits end with all of those abnormal characteristics that comes with smoking the rock, and I knew what T. was setting himself up for, I told him, "I'd check back later in the day and left."

Being a bit spooked myself, I stopped at the neighborhood market a block from T's and bought a 40 ounce of Miller draft beer, this always balanced me out mentally, and would keep me on my toes while I was selling rock.

I walked back to the C street park and hung around for a minute, all the while looking out for the cops, when everything looked clear I began selling rock.

At first it was slow, 5 dollars or less, then gradually it picked up, one guy whom I did not know and whom had been watching me came up and asked.

"Hey G. (gangster), you need someone to watch your back for you, I'm the man, plus I will bring in the business for you too."

I thought for a moment.

"Well, yeah man you might be usefull to me, and when were done I'll look out for you swell."

At first I didn't trust the guy, due to the systems undercover techniques of entrapping a dealer for rock trafficking by sending a decoy in on him.

The guy was a white dude and he also had an automobile, the car would come in handy.

I came up with a remedy for my indecisiveness of being able to trust this white guy, we walked to his car and I gave him a piece of rock.

"Hear dude let me see you hit this piece rock."

He put the piece on a makeshift pipe, lit it, and took in the combustion of smoke, I know how to recognize someone fabricating a reaction from a rock high, but when he exhaled, his reaction appeared authentic; his eyes were big and he was silent.

That wasn't quite good enough though, I then came with, "let me see your I.D."

He came out with a Nevada drivers license, so I decided that he was safe.

The white dude drove around to different spots for me to sell my rock, gaining my confidence with every minute that passed by wanting to pull over constantly to take a hit on the pipe.

I thought to myself about how I was starting to see an influx of whites getting into the rock scene, and that although the plague was designated to deprave Black Americans, it was now pulling in whites and other ethnics as well.

After selling all the rock that I had, I told the guy, "run me by my partners place," when I got there I gave T two hundred and thirty dollars and ask for 10 more dubs.

He was by himself this time and was still smoking rock, he took the money without even counting it, stashed it in his pocket, took another hit, sat there for a moment, then stood, went into his sock and came out with the dubs.

I boosted his spirit by saying, "T. I rented a car and will have some women for you when I return."

I left and went back to where I'd left the white guy, a block away, when I arrived back he was in there smoking on the residue from the pipe and waiting for my return.

I was somewhat comfortable with the white dude at that point, so it was time to make another deal on renting the car, this time I would be the only occupant.

"Hey dude would you be interested in renting out this car for a few hours, for a rock"?

"Oh yeah G, I'm cool with that."

On the way back to the park I gave him the dub and a time in which I'd be back, dropped him, and left.

It was 5:00 p.m., later that evening I stopped by a high school friends house named Jeff in the south area to see if he might be interested in buying some rock.

Jeff had started smoking rock back in the early eighties and had never stopped, he'd started working for Campbell soup right after high school.

In 1985 he was discharged from the Company for not showing up to work because of his rock smoking binges; like myself, up until that time period, he'd been a viable employee for the Company.

He lived with his mother and two sisters in the same house He'd resided in since high school, we were somewhat running pals back then.

I knocked on the door and his mother answered the door, she was still pretty as ever, I remembered back to being at his house and I would enjoy looking at her because she was so pretty.

"Hello Miss Brown is Jeff was around"?

"No he's not Siege, he's down in L.A. visiting one of his sisters for the summer."

Back in time his mother was aware of his smoking refer and didn't say much about it, because it wasn't considered a heavy drug.

I acted cordial and respectful with Miss Brown while we stood at the door and chatted with each other, I told her that I had something I wanted him to check out, and that I'd check with him when he got back.

She inquired, "what is it that you wanted him to check out"?

Not knowing exactly how to reply, "just something for the head".

"What kind of something for the head?", she asked, I had remembered Miss Brown of being kind of up on things back in the day, she knew all of the drugs that were out there.

"Some cocaine," I politely said.

To my consternation she said, "do you have some rock with you"?

"Yes I do," and she invited me in.

Once inside came the question, "can you sell me a twenty rock"?

This ungodly substance was not only playing host to young Black Americans, but to mothers, fathers, and the sophisticated elite Blacks as well.

It was shocking, I hoped that she wouldn't, or hadn't fallen into that business of trading sex for rock, because rock has no conscience when it comes to it's client, and what they'll do for it.

This was very unsettling news to me, I felt contrite about this and was reluctant selling it to her, but I did, if I hadn't she would have just gone elsewhere to get it, I brought out a dub, took her money and left.

All evening I thought of how truly devilish this rock had become in the way of manifesting itself in a profound way upon and into the lives of Black Americans.

I had kept the white guys car until that next morning, when I went over to the C street park to look for him, he wasn't there, I waited fifteen minutes for him and then left.

Keeping the Mazda until that afternoon, then resuming my search for him with no avail, and not knowing what was going on I kept it and waited.

T had went to work that morning, but before he left for work, I'd went by and dropped off the profits of the sales, and picked up five more rocks.

My money was building, and I was feeling good enough to treat myself, I rode around drinking and taking hits on the rock, evening came, and I still had not located the white guy.

The idea of picking up some women came into my mind, and I drove out to the Del Paso Heights area to fulfill that quest.

It was about 8:00 p.m., I pulled into the self service Shell gas station on West El Camino, and Del Paso blvd to get some gasoline.

At the gas station there were a couple of ladies parked at the phone booth sitting in a small truck, after pumping the gas I drove over and pulled in next to them.

We acquainted ourselves, they'd been sitting there having a drink while waiting on a return call from the booth.

One of the girls commented that the guy they were waiting on to call was playing games by not calling them back, and said to the other girl that they might as well get with me and have some fun.

Everything seemed to coming together for the plan that I'd had, when all of a sudden a police squad car pulled up, and parked in a vacant lot across the street, they usually did this to do their paperwork before changing shifts, but it wasn't a shift change yet.

Then another one pulled up behind me in Burger Kings parking lot and sat with his lights on, I took notice of it and got that feeling that something was wrong.

I didn't know if the car was reported stolen or not, but I told the girls that I was going to leave, I started it up and began pulling away, but to my right side a third unit pulled right in front of me.

He got out drawing his weapon on me, and ordering me to place my hands out of the window, then to slowly open the door, step out of the vehicle, and to lay on the ground.

Luckily for me I'd sold all of the remaining rock I had, but there was still a half of a dub left that I hid in the cars door panel when they'd pulled up on me, and drew their guns.

Once in their custody on a charge of Grand theft auto, they searched the vehicle but did not find that piece that I'd hid in there, or I would have gotten an additional charge of possession as well.

On the second day of being in jail I was arraigned in court, and I plead not guilty to the charge.

I could beat this case, the plan was to fight it to the end, because the car was a rental for rock, the guy probably wouldn't even show up at court, I had to gamble on it.

While in jail, I came into contact with success, saying that he was about ready to start his trial, and that they'd already offered him a deal of eighteen years but that he'd turned it down.

I remained in custody for 2 and a half months fighting that case, getting ready to go on to trial, on the day of selecting a jury, the D.A. dismissed the charge as a result of the guy not showing up for court, I thanked GOD.

It was mid June when they released me, the weather was warming up, it felt good to once again be free, I reflected back, and to date, every period of incarceration I'd done was either directly or indirectly as a result of my rock cocaine addiction.

But my calling to quit that shit hadn't arrived in my life yet, I would still subject myself to a few more ill fated encounters behind the rock before finally seeing rock as the culprit in the downfall of my life.

A visit to T's place was in order, it was a weekday, early afternoon, when I got there he answered the door looking uneasy, with a few people sitting around smoking on the rock.

"Hey T. aren't you supposed to be at work"?

"I called in saying I wasn't feeling too well and couldn't come in today."

"Let me give you a bit of good advice I've been down the road that your on, with S.E.C., and look where I'm at today, you better get some more control T. or your going to be sorry, take my word."

He had heard about my fall from a lucrative position with S.E.C. form other people who knew us both, and now he was hearing it from the horses mouth in hopes of sparing him from going through the same misfortune.

"Where have you been man," He asked?

"I got caught up in that rent a car that I had, and went to jail on a G.T.A. charge (grand theft auto), I just now got released".

"Here's something to blow your hair back on your first day of freedom," and he threw me a dub.

Reflecting back to when I was at the Starting point rehab, they stressed how when being off of a drug for a while, then starting back on that drug, the intensity of it is great, and it held true because after that first hit I craved more right away.

I sat down and engaged myself with some rock smoking that would last all that day, there were two guys and two girls there, sex was not in the scenario, but by it being early in the morning, I'd assumed that they had all already been there and done that the night before.

Jail was a hardship for anyone to endure, as it was certainly proving to me, I was already on probation for possession, and was avoiding violations of a dirty drug test by not smoking rock 3 days prior to testing, in addition to drinking vinegar and lots of water to help flush my system out.

My P.O. didn't violate me on this incarceration because I beat the case, but I'd be chancing it if I let the overwhelming sensation of the rock run it's course with me from this point on.

That evening T brought up that he was operating in the red behind my going to jail and being out of circulation, he also admitted that the people he was associating with were bringing him down.

After the rock was gone and everyone had left he confessed to the calling in on his job more than once in the past, but stressed that he was in control.

T. stated, "I have a hundred dollars to my name and I'd like to get us back into the click of things again, that is of course if your still up to the mission."

"Yeah I'm still in it", I replied.

We sought out someone whom could accommodate us in the purchase on another ounce, the hot weather brings people outdoors, when we reached 17th and Capital streets it was congested with street people.

We didn't need to asked where the rock was this time, it came to us in abundance, we jumped at the best deal and headed back to his apartment to break it down.

I could see the beginning of the end to T's downfall, it was like looking into a mirror, and as a friend all I could do was to speak on it and continue to warn him of the consequences, the rest would be up to him.

Before packaging up the rock we sat down to try out the product, before long we'd smoked up a dub, I intervened and said we needed to start cutting down the dubs before we smoked too much of it.

Remaining silent for a while, he finally started in and chipped up some pieces into dub rocks.

When he'd finished he gathered up all of the crumbs and began to scoop them up and onto the pipe, out of the quarter ounce twenty dubs were cut, he gave me eight to sell and then went back to smoking on the crumbs.

Not wanting to hang around and keep smoking rock I collected up the rocks, told him "I'd be back later" and left his spot.

I went to the usual location back down to the C street park, when I got there, Lou, a guy that I'd met in jail on a same charge as me, was there drinking alcohol and waiting for the opportunity to hit on some rock.

He came running up to me, "hey Siege you made it out huh, that's always a good thing."

"Man please tell me that you got a hit for me my brother."

"Your in luck", I retorted.

As fiendish as he was acting, if he'd been challenged to jump in front of a moving automobile to receive a hit, he be a dead man.

Chipping him off a piece, I stated, "earn your wages and bring in some business", and off he went to a corner, blazed up the piece, and afterwards coming back truly sparked from the hit.

He went off on a search for some customers and summoned up 3 buyers in all, and all three only bought pieces of a rock which totaled a dub.

It was evening and the rock stars(rock addicts)were coming out and onto the scene, I ended up selling all that I had.

Instead of going back to T's, with the profit I bought another quarter of an ounce myself.

I improvised and went to a spot where Lou knew to break down the package, which was a females apartment. I noticed immediately rock paraphernalia laying around and the place was dirty, but it would have to do for the spare of the moment thing.

I finished doing my thing and was about to leave when someone knocked on the door, the woman answered and let in a black guy, he was looking to rent out his 87 Oldsmobile Delta 88 for a dub.

The thought running through my mind was, here is another trap that the devil is sending my way, but than maybe not.

I asked the dude, "where is this car your talking about?"

"Just parked outside, look out of the window."

I looked out and saw an elegant looking gold colored Olds Delta, it had been a while since I'd driven a luxury car which was what I liked to drive in, so I took another gamble of the dice and rented it.

The dude and I agreed on a dub rock until 2:00 a.m. and we exchanged commodities, I got behind the wheel and Lou was my passenger.

Driving that automobile to me was like the feeling a kid gets when they get a new toy, I drove through just about every black community in Sacramento, hoping to either sell some rock or pick up on some females.

The prospect of selling rock was good, and I gradually sold all of the dubs and had to buy another package, but time was running out and it was nearing the 2:00 a.m. mark.

So I went back to the girls apartment, but nobody answered the door, nor was that dude whom I'd rented the car from in the vicinity.

I sat out in front of her complex for thirty minutes, still neither one of them showed, so I drove to Del Paso Heights and bought a half of an ounce, and while riding around in the area I spotted a cute young white girl walking by herself.

Her being out like that early in the morning by herself meant one of three things, either car trouble, she was rock hunting, or out on a pussy selling mission; I went with the second theory, and stopped to check her out.

My hunch had been right, she got in and I drove off. T would like this one, she resembled the singer Madonna, and had a body like fisher(top of the line) so to speak.

Going straight to his place, I drove by the black girls apartment checking to see if the guy who the car belonged to was there, he wasn't, but the girl was.

She said he had stopped by not long ago, which at that time was 3:00a.m. and said he'd be back a little later, I didn't trust leaving the car with the girl because I did not get it from her.

Rock stars are irresponsible, had I left the car with her she could have rented it out, lied and said that I'd never brought it back, and the blame of anything happening to it would have been on me, so I left driving over to T's.

He was still up smoking, and was grateful when he saw the white girl I'd brought back, she was a freak.

He gave her a hit, she came alive and began undressing herself, once naked she was game to serving all three of us at the same time.

After the foursome, Lou and I had to go back over to that girls house to catch up with the owner of the vehicle.

"Hey Siege you can leave this young lady here with me until you come back", T hollered out.

"OK, that sounds like a plan," I'm out of here.

Getting to the apartment, dude still hadn't shown back up, it was 4:30a.m., I'd left most of the rock with T except for a couple of dubs.

Freaking with that white girl had been exciting, and only prompted me to go on a search for other females, the only other location where I could find those types of ladies close by was Broadway and Stockton blvd.

Lou and I left out headed to that location, driving down Broadway a few blocks from Stockton blvd, I noticed off to one side of the street some yellow lights that resembled those of police cars.

As I passed the street I kept watch in my rear view mirror, and my sixth sense was on cue because those yellow lights that I'd seen earlier turned the corner, and the headlights flashed on.

The cop car wasn't speeding upon me, it trailed back a little, I suspected that they were running a make on the car, but then as if confirmed by a dispatcher, it sped up.

I turned on to Stockton blvd, still watching through the mirror, it turned the corner too, as it turned the corner behind me I could see the black and white paint on the squad car.

Driving safely using my signals, I turned off of Stockton blvd and onto a side street into the residential area, not even five seconds later it followed, then another, and still another one, all turning on their top lights lighting up the area with red and blue flashing lights.

I pulled over cursing and trying to stash the two rock dubs deep into the front of the seat of the driver side without displaying furtive movement.

They got onto the bull horn and ordered "Driver, throw the keys onto the pavement, open the door from the outside, slowly, with your hands out, lay on the ground.

The owner of the car must have reported it stolen after he'd finished smoking the rock in order of relieving himself of any further liabilities that might occur while not in his possession.

Reporting cars stolen after the addict had smoked the rock was fast becoming a trend at that time.

The police repeated the order to Lou, we both lay spread out in the streets while they searched the car, after fifteen minutes of searching, one cop came over to us with the two rocks, charging us both with Grand theft auto, and possession of a controlled substance, and we were off to jail.

At the preliminary hearing, the prosecuting District Attorney came with a deal, they would dismiss the Grand theft auto, if I accepted a guilty plea of possession of rock cocaine, and I'd receive a year lid in the County, and probation.

I took the deal, Lou was given ninety days in jail and probation for his being an accomplice.

This rock was always the culprit behind my incarcerations, this would be the longest time of confinement yet, I would do eight months out of the twelve.

Passing back through the County jail I ran across Success for a third time. He'd lost at his trial, and received a 96 year prison term, his crime partner received 84 years for his part in the crime, and both were awaiting transfer to the California Dept. of Corrections.

He didn't seen to be affected at the time by his long prison term, but did say that he regretted having smoked rock that night because it had made him irate and impulsive which caused him to do what he did.

I said a prayer for him and wished him luck, he would need it being behind the walls of where he was headed to; Pelican Bay.

After a few days in the main jail downtown I was transferred to the County branch jail in Elk Grove, Ca, where I'd finish my time out.

Each encounter in the system brought me more aware of the disparities of justice rendered down to the Blacks in America, in contrast to the whites by the State of California's Judicial system.

I felt it was a wave sweeping California's Judicial system, as well as the authorities of the law with their intent to imprison Black men, and the rock cocaine was the means through which it was getting accomplished.

My prior terms of confinement, as well as this current one would increase my faith in GOD, and intensify my relationship with him; with the growing wickedness in the world, GOD was to be my only refuge.

It wasn't known to me then that all those small periods of confinement in the County jail was conditioning me for serving even longer terms with the California dept. of Corrections prison system, unless I changed my lifestyle.

Serving out my sentence of eight months in the County jail taught me discipline, as well as letting me feel how naturally good my body felt without the contamination of rock cocaine in it.

I was healthy in mind, spirit, and body when they released me on March 15, 1991.

For the first time since I'd began smoking rock back in 1980, I showed diligence in attempting to remain off of the rock cocaine through self will, and taking up residence in a drug rehab program that the Salvation Army provided for addicts called A.R.C.(adult rehabilitation center).

It was an in house program, subsidized by the Sacramento County, of whom gave an allotment of one hundred and eleven dollars worth of food stamps for each addict placed in the program.

The center accommodated a total of one hundred men in a dormitory type living arrangement, and the quality, and quantity of food was superlative.

The center was very sanitized, with amenities in the way of weights, a 50 inch T.V. screen showing current movies twice a week, a music system, and washers and dryers.

I had already attained while in the County jail, a muscular physique from weight lifting, however, the high carbohydrate intake of food in jail only sustains one, now with the good nutritional food being served at A.R.C., my weight increased by fifteen pounds.

I weighed 185 pounds of good healthy solid muscle and I felt and looked good all over.

There was a 3 month restriction period for all newcomers, this meant that you could not leave the grounds for any reason unless you were going to work, or with staff, and then had to return back, one was allowed to call family or friends though.

The Salvation Army had a thrift store located on 16ᵗʰ and D streets, 5 blocks from the rehab center, and a block from the C street park.

The thrift store provided work for the recovering addicts, we weren't paid cash though, it was a means of preparing us for the work force upon completion of the program.

5 days a week two shuttle vans transported the workers to and from the store, we would work alongside the free staff whom were paid.

I worked in the shoe dept., but had access to all of the other dept.'s, which in turn enabled me to rebuild my clothing attire.

One would be surprised at the quality of clothing and other items that wealthy people either set out to be picked up, or dropped off themselves to the Salvation Armies donation centers.

At the end of a month in the program I had accumulated two leather tot bags, 5pairs of assorted colors 501 jeans,6 different stylish shirts, 3 pair of brand name tennis shoes, and 2 pairs of dress shoes.

One month after new arrivals enter the program their allowed to leave the grounds one day out of a week on a pass, when they return, their subjected to a breath analysis or drug test.

I took my weekly pass, while out I drank a can of beer, upon my return they tested me and the test registered a decimal over the normal standards.

They suspended me from the program for one month, after which I could be reinstated back if I wished to do so.

I thought the regulations of the program to be a bit stringent and decided not to return back to it.

I gathered up all of my belongings and left, I felt good being off of the rock for all of those months, but now the devil would put it before me again to test my strength.

MANIPULATING THEIR TRAPS

I now had extra baggage to carry around with all of the things I had collected while in the program, I had to find a place to store it all, I knew of an apartment complex that I'd been in before once while smoking rock.

It had a basement with a dug out section of dirt beneath a staircase, I went there and hid my belongings, they would be safe there.

I hit the scene, not really with the intentions of getting involved with the rock, however, the devil is crafty, tricky, and knows how to lure one back into the business.

These two young rock dealers approached me and asked me if I knew of a toss up that they both could ravish together and offered me a rock if I could find them one; that was bait one from the devil.

I told them I'd check it out and get back to them, I had no idea of where to look for a girl for those youngsters, and wasn't even concerned with trying to find one.

I walked away, several blocks down, a decent looking black girl propositioned me with sex if I'd smoke some rock with her; that was bait number two.

Each phase of the devils plan for me was a bit more tempting than it's predecessor because the bastard knows mans weaknesses.

Defeated in my attempt to stay off the rock, I brought the proposition to the young dealers; both parties, the girl and the dudes accepted, I got my dub and was getting ready to leave.

The dealers were from the Oak Park area, wasn't familiar with downtown and needed a place to do their do with the toss up.

They offered another rock for that accommodation, I mentioned the basement where my belongings were hidden, there was also an old mattress there too.

They settled for that and gave me another dub, and we all headed for the spot, when we got there I showed them where to take care of their business, and made the stupid mistake of mentioning to them that I'd be over behind the stairs where my belongings were at.

It took them no longer then twenty minutes to do their thing with the girl and they departed.

Before the girl left I ask, "hey sis can I use your pipe to take a hit on one of these rocks"?, I was curious as to how it would effect me after being off of it for months.

I took a hit from one of the rocks I had gotten, prior to that hit of the rock I'd had no sexual attraction to this women, but after that hit all of a sudden I became lustful towards her.

She in turn reciprocated my gestures at her to have some sexual fun and produced a condom, we then both laid sown onto the mattress and engaged ourselves in each other.

It had been a while since I'd had sex, so I was deserving of and in need of it, but what mystified me was how, prior to taking that hit, I had no interest in ravishing this woman, yet after the hit she appeared sexual to me.

The whole ordeal was the works of satan, and affirmed my ever growing belief that rock cocaine is truly the works of the devil.

The girl and I, which I hadn't even gotten her name, finished doing our thing and went our own ways.

It was almost June, the sun was warming up, I went to my apparel and changed into something that would fit for summer.

Not having any money on me made things worse, I still had a dub and a half of rock left, selling off the biggest piece would provide some pocket change.

Soon I would have to go and re-apply for G.A. at the County welfare dept.

Walking down 17th street minding my own business, two guys pulled up on me in an old 72 Nova, they were both kind of heavy set dudes, and given their appearance could pass as rock smokers.

One was white, the other Hispanic, they ask, "hey dude where can we buy some rock at," I'd been locked up for almost a year and wasn't up on who was out there selling rock.

I'd heard that the authorities were practicing entrapment tactics by buying rock, and at a later time indicting you to appear in court on a sells charge.

Or setting up reverse stings, where they would raid a rock house, take it over, sell you some rock and arrest you before you left the house.

I thought all of this to be an aberration within the authorities of the law, an indication of signs of decadence within the systems ability to utilize thorough policies, and man power on capturing suspects, rather than resorting to insidious practices, and/or measures to imprison black men for selling rock cocaine.

I needed cash, and after a minute of hesitation, climbed into the back seat and told them to make a block.

We drove off and around the corner, I pulled out one of my rocks, the passenger looked at it, and they bought the dub rock.

I felt better now, I had some pocket change, they pulled to the curb to let me out, but for some reason stalled on letting me get out of the car by asking, "can we buy another one,"?

"I said yes, but it is small,"

"let me see it anyway," was there response.

I pulled it out and they bought it too, my suspicion was growing now and I demanded to be let out, the passenger door opened, but before I could get out of the car two uniformed cops were standing on both sides of the vehicle.

They had just pulled up behind the Nova, but I hadn't noticed them with my back to the window, that was why I'd been delayed, waiting for the uniformed cops to arrive.

The excuse the cops used for pulling up on the Nova was that the tags were expired and they wanted to run a check on the vehicle.

Another unusual turn of events took place at that moment, when they asked the driver, the passenger, and me for I.D., the one officer went back to the patrol car while the other remained by the Nova.

When the officer came back to the car he said that the vehicle could not be moved because the tags weren't current and that we'd all have to foot it.

I felt all that was happening to be very peculiar and was relieved at not having been busted for those sales, I got out and left walking.

I didn't know what to make of the incident and eventually forgot about it.

A lot had changed and happened since I'd last been out there, later that day I ran into T, I'd thought of how he'd been fairing along while I was in jail.

As we talked T told me that the U.S. Postal service had terminated his employment with them because of his excessive absenteeism.

He'd sold his Cadillac Seville to a rock dealer for $400.00 worth of rock a few months back, and that he was now homeless and sleeping where he could.

He went on to say that he was appealing their action because of certain rights of his being violated in the process of their termination of him.

He hit home with what he was saying as I reflected back on my tenure with S.E.C., I didn't know all of the circumstances involved in T's situation, but wished him luck on it anyway.

In most every aspect of the current state of depravity among Black Americans, rock cocaine was culpably involved it seemed.

T mentioned that he was working at a day labor program at the Loaves and fishes agency, which paid daily when they had work for the workers.

He wasn't working on this day, but had saved some of his money from the day before to allow him to buy his wake up rock for the day.

He ask, "is there anyone around selling,"

"I just sold what I had left," and elaborated on the peculiarity of the whole scenario that had just taken place with me with those dudes and the cops.

He said that it was probably a tactic they used to get a make on me, and that I could probably expect to be indicted in the near future, because that was how they(the police) were getting people now.

I wasn't happy to hear this bit of information, but it was a done deal and nothing could be done to reverse it now.

I suggested to T that we hang around and more than likely someone would come around with a fix for him.

I sympathized with him on the hardship he was going through with the lose of his employment with the U.S. postal service, and extended warm comradeship to him because I'd been down that road before.

I refrained from stressing the fact that I'd told him to be careful, that would have been like hitting below the belt.

We continued to walk slowly while talking, coming upon a neighborhood market I acted on a notion to buy us both a 40 ounce bottle of Miller draft beer, maybe this would help to temporarily relieve some of the anxiety he was feeling.

We drank and discussed the prospect of goals of our individual futures, and groped over what was happening to Black America, and what it was all going to add up to in the end.

Nearly half way through the drinking of our beers a shady looking Black guy walked up to us claiming that he had fat dub rocks for sale, that was T's fix for him.

The guy pulled out a bag of rocks, they looked authentic in the plastic bag, T handed the dude his only twenty dollar bill, and took a rock.

He immediately said, "this shit feels funny in my hand; like wax or soap," he tasted it, and discovered it to be a synthetic remake rock of soap and wax.

"Son of a bitch, give me my money back," T demanded, the dude became arrogant, so I intervened and was ready to take back his money.

The dude said, "that rock is the real deal you just bought," and pulled back his shirt in front to expose the handle of a 9mm hand gun in the waist of his pants.

He went on to say, "ya'll can try and take this money off me if you like," and turned around and walked off.

We had been beat point blank, more or less a cunning holdup type of style, but we were out done because of the pistol he was wielding on his persons.

This kind of fraudulent rock selling was also on the rise, it certainly was an attributing factor in the many Black on Black homicides in America.

The ruthlessness brought about by the rock cocaine business among Blacks paved the way for calamities within our race of people.

That dude was on a suicidal mission, luckily for him that both T, and I were the civilized type, and weren't in possession of guns ourselves, otherwise the situation could have turned fatal.

There are the type of individuals out there that are hardcore with their reactions and it surely would have ended up being curtains for one of them had that dude pulled that shit on one of those kind of people.

T chalked up his lose as a lesson of the many perils of the rock cocaine business, he was now broke, and not a hustler by nature, decided to count the day as over for him, and said, "man I'm done now, I'm going over to another one of my friends place to see what he has going," and was preparing to leave.

"wait a second," I said, went into my pocket and came out with $10.00 and handed it to him, wished him well and we went our own ways.

I wasn't doing good myself, but what I had over most rock smokers was a healthy mind and body, and it showed because I stood out from everyone in the business by the way I carried myself mentally; I was not a fiend for rock.

Having a little over twenty dollars on me and no place to go, I roamed around downtown, on my trek I was receiving extraordinary attention from the opposite sex most everywhere I went, I guess that was due to my being fresh out, and rejuvenated in mind, body, and spirit.

While roaming around one young lady caught my attention as much as I caught hers.

It was a mutual attraction and as we approached each other I noticed she was a classy act by the attire she was wearing.

She was pretty, with a high yellow complexion, had a small afro hair style, keen features with a touch of facial makeup, and a body that was remarkably well sculptured.

She wore a nice fitting pair of 501 jeans, a navy blue short sleeved button up blouse, and a pair of casual women's tennis shoes.

Upon reaching each other I complemented her on her appearance, she thanked me and returned the complement of my style of dress as well.

We exchanged names, she introduced herself, "Hi I'm Terry,".

"I'm Siege, nice meeting you," "where are you headed right now" I asked, she replied, "just out walking," I said the same and asked, "could I join you on your walk," she accepted, and we strolled together to got better acquainted.

It was early evening, there was still some daylight left, although the sun was steadily setting.

She was a single woman, with mental impairments and receiving Social Security benefits, I couldn't detect right off any mental challenges in her, and did not question that issue any further, but rather, changed the subject.

"You know I'm so tired of meeting no good men, but I sense something unique about you which was why I was receptive of you," she stated.

I thought the gesture was a good sign for me to a new beginning with a decent woman, and went on to explain my situation to her.

I divulged to her my hardships behind my rock cocaine addiction, she was sympathetic towards me and expressed grief at how rock was destroying Black people, but added that she too was a recipient of the rock cocaine plague, and was now trying to refrain from using it.

I spoke on about the A.R.C. rehab program and how I was ousted from it, and that I was now homeless and waiting in line to get into the Salvation Army shelter.

Terry, in response to my unfortunate situation offered me to stay at her place with her for the night.

I gratefully accepted the offer and assured her that when I was able to, I'd accommodate her financially.

I told her of my belongings and where I would have to go to pick them up.

We headed to retrieve my property, when we got there, both my leather bags were gone, I suspected right away that those two youngsters had searched the place until they'd found my bags and had taken my possessions.

There was nothing I could do but accept the lose and move on with my life, I was distressed behind this event; the devil and his substance(the rock), had caused me to lose my possessions.

Looking at the brighter side of things though, GOD had sent a decent woman into my life whom was willing to take me in off of the streets, thank GOD for serendipity.

Her place was neat and organized, she didn't have any children so there was no infringements, we sat down and talked for a few hours.

She openly explained her mental incapacities saying that it was due to a rape she'd endured a couple of years back when she'd went into a house with two black guys to smoke some rock.

While smoking on the rock the guys wanted sex, but she refused, they both had severely beaten her causing an eye injury that required surgery, and then raped her.

The incident sent her into shock and brought about a neurology disorder which in turn rendered her incapable of functioning normally in society.

The more stories I'd hear about the horrors of rock cocaine, in addition to my own personal experiences, really necessitated some interdiction on this rock cocaine plague.

I verbally comforted her and reassured her that she was in good company with me in her place, we went on to share experiences back and forth and into the early morning, finally she went off into her room, I sat on the sofa until I dosed off to sleep.

She awoke at 11:00 a.m., and fixed both of us something to eat, after eating I invited her to accompany me on my trip down to the County Welfare office so I could re-apply for the General Assistance program and receive aide.

Terry and I had to wait at the welfare office until 3:00 p.m. before I was interviewed by a social worker.

Because it was near the end of the month, the County cut me a check right there that day for the rest of April, and all of May, I'd have to wait another 2 hours before the check would be ready for pick up.

There was a city park a block away, I took her by the hand and we walked to the park to kill some time before going back to the County welfare office.

Two hours passed quick and we headed back to pick up my check, the County had cut me a check in the amount of three hundred and sixty eight dollars.

After cashing it I ask her, "would be interested in a room-mate,"?

"I'll give it a try," she replied, so we came up with a plan together where I'd give her a hundred dollars for the last ten days of April as a trial run.

We stopped and ate lunch at Jim boys tacos then headed for her place, along the way Terry commented "can you buy us a rock,"? I neither agreed, nor disagreed with the idea, I let the choice be hers alone.

She went straight to the source, when we got to her place she went right to her rock utensils, put a piece on the pipe and took a hit.

Following her exhalation, for a moment she sat silently staring at me, I was standing motionless, it was when I moved to seat myself that she jumped up and came very close to me as though she was frightened by something, and began clinging to me like superglue.

Every step I took, she was like my shadow, this disturbed me and I ask her what was wrong, she couldn't speak though because she was spooked, and she just clung to me until she'd calmed down.

I gathered that either she was flashing back on the trauma she'd been through in being beaten and raped, or possibly it was the Ill reactions of paranoia caused by the fabricated rock cocaine that was being filtered into the black communities now.

I remembered an incident before I'd went to jail involving a guy downtown at the C street park one day where the guy, prior to taking a hit of the rock was socializing and acting calm with everybody around him.

But soon after taking that hit of the rock, he became irate and paranoid, and for no reason the guy just took off running with the pipe in his hand as fast as he could go.

I'd remembered another incident that was unusual as well where a fellow had just bought an ounce of rock, when he got back to his own place he took a large hit, and for two hours after the hit stood by his window peaking out of the curtain.

If this was the way that rock cocaine was effecting one's natural state of being in the 90's, what possible means of satisfaction could one derive pleasure out of smoking it.

After an hour or so of comforting her, she calmed down and relaxed, but still felt unsafe as though she feared for her life.

I thought this to be a peculiar reaction of that rock cocaine which was prevalent among rock smokers as I was beginning to take notice of.

It was beginning to produce a stage of paranoia that could lead one to act prematurely on assumptions that there in danger, and in turn provoke them to act irregularly.

I talked her into a state of calmness and told her to put smaller pieces unto the pipe, which might help to decrease her state of paranoia.

Terry was a good woman and I liked her, I took a hit myself to help alleviate her feelings of insecurity, she then took another hit of the rock, and although she was a little calmer, still displayed the same reactions.

I knew I couldn't smoke rock with her, furthermore, she be better off leaving the substance alone period.

When we finally smoked what she'd bought things seem to return to normal, we laid back and watched television, talked a little, then made some good loving.

I felt that she was a woman I could try to have a life with, that was if her addiction to the rock wasn't chronicle.

Our relationship was going smoothly up until when she'd smoke rock, her paranoia worsened every time she smoked, after we were together for a couple of months, with no success at getting her to curtail her binge smoking, we mutually agreed that she check into a rehab center, to my surprise, she'd done this before several times.

It was July, her in-patient rehab program would last for 3 months, I couldn't keep up the bills by myself on General assistance, so she put her things in storage, told me to stay in touch, and to wait for her by being there when she got out of the program.

Being preoccupied with hustling and smoking rock myself, I found little time to stay in touch with Terry, but I was glad that she sought help for her addiction.

In her case, as in the cases of many other Black women of her stature, it would be a tragic loss if they didn't try to help themselves with their addiction.

One night while out hustling I was put up on another kind of con game by a guy I'd smoked rock with earlier that evening.

The con consisted of hustling homosexuals without ever becoming sexually involved with them, the trick was to hang around the nightclubs they frequented until you were propositioned by them.

Once in their company, because you were a new face on the scene, you'd use that to your advantage by employing the tactic that you'd like some marijuana to relax you, then finesse them into giving you the money to buy a bag of it.

They'd give you twenty or thirty dollars up front then drive you to buy it, you'd give a fictitious location, go there, get out like you were going to make a buy, go through the front of an apartment complex, and exit the rear through an alley and take off.

I acted out this scenario a couple of times at a gay nightclub in downtown Sacramento and both times were fruitful.

This wasn't an occupational hustle that I would undertake extensively, only at times when all else failed, and it was late at night or early in the morning, and it always brought dividends.

Thus I was subjecting myself to being affiliated with that kind of a lifestyle, the necessity to get some money for my rock habit over-rode the stigma with which I might perhaps be labeled with.

This among other things, are what demoralizes ones character when their caught up in the rock cocaine business.

Myself, as well as other patrons whom cater to rock cocaine fail to realize what the substance entails and these crucial effects that befall them when they succumb to it.

On two other occasions I orchestrated the plan of luring in gays and capitalizing off of them, both encounters, through cunning tactics, and calculated timing, I made off with several hundreds of dollars.

Although I wasn't forcefully taking money, nor robbing them, I was paving the way for bad karma unto myself, they would openly give money to me on the promise that I would allow them to get sexual with me, but I never came through on my end of the deal, and in the end I would disappear on them.

In August, one month after Terry checked herself into a rehab program, I was staying wherever I could; at the Salvation Army shelter on and off, in rock houses, walking the streets sometimes all morning long, and sleeping in downtown apartment building laundry rooms.

One day while at the Salvation Army, I ran into a guy I'd hung around with as a child named Jesse, he'd become homeless as a result of his rock cocaine addiction.

He was an amicable person growing up, but had a birth defect in his right arm that left it extremely bowed, I remembered as kids he had an inferiority complex about his impairment.

As we talked Jesse revealed to me that he had tried to commit suicide by drinking some liquid Drano, he claimed he was tired of living the way he was, smoking rock, physically impaired, and no means of income.

The doctors saved his life in the nick of time, and he underwent reconstructive surgery of his throat and relative neck area, implanting synthetic human like plastic tubing in his neck.

After months of being hospitalized he applied for S.S.I. and Section 8(a Government allotment for cheap housing), and was granted both.

He resided over in the New Hellveisha projects off of Broadway, he lived by himself in a one bedroom, he invited me to his place to have a drink with him.

Despite the surgery he'd had done to his throat area he was still able to drink moderately, and mentioned that he still smoked rock.

On the way to his place we laughed about things we'd done as kids, it was great to see him after thirty years, but he was apparently a lonely person, he didn't have a girlfriend and wasn't gay, but kept to himself all the time.

He said that when he got the urge for some sex he resorted to hooking up with a toss up and satisfied his sexual desires that way.

He offered me shelter for one hundred dollars a month, and I accepted his offer.

GOD was looking out for me and would keep the blessings coming in, in other ways for me, my only misfortune and downfall would be rock cocaine.

Things were going well living with Jesse, we kept food in the apartment, everyday we both went our own way.

His place was bare of furniture so whenever I came across anything that could be utilized in the apartment, I picked it up and brought back to his place.

I'd been there a couple of weeks, one morning after coming from my probation officer walking back to his place, a jazzy looking female next door to Jesse's kept looking at me smiling, I was flattered but kept on up to the apartment.

I went in and came back out to the back porch carrying a pair of my Tennis I was going to sit on the porch and clean mud off of.

As I was cleaning my shoes she appeared from out of nowhere and struck up a conversation with me, she introduced herself, "hi I'm Lea, I've never seen you around here before."

"When a nice looking Black man shows up around here it's a treat for the single women in the complex".

"Thank you for that compliment, by the way my name is Siege."

She was a beauty, reminding me somewhat of a young Gladys knight, she was living there with her boyfriend at his sisters apartment, but had broken off their relationship due to his infidelities with other women.

I mentioned to her about Angie and how I had played myself out of her behind staying out late, although I wasn't cheating on her, I declined to state my reason of rock smoking as being what led to our separation, I blamed it on drinking and kicking it around with the fellows.

I spoke on how the family institution should be held in high regard and treated as something sacred, never to be taken for granted, further, how I more importantly missed my children.

I gave a description of Angie and the kids to Lea, and to my consternation, she replied that she had baby sat my kids one day for her boyfriend, and that Angie was the girl her boyfriend had been spending time with.

What a coincidence I thought, the irony of all this was a bit shocking, essentially, this strengthened the chances of Lea and I getting something going even if it was to settle the score by dating each others X's.

This was just a thought in my head, I recognized a lot of potential in Lea that could make my life relatively happy if we did get together.

I was a domesticated man by nature, and yearned to have a decent woman in my life again, but I couldn't have this and keep smoking on the rock too.

The two do not co-exist, if a woman is morally sound and doesn't use drugs herself than a relationship with that woman will be void, this is what I'd have to come to terms with if I was going to find happiness in this life.

Over the next few days Lea and I got closer with each other, I put her through the test by trying to seduce her into bed to see what kind of a woman she was.

She passed the test with flying colors, it wasn't until a couple of weeks later that she showed up at my residence at Jesse's while he was away that she whole heartedly gave herself to me.

Once again I'd met a good woman, this time I hoped there wouldn't be any skeletons in the closet that would later hinder the relationship.

Everyday Lea came over to the apartment to see me, she made herself useful by cooking meals for Jesse and I, and cleaning the place up.

She too, like Terry, was on S.S.I., I didn't go into why she was on it and I thought it better to leave it unquestioned, she was also waiting on the Section 8 housing program herself, that was due to place her into a unit for Senior citizens and/or disabled people very soon.

She ask me, "would you like to move in with me,"?

since I had no place to go, I replied, "yes I would love to," it wasn't my intentions to desert Terry, because I liked her too, but anything could happen within two months, furthermore, I had to suffice for myself as I went along, because of my unstable lifestyle.

Lea spent nights with me on and off, when she did, Jesse being the nobleman that he was, always let us sleep in his room and he took the living room quarters.

Women and girls would either show up, or be there some times when she came over, but the type of people that they were left little for one to desire.

These were the people that Jesse knew and allowed to come in and use his bathroom and/ or smoke rock.

Lea was fairly perceptive, although she suspected as much, never linked me to the trafficking or involvement with the smoking of rock, I'd never given her a reason to suspect me.

She took note of the traffic in, and out of Jesse's place, and commented that she wanted to get me away from that kind of activity, and hoped that soon her housing would come through for her.

In late August of 1991, the housing Authorities of Section 8 sent her notice that they had an available unit ready for her, I'd been with Jesse for three weeks.

I told him I was moving out, but that I would stay in touch, I didn't have much to move, just a bag with what clothes I'd accumulated again after those youngsters had stolen my other bags of belongings.

As for Lea, she wasn't allowed to get any of the furniture she had bought out of her X's sisters house, because of her having broken off the relationship with her X.

We moved into the apartment on the first of September with no furnishings, but we had each other, plus some much needed peace of mind, and that suited us both fine.

We started getting closer with our much enjoyed privacy, Lea had one close girlfriend whom would either call or come bye to visit occasionally, other than that it was just the two of us there most of the time.

She wasn't big with having a lot of company over, and neither was I, I'd learned years ago from my father in my younger years to never entertain my friends at my home around my woman and/or children, and I'd always lived by that rule.

We took walks together, went shopping, cooked, and pretty much did everything as a team, I was loving this union we shared together, when I got urges to smoke rock I'd leave and do it away from her, when I felt like I'd done enough and was back to normal, I'd return home.

Sometimes I'd stay out late, not to often, but when I did, she'd always question my whereabouts, that didn't bother my when she did this, I'd always give her a story that was satisfying to her and that would be the end of it.

Lea would bring up the issue of rock cocaine sometimes, I'd wonder to myself why she was being so inquisitive about this, one evening as we sat at the dining table we'd just bought, she ask me to go into her purse and get out a pack of Newport cigarettes and light one for her.

While in her purse rumbling around for the lighter I came across a straight shooter(glass stem rock cocaine pipe), I ask her, "what is this doing in your possession"?

She replied, "it belongs to my Uncle, he'd left it in there and I was going to return to him when I got the chance to."

I'd met her Uncle once and he did smoke rock, but the discovery of a rock pipe in her possession still left skepticism in my mind as to the possibility of her being a closet smoker.

From that point on I found it necessary to play her close on this issue, later it would all come to light, when one evening her Uncle showed up with a couple of dub rocks and broke her off a piece of one of them.

Lea had kept her rock smoking concealed from me quite well up until that point, but after it was revealed it was as if she felt less than an adult because of it's revelation.

After that discovery we'd sometimes smoke rock together, and the alteration of character brought about from smoking rock would create uncomfortable feelings between us.

Lea would complain that I would act strange, a strangeness as if someone, or something was coming to get me, which was in all actuality true, and she didn't say anything more about it once it was said.

I hadn't reported to my P.O. as required to do every week, it had been a few weeks, there was probably a warrant out for my arrest.

I had given my P.O. our new address when we'd moved in there, but hadn't seen him since,

Because of that I was kind of on edge in my demeanor, in addition to that she was displaying an attitude that I had cheated her out of some of her rock we'd later bought together.

Rock was the devil's playground in every aspect of it when we did smoke together, bereavement was the state of mind we both experienced when we did smoke with each other.

Our togetherness was breaking apart with each encounter of our smoking rock with one another.

I had to put a stop to this madness, so I stopped smoking the rock with her and started going off to get high, she then complained that I was staying out to long at times, it seemed that I couldn't win for losing.

On October the first my P.O. came by with two other officers looking for me, later that day when I came home Lea told me that they searched the place and told her that they were going to arrest me when they caught me.

Now, despite our quarrels, I had to stay away from the place in order to avoid going back to jail, I told her I was sorry for the way things were turning out for us, spent a little time with her, gathered up my things said goodbye, and left her place on the run from my P.O.

Before I left I explained to her that she did not need to be subjected to that kind of bullshit on my account, and that if she in the near future wasn't with anyone, and I was past the stage of the system being in my business we could try it over again, I closed by saying, "I really have deep feelings for you."

She cried while kissing me before I left her apartment, and told, "please be careful out there."

I evaded capture for three weeks after leaving her, I was hustling, smoking rock, selling when it would help to insure my next package of rock, and occasionally going by Lea's when I was tired and needed some down time.

On October 21rst, 1991, at 1:30a.m. I was walking down 16th street with a female and two guys whom I'd just sold two dub rocks to, and was en-route to buy my next package.

I noticed a police car pass by, I got a feeling that they would circle the block on us, at that hour in the morning 4 people walking drew attention, but before I could break away from them the police car was creeping slowly upon us, with a full view of our every move.

The squad car pulled up to us and stopped, the doors flew open and both officers approached asking everyone for their I.D., one gathered up all the I.D.'s and took them back to the patrol car to run checks, the other stood watching us.

Twenty minutes later the one came back with all the I.D.'s in his hand and said everybody was clear except me, and told me I had a twenty thousand dollar warrant for possession of a controlled substance and ordered me to place both hands behind my back.

At that instant I thought of breaking to run, but weighing out the odds of receiving an additional charge, I simply did what I was told, after being cuffed they placed me into the back of the patrol car.

I watched from the patrol car as the others were told to leave the area, on the one hand I was indignant because my freedom was being taken from me, but on the other hand I was tired of running and hiding, so it was a relief.

Back in the County jail once again brought with it a reaffirmation of the white power structures willful intent of incarcerating the Black man.

Discrimination against Black men within the criminal justice system was in full force and being carried out on a daily basis in the County courtrooms.

Lengthy sentences were being served out in both the County courthouse, and the State's custodial facilities(State prison) to Black men for mere minor possessions of rock cocaine.

The main jail was full of Blacks, rock cocaine was the main culprit behind many of the arrestee's in one way or another.

Either some were unjustly searched and arrested for having rock on their person, or others were arrested after committing an illegal act to support their habit.

Rock cocaine was subjecting Blacks around the Country to dire consequences in increasingly significant proportions, was my sentiment, as I too became a recipient of the power structures full pledged attack on Black men to, imprison them by and through the rock cocaine.

I was fed up with Sacramento Counties petty tactics in dealing with me on probation, and had it set in my mind of getting prepared on entering into the States prison system.

Both agencies, the County and the State, racism existed on a profound level, but with the State you were given more lead way in governing yourself on parole, and the State was less petty.

On my third court appearance I took a deal of 4 years in State prison, with credit of time served from previous jail times in custody that added up to a year.

On this incarceration I'd only been in jail less than three weeks and had taken the deal of 4 years with the State prison system and was ready and waiting on the transfer to the California dept. of Corrections reception center at Vacaville, Ca.

While in the Sacramento jail an ex San Francisco Forty-niner football celebrity had entered the judicial system, his charge was robbery of customers at their banks automated teller machines.

There was no doubt in my mind that this ex professional football star was a victim of the rock cocaine plague too, he'd just let it get out of control and went too far on his missions to obtain more funds to support his habit, which in turn would send him off to prison for a term.

I'd heard that he was smoking rock pretty heavily, which was ultimately the reason he was forced to leave the pro team the S.F. Forty-niners.

It was said that even after going into rehabilitation, he went back to the rock right after being released from the rehab.

I saw him once in the County jail, he'd had a sling on his arm and was bruised up pretty badly, it was alleged that he'd given up his Super bowl ring for a few grams of rock to some youngsters in the Glen Elders area.

After smoking up all of the rock he went back to them and tried to take back his ring, but that those youngsters had jumped him and beat him down in his attempt.

Rock cocaine never ceases to conquer, but my primary concern was with how this drug seemed to impinge upon Black people in such a luring manner.

I pondered with the thought that the power structures virulent behavior, and/or attitude towards Blacks led them to conduct a scientific study of the genetics of Black people so as to produce and administer a concoctive formula into cocaine that lures and attracts the Black race of people to this substance.

At the same time the NFL's superstar was brought to jail on Robbery charges, another bit of shocking news surrounding rock cocaine hit the National headlines.

Our Nations Capital, Washington D.C.'s Mayor Marion Barry was set up by F.B.I. officials and caught on camera in a motel room smoking rock cocaine with a prostitute.

This despicable type of entrapment of a highly notable Black public official was an injustice purposely promulgated by the power structure to make his character ignominious as a Black figure head in American society.

As I watched the incident on National Television in the County jail, it was equally disturbing to learn that the Black prostitute played a role in the entrapment and filming of Mayor Marion Barry on camera.

It was bad enough that Blacks were caught up in the many perils of rock cocaine by their own will, but was even worse when the power structure in America uses one Black against another as a means of incriminating the one.

This Country was founded upon that very strategy among the slaves, where the slave master had the field nigga and the house nigga the two were in constant rivalry with one another and that kept order for the slave owner. It's unfortunate that Black people are still pragmatic of that system of things.

What was even more of a mystery was that this rock cocaine was steadfast in luring in a prominent Black National official of that caliber and stature, which is what makes me feel as though there is something in the rock cocaine that has been fabricated to genetically attract Blacks as a consumer.

Never before has any drug had a profound effect upon a race of people as has the rock cocaine, heroin was an addictive substance, but it wasn't phenomenal, nor did it attract high up Black figures as one of it's users.

Black America continued onward in it's viabilities as a whole, the heroin only captured the lower echelons for the most part, blacks as a whole weren't drastically hindered or obstructed behind it.

I groped over the possibility that through rock cocaine there was a conspiratorial genocide geared towards Blacks in America.

Back in the mid 1980's, or there about rock cocaine was culpable in destroying the careers of Black actress/ singer Irene Carr, actor Todd Bridges, and actress Ola Ray, whom for the record is a native of Sacramento, Ca, whom I'd went to school with.

This insidious kind of approach imposed against Black America by the power structure in this Country is a travesty of justice of the constitution of rights in America, and is a reality check that exemplifies how this Country is still geared towards oppressing Black Americans.

I was indignant behind the stigma of egregiousness that has been labeled on Black Americans, and to add fuel to the fire sort of speak, I was caught up in this refutable blight.

In mid November my mule, sort of speak, California dept. of Corrections (transportation bus) came to transport me to the 40 acres of land(Vacaville's State prison reception center).

When I got there, having never been to prison, I wasn't surprised at seeing what was actually proving to be true, of hearing that the prison system was heavily populated with Black men.

It appeared that the general reception center population was sixty percent black.

Seeing that many Blacks incarcerated in the penal system was pragmatic of a modern day slave plantation, some of the Blacks in prison, as with other ethnics, were there for a crime deserving of punishment.

But as I mingled around and talked to others, discovered that a good percentage of Black men, like myself, were there for small amounts of rock cocaine possession.

This was the means through which the power structure of this Country could eliminate the Black male from the mainstream of American society, thus stifling the reproduction of the Black race, even further, leaving the Black woman and children to fend for themselves in a white society.

After 2 months in the reception center at Vacaville State prison, I was interviewed by a counselor and recommended to finish out my sentence there, a few days later I was sent to the mainline and into the general population.

It was a New Year, 1992, I'd been in the general population for a couple of months, I was witnessing the harsh reality of just how deep racism was in prisons.

Not just between the different ethnics that make up the population, but even more so by and through the correctional officers that work there.

The white C.O.'s, (Correctional officers), and some black ones would discriminate and show their disdain towards the black convicts in most every given opportunity.

White C.O.'s would secretly slip the Arian Brotherhood convicts,(white prison gang),kitchen knife's before a race riot would start, so as to give them the upper hand in the battle.

Or they would unlock a black convicts cell, catching him off guard and let three or four A.B.'s(Arian Brotherhood) make a hit(commit a stabbing or killing), and turn their back on the incident while it's happening.

These were some of the many stories I listened to while in Vacaville, the white C.O.'s would give extended privileges to their own race, while on the flip side of this, most black C.O's would make life tough on their own race, and constantly brown nose their white co-workers as if to receive brownie points from them.

I also noticed a few black woman correctional officers either married to, or dating white C.O.'s, for a time there I'd thought I had been placed in a time warp and transported back into slavery and was on the plantation, where the black over-seers were token blacks trying to impress their master, the white boy.

And to compound the situation even more some of the black woman correctional officers would look down upon the black convicts, but butter up to the white ones making their life in the system as easy as possible for them.

Not only were blacks being subjugated by and through this rock cocaine, but also victimized by token blacks once they were in the system, this kind of double jeopardy was a rude awakening for me.

While serving out my sentence in Vacaville, in March a warrant from Sacramento was issued and sent to me, I had no immediate idea of what it was for.

The penal code of the warrant was 11352, which is sales of a controlled substance, but I still couldn't discern it's origin.

Everyday leading up to the court date I'd question associates there about that penal code and they'd all tell me it was for a drug sales charge.

I was slated to appear in court on the 15th of April, a few days prior to that date they shipped me back to Sacramento.

CAUGHT UP

On the court day, standing before the judge, the district attorney read to me the charge, and briefly gave me an account of the sales transaction and how it had occurred.

It turned out to be those very two fat undercover cops that had pulled over to me in that Chevy Nova and ask if they could they buy some rock.

As the proceedings went on at the prelim hearings, it was revealed in court that the two undercover cops were wired, and that everything that was said in the car while we were talking was on tape.

At my next court appearance the D.A. offered a deal of 3 years, to be ran concurrent with my present sentence, I took the deal since they had a solid case against me, it would have been senseless to have fought those odds.

More than anything, what was unsettling to me was how the authorities were now incorporating aberrant techniques and stealthy measures to incriminate and convict blacks involved with rock cocaine trafficking now.

The sentence of the new conviction didn't change my release date, because it was ran together with the current conviction I was in prison for, more disparaging though was the fact that I now had a sales conviction on my record.

The power structure in this Country can hold your criminal record against you causing perhaps the doors to a prestigious employment position, a scholarship, etc, to be closed shut.

Obviation of blacks in America was on the increase, and the most significant way it was being accomplished was through the rock cocaine.

I stayed in the County jail for a period of three weeks and was brought back to Vacaville State prison.

I phoned my mother and family and told them of the trickery of the system and how they'd entrapped me with a sales charge, thus giving me another felony, she wasn't happy to hear about it, primarily because of the things that were happening out in society behind the rock cocaine.

She told me that Holly was doing good and staying clean, but that my youngest brother Chance had begun renting out his 86 Honda Accord for rock to the dealers, and on one occasion had to chase down the car because the youngsters kept evading him.

When he finally caught up to them they took off while he tried opening the door handle, dragging him a few yards before he let go of it, and that he'd gotten bruised up pretty badly from the ordeal.

A few days later after not knowing where his car was, he was informed by the police that they'd found his car flipped upside down, totaled out, and abandoned.

Rock cocaine was a devilish plague and was now playing host to my youngest brother.

Chance had married a young lady whom was a registered nurse in the Army a few years back, she was stationed in Germany, so for the past 3 years he'd been away from the States and most certainly wasn't involved in drugs over there.

It wasn't until he came back to America a few months ago that he began using rock cocaine by being introduced to it through someone he'd grown up with there in Sacramento.

Around this same time singer Rick James hit the headlines, being charged with assault with the intent to commit great bodily harm, a charge that was conduced from his state of delusion as a result of incessant smoking of rock cocaine.

It was surfacing more and more that Blacks were being systematically victimized by and through this rock cocaine plague.

Then amidst the warfare of the rock on Blacks, there was still the ever increasing need of the young Black gang bangers to unify themselves, and to realize that the war their in, is not against each other, but rather, stemming from the control, and distribution of the rock cocaine business.

An incident happened at Vacaville prison where some bloods and crips had some quarreling amongst each other, supposedly over the wearing of some blue tennis shoes.

An altercation followed where sugar, a crip, knocked out a blood on the main yard, sugar was to be released in three weeks prior to that incident.

Two days later, blood members ran up in I wing(housing unit), and stabbed sugar to death, stabbing him in the eye, and right through his heart with a makeshift shank, killing him instantly.

This type of malicious behavior acted out on each other is ridiculous and unnecessary, these senseless acts, in conjunction with the rock cocaine epidemic waged against Blacks will certainly place the Black man into an endangered species category, on the brink of extinction.

In mid summer in Vacaville prison there was a letter being passed around to the Black population by other Blacks, that should have served as a wake up call, or a reality check to all Black men.

It read "we would like to personally thank all of you bloods and crips gang members for doing such a wonderful job of killing up each other, your doing our job for us, pretty soon, with many of you niggers gone to prison for life, or safe in the graveyard there won't be many of you left on the streets."

"Then we can go back to raping your nigger women and children because you won't be there to protect them, so keep up the good work boys, thank you sincerely," the K.K.K.

I wasn't certain of it's authenticity of origin, but nevertheless, a statement of that magnitude should of served to alarm those young Black gang-bangers to the seriousness of such a projected proposal.

After the effects of that letter had died down the gangs began to slip again, and went back to feuding between one another, as if that letter was insignificant to them.

While in prison I had singled out and associated with two or three individuals, not one of them were under thirty years of age, one in particular, K.J., I became real close with.

He was in prison for possession for sales, he too, was a resident of Sacramento, we were housed in the same bungalow building.

As we got better acquainted we discovered that we both knew many of the same people in our town.

K.J.'s woman had a friend whom was single, lonely and wanted to correspond with someone whom was in prison, so he mentioned it to me to see if I would be interested, I accepted the invitation.

He said her name was Jamie, she was an older woman of 39, at that time I was 34 myself, I preferred older women though more or less anyway.

She was a little on the heavy side and had 6 children, five girls and 1 boy, he added that she had a sweet personality, but just didn't go out much to meet people.

One day when K.J. called his woman, he had her to go over to Jamie's house, which was right across the street, to get her, so we could become acquainted.

When she got on the phone, she sounded like a sweet person, she gave me her phone number and address and told me to write her an introductory letter giving a description of myself, and that she would do likewise.

Having a woman to correspond with on the outside helped with the passing of time, since I was single as well and wasn't corresponding with anyone on the outside.

As we communicated with each other we got closer and learned that we both had a few things in common.

We both were homebody's, liked some of the same kind of foods, and like to travel and see other places the world had to offer.

She mentioned something that kind of gave me the notion of breaking off the corresponding with her though, she said that her daughters, all ranging between the ages of 15 to 22, were all dating either a blood or a crip gang member, and that she had become tired of all of the riff raff that goes on around her house when they showed up.

She lived in the Oak Park area, and went on to say that she wished she had a man to take control of her domain and to put his foot down whenever things got out of control.

Despite the problem that existed among her daughters boyfriends, more importantly, I needed a residence with which to give a parole officer when I was released, so I went along with the playing of a father figure for her.

Jamie eventually sent me some pictures of her and her children, they were a nice looking bunch and so was she, I had a photo of me taken on the yard and sent it to her as well.

The bond between us was strengthening, she sent me money orders to go on my books, hallmark cards, and quarterly packages with a few treats in them.

Whenever I called, some of the kids would call me daddy, especially her son.

This made me think of my youngest son council whom I wrote letters to and called occasionally to check on.

Mary, on the other hand would not let my older son, siege II keep in contact with any of my family, she would be held accountable for that to GOD.

I was faring along pretty well with prison life, I was assigned to the maintenance dept. as a carpenter in the vocational training trade.

I became skilled in the trade of laying cement, putting up chain linked fencing, laying floor and acoustical ceiling tiles, and repairing sheet rock panels.

I received a monthly pay of fifty eight dollars, I didn't have to go to the canteen every month because Jamie was sending money and packages to me, so I was able to save up my money.

3 months prior to my release, my points dropped, changing my prison status to B1 custody, meaning that I could go to a ranch outside of the prison walls.

I was transferred to Vacaville's ranch, and placed on the off grounds work detail crew; a crew that went outside to the California State mental hospital in Napa Valley to keep the grounds clean.

Five days a week, a correctional officer drove a crew of 9 men twenty miles to Napa State hospital to mow lawns, pick up trash, and other small deeds.

Getting to go to the outside world everyday really helped the time to pass for me, my release date of March 1rst, 1993 was finally upon me.

Tasting freedom was exhilarating, I'd been locked away from society for 16 months, the longest period of incarceration for me to date, while in prison I'd saved up nine hundred dollars which was enough for me to make a fresh start out in the world.

The state parole shuttle bused me to the Greyhound bus station and made sure that I boarded the bus.

Arriving in Sacramento, Jamie, and her youngest daughter Tam, were there to pick me up.

They hugged me a while before we all got into her car and left for her house, when we got there I met all the rest of her kids, they were all nice and respectable kids.

Her youngest and only son Mark really took a liking to me, he was happy that there was now another male figure in the household.

Jamie's husband had overdosed on heroin a few years back and she'd never dated after his death, so for Mark it had been living a life with all females.

Jamie had told her kids that she was going to let me stay there, and they were all happy for her that she was finally coming out of her shell and wanting to have another relationship again, plus, they'd all gotten use to my voice whenever I'd called from prison wanting to talk to their mother.

That night Jamie prepared a big seafood dish for me since I'd told her that any seafood was a favorite for me.

After eating we all sat around and talked, one of her daughters boyfriends was over and right away I got the feeling of despair from the bad vibes I was feeling from him.

The guy was a blood, he had no respect for anybody, he sold rock cocaine out in front of their house, and always had a gang of his homies out in front with him cursing and drinking forty ounces of Old English 800.

As days passed I came into contact with the other daughters boyfriends from both, the crip, and bloods gangs, a couple of the guys seemed to be alright when I'd met them.

They seemed to respect Jamie's house when they were around, and when one of the other girls boyfriend of the opposite gang were over, they'd avoid any confrontations around the house just to keep the peace.

I really cared for Jamie, one day her and one of her daughters went shopping, I had no idea what they'd went shopping for, but when they returned Jamie laid out 4 pair of dress slacks, 3 dress shirts, and different colored under clothes that she'd bought me.

I thanked, and kissed her, and later that afternoon showed my appreciation of her by cleaning up her backyard, which was full of junk and debris that had collected over the years.

As time passed her daughters boyfriends offered me rock in order to gain favor with me, initially I declined all offers because I wanted to stay clean, but one day I accepted an offer and it all started to get bad after I did that.

Gradually I began to sneak out into the backyard shed and lock myself inside and smoke whatever the youngsters would give to me.

Each encounter increased my urge to want more, the money I'd saved was put up, Jamie had told me to spend it on myself, that she didn't need my money.

One evening I asked her if I could use her car, I gathered six hundred of the dollars I saved and went out in search of an ounce of rock cocaine, in hopes of maybe selling so as to double my money.

Not knowing where to go, I went over to 2nd Ave by Sacramento high school, an area known to have large amounts of drug activity in it.

I saw a female and a guy standing around out in front of an apartment complex, I'd been out of circulation for 16 months and wasn't aware that Blacks were jacking each other now(robbing for either rock or money on sight).

I got out and asked, "say where can I buy an ounce?", I could have gotten an ounce from one of Jamie's daughters guys, but didn't want Jamie to find out, so I took this route instead.

The couple replied, "come on up to the apartment," I followed behind them on up to the building.

Once inside there were two other dudes in there that I didn't know, the female said, "I'll be back", and left, I started to get an ill feeling about all that was unfolding before me.

My six sense told me to get out of there, I got up and said that I'd left something outside in the car, and walked out.

I got into the car, the ignition wasn't working in the car so a screwdriver was used to start the car with.

I searched eagerly for it, time was crucial, I finally found it and brought the engine to life, was backing out and leaving when the female and four dudes came running up to the car.

The female opened the passenger door and sat down leaving the door open, two dudes came around to my side saying that they had the once, while another remained standing outside of the opened passenger side door.

Right then I should have said that I had forgotten the money or something, because they all began talking to me at the same time as if to confuse me.

Before I could call it off and move on, the guy whom had been standing on the passenger side of the car dove into the car and was trying to turn off the ignition, but there was no ignition keys for him to do so, out of reaction I mashed the accelerator to the floor.

The car took off, I was in an alley where it was all gravel, the guy whom had dove into the car, and I were struggling with the stirring wheel as the vehicles speed increased.

The car zoomed across a street and on into the next alley way, suddenly the automobile began veering to one side as I was losing control of it, that was the last thing that I remembered when coming to consciousness as the paramedics were placing me on a stretcher.

The paramedics told me that my car had struck a utility pole and that from the looks of the shape of the vehicle that I was lucky to be among the living.

The front end of the car was completely demolished, the engine had come through the dash, and front floor board, they had estimated my traveling speed on impact at forty five miles per hour.

The utility pole was broken in half and had to be replaced in able to restore electricity to the neighborhood.

I was thrown from the car on impact, the other two would be assailants were injured also, my money was still in my possession.

They transported me to the U.C.D. Medical center, there was so much blood soaked within my clothes I thought that I was seriously injured, but numb to any kind of pain.

After a lengthy examination by the Dr., I was told that aside from multiple facial and exterior cuts and abrasions that I'd only come out of it with a broken wrist.

I noticed that I couldn't move my right hand, and after looking at it I saw where my hand was nearly an inch off center and to the left of where it normally should have been.

Jamie was notified about the accident and immediately came to the hospital, when she got there she became hysterical upon seeing all of that blood, but calmed down when she learned that I was alright.

News travels fast though, although she was called and informed about the incident, I had no idea of how she was informed because I hadn't told the hospital of Jamie yet, nevertheless, she arrived there just after I'd been brought into the emergency room.

She too was telling me that when she'd looked at the vehicle she thought that I'd been killed in the accident because of how demolished the car was.

She also said that she knew of the people whom had jumped into the car and were injured along with me, and that they were no good people.

She said that the female came out of it unhurt, but that the guys leg was severely damaged, possibly leaving him crippled for the rest of his life.

I hated wishing bad on anybody for whatever the reason, but silently I thought to myself that it served that bastard right for what he was attempting to do to me.

After the nurses cleaned me up and put a temporary cast on my wrist they registered me into a room, when Jamie and I were alone she asked, "what had happened"?

I deviated from the truth a little by saying, "I went to buy some weed, and while doing so I flashed my money and the dude dove into the car," "I reacted by speeding off trying to get away but ended up hitting a pole in an alley."

She believed me and commented, "both that dude and girl are bad actors and you shouldn't have trusted them to do nothing for you."

I remained in the hospital for three days, and was given an appointment when I was released to go and have a real cast put on my wrist.

Jamie was without transportation now because of my furtive mission to buy an ounce of rock cocaine, when I was discharged from the hospital and got back to her house I gave her the whole six hundred dollars that I had left.

Her car was an 81 Buick Regal, and wasn't in to good of condition anyway, now she could use the money I'd given her as a down payment on a better car.

A week later she bought an 84 Mercury cougar from a used car dealer, I felt relieved that something good came out of all that had happened as a result of my misdeed.

After that terrible incident faded away, one school morning we laid in bed together talking and watching the T.V., Jamie kept hearing a bumping noise upstairs, soon after she said it I heard it too.

It was 1:00a.m., she ask me, "can you go upstairs to my youngest daughters Tamie's room to see what's going on in their please".

When I got up there and opened up Tamie's door, before I could even turn the handle to open the door though, there was some shuffling noise's going on, as I turned on the light some young blood was sitting up on the edge of her bed with his shoes in his hands.

I rushed him off, but not before telling the youngster never to let this type of action happen again, then Jamie and I restricted Tam.

A week later after sneaking out and buying a couple of dub rocks from one of her other daughters boyfriends, I got into an argument with that same dude that almost resulted in a confrontation, because he'd told Jamie about my buy.

It had almost been a month since I'd been out of prison and living with Jamie, and the tension with one of her daughters gang member boyfriends was building.

I was beginning to feel uncomfortable being there, besides that, my parole officer knew where I resided at, but hadn't done a house visit yet.

I didn't need this kind of an impression to be seen by him.

The next day I explained to Jamie my intentions of leaving, although she was hurt by my decision to leave, she went along with the idea.

After her husbands overdose she'd made a self vow to never get to serious with a man on any kind of drugs.

I gathered up all of my belongings, hugged and kissed her and the kids and left her house.

It would have been nice if our relationship hadn't of taken a turn for the worst at the onset, by her children's associates, and my urge to still participate in rock cocaine use and trafficking.

I had saw my mother and youngest son a few days after I was released from prison, but only for brief moments, now I wanted to spend a little more time with them.

I caught the bus and went to see them, my mother hadn't seen me since I'd been in that car accident, she knew me so I couldn't even fix my lips to lie to her about how things had happened.

She came right out and said, "you'd better change your life around before it's too late, you've already lost good employment with a good company, lost your family, been imprisoned, and now almost lost your life in an accident from would be robbers, what's next, death?"

She went on to say, "the time has come for you to open your eyes and to start using your GOD given senses to discern how truly pernicious rock cocaine is, and will continue to be."

Chance my brother, after the wrecking of his car had turned away from rock use, my sister Holly had resumed using again to the point that my mother had to place her into a boarding house because she could no longer deal with her.

Holly caused disturbances there by smoking rock in her room, and was forced to leave there by our older sister, she was now out there homeless until our Father, Mr. Black could locate another boarding house that would accept her.

It was a Friday, I'd spent the weekend with my Mother and family, and in the process seen Angie and my kids.

Angie had met a fairly decent guy and they were getting serious about one another, I thought that was good for her.

I had run off one of the other guys she'd been involved with because he didn't seem to good for my kids, so I didn't interfere with this relationship.

Over the weekend my Father, Chance, Elaine, my second eldest sister whom resided in Los Angeles, Ca, and works for the Criminal Justice system, and myself all sat around and drank some Rhine wine and talked the day away.

Elaine was the back bone of our family, very educated with two degrees; one was a P.H.D. in business administration, the other was a Master in Criminology.

She was all business and very devout with her relationship with our GOD, she took control of any and all serious family issues whether they were legal, or trivial, always giving her final assessment and input on the matter, and, she was always there giving the family her full support on any problem that arose.

I enjoyed being around my family, drug free for the moment talking and drinking wine and beer, that Sunday evening I decided to go back to the downtown Sacramento area so on Monday I could tell my parole officer that I was no longer living at Jamie's address anymore.

I also wanted to start looking for Holly whom my Mother had said was now living at the Salvation Army shelter for women.

When I got downtown it was 7:00 p.m., it was the month of April, daylight savings time would come next month in May, so at 7:00 it was still light outside.

I'd left half of the clothes that Jamie had bought for me at her place, and kept only an exchange outfit which I'd left at my Mothers place.

I didn't know where to look for Holly, I thought I'd try the Compton's market area, an area frequented by most of the rock stars(rock addicts).

When I got there, a few people were standing about either hustling, drinking alcohol, or waiting for an opportunity to present them with another rock cocaine hit, the usual formalities typical for that location.

Approaching the corner of 17th and Capital streets I bumped into a young lady I'd known for many years, I knew all of her brothers and had went to school with them, her name was Roane.

I'd been in the company of Roane once before back in 1989 in the downtown area, she was a sophisticated looking black woman in her early forties, and worked for the State dept. of Agriculture.

I'd seen her in the downtown area one afternoon dressed to the T, in a long blue knit body fitting dress that came to her ankles, and a matching pair of women's high heel pump shoes.

She was searching for some rock, we got together and I had ended up buying the rock from someone for her, she gave me a piece and went on about her business.

At that time she was seeing somebody, I'd never forgotten how dazzling she'd looked that day, and told myself that one day she would be mine.

She was the type of woman that dated guys that were otherwise decent men, but weren't academically motivated to excel in life, in other words, indigent hustling type dudes.

As pretty as she was intelligent, I could never understand why she catered to such types of men.

She had a golden hue to her complexion, with a shoulder length perm hair style, wore designer made prescription glasses that accented her facial features, and had a figure that turned men's heads, and was always adorned in fashionable attire.

I had heard from people that she was a closet rock smoker, and a chronic functioning alcoholic still maintaining in society, but to look at her one would never suspect that in her.

We greeted each other with a hug and a kiss and began talking, she lived two blocks down the street from the Compton's market in a security building, was still working for the State, but hadn't been going to work for the past month because of her rock smoking binges which kept her up long mornings getting high.

The guy she was with was in prison for a spousal abuse charge on her, she claimed she wasn't sure about going back to him when he was released.

At the moment she was living alone but was seeing some older man that would come by just to have sex with her, but he wasn't helping her out financially, and that she was tired of that arrangement with him.

I thought that maybe now was my time to make my move on her, she had stopped at the market and bought herself a half a pint of Vodka, her drink of choice, and was broke, she was also a couple of months behind on her rent.

I stated, that I'd just gotten out of prison for drug possession and that rock cocaine, and California's judicial system, are unjustly locking up black men.

Furthermore, California's judicial, and penal system is in all actuality an industrial racketeering business for the State, with Black men being their commodity.

Becoming more indignant about this issue, I changed topics and began explaining what had happened to my wrist.

I told her that I'd felt obligated to give Jamie the money because I had wrecked her only source of transportation, and that I had some money left on me with which to get a room with.

She unscrewed the cap off of the Vodka, took a swallow and passed it to me, I did not, nor had I ever drank Vodka straight from the bottle like that, but took one swallow, and gave it back to her.

She put it back in her purse, paused for minute then said, "if you'd like you can give my some money, and stay at my place,".

I asked, "how much would you want, and for how long".

She replied, "one hundred dollars for the rest of the month".

It was April 7th, I agreed to that and we both walked on to her place.

The living room had one couch that let out into a bed, there was no other furniture in the living quarters, her bedroom though was furnished with a king size bed and a matching dresser with night stands, she had a black and white T.V., that she carried from room to room.

As we sat and drank on the Vodka she brought up the idea of buying some rock, I didn't object to it, and counted out and passed her the hundred dollars, a few minutes later we were out on a search to buy some rock.

We found a dealer and together bought a hundred dollars worth from the youngster, stopped by Compton's market bought some more alcohol, some groceries, and headed back to her apartment.

I asked Roane, "have you seen Holly around anywhere"?

"I've seen her a few times in the area, but I haven't seen her today anywhere," was her reply.

Back at her place as we commenced to smoking the rock, that usual feeling of lust began surfacing on me, and I suggested that the two of us parade around in our birthday suits, she obliged and began to undress herself.

We partied together all morning long, enjoying good sex on and off, and in many different positions, all throughout the morning different guys would ring her apartment buzzer to be let into the building, but I took control and told her to not answer their call.

After being coached by me the first time, the door buzzer rang, I took it on myself to just get up, get on the intercom and tell the dudes that she wasn't available, and to not come back by.

That morning she didn't get up to go to work and I didn't force her to, but assured her that I was going to see that she started going if I had to walk with her in the mornings.

Her job was only 8 blocks away, so it wouldn't be a problem if I had to escort her there.

As the days passed we were always seen together, I'd walk her to work, meet her for lunch, and be there when she got off at 5:00p.m..

The guys in the area whom had either been with her previously through the rock/sex exchange game, or were attempting to try and get with her, after seeing me around her all the time began backing away.

It was being spread around that I was her new man, and despite my handicap of a broken wrist, I was a 190 lbs of muscle I'd acquired from prison, so most guys gave a second thought to me being a push over dude.

After a few more weeks they stopped coming to her apartment, the older man whom just came around for periodic sex was allowed to still come by once a week and I'd leave the place so they could do their business.

This happened twice, every time after he'd leave she'd have nothing to show for her services rendered, the old guy knew she was having problems financially, but still never offered to give her any kind of help.

The third time he showed up I didn't leave, but spoke on this issue, telling the guy that he wanted to get something for nothing from this exchange, and that unless he started paying for services rendered, there would be no need for him to come by anymore.

The old dude called her the next day on her job and told her that he wasn't going to be coming around anymore, and that there thing was over.

She went on to say that she was both glad and sad, by that she meant that she didn't have the nerves to end it herself because he kept promising her that he was going to help her, and then go and by her some Vodka to smooth her over.

She thanked me for taking control of the matter and ending it for her, I stressed the fact that he was using her as long as she was going to let it happen.

That next morning after walking Roane to work I stopped by the County welfare office to apply for the general assistance, from there I went to my parole officer to give him the address to where I was now residing at.

At noon I went to her job to meet her for lunch, she introduced me to her co-workers, where several of them commended me on my success at getting Roane to start coming back to work again.

They were the few close friends of hers that knew the reasons why she wasn't showing up to work, had tried to turn her around, but were all unsuccessful at it.

Roane had confided in them, she had also let them know that I was new in her life and was the reason why she'd gotten herself back on track again.

I thanked all of her co-workers for their praise's of me, and could tell by the look on the face of Roane that she was appreciative of me as well for what I had done for her.

She had been forging fake Kaiser hospital medical appointment slips to cover her absentee's when she did show up at work for a day or two, but then after that, start the whole process all over again.

Her supervisor and superiors were all starting to get wise to her ill deeds, I had come into her life just in time, and had spared her of possible termination of her employment with the State, which they'd put in motion already.

Other people can usually recognize faults in one before that person realizes it themselves, I noticed the deterioration of her appearance as a result of the excessive drinking of Vodka straight from the bottle.

Everyday when I met her at 5:00p.m. she would stop at a liquor store after leaving work and buy her a pint of Vodka, I intervened sometimes by stopping her and suggesting that we buy either Miller beer, or some Morgan David wine.

The same effects were derived at, or so I felt, but without the chronic destruction of her liver, or other organs.

She always went along with that approach of mine, and gradually her arrogant personality when she drank Vodka begin to subside, plus she felt better afterwards.

I was making progress with her, the rent on the apartment she lived in hadn't been paid in two months, the sum total amount needed to bring it current was eleven hundred dollars.

She hadn't been going to work which meant that her paycheck for the month of May wasn't going to nowhere near cover rent, which in essence would put her back another month in the hole.

Her landlord was being patient about her back rent, but assured her that if it wasn't paid in full come May, that he would get a lock put on her apartment along with an eviction notice from the Sheriffs Dept., and then auction off her property to pay for her back rent.

She ask me, "Siege can you start looking for another place somewhere downtown close to my job, and we'll vacate this place before he's finish with his eviction plan."

"I'll be out there on it everyday while your at work sweetie," I responded with.

Everyday while she was at work I went out in search of another apartment to rent, around April the 25th I located one that was within a block from Regional Transit's light rail station, it was another security apartment complex similar to her present building, though not as elegant looking.

That evening after her job we both met with the lady resident landlord with our credentials, and used her mother as our current landlord as a reference.

The next day I checked with the landlord about that apartment, she gave us a thumbs up approval and said that we could move in on the 1rst of May.

Roane's mother liked what a swell job I was doing in rejuvenating her daughter, so she put up the needed money for us to be able to move into this new place in May.

On the 1rst of May we successfully moved out of her current place without her manager even knowing that we had, and got settled into the other apartment, we now had a fresh start.

A week after we'd moved out of the old apartment a young Black man living in that same building was killed by another Black man for not sharing his rock cocaine with him.

The story was that the two had been smoking together, but when the rock ran low, the deceased stopped sharing what was left, they had supposedly just met one another.

The assaulter beat the deceased unconscious with a tire iron, ran him through the chest with the tip end of that tire iron, then through him over the 3rd floor balcony of the apartment balcony.

The assaulter, after committing the murder fled the scene, but began boasting to someone about what he'd just done and was later arrested and charged with first degree murder.

Rock cocaine had laid claim in destroying the lives of two more Blacks in America.

At the same time that incident happened, I had finally came into contact with my sister Holly hanging around the 17th and Capital streets area, she appeared to be surviving well and learning the do's and don'ts of that location.

She mentioned of a high school associate of mine named Mic, whom had also went to Consumers River College with me back right after graduating from high school.

Mic was the all State collegiate track star, and long jumper, training there at the college, while furthering his education their on campus.

He had just been sentenced to three years with the California Dept. of Corrections prison system for a small possession of the rock cocaine.

I knew Mic well, he was from a good family, and had been raised with good morals, was a decent and respectable individual in the community.

We'd run into one another a couple times back in the Oak Park area, both of us on rock cocaine missions at the time, the last time I'd seen Mic he had mentioned to me that he was on probation for possession of rock cocaine, and that he had to refrain from smoking 3 days prior to his P.O. testing him.

Mic was a nice looking easy going type of person, somewhat like myself, neither of us were prison types, as was true of many of the Black men whom were caught up in the smoking of rock cocaine.

Unfortunately the cynic ethos of the white power structure is a preponderance that indoctrinates imprisoning Black men into the penal system for trivial rock cocaine cases.

I was now starting to see the invisible cloak of injustices that permeated throughout the California judicial system with regard to the sentencing of Blacks for possession of small amounts of rock cocaine.

I felt for Mic, and was sorry to hear that news, like myself though, the County probation dept., after they've finished sending you back and forth to jail, they give a bad report of your tenure to the judge, thus rendering you unfit for probation, with a recommendation to the judge that you become a ward of the State's prison system.

I gave Holly our new address and told her to stop by anytime, she didn't drink alcohol which was a good thing for her, so I bought myself some Morgan David wine to sip on, and share with Roane when she got off work that day.

Holly and I walked and talked for a few hours before she said she was going to get started on panhandling some money for a few hours to get some rock with.

I didn't like how she was now living, and before parting from her I chastened her thoroughly about the way she was living, and gave her 5 dollars, told her to come by our place, then left.

Later that night she showed up at around 1:00a.m., I waved her in, gave her a blanket and she fell asleep on the floor, later that morning she got up, cleaned herself, washed her clothes, and took off around noon.

Roane, and I had become a unified team together, we had lucked up at a garage sale and got a deal on a nice looking couch and chair set for $20.00, our apartment was slowly coming together.

We had almost become inseparable, always together, we got along fairly well except for when we'd smoke rock and/or drink alcohol together.

The rest of the month of May went without incident, June brought chaos though, Roane received a full paycheck, plus I had my general assistance check.

The bills were paid, groceries were bought, but we had an excess of money now with which to do as we pleased, which was rock cocaine, and Vodka liquor splurging.

Together we indulged ourselves, Roane would become obnoxious under the influence of the rock and Vodka, in conjunction with a subtle form of paranoia, which later that evening led her to dialing 911 for no apparent reason.

There was a knock a the door, along with the sound of police radios, I ask, "who is it"?, and they replied, "the police open the door," so she opened it.

When they entered one officer ask, "what's the problem,? were responding to a 911 call", I replied, "there must be a mistake with the number that was dialed," but they gave me the correct phone number as the place of origin.

Roane denied having called 911, and said, "it must have been a mix up somewhere within the system officer."

Before they left they looked around the apartment, luckily for us all rock paraphernalia was either put away, or camouflaged.

I suspected that she had dialed 911, but couldn't be sure of it, even further, as to why she would have even called in the first place.

I would have to watch her more closely now when she was drinking Vodka and smoking rock.

In addition to our personal problems, the apartment complex in which we lived turned out to be a haven for drug addicts, and dealers of every kind.

I didn't detect this when we filled out the tenant application forms because it appeared to be a peaceful complex during the daytime, no loitering or anything going on that alarmed me to this.

Drug trafficking was thick in the building on the 1rst, and there after during the night hours.

I found there to be mostly rock cocaine on the premises, but heroin and crank could also be purchased, but a more diligent effort of search was needed to locate those substances in the complex.

I had tried to avoid moving into that type of an environment, I had no way of knowing of this activity because the signs weren't present, plus time was a factor in our having to vacate the other premises before being evicted. This type of a living environment was a precarious one, and would subject us to untimely, even perhaps ill fated events while living there.

A few days later, Roane, after smoking on some rock and drinking Vodka again pressed 911 on our touch tone phone, this time I caught her while she was hanging up the receiver.

Twenty minutes later the police were at our door once more, I let them in and the routine questions were asked, she lied this time though and said that we'd been arguing and she thought that it could lead to some violence and pressed 911.

The police suggested that one of us take a walk and let things cool off, my being on parole could have brought a automatic arrest for me just for coming into contact with the police, so I agreed with them and stepped out of the place for a while.

After being gone for a few hours I returned, Roane was there laying back drunk and high, I decided to wait until later to ask her why she always dialed 911 when she's under the influence of alcohol and/or rock cocaine.

The night passed and returned to normal, I shot the question on her of why she did that.

She exclaimed, "most all of my previous relationships the men abused me physically, in addition to that I was raped once at knife point while smoking rock with a guy, and on another occasion I had barely escaped a rape of two guys while smoking rock with them, so I go on the offense at times".

Although I'd never gave her a reason to feel that I'd beat her; when she smoked rock she claimed she experienced flashbacks and paranoia sets in which causes her to feel threatened.

I assured her by saying, "well I'm not a woman beater, and that before I'd commence to start hitting on you I'd leave the relationship".

I felt sympathy for her and ask in a pleasant voice, "could you please refrain from calling 911 since I'm on parole, and when ever you feel that way, to just ask me to leave, or try sitting down with me and talking about it".

This irrational action didn't cease there though, it was to become a weekly pattern at least one day out of a week, sometimes twice a week she'd hit the 911 pads on the phone while under the influence.

When the police would come out they'd see that she wasn't bruised or battered and ask one of us to leave, they came to realize that she was the one always under some kind of an influence of something.

Despite my being on parole the cops would seem to understand the situation and give me a pass, but would remind me that one day I'd go to jail.

Aside from the police coming to that complex for us, either they themselves, or the paramedics would frequent the building on a regular basis.

One woman overdosed on heroin and died there, there were gang related fights, a child injury, or an elderly person would need medical attention, that complex was a very bad omen of sorts.

A couple of months passed, although I was escaping the possibility of going back to jail behind Roane dialing 911, it was getting out of hand now.

To intensify things, my sister Holly would come by smoking on rock and sleeping over, Roane, and Holly didn't particularly like one another.

It was like being between a hard place and a rock so to speak, not wanting to sway to one side or the other in defense of either of them, but trying to be fair to both at the same time.

Roane didn't want Holly to stay over and smoke rock, which wasn't that often, I took sides with my sister on that issue, and went on to mention that I put up with her dialing 911 when she was high, so it was no harm in my sister coming by and doing her thing occasionally.

I won the round with that statement for the time being, but it was fuel being added to a simmering fire.

In early August after our payday we got together with our funds and bought a half an ounce of rock cocaine, the plan was for me to sell while she was at work and make some extra cash.

At the outset it was going according to the plan, but Roane would smoke a rock and ask for another one, by late evening we had broke even with a few rocks left.

She kept on nagging me for more to smoke on, finally, but not giving in to her though, I separated the money made and the remaining rock down the middle.

She wanted me to set up a deal to buy another half an ounce, I'd become both bothered and tired of the whole affair and decided that I would take a hit before I went to pick up the next package.

I felt that taking a huge hit would spark me into a different frame of mine, I chipped off a boulder of a hit and inhaled as much of the combustion as I could.

I held it in my lungs for as long as I could and then exhaled, blowing out the smoke was the thing that I remembered doing as I slipped into unconsciousness from an overdose of that rock cocaine.

The paramedics came and I was en route to the U.C.D. Med center in an ambulance with tubes running through my nose.

They registered me into the E.R. section where I remained for several hours while Dr.'s checked my vitals, put me on a monitor, and watched me.

Several hours after being under observation, and some test ran on me, I was released, the paramedics had torn off my designer shirt in order to administer the necessary treatment to that region of my body.

At the hospital I was given a robe to wear, when released there was no one readily available to pick me up which meant if I wanted to leave I'd have to do so in hospital garb.

I walked from the U.C.D. Med center to our apartment, which was about a mile from where we lived, all the while the hospital gown making me feel uncomfortable.

I had to thank GOD for bringing me through what I had went through that day.

I'd been blessed in light of the recent cocaine overdosing deaths of the two upcoming superstar sports figures Lyn Bias, and Don Rodgers.

Both were top sports draft picks in their particular fields and were ready to begin their careers until there encounters with the rock cocaine ended it all.

I am a witness to several people whom I personally know that have went mentally insane as a result of their over indulgence of smoking rock cocaine.

One nice looking Black female I'd smoked rock with several times before I went to prison was a complete nut case when I got out. and ran back into contact with, she held conversations with herself, was desultory, and listless.

The physical and mental impairments that inflict the body and mind of someone smoking this rock cocaine continuously is certainly something akin to playing Russian roulette with ones own life.

When I returned to the apartment Roane was sitting in the living room smoking rock with some of the other tenants of the building, not one of them seemed to be interested in my being alright, but I understood their un- attentive state of being.

I came to know rock cocaine as being the demonic substance that it is, and realized that being under it's influence alters ones state of being dramatically.

I went to the bedroom and laid back on the bed thinking about my near death overdose, plus what all I've been through behind my rock cocaine addiction over the years.

I was cutting it very closely this time and cheated death once more, GOD had spared me again, how many more times would GOD give me a pass?

It was time to start accessing my worth as a human being, and not continue to be a servant of the devils by consuming his poisonous candy the rock.

Roane finally came into the room an hour later after everyone had left, looking at her, I couldn't see a future there, maybe it was time to assess her worth to me.

Aside from the power structure imprisoning Blacks behind the rock cocaine epidemic, I didn't need the aide of a Black woman trying to put me behind bars again too, especially if I wasn't deserving of it.

For the time being I had to go with the flow of things and play it all by ear.

For a few days everything went smoothly, then, she went back into her mode of dialing 911, the consistency of her periodic summoning of the law made me feel as though she was purposely trying to get me out of the picture, so as to prepare for the guy she'd sent to prison to come back into her life.

The dude was up for release in August sometime I'd learned, yet she claimed to be through with that person, women are experts at deceptions though.

I talked with her on the possibility of her wanting me out of her life after the police left the last time, letting her know that all she had to do was tell me so, and I'd be gone, but she insisted that that was not the case.

On August 21rst, we walked to a convenient store at night to buy some cigarettes and wine, Roane had been drinking Vodka while at work and was her obnoxious self in full, I let her go in and buy the items while I stayed outside and smoked a cigarette.

It was taking her a long while to come out so I went in, to my surprise she had dialed 911 and was standing in the store clerks backroom talking to the police dispatcher.

I made her hang up the receiver and escorted her out of the store, as we were walking and somewhat arguing a police cruiser pulled up, the officer got out and ask, "what's the problem?", we both at the same time retorted, "there's no problem."

The police questioned her about the 911 call made from the store, she stated to them, "we had been arguing just a little, but that it was over with."

The police knew I was on parole, and placed me into the back of the squad car, so as to question her more intensively alone, that tactic of dividing and then conquering by the system is as old as slavery itself.

After 10 minutes of interrogating her the cop came back to the car and said that I was under arrest for spousal abuse.

Another cop had come to the scene whom was a racist, and after looking at a chapped and peeling part of her lip, claimed it to be a healing bruise.

Roane had been cajoled by those cops when they separated us and put me into the car, they must have convinced her to press charges on me, so now I was headed back to the slave plantations of C.D.C.

When I got to jail I called her and asked, "why did you do this to me?"

She replied, "we needed a break from one another," I called her a bitch for that and then realized that she was in fact making room for that other guy.

"I'm not going to follow through with pressing any charges on you though," at that point it didn't matter because I would still come out of it with a parole violation.

A couple of weeks later I called her place again and sure enough the dude answered the phone, after that call I was only concerned with her really not pressing any charges, cause our relationship was truly over at that point.

I felt that the ploy she had used to get me out of the picture was a dirty one, but life is full of lessons to be learned though, this one incident just taught me more about the treacherousness of a woman.

The machinations of the law enforcement officials, the district attorneys, the public pretenders, and the judges, not only in California, but the Country as a whole, it appears, have become relentless in their pursuit to imprison the Black man.

I knew that she wasn't going to press any charges so I prepared myself for a jury trial, at the prelim the D.A. offered my a two year deal, and I refused.

The D.A sent a subpoena to her job ordering her to appear in court to testify, she came on that date and said that she wasn't going ahead with pressing any charges because I hadn't struck her.

The District Attorney still wouldn't drop the charges against me though, and I then became aware to the cynicism, dogmatism, and racism within this Countries judicial system when it's trying to incriminate a Black defendant in court.

Although Roane gave an oath to the D.A, and the residing judge that she was not pressing any charges, they bluffed her by threatening to charge her with perjury.

On the defense end of things the public pretender went on to say that Roane didn't have to press charges, that the D.A. would pick up the charge and could convict me and that it would be best for me to take the offered deal of 2 years.

I guess the judicial system feels that all Blacks are ignorant to the practices, and legalities of the courts, thus prompting them to be cajoled into accepting fabricated and warranted sentences.

I applied my GOD given common sense to the matter and suddenly realized that in every crime there has to be a suspect, and a victim, the victim is whom gets upon the stand at trial and testifies in the courtroom, if there is no victim to testify, then there can be no trial; case closed.

I told the public pretender, whom more or less works side by side with the D.A in getting convictions for the court, to kiss the nastiest part of my crack, and all the while praying that Roane remained resistant to the cajoling of the D.A., and said lets go to trial.

A month passed, the screening officer for the California Dept. of Corrections offered me a nine month violation, I turned it down, and would go to the board of prison terms since I hadn't done anything.

While in jail my cell mates came and left the cell, some of which spoke on their arresting charges.

Most every Black man in the County jail was there either directly or indirectly behind a rock cocaine charge.

One cell mate in particular spoke on his charge of robbing several Sacramento Bee newspaper boy carriers when they were delivering their newspapers, for such an act as that, he deserved to be locked up.

Rock cocaine, A.K.A.,(the devil)had made this guy so desperate to ingest his poisonous candy that he belittled himself to rob young helpless boys to support his habit.

After hearing that, I knew the time was near to put the devils substance(rock) down for good before it would get to far out of control for me.

The dude had never been to prison, the judge gave him 8 years for his crime, which was a just sentence for the kind of crime he was committing.

I stayed in jail standing firm in my fight for justice against this fabricated charge, 2 and a half months after being in jail, and not breaking to the system, the day before I was to select the twelve jurors, the D.A. dismissed the charge claiming lack of evidence.

My next challenge was to go before the board of prison terms to see what they had for me in the way of custody time.

A week later sitting before the board I explained my reason for wanting a board hearing, sitting in front of what appeared to be all racist white males, I was given a 12 month violation, with a comment that I must have been guilty.

I thought that to be a bias and unfair violation term, but there was nothing I could do to counter the power structures decision to place me back on the plantation(prison).

At the same time, but after me a white boy went before the board for the same charge, yet, he actually had busted his wife's lip, and she too, didn't press any charges, he came back saying that they gave him a 4 month violation.

After hearing that I thought to myself that racism and discrimination was very much active and thriving in California's judicial and penal system.

But consolation behind all of this came to me in the way of knowing that GOD sees all acts of unrighteousness, and just as the white man oppresses with his wicked laws, and is bias and unfair with his judging of blacks and minorities, so too will he be judged in the same fashion by our creator.

The distinction of punishment will be significantly different though, the eternal punishment from the wrath of GOD will be both merciless and endless.

With a twelve month violation, and getting credit for half time I would stay imprisoned for 6 to 7 months providing that I received some type of a prison job starting out my violation.

But with California's attitude towards locking up Blacks and other minorities, the prison system was overcrowded, which meant that I would be serving out the full 2/3rds of my violation which was 8 months.

I did the 8 months violation and was released, I went to my parole officer and asked if I could be placed in a half way house, he checked his area for an available slot.

He came up with one located on 27th and Broadway, made the call and sent me over to get registered into the house.

SELF INTERVENTION

Walking up to the old Victorian styled house, I thought I'd have a fresh start at cleaning up my life, it was a clean place, well integrated ethnically, and from the looks of the neighborhood, it seemed to be drug free.

There was another house right next door that housed S.S.I. recipients.

The residence though, as I later thought it to be, were like the distinctions of between daylight and nighttime, this differentiates the habitats of a community.

As night fell, the traffic around those two houses got heavy, across the street was an apartment building with about twenty units in it, I learned from one of the other parolee's that the complex was a haven for young rock dealers, and toss up's(rock cocaine prostitutes.)

I also discovered that rock cocaine was being smoked in both of the houses, one S.S.I. recipient named Doc ask me if I had any rock for sale as I walked between the houses.

My hope of having a chance to change my life and put the rock behind me was shattered now, and a week later I took that first hit of the rock.

Trying hard to refrain from it was now impossible, as it was before me and put in front of me everyday now, and Doc would always seek me out and give me a hit whenever he had rock, I was in line for another fall.

Before I fell back into smoking rock, I'd taken the liberty to get my general assistance started up again, everything else was secondary to doing that.

At the halfway house there was another Black guy whom I associated with named Duke, Duke was an avid rock smoker and he'd become suspect by the staff of smoking the substance in one of the rooms of the house.

The staff scrutinized my every move because of my association with Duke.

I knew the time was near for me to make plans to get out of that house before getting caught up in a cross and being reprimanded by my P.O.

I was smoking rock true enough, but not in the halfway house, and for the staff to suspect me, and watch me constantly, I might as well fulfill their suspicions of me.

That next night while in downtown Sacramento, I ran into a young lady that I'd had a crush on, but never had gotten the opportunity to be with.

I'd not had the leisure to satisfy my sexual libido thoroughly yet, since my release from prison, now was the time for it, I propositioned her, "hey sweetie you feel up to going to my place to smoke some rock and get kinky,".

she accepted my invitation, by replying, "lets do this thing handsome".

When we got to the house it was dark out, I snuck her up to my room, my room mates were both gone, we both took our first hit of the rock, then in a rush fashion we had sex, both reaching our orgasm at the same time.

A staff member could have come into the room at any time, but I no longer cared about their regulations anymore since I'd already planned to leave.

With a rock trafficking apartment complex across the street, and rock smoking going on in both the halfway house and the house next door what kind of a rehab chance was I to have, it was all a trap and I wanted no parts of any of it.

I successfully pulled off smoking some rock and getting sexed in the room without getting caught and was gratified at having put one past the staff for their accusations of me.

I wanted to see the young lady again but under different circumstances, but it would have to be some other place and time, so we kissed and she left.

The next day staff gave Duke the boot and warned me, I responded by saying they had no just cause to suspect me of drug use just because of my association with duke without any concrete evidence of it.

I told them to shove that room up their ass because I was in fact leaving as well, I gathered up my belongings and left the place.

Having to start out fresh again I went to the Salvation Army in order to have shelter for the time being.

At Sallies (Salvation Army) I ran into Roane and the guy she'd sent to prison, and whom she was waiting on to return.

He was a heroin addict, and not only had he caused her to loose her State job by not getting after her to go, but had also drug her down to the lowest part of life that one could get to, they were both living where they could.

I hated seeing her in that predicament, but karma has a way of getting back to one in one way or another, she had done me wrong despite my helping her, now she was reaping what she'd sown.

She couldn't even look at me when our eyes met, I was looking healthy and good, had my body toned up with muscles, a big full natural hair do like the ones the Jackson Five wore back in time, I was the center of attention.

It paid off for me too, while hanging around Sallies and looking like I'd just come from the era of the radical 60's and 70's, with the huge afro and muscular physique, a Black woman came up to me out of nowhere and introduced herself, "hi I'm Kat".

Her next words were, "you are so very nice looking, are you new in town because I've never seen you before,"?

I replied, "no, I've been away in prison for a few years, and thank you for the compliment you just gave me, by the way my name is Siege".

She was diligent at keeping my attention on her because she kept complimenting and inquiring about me.

She was an ordinary looking woman, not much my type, nevertheless, I remained cordial to her as we continued small talking for a while.

She invited me to accompany her to the C street park to smoke a stick of refer with her.

Weed wasn't my thing, it had been years since I'd hit a joint of weed, so I cut the meeting short, and excused myself.

My reason for being at Sallies was to get on the list for a bed there at the shelter, time was crucial so I cut our conversation short by saying that I had some urgent business to tend to.

Before I left she went into her purse, brought out a pen and some paper, wrote down something and handed it to me, and at the same time saying, "this is my address, I would love the chance to be in your life, you could call me when ever you'd like to, I'll be waiting."

I would take her up on her offer later, several days had passed before I finally went to her studio apartment on 26th and Broadway.

Upon opening her door she said, "I've been waiting for you to show up".

I was reluctant in doing so though because of the way my luck had been going with women the past two years, I was homeless though and she was offering me a place to stay.

As we talked I learned that she too had recently been released from prison for drug possession, and she was on Social Security Income.

Her drug of choice was the all too familiar rock cocaine, which like me was what had sent her to prison.

We had that much in common, I hoped that this arrangement wouldn't end up as all of the others had behind the rock cocaine.

Our union together got off to a good start and stayed that way for about a month.

It was June when all hell broke lose, I hadn't been smoking rock that much, she would smoke with her uncle every time she went down to Sallies.

Her uncle and his girlfriend of whom had just gotten out of jail started coming by the studio with rock, and needing a place to stay, would crash out on the floor.

Before anything was said about it they had gotten comfortable living there as if it was their place too, and every day her uncle and his other half would go out hustling and come back with a bunch of rock.

My being the man of the house I was always given my share of the rock by her uncle, as a means of compensation to us for their staying there.

From that point on it would get worse before getting better, I eventually began hustling at times with her uncle, Kat, or all by myself to get money for the next hit of rock.

Kat, I'd found out later was at one time selling sex to support her habit, in between her monthly S.S.I. checks, she'd turn dates, and to justify her actions she'd give me half of everything she brought in from her dates.

In addition to the excessive rock smoking binges that we went on, the consumption of any and all types of alcohol was flagrant, this in turn enhanced my already present addiction more so to the rock cocaine.

Where I resided was within blocks of the halfway house that I'd just left from, I'd constantly see Doc on his rock searching missions all hours of the day, night, and early mornings.

It was easy to stay high on some rock, in between my own hustling, I'd get catered to with rock either by Kat and her clan, or by Doc.

For the first time since I'd lost my job at S.E.C., and my family, I was going way overboard again with the excessive smoking of the rock, and I didn't like it.

There was a liquor store on 19th and Broadway where most of the transients would hang out and panhandle, that location which was up the street from where I was living would become a habitat away from the house where I could bolster my hustling.

I met a guy named T-dog up there while at the store one evening, he was a part of the landscape so to speak, because he was there from sun up to the stores closing hours.

The owner had consigned him to sweep up the parking lot as an incentive to help T-dog with his alcohol addiction, afterwards he would panhandle there.

T-dog was also on S.S.I., and lived by himself a block from the store.

He was a young dude of about 27 years old, but was chronic alcoholic which made him look older, he was also a blood who went solo.

He was a comedian at heart and kept people laughing at his antics, even the people he panhandled from and they would fill his pockets with dollars and/or change.

He and I instantly clicked and became good friends and hustling pals, we'd usually split up and I'd take one side of the liquor store and he'd take the other and we would rake up together about 75 dollars on a good day.

The situation at Kat's place got worse by the day, she would sometimes wake me up from a deep sleep and ask me to leave for a while so she could turn a date.

I didn't mind that so much, but when I began to hustle with other women, she get upset and become belligerent, I had figured her to be the domineering type from the beginning, she wanted her cake and to eat it too, but that wasn't going to fly with me though.

Two positive forces always would clash in life no matter what the scenario was, so I anticipated that this union would come to an end in a matter of time.

We both continued to do our own thing and the clashes between us escalated.

My brother Chance had been dropping by at times to check on me, after the incident with the renting out of his previous vehicle he'd gotten himself together and was doing well.

Although he and his wife had separated, he was employed with Methodist Hospital as an orderly with a decent income, and had bought a 1985 535 I BMW.

When Chance came by Kat would always try to butter Chance up some kind of a way as if to try and make me jealous.

Chance liked to drink, he had backed away from the rock, but would occasionally indulge himself when he came by our studio, I would always warn him of the consequences of the rocks wrath and never instigated him to indulge in it.

He was starting to drop by our place more often during the days since he worked the swing shift, and at nights on some of his days off, if I wasn't there when he showed up he knew I'd be down at the liquor store and would go there.

There was a cute Mexican woman who worked there at night, both Chance and I had developed good relations with her and she'd give us credit there.

One night on Chances off day he came to our studio looking for me, I wasn't there so he drove down to the liquor store where he knew I'd be, when chance entered the store he and Pam hugged and kissed each other.

Pam knew us both individually, but not as being brothers, so when he went on to say that he'd stopped by my studio, Pam looked puzzled and ask if we knew each other, at the same time we replied, "were brothers."

Her lips dropped as she told Chance, "your brother and I talk and socialize almost every night, it's co-incidental that you two are brothers."

In another revelation all at the same time my lips dropped when Chance said, "yeah bro Pam and I are involved with each other," and at that statement we all laughed at the untimely co-incidence of the whole thing, but silently I thought to myself that this arrangement could become an ace in the whole for me.

The two of us hopped into his BMW and went back to my place, Pam had given us both an abundance of alcohol, Kat was in there smoking on some rock with her uncle.

Her uncle's girl had been arrested earlier that day for petty theft, they were both finishing up what little bit of rock that was left, and neither of them had any money to buy more.

Chance feeling kind of good with all of the alcohol that Pam had given him stated, "I wouldn't mind smoking a little bit of rock himself."

She had given him two fifths of Smirnoff's gin, four bottles of 40 ounce Old English 800, two fifths of Christian Bros brandy, and several packs of cigarettes.

I knew we could take half of the alcohol to any of the young dealers in the Oak Park area and trade it for some rock cocaine.

I nudged Chance and ask him to take me to Oak Park, we made the trip and came back with a twenty dollar dub rock, but it didn't go far with all the mouths that was there, so when it was gone Chance left to go home.

Kat went out on the Broadway strip to sell some sex, while her uncle and I just lounged around the studio waiting for her to return.

A change of venue was in order in that dwelling, because I was growing sicker of the arrangement there by the day, the place wasn't designed for it.

The first of June came and along with it more chaos, the phone had been put in my name, and her uncles girl was running the bill up calling constantly, they said they would pay the phone bill, but you know how promises go.

Around mid June Kat threw me out because she'd seen me walking down Broadway with another woman, so I went up to the store and hung out with T-dog.

At 2:00a.m. when the store closed T dog let me crash at his place.

His apartment was trashed and empty of furniture, he hadn't paid his rent in two months and was being evicted, it would be any time now that he'd too be on the streets.

The next afternoon, Kat knowing where I hung out at came looking for me, she found me at the liquor store and told me, "please come back home."

Reluctantly I walked back to her studio with her, when I entered the place there was a full entertainment center along one wall, complete with a 19 inch remote color T.V. set, a dual cassette recorder with speakers, and a V.C.R.

Earlier that morning she'd called a Renta center and had them deliver the whole system that she'd previously ordered from them.

Coming back to an entertainment center somewhat eased my frustration that had been slowly mounting, due to her domineering personality.

Back to my main issue though, it seemed that Black Americans had become such a profound consumer of the rock cocaine until it was almost impossible to escape from it's clutch.

In the small 10 unit apartment complex our neighbor Tone, whom was a working man, had often sent either myself or Kat to pick up rock for him.

He, in turn would either smoke with us or chip off a piece for the both of us.

Aside from my own sources from which to obtain rock, the prospect of rock outside of my own realm was abundant, and it added to the growing increment of my consumption of rock cocaine, thus rendering me susceptible to the unknown circumstances of the rock cocaine trafficking scene.

After a few days of harmony in our household, the shit hit the fan again, this time she threw my clothing and tot bags over the balcony and unto the ground, this time I quietly gathered up my things and left her place for good.

I went to T dogs, that next day Kat's uncle saw me at the liquor store and his exact words were, "Kat's parole officer came by her studio to let her know that she had given him a dirty test, and warned her not to get another one."

Kat had become distraught over our breakup, and had started going overboard with her usage of the rock cocaine.

A week later I went by her studio to see how she was doing, she had sold the entertainment center to a rock dealer, and was hiding out from her P.O.

A couple of weeks later her uncle told me, "hey Siege her P.O. and another female officer came by the studio and caught Kat there smoking rock, and arrested her on the spot."

I found out later that Kat was given a year violation and returned to California's Rehab center for women.

Back at T dogs place, he suggested that I apply for S.S.I., it didn't seem like a bad idea considering how my life had become out of control with rock cocaine, and alcohol.

The next day T dog took me to the Social Security Office and I started filling out the paper work, having been to prison would strengthen my chances of getting approved.

A CALL TO RESOLVE

Being around T dog certainly meant getting drunk and smoking rock everyday, because our daily agenda was hanging out at the liquor store.

It was fun though because we met a lot of different people, but that too soon got old.

One day a white man came into the store, he wasn't a regular patron there, just a pass through, he and T dog had joked with each other before, on this day though he was looking for T dog to put him to work.

The man was the sole owner of a boat shop off of Garden Highway near the Sacramento river, he sold, detailed, and did maintenance work on boats, and was in need of someone to buff some speed boats for him.

It was the beginning of Summer, so that type of work was plentiful, T dog wasn't around that day, so after talking with me briefly he ask, "hey young man would you like to go to work for the rest of the day?"

"Heaven yes, lets do it, I need the money", we hopped into in Honda Civic and headed for his shop, it was 1:00 p.m. at that time.

The man introduced himself, "I'm Bob," going on to say, "I'll pay you fourty dollars to work from 1:00p.m. to 5:00 p.m., and if I like your work I'll keep you on permanently, starting you out at 7 dollars an hour."

I washed and waxed a metal flake speed boat, I finished just before 5:00 p.m..

When the owner arrived to pick it up, he was very impressed with the job that I had done and told Bob as much, the owner thanked me personally and tipped me 10 dollars as he was loading his boat unto the trailer.

Bob liked my workmanship, and also gave me an extra 10 dollars along with the thirty, "so what do you think about signing on permanently with all of the benefits?", he asked.

I was gratified that employment had happened my way, but became reluctant to take the job because I had earlier filed for S.S.I., "can I give you that answer in the morning?", I replied.

"Sure, just be sure that this is something you'd like doing, because our outfit travels around the Country, and you'd be on the go."

I had mixed feelings about all of this, plus I had no way of getting out to the work site because no buses went that way, and I mentioned this to him, he replied, "I can pick you up everyday at the liquor store."

We agreed that he would pick me up at 7:30a.m. every morning through the week, that night I went on a rock smoking binge that went into the early morning hours, and so I wasn't able to meet Bob that morning.

That afternoon as usual Bob came to the liquor store to see what had happened, I gave him a sad story, he bought it and said, "O.K. Ill see you tomorrow morning."

I really didn't want to nullify my chance at getting approved for S.S.I., and wasn't eager to go to work anyway, that of course was the rock cocaine induced mentality talking to me telling me to take the easy way out.

The next morning came again, and due to my having drank a lot of Vodka and smoking rock I missed Bob again, and that day he didn't come back into the store at noon.

The following day he came by the store at noon and pulled me to the side saying, "listen your a very good worker, and I don't know what's getting you caught up where you can't go to work for me, but when your ready, seriously ready to work, let me know."

We shook hands, he talked to the store owner a brief minute and then left.

I had let rock cocaine and the comfort of an easy way out of living off of the hope of receiving S.S.I. in the future deprive me of a chance at prosperity.

After I'd worked for Bob that one day, and before the owner of that boat I'd buffed showed up, Bob sat down with me and laid out what the job entailed.

Which was attending boat shows with all expenses paid, traveling around the Country with him and other employee's doing work and/ or appraising boats, and doing boat repairs, all of which would be a very exciting career, reflecting back, I was stupid as hell for passing that opportunity up.

The combination of heavy drinking and the smoking of rock cocaine that I had embarked upon with T dog had played a big role in my lack of enthusiasm for making a better life for myself, and in turn passing up the offer that Bob had presented to me.

This was the typical response of most rock cocaine addicts to the prospect of making a better life for themselves, and afterwards I kicked myself in the ass over, and over for blowing that possibility for myself.

Later that day, still sulking over my lose, T dog and I panhandled enough money between us to go and get a quarter of an ounce of rock cocaine.

I was still catering to the substance that was little by little continuing to destroy me, now, I'd made room for it to make decisions for me as well.

Chance my brother was also backsliding, he'd went by the studio looking for me, learning of the breakup between Kat and I, he drove down to the liquor store where he found me.

He explained to me that he'd been up all night and morning smoking rock and drinking alcohol and hadn't even reported in to work the day before.

He ask, "hey bro can you drive me around so that we could talk about what I should do, I'm tired and just wanted to sit back with open ears and get some good advice from my older brother whom has already been down that road."

I got behind the wheel of the beamer(BMW) and begin putting things as best I could into the proper prospective for him on what he should now do.

We drove around town for several hours before returning to T dogs place.

Chance left and went to his own place to catch up on his R&R, and to get the story he was going to give to his boss down packed before he went back to work.

As the days passed T dog was converting his vacant apartment into a place where rock could be smoked at all times, women were in and out around the clock, getting tossed up behind their need to get that rock high.

If I wasn't bringing a female by there, T dog was, there was just about around the clock kinkiness going on there.

Aside from our own rock cocaine induced libido, woman would come by willing to have a good time with us, as if they too were geared sexually for the good times.

But then most of those females were into it so that they could not only get high, but also have a place to lay their heads for the night when all was done.

Chance came back by a week later saying that the situation with his job played out smoothly and that things were back to normal, he was in his uniform and it looked good on him.

He drank a beer and left, he knew now where I would be if he needed me for anything, the only problem I foresaw with him coming by T dogs now was that, his being separated from his wife, and seeing all the women in and out of T dogs place could be a temptation to great for him to resist.

With that activity going on at T dogs vacant spot, my smoking of the rock got worse, as did my state of mind when I smoked; I soon started experiencing feelings of paranoia that led me to suspect any and everyone whom would appear at the spot.

It always seemed to surface whenever I would begin smoking the rock.

Always suspicious that something, or someone was out to get me was the state of mind I'd be in after taking a hit of the rock, it was almost to the point where I was delirious.

My state of deliriousness at one time caused me to retract from an act of sex I was about to engage in with a female after she'd gotten undressed.

I was partially clothed and continuing to undress, soon after taking a hit of the rock I became paranoid, hurriedly dressed myself and ran out of the room leaving the girl nude and befuddled.

Standing outside T dogs place scoping the area for would be assailants, or the police for nearly an hour, I went back inside claiming that I didn't feel right, perhaps it was my conscious of what I had been doing with all those different women that wasn't right.

This anomaly of paranoia that was starting to surface when I smoked rock, I couldn't differentiate it from being either the ill effects of long term rock smoking, the ingredients of the fabricated rock that was now coming unto the streets, or nerve damage caused from excessive smoking of rock over the years.

Something was beginning to take it's toll on me though, and it was causing me to act unusually abnormal whenever I took a hit on some rock cocaine.

My sister Holly, I was told by my mother when I phoned home had been arrested downtown for 0.03 grams of rock and was in jail for possession.

The next day I went to visit her at the jailhouse, she'd been in custody for almost a week, she told me that the district attorney had offered her a deal of 6 months in prison, but that she was going to fight it because of the amount it was, plus she'd never been in prison before, and I told her to follow her first mind.

The racial discrimination and injustices that are practiced within the law enforcement, and court systems in California had to be a travesty for them to want to spend tax payers dollars to send Holly to prison on a first time possession charge of 0.03 grams.

I told her not to worry, not to take any deals, but to just ride it out for a little while and everything would work itself out for the better in the end.

While visiting Holly she gave me some shocking news on a couple of my long time acquaintances whom had suffered drastic consequences as a result of the rock cocaine syndrome, one was fatal.

Both were middle school friends from good family backgrounds, both nice looking guys, and both, in their latter adult years had become successful panderers, however, eventually fell prey to the rock cocaine epidemic.

The first, D.W was found dead on the top of one of the skyscrapers in downtown Las Vegas from an overdose of rock cocaine, laying at his side was drug paraphernalia and a large quantity of rock cocaine.

When Holly told me the story I suspected fowl play immediately, it appeared more of a hit job, I knew D.W well and that was out of character for him, the police probably set that up because he was pandering his girls up there and was making big money, so they took him out.

The other acquaintance was T.R., also a top notch panderer, the best at his game, he was transporting a key load of cocaine up through Canada, was caught and sentenced to ninety two years in the Canadian prison system.

Both of these two fellows executed finesse and smoothness to their games, traveling around the Country right after high school with a half dozen or so women, doing what they did best, pimping.

Nevertheless, and regardless of their profession, they were decent dudes though, and it was an unfortunate demise that befell both of them.

After the hearing of that news, I just shook my head and sat pondering on the future of Black Americans addicted to this nefarious substance rock cocaine, and how many other tens of thousands of Blacks either had, or would meet terrible ends similar to the two just mentioned.

I stayed the whole hour of visit time talking to Holly, telling her it would work itself out, all the while conveying to her that the power structure in America was attempting to recreate a modern day slavery, primarily of the Black people, but that this time there would be other poor minorities in the midst, and the means by which they're accomplishing this is through rock cocaine.

I told her, "sis you'd better get wise to their scheme of things and let this period of incarceration be a lesson for you".

I wasn't in the habit yet of practicing what I preached, but at that point I felt compelled to forewarn my sister, and as many Blacks as possible of the systems wrath, and full pledged machination to divest Black Americans.

I left the jail, Back at T dogs place it was like Graham central station, there were rock smokers inside, and out in front of the complex, some were looking to score, but were either short of money, or didn't know who had rock for sale.

I immediately responded to their distress by collecting all of their money and making a run to my source to purchase the rock, some were hesitant to give up their money, but after learning that I was the man of the house they kicked in.

This would become a new market for me in between my own pay periods from General assistance, or hustling; I called it hustling the smokers.

In effect, I was the middle man and would always make the buys, and would come out ahead with the excess of rock cocaine without even contributing any funds of my own.

Aside from that hustle, I could at almost any time go by the liquor store and get alcohol from Pam for free which I could trade for rock.

In essence, this just caused me to slip deeper into the devil's grip of me, which would led me back into the mode of hard core rock smoking.

I was not only destitute behind smoking rock, but was finding it hard to shake that feeling of paranoia when I did smoke.

I was becoming decadent, the rock was debilitating me but I still found it hard to break free of it's clutch.

Something would have to intervene soon and save me, it would have to be through the love, grace, and will of the lord our GOD to avert this vicious cycle of doom.

Weeks passed, my itinerary remained the same, drinking alcohol, smoking rock, and hanging out at the liquor store.

It was mid August, summer would be over soon, T dogs apartment manager had finally got a sheriffs order to remove him from the property and to lock up the apartment a week following the order.

T dog and I were now on the streets and we continually hung out at the store, each going our own way in the early morning hours, I took to finding unlocked apartment wash house rooms to sleep in.

One afternoon while at the store, a young white alcoholic transient showed up on the scene, he was broke and wanted a drink, "hey brother I can boost any kind of cassette music from Tower records, but I don't know who to sell them to once I get them."

I had my thoughts on smoking some rock so I went along with him giving him a list of some rap tapes to get.

"Listen dude if you can get me 5 of various rap cassettes, I'll buy you a pint of Vodka."

"Lets get going then brother", and we headed off towards Tower records.

I could get the Vodka from Pam at the liquor store, and I would take the cassettes to one of the rock dealers on 27th street across from the halfway house to get the rock.

I went into Tower records with the dude and picked out 5 cassettes, and stupidly stayed in there with him while he began stashing them on himself.

We both headed towards the exit door, passing through the upright security detectors, the alarm went off and the cashiers snatched him before he could leave.

5 minutes later I walked up to the white boy and the security like a fool, and I too was snatched and detained and we were both taken to the back of the store to await the police.

The store clerks alleged that I was the main conspirator of the theft plot,

when the police came the clerks gave their story of my being the mind behind the plot, the white dude was charged with petty theft, and I was charged with conspiracy to commit theft and was taken to jail.

Back in the jail system once again, the D.A. came to me with a 6 month County time lid, although I hadn't stole a thing, I reluctantly took the deal.

I could have fought it and maybe even won, but not having any place to lay my head at the time, maybe a break from the destructive life I was living was in order, my P.O. didn't violate me since it was a misdemeanor, so I'd just have 4 months to do on 6.

Once again I was seeing, and reflected on just how racial and unjust the power structure is when it comes to incriminating Blacks and other minorities as opposed the whites.

The white boy I'd found out, whom was already on probation for previous thefts was sentenced to two months in jail, whereas I received 6 months.

Two months into my sentence my brother Chance was arrested for a D.U.I.(driving under the influence), where he was involved in an accident in which no one was injured, but he'd totaled out his BMW.

I would wait to hear from him before I passed judgment as to how it actually happened, but for some reason the pieces of this puzzle didn't fit right from what I was told from my mother when I called and talked to her.

Holly was fighting her case and was still behind bars, and now both Chance, and I were as well.

Chance ended up taking a year lid deal in the County jail and was transferred to Rio Consumnes correctional center, an extended branch of the main jail which is out in Elk Grove, Ca., which was where I was at.

When we were united at the branch jail, Chance began explaining to me how it all happened, "bro I had been smoking rock and had picked up a cute toss up so I could enjoy some female company."

"It was at 2:00 a.m. when the accident occurred, I was coming upon the Stockton, and Fruitridge intersection, the female had put the rock pipe to her mouth and was lighting it with a lighter."

Stockton blvd is one of the many locations for prostitution in Sacramento, as it is also highly traveled by both the police, and sheriff units because it's where city, and county boarders cross each other.

"When I saw her lighting up the pipe like that, I took my eyes off the road and tried stopping her activity, and without seeing that the green light had changed yellow on me, I kept going into the cross lanes of traffic."

"The light had turned green for the cross traffic, and before I knew it I'd made contact with an oncoming vehicle, that upon impact demolished my whole front grill and left quarter panel."

"When the police arrived on the scene, I'd already disposed of any remaining rock cocaine, and paraphernalia, but I'd had an open container of alcohol, and some cups that were tossed all around the interior of the car causing it to reek of alcohol."

I responded by saying, "Wow my little bro, I knew it would come out better hearing it from you, because Mother made it sound slightly different, but nevertheless, you went bad with this incident, chalk it up as a lesson, and move on."

As a result of the accident and his incarceration Chance destroyed an expensive automobile, and quite possibly his employment with Methodist Hospital, that, he would find out when he was released from jail.

Now there were 3 family members in jail either directly or indirectly behind rock cocaine.

"Your learning some of the many perils that's associated with this wicked rock cocaine," I chided.

Finalizing my admonishment to him I closed by saying, "rock is a tool of the devils that the white man is utilizing to disrupt, and destroy Black people's lives."

His face and arms had healing scars from the accident, other than that he had a lot to be thankful to GOD for in coming out of that accident alive and in one piece.

I finished out my time without incident, and was released on December 23, 1994, the 4 months I'd served in the Sacramento County jail brought me back to the reality that every imprisonment of mine was due to rock cocaine.

I was now ready again to try and relinquish the hold that rock had on me.

I would pick up my G.A. check for the month of September which had come to a friends address I was using for that purpose, and get a room for a couple of weeks.

I would still go forward with getting the S.S.I., yet I would try to work odd jobs to sustain myself until the S.S.I. was approved.

I picked my check up, but had problems cashing it at the cashing outlets, simply because it was almost 6 months old, I was told by all outlets that a bank would have to cash it.

It was 5:30 p.m., Friday, I had a friend drive me to the Bank of America on Stockton blvd, making it there at 5:50p.m. I was able to cash it.

Ironically, I was looking at the intersection where Chance had totaled out his BMW.

On this corner of Fruitridge and Stockton blvd there is an Arco a.m./ p.m. mini mart, walking up to that store after cashing my check a young Black female pulled up to the gas pumps in a Datson 280 ZX.

Having been away from society for several months and away from the opposite sex, she was a beautiful sight for my eyes to behold; when she stepped out of her car her body was even more enticing.

She was jet Black, and lovely, with Barbie doll features, as she walked up to the store I joined her, and stated, "I'd love to pump your gas for you young lady."

"You sure can good looking, and thank you for wanting to," was her reply.

I bought some beer and cigarettes, and handed her a five to put with her two dollars.

While I pumped the gas she introduced herself, "by the way, I'm Betta, what do they call you?"

"They call me Siege," I retorted, looking at her I could tell she wasn't a naïve woman, and had been around as I noticed the way she asserted herself in our conversation.

I finished pumping the gas and ask, "what's your plans for the evening?" "Just out driving around, nothing in particular planed."

"Mind if I join you on your ride this evening?" I ask.

"No, your very welcome to join me, but before you get in my car I'm going to have to pat you down to see if you have any weapons on you that could hurt me."

From having just gotten released I was pretty muscular, and to her that could have represented violence, "go ahead and do your thing if it puts you at ease," was my words to her, and she commenced to patting me down like a cop.

I passed her test, we hopped into the car and took off, while driving around and talking, she blurted out, "I'm a single woman, and you're a very handsome man, I was hoping that you'd say something to me when I got out of the car, I'm glad that you did."

"I'm from Fresno, Ca, down here visiting my brother, but I'm going back there in a couple of days."

The subject of rock cocaine came up in our conversation, and she blurted out, "you know I smoke the stuff, and I wish I had some money with which to buy some now."

I thought to myself for a minute that this had to be the devil coming at me like this by sending a lovely Black woman into my life, and tempting me to start smoking that shit again after I'd vowed to refrain from smoking it when released this time.

The devil is a very crafty bastard, and knows everyone's weakness, he played on mine this time and led us to get two rocks and a motel room.

For the most part I stood up under my plan to back away from smoking rock, I took one hit and gave all the rest to Betta.

While smoking on that shit she went through the common motions of looking around, and becoming real quiet, the behavior one exhibits while under its influence.

It was weird to me how peoples personalities changed after taking a hit on some rock, but then, that's the devils candy and it controls it's user. After several hours of abnormal behavior from Betta, she finally came down to earth, and climbed into the bed with me.

We made sensuous love together, she whispered, "It's been a while since I've had any sex, and the sex you've just shared with me was splendid, I'd like to have you in my life Siege."

"I am trying hard to break free from this devils rock, and I would need for you to want to do the same if your serious about wanting to be with me."

We awoke the next morning to see a middle aged Black woman standing outside in the motel parking lot with four young children ranging in age from two to seven, the woman, as well as the kids were all dressed raggedly.

She approached, "could you people please give some money so we could buy some food with?", I motioned to go into my pocket to produce some bills for the lady, but Betta stopped me saying, "all she's going to do is spend that money on a hit of rock, the kids won't get no food from it."

It turned out that Betta knew the lady, and that her predicament was brought about due to her addiction to the rock cocaine.

She also knew that the woman had been evicted because she'd smoked up the rent money, and this day was their last day in the motel, so they were all homeless now.

Betta had a step brother who lived a few blocks away up Stockton blvd in a residential area with his wife, feeling sorry for the woman and kids she offered to take them to his house where they all could clean themselves up.

Her Datson 280 ZX was small so she took the woman and kids there while I waited for her to return.

After they pulled away I became indignant and displeased at how un Godly and vicious this rock cocaine was, at how it led one to totally disregard their responsibilities, even further, of how it caused one to do the things that they do while under the influence of the substance.

Betta came back, picked me up, and we went back over to her step brothers house, his one bedroom apartment was small and I saw right off that it was a flop house.

He introduced himself as Ken, there was a younger guy laying around with his white girlfriend, the woman and kids were sitting on the floor in the kitchen eating scrambled eggs and toast with a glass of milk.

There were 40 ounce bottles of every kind of beer laying around, as time lapsed I learned that everyone in that house drank alcohol and smoked rock.

The white girl was a prostitute, and would go out every night to make money for the nights rock and liquor to appease her nice looking young Black pimp.

They gave Ken money here and there, in addition to getting him high on the rock they'd bring back so they'd have a place to crash at.

The woman whom Betta had brought there with her kids was discussing with Ken the possibility of her and the kids staying there until the New Year, promising him that she would pay him when she got her Welfare check, and he gave his OK on that.

I later found out that Betta was also staying there on and off, and in between staying with other relatives in the Sacramento area.

She was now claiming me as her man and said that I'd be staying with her wherever she stayed.

For the rest of the month of December every night that we were there, rock was smoked, and alcohol was consumed, me, still sticking to my pledge would take one hit and back away.

The living conditions were cramped, plus different people were in and out all throughout the day and night.

Ken's wife worked for a convalescent hospital so she was gone during the day, the activity during that time was rampant, when she returned home at six in the evening most of the traffic had dispersed.

His wife smoked rock, but only with him, and very infrequently, she didn't take well to all of the extra company hanging around, and everyone knew it because that was the basis of hers and Ken's every argument.

At times his place was so congested that Betta and I had to sleep huddled on the sofa together, this was not only very uncomfortable, but it didn't leave much in the way of privacy for us from the unknown strangers coming and going.

The first of January finally came, the woman cashed her check, paid Ken his due money, bought her kids a few pieces of clothing, stacked up Ken's refrigerator with food from her food stamps, and went straight to the rock man to make a purchase.

As a result of the woman's mismanagement of her funds she would later not be able to move from Ken's place.

Ken and his wife were comfortable with her giving them the extra money and food stamps, so she ask for an extended month of being there.

That's exactly how it turned out, the woman ended up smoking all the rest of her money up on rock with Ken and his associates.

Betta called her brother and ask if her and I could stay at his place for a little while and she'd pay some of his rent out of her S.S.I. check, he gave his OK, so we left Ken's place and headed out to her brothers house.

His place was a fairly nice and roomy one, he was a family man with a wife and 4 boys, he didn't use the rock, had been down that road before and had long since quit, but he did drink beer, it was a relief being there.

I kept a tight reign on Betta, going with her wherever she went, not letting her have time to slip away and smoke on the rock.

After learning that the child protective agency had taken away her 4 children from her in Fresno, Ca for neglect, it had become a mission for me to help her and myself in staying off the rock.

After that phase, I'd planned to get her into some kind of a rehabilitation program so she'd have documentation of her completing the program which was required to assure the return of her children to her.

She drank alcohol while she drove her vehicle, and on one occasion she was pulled over by the police, she didn't have a California driving license, so the officer cited her for driving under the influence and told her to leave the car parked where it was.

My license had been suspended earlier when I had wrecked Jamie's vehicle after getting out of prison, so I couldn't drive the vehicle either.

She waited an hour or so, went back to her ZX, got in and snuck it away.

I was doing a swell job of keeping her away from the rock, I felt that she really wanted to quit using it as well, however, once a week we'd buy a rock, smoke it and wouldn't buy anymore.

The first week of February at 12:00 a.m., a block from Ken's apartment, which Betta and I were en route to, a C.H.P. officer stopped her, claiming his reason for the stop was due to her back taillights being out.

The officers found an open container of alcohol in the back seat, they checked our I.D.'s, finding me to be on parole, and her having just been cited last month for a D.U.I.

The C.H.P. officer called a towing agency to come out to the location to tow away the car, handcuffed and arrested her, put the cuffs on me, but later removed them and let me go.

The next day, by her not having a criminal record she was released on her own recognizance.

She didn't have the money at the time to retrieve her car from the tow yard, and as each day passed the cost went up, so she would lose the car to the tow yard.

Together, we both decided it would be more convenient to be located closer to town, her brother Randy lived 20 miles out in the town of Elk Grove, Ca, so we both checked into the Salvation Army shelter for couples.

In mid February when she was to appear in court on her citations she purposely did not go, I urged her to, but she was adamant about not going.

One evening as we strolled down the K street mall together, a bicycle cop rolled up on us and ask both of us for our Id's, his reason, a fictitious one, at best, was that we fit the description of a pair selling rock cocaine on the mall.

Young Black gang bangers, and young Black couples had in fact taken over the mall selling their rock cocaine 7 days a week, however, we didn't fit that category and the cop knew it, this was just plain police profiling, and harassment.

He ran checks on us both, a warrant showed up for Betta and the cop called a unit to come and pick her up, I had warned her about this but she was defiant.

I went to her court date, the judge sentenced her to sixty days in the County branch jail, I visited her twice a week in the main jail downtown until she was transferred to the branch to finish out her time, after the transfer we corresponded through mail.

I needed to get back on General Assistance again, but needed someone's address I could use saying that I was renting a room from them.

Not having much else to do I went to the Biltmore hotel on 17th and J streets, I was now back in the location of Compton's market which was two blocks down the way.

The Biltmore was inhabited mostly by S.S.I. recipients, also a haven for drug addicts, drug dealers, and prostitutes.

I went inside and was immediately ask by a lame looking White dude, "hey man you have any roc for sale," I replied, "no, but I can get you some up the street," "lets go for it," he suggested.

We walked down to Compton's market, I got the dudes money from him and found a youngster that I scored the rock from.

"Dave's my name," he invited me in to his place, "would you like to smoke on this with me?"

"Yeah why not", while getting high the idea of using his place as an address came to me and I ask, "say Dave would it be alright if I used your address as a place to receive my mail at"?

"Yeah that would be cool with me."

Dave was kind of timid, people came to his room to smoke rock and crash out, he reminded me of another Auto, only he wasn't a paraplegia, he was a rock star, which was why people came by and used him as they did.

The hotel was owned and operated by a slumlord, a few weeks ago, a roughneck Black girl had kicked Dave's door off the hinges, and splintered the door frame, and the owner still hadn't repaired it yet.

Dave was like a loner, there was nothing of value in his room and it was filthy, I had to reposition the rooms door as I left.

I saw an opportunity to gain favor with Dave by acting as a rock dealer, this would eliminate all of his undesirable, and intrusive company, I could then sleep there periodically and cater to his needs all at the same time.

I presented my idea to him, and he went for it, one by one I stopped all of the traffic, unless he gave the OK on someone, and I in effect had secured a place to lay my head.

The next day I went to the welfare office to activate my G.A., walking back to Dave's room I was pulled over by a Jimmy Durante looking white man driving an old Toyota Corolla.

The man flagged me to approach his car window and ask, "do you know where I could buy a gram of rock cocaine at?", "you can smoke it with if you'd like to", my alarm antenna went up with that invitation.

Something seemed peculiar about this character, right off I couldn't discern that he was gay, he almost pleaded with me to take him to score some rock.

Once inside the car though it all came to light, he complemented me on my masculinity, and good looks, saying, "I just got a pretty big settlement, I have eight hundred dollars on me to splurge with someone."

He was forthright and un-inhibited with his desires, saying, "I like the way you look, and want to suck on your phallic, and then be sodomized afterwards."

DECADENCE AT IT'S BEST

What a weird one he was I thought to myself, but then my mind saw dollar signs, and I began masterminding my scheme to get some of his money.

I said to him, "your request is going to cost you dearly, because 1rst, I'm neither gay, nor by-sexual, secondly, I don't know you personally, if I was that way."

"The money is no problem, I'd like to spend a lot of it on you", he replied with femininity, I and I knew that I had him them.

We went to a rock house downtown, I came right out with it, "for starters lets get an ounce which cost 5 hundred dollars," he forked over the money to me.

I bought 2 hundred dollars worth of rock and kept the other 3 hundred, when I got back into his car I showed him the rock, he was satisfied with it, so I gave it all to him.

"Can we go to my motel room located downtown?", he asked while taking a hit of the rock, I went along with his proposal.

In his room I would implement phase two of my plan, "can I please suck on your dick?", was his next question, cunningly I pulled it out and his eyes lit in anticipation.

But before he was able to seize it I put it back into my pants, he looked disappointed at this, I baited him in a little more by saying, "I'll sodomize you all morning long, but this ounce isn't going to be near enough, we'll need another one."

I lied, and said, "my drug connection is leaving soon and that before I do anything more with you, I want to go back and get the other ounce before the connect leaves his place for the night."

The trick man was hungry for a big Black dick in his mouth, and ass, so he hopped right up, went in his wallet and pulled out 5 more hundred dollar bills and gave them to me.

I repeated the process at the rock house, I now had 6 hundred dollars to myself, the trick was again satisfied with the quantity I came back with, now I would put my last phase of the plan into action.

I mentioned to the trick that I had a wife whom smoked rock, and that in order for her to allow me to stay gone all morning, I'd have to give her enough rock to sustain her while I'm away.

I had the trick take me to the projects off of Broadway, and told him to give me half of the second package of rock so I could give it to her, he did, I got out, said wait till I come back, I stood off out of sight and watched him for about ten minutes.

I then returned to him with a story that my wife had been jumped by a gang member and that I couldn't leave her like that, but that after I saw to her needs I would come by his room in a few hours.

His mouth hung open, he was speechless, I patted him on his head and said good things come to those who wait and I left his presence, never ever planning on seeing him again.

I had manipulated the trick without creating any kind of animosity, now I could get a package and start doing a little selling around Dave's place myself.

I caught the Regional transit bus line back to the Biltmore hotel, Dave was inside cleaning the residue out of his rock pipe, I threw him a fat rock, his eyes lit up like sparking diamonds.

I didn't relish the idea of doing that trick the way I had, because I do believe in the Karma theory, but being able to capitalize on an opportunity presenting itself to you, and without applying any physical force, I had to act it out.

I was once again caught back up and into the rock trafficking dilemma, Dave sat back and smoked his rock contently, I left him to enjoy his rock and went to spend three hundred of the money on some more rock so I could have a decent supply with which to sell.

Returning back an hour later there were several customers waiting outside of Dave's building to buy some rock, I started selling and by midnight I'd made two hundred dollars.

Stray females came by Dave's room, some of which I traded rock for sex, this would become an endeavor I'd play out every time a sexy, and cute female showed up.

The rest of the month of February I satisfied my sexual libido in abundance, there always seemed to be a lovely lady lurking around somewhere in the building.

My own habit of smoking rock later began to resume it's normal course, and I soon just started breaking even on my purchases of packages, profits were no more.

When Dave received his S.S.I. check, I, through finesse and cunning connived him out of two hundred dollars, with that and my G.A. check I could bring myself back up to paar.

But first I wanted to improve my appearance, so I bought some new attire, a pair of grey 501 jeans, a knit sweater and a pair of penny loafers, the remaining 3 hundred dollars all went towards the purchase of a cocaine package.

Later I reneged on my promise to give Dave half of the rock I'd bought, and instead gave him a few rocks, assuring him that I would cater to him as he needed more.

Rock was influencing my personality causing me to make rash decisions when dealing with individuals whom had my best interest in mind, I was letting the rock dictate my lifestyle all over again, and it would cost me later.

It was the first week in March, there was money to be made, I sought out to get it, the first spot on my agenda was the C street park.

En route to the park, walking on 16th and I streets I came upon two Black men in the middle of that main through fare street, 16th, both wielding knives, and both trying desperately to slice the other to death.

The two had the traffic backed up for two blocks on that main street, viewing the scene while standing there watching and listening, I overheard one telling the other, "motherfucker you ran off with the twenty dollars that I gave to you to buy some rock with, now I'm going to cut you every way but loose".

The other replied, "bring it on sucker, cause I'm not giving back that money, lets do this, either your going to kill me or I'm going to kill you", and all the while slicing at one another while they dialogued back and fourth.

As sirens drew nearer to the scene I thought it best that I continue on about my business since I was carrying so much rock on my person, walking on, I dismissed the incident as another fallible disruption between Blacks caused by the rock cocaine.

The rock was culpable in most all disharmony created among Blacks, and it certainly was fast becoming the most detrimental of all controlled substances.

In view of what I'd been through behind the rock, and the things I saw on a daily basis as a result of rock use amongst Black people, it disturbed my heart to think of where rock cocaine was going to lead Blacks in America in the future.

C street park was ripe and ready for business, it was a 2 acre block park, every section of the grass area was clustered with people sitting around with some type of an alcoholic beverage before them.

Making my way through the people and stating to them that I had fat ones(rock), I sold 4 of them, I even made small sells with the loose crumbs, and smaller rocks.

At the north end of the park there was levy, one has to walk upgrade to reach the top, Southern Pacific railroad tracks run along the levy where Amtrak trains runs the course several times a day.

Adjacent to the tracks is an old abandoned steal mill yard, and acres of dirt hills and gravel that lead to the rear of the Salvation Army.

On the bottom side of that levy across the street from the park are warehouses for a trucking company, transient drug addicts, and alcoholics sit along side the building and drink or get high smoking on the rock.

Upon the levy people sit on a concrete wall viewing the length of 15ᵗʰ street keeping an eye out for the police, elevation of that wall is twenty feet above ground level, so the view of everything, even Sacramento's skyline is accessible.

I made my way up there and sold 6 more rocks, walking along the levy next to the concrete wall I heard a pssst psssst, I looked down by the warehouse building and saw a young Black pregnant girl, and two Black dudes flagging me to come down there.

One of the dudes wanted to buy a ten dollar piece of rock, the other dude and the girl were on the side of a trash bin, as I moved closer I saw that the girl was giving him some head.

I sold the ten piece, and ask the girl, "how many months pregnant are you", she replied "eight", I then ask, "do you know that your infant baby is smoking rock right along with you" she answered, "I've only been smoking a few months."

I then ask, "why are you belittling yourself by sucking a dudes dick in public", she became silent, I told the Black dudes, "you cats are in violation on two accounts by committing this act," making them both feel stupid and small.

I coaxed her into accompanying me by saying, "hey young lady I'll give you a piece of rock cocaine," and told the guys, get yourselves an un-pregnant toss-up to degrade, I have something better in mind for this young Black woman."

She amicably moved close to me, leaving the dudes looking disgraced, as they walked away I told her, "I rescued you from the ungodly wrath of the devils rock."

And although I wasn't pragmatic of giving drugs to pregnant woman, I would make it worth her time if she carried my product, the rock, on her while I was doing my business of selling.

I bought her something to eat, afterwards, we went downtown to the K street mall to try selling off some of the rock I had left.

She was feeling good in the company of me, and after a couple of sales I had made, she joined in and took to selling the rock as if it was her own, giving me the money after every sell.

It was 3:00p.m. when I'd rescued her, it was now 9:00 p.m., I'd made 400 dollars, with 3 rocks left to sell, it had been a good days work.

"Where are you staying," I asked, "I'm homeless" she exclaimed.

I went to the Biltmore, and instead of going to Dave's room, I got a room for us for the night.

I gave her 10 dollars and one of the rocks, and explained to her that I was against pregnant woman using drugs, especially the rock, but that if I'd have given her twenty dollars and sent her on her way, she'd have bought rock with the money anyway, so why not just do it this way, "thank you for rescuing and caring for me", she responded.

She hugged and kissed me, "I've never before in life been treated this way by any guy whom acted like he cared for me," she stated, then ask, "can I be your girl?"

"I have a woman whom is in jail, and she'll be out soon," I went on saying, "you need to respect yourself more because your a pretty girl, and you also need to take on the responsibility of motherhood for your unborn child".

As the nightfall progressed, laying around the room together she offered me some sex as a gesture of gratitude for the way I cared for her, I refused it.

Apparently she was used to men abusing her, which was pathetic, I offered her compassion, hoping to introduce her to the up side of a relationship.

She awoke early that morning saying, "I have an appointment to be at with the County welfare office at 8:00 a.m. to pick up my A.F.D.C.(aid for dependant children) check.

As she was leaving, I said to myself that I'd never see her again, "good by young lady, and take care of yourself and that baby," I told her as she left.

Later, some three weeks later, I was told by someone when I inquired of her whereabouts that she had had a baby girl and was seen up and around the C street park with her infant, smoking rock.

Having been down that road from a man's perspective of it, and still fiddling with it here and there, I knew how hard it was to break that cycle, I had to just shake my head to the decadence that was taking hold of Black men and women who smoke rock cocaine.

Back at Dave's now and having been in several disputes with him regarding how much he'd been given back from the money he'd given to me to buy a package with, I had to keep feeding his habit.

I'd probably not totally given back to him what he'd invested, but assured him that his return from me would soon be balanced out after my next purchase of a package.

I would constantly give him pieces of rock here and there to keep him quiet, but it would never be enough to satisfy his need, realizing this, he began distancing himself from me.

I needed him more than he needed me, he had the roof, but now, every time I wanted to ravish a toss-up, or rest my head, he would hold out his hand for his due rock.

It had now become a due onto others as they due onto you sort of attitude that Dave was acting out, and I understood and respected that, and when either one of those needs presented themselves, I had to pay the piper so to speak.

It went on like this between Dave and I up until Betta was released in mid April, she got out and came looking for me, we kept missing each other by minutes in traffic though.

People would tell me Betta was at Sally's waiting for me to show up, I would show up minutes later, and she would have just left.

When we finally did meet up she was healthy looking, almost plump, she claimed to have been into the word of GOD while in jail and no longer wanting anything to do with rock cocaine.

I commended her on the conversion and told her that I'd started selling rock while she was away, but that I would keep it away from her since she was now out and back with me.

Betta had gotten a bus ticket to Fresno, Ca earlier that afternoon and was leaving to visit her kids for a couple of days, her bus was leaving in an hour so I went with her to the Greyhound bus station.

She spoke sincerely on wanting me to leave rock cocaine alone also, now that she had, and gave me an ultimatum of her, or the rock.

Leaving my embrace and boarding the bus her words were, "you let me know which it's going to be when I return back in a few days.

My cash flow from selling rock had dwindled drastically, mainly because of my excessive indulgence in toss ups, where, while tossing them up, I would smoke rock right along with them.

When Betta departed I'd only had three dub rocks left, and fifty dollars to my name, by midnight, I acted out another scene with a pretty toss up, and that depleted the remaining rock that I had left.

I got a room for twenty dollars, spent my remaining thirty on rock, and eventually smoked that up.

Being sprung off of the rock and discouraged by the unfolding events, I hit the streets conspiring out a plan to come across some more cash.

The Greyhound bus station had seemed easy enough hustling grounds before, it wouldn't hurt to try it again, I set out for that destination.

There's always people of all sorts hanging inside of the building, and out front of the terminals, one young lady in particular caught my eye.

She still looked the same after all those years since I'd dated her in high school.

The thought crossed my mind of what she could possibly be doing out here this late by herself, I called out to her, "Donna," she turned and came up to me.

We hugged each other briefly, I ask, "what are you doing at Greyhound of all places this late at night," "my boyfriend made me mad so I got on the Light rail system and came downtown to cool off", she replied.

Deceiving her, I said, "I just got out of jail and need some money to catch a cab to the south area," she didn't use drugs, and perhaps didn't suspect that I did either.

"How much do you need," she asked, "twenty dollars," twenty was all she had until her A.F.D.C. check came, but she offered half of it to me.

She gave me the twenty and told me to go and get change at the Royal motel next door to Greyhound where there was a snack bar and cigarette stand.

While inside the snack bar thinking of what to buy, the temptation to keep the twenty overwhelmed me and I split the scene through the side door of the building.

The scandalous behavior that comes to surface when smoking rock, I was slowly succumbing to, later that morning I sat in my room, having come down off the high of the rock I'd bought with Donna's money.

My conscience was eating at me for what I had done, though it was a little late to remedy it.

In all actuality I would sooner or later have to decide which was more important, life without the rock, or destruction and/or death with it.

Betta returned from Fresno and came to Sally's looking for me, but to no avail, I'd been told by the staff when I showed up down there a couple of days later.

I phoned Ken's place, I had a feeling she might been there, and she was, talking with her I said, "I'll be there in about an hour.

Knocking at Ken's door for nearly 5 minutes, Betta finally opened it, I knew right away that she must have slipped back into smoking rock, the signs were visible, her looking around aimlessly, strangely silent, etc.

I ask, "have you been smoking rock?", "yes," she admitted shamefully, and went on to say, "my sister in Fresno got me back into it," I immediately stated, "leave this place now," but she refused.

Then I gave her an ultimatum by saying to her, "when your ready to stand firm on your vow of staying off the rock come back to Sally's where I'll be waiting for you."

A few days passed before she showed up at Sally's, the first thing that came out of her mouth was, "I missed you and wanted to be by your side and, am ready to do the right thing with you."

The month of May was a week away, she mentioned of going back to Fresno to pick up her S.S.I. check and visit her children again, this trip she wanted me to accompany her.

She got 40 dollars from her brother to pay for our fare there and we went to the Greyhound bus station to board the Fresno bound bus leaving at 3:00 p.m.

I'd never been to Fresno, Ca, when we arrived there, the change of scenery was pleasant, the town was not quite as big as Sacramento, but it covered a lot of area.

I met her Mother and Father, and later her children at a foster home facility.

They were all cute little kids and I took a liking to them right away, she needed to really clean up her act and get them back into her life right away.

The first couple of days there went pretty smoothly, on the 3rd day she left and went to her sisters husbands to get some rock and stayed there all morning, leaving me with her parents.

When she strode in the next morning at 8:00a.m., I was upset about it and told her, "I'm leaving," "please don't do that", she begged me, which kept me there.

Everyday after that she showed her ass in some defiant manner, it was her town, I really was bent on leaving now, but was unable to for the lack of money to buy a bus ticket with; never be at the mercy of anyone.

On her check day, she bought our tickets and we headed back to Sacramento, we arrived in Sac at 5:00p.m., she wanted a place for us for a month, I had earlier told her about Dave's place and how much he paid a month at the Biltmore hotel, and suggested that we try there first.

There was a room available for two hundred dollars a month, she rented it and although it may not have been the appropriate place for us to reside, it was the only one with a reasonable monthly rental price in the area.

I went to Dave's and picked up my check from G.A. and my food stamps, and we stocked up the place with non perishable foods, everything seemed to be getting back on track with us.

However, being in a building which was a dwelling for rock smokers would be a challenge for the both of us, it would either make or break us.

My sister Holly was finally released from the County jail, the D.A. had tried to convict her, but because of her mental status as a result of the car injury, she was deemed incapable to stand trial, and was given time served with 3 years probation.

Nevertheless, the system had taken 9 months out of her life behind rock cocaine, she was now ready to turn her life around by starting out fresh of not using the rock cocaine.

When Holly and Betta would meet later, Holly immediately disliked her, her reason was that she wasn't my type, and appeared to be superficial, maybe she saw something I didn't, women can usually see through each other's exterior.

I was glad she was free though, and that small period of incarceration had turned her around.

Betta and I refrained through the first two days form using the rock by enjoying the feeling of being together in our own place, but the idle time and boredom took over causing us to fill that void with something, and that something, was the rock.

Creativeness to seek out other avenues of recreation to avert the urge to smoke rock had escaped us.

Even further, the constant temptations brought about by rock stars in, and out of the building, approaching us asking do we have a pipe, led us to buy a rock, sit back and get high together.

That just opened the door for us to feel comfortable smoking again, with the rock you can never get enough, it keeps you wanting more, that's one of the many wicked aspects of it.

Our indulgence of it gradually increased, as did the other ungrateful elements that comes with it; people coming by to use our space to smoke the rock, to use our pipe, etc.

On May 7th at 2:00 a.m., we bought a rock, I'd been drinking all day and wanted to come out of the stupor I was in from the alcohol, so I put a large piece of the rock onto the pipe and hit it.

After exhaling the smoke I became extremely paranoid and told Betta, "I need to take a walk and get some air baby, I'll be back, and left the room."

Walking down 16th street I became unsteady on my feet, almost losing my balance several times, an officer pulled along side of me and stopped, got out and called me to his car, getting to his car he told me to put my hands on the trunk, I complied with that.

He grabbed my hand and began to put the cuffs on me, I pulled away asking why I was being cuffed, I was told to place my hands back onto his cars trunk again.

This time I was cuffed and placed in the back seat of his squad car, after running a clean check of me, I was let out of his car, still cuffed though, as we both stood in silence for a minute.

I asked, "what's going on here with the cuffs on me?", he replied, "your drunk in public," not saying anything more, after several more minutes passed I started to walk away, he grabbed me and through me to the pavement.

5 more units arrived to the scene, that officer and 5 other ones lifted me off the ground and carried me to another awaiting squad car.

I still wasn't being told why I was being arrested though, because of my being so delusional from all of the alcohol, and the rock, I didn't ascertain that it was for being too drunk.

On the way to that awaiting squad car, another officer looking like he was overdue for his retirement stood by near a street sign at the rear of the car I was to be placed in.

As I passed the old cop he sprayed me in the face with pepper spray.

At this point I was unsure of their true intent with me and became resistant to their will as they tried placing me in the back seat of the police car, a struggle ensued and the 5 officers began wrestling me to the ground.

Still resisting their force, they smeared my face into the pavement causing multiple abrasions, one put his knee into my back, after that they drug me to the squad car.

After about ten minutes of police brutality where I received bruises to my knees, arms, and shoulders they hogtied me and put me into the squad car.

Once inside the car and lying face down, one of the officers punched me in the back of my thigh as if to give me a charley horse while I was hogtied, and made the statement of, now we have to find out where to take this scum and shoot him".

I suspected the reason why a statement like that was directed at me, was, like the Rampart squad whom were corrupt in Los Angeles, Ca, the cops now are taking their authority beyond it's limits and trying to exact their convictions in the streets.

In light of the Rodney King beating by L.A. police, I felt threatened by these public servants of society and reacted the way I did to them.

Nevertheless, I was arrested and booked into the Sacramento County jail under the charge of battery on a peace officer, and resisting arrest.

I couldn't have struck anyone of those cops due to my restraints.

I was taken to the infirmary ward to recover from the inflicted wounds, as I lay there in pain, I felt an injustice was in the making, yet, I had no immediate solution of how to counter it.

I knew this to be the very type of injustices Black men were becoming subjected to in America by and through the police and the court systems.

The officer had lied, it was a fraudulent attempt by the authorities to remove another Black man from society by incarcerating him into the California prison system, otherwise known as modern day slave plantations.

I was set on fighting the fictitious charge of battery on a peace officer, but was deterred by the public pretender when he told me that I could face a maximum of 11 years in prison if I lost at trial.

At pre-trial hearing the officers held firm in all of their allegations, even sweetening it up some, the D.A offered me thirty six months at 80%, not knowing the boundaries of the laws, and even further, being misinformed by my counsel, I took the deal.

At sentencing my counsel hadn't advised me that I was to receive a second strike, when at sentencing the judge stipulated this as part of the plea bargain I'd accepted earlier.

In fact, my counsel had stated to me that I would not receive a strike due to the un-seriousness of the charge.

In effect, I was Ill informed and deceived into accepting a guilty plea.

From these types of aberrations of justice that is pragmatic of the judicial system, and authorities of the law, the District Attorney's, and on down to the public counsels, I collectively knew why so many Black men were behind prison walls in this Country.

The new breed of racists authorities on patrol in America prioritize the mission to arrest and /or harass Blacks, then once they are placed at the mercy of a court system by a judge for further prosecution, the D.A.s', and public pretenders finish the kill through insidious deception in the court rooms.

By the statement made from officer red when I was arrested, of now we have to find out where to take this scum and shoot him, it's not unlikely for cops of this kind to purposely assassinate unarmed

Black men out there on the streets, and the courts would render it as a justified homicide.

I wrote a letter to Betta telling her to go on with her life, she wrote back saying she was returning to Fresno, perhaps it wasn't meant for us to be.

The carelessness brought on by my over indulgence in rock cocaine consumption had victimized me again, this time I'd have to be confined in a prison cell for thirty two of those thirty six months with California's new law signed into effect where an inmate does 80% of their time.

Leaving the County jail after two months I was sent to Northern California's reception center at Tracy's duel Vocational Institution.

In my three months housed there, it was phenomenal as to how many Black men had fallen up under the three strikes law, most of which had no less than 25 years, and most were for mere petty crimes.

I thought it was an invasion on justice of how the State could just take away someone's life like that.

And by my alleged conviction the system was planning to include me and many more Blacks into their scheme of lengthy imprisonment.

From Tracy I was transferred to Folsom State prison, Singer Rick James was serving out the rest of his term there for the cocaine induced rage of sadistic sex and torturous abuse on a woman while they smoked rock cocaine together.

I met him the following week after my arrival there, I shook hands with him and we talked briefly, he stated that he was so in a state of delusion while smoking grams of rock cocaine that he wasn't aware of what he had even done.

Going on to say that rock cocaine was an evil epidemic that will destroy humanity in America, and that he would never again belittle himself by indulging in that substance.

We would talk occasionally whenever the opportunity presented itself, but by us being housed in different buildings, it wasn't too often that I saw him, furthermore, he was somewhat secluded, and didn't even eat in the cafeteria.

Rick didn't look at all the way I remembered him to look as a musician with the long braids and slender build, he was instead kind of plump, with a small afro and short in stature.

It was a pleasure making acquaintances with the celebrity figure just the same though.

While at Folsom I took to reading books, there wasn't much else to do being locked in a small cell where if one extended both arms out they could touch both sides of each wall.

I read the autobiography of Malcolm X, Waiting to exhale, Luring and Loathing, by W.E.B. Dubois, the Isis papers, by Dr. Francis Cress Welsing, and a Black Panther Documentary titled a Taste of Power, Elaine Brown.

These books helped to solidify in my mind the theories that the White man in power is nefariously devilish and that with his reign of power he brings strife, dissention, chaos, racial inequality, and injustices to all people of color, and that this is an innate part of his nature as he exist on this earth.

I am not a prejudice person in any sense of the word, and I don't despise White people as a whole because I've had some great white male and female friendships.

I resent the white male power structure in this Country, for their cynicism, and evil will that dictates and brings to fruition the unjust fates of Black people and other minorities.

There is no measure of fairness dispensed to Blacks in many realms of the white ruling Classes, and now, rock cocaine affiliation and trafficking by Blacks has prompted the power structure and white America to undermine Blacks as a whole.

SELF RESOVLE

I'd read in a newspaper article written by Congress Woman Janet Reno that Blacks getting caught with small possessions of rock cocaine were sentenced more harshly than whites getting caught with large quantities of powder cocaine.

The disparity of penalties are to far and great in between, regardless of what each substance causes to happen in our society, both are from the coca plant, therefore the penalties should be the same for both substances. A year into my term I was transferred to Avenal State prison, it was March and Summer was approaching.

Avenal State prison is located dead center of California's pastureland.

When Summer came, so did the immense heat, this particular prison, although still the California dept. of Corrections, is operated by the small town residents, and bordering county residents.

Dogmatic and racist was the best terms to define the ethics of correctional officers, Sergeants, and on up to the Warden whom all enforced their rules and regulations with antics that were akin to a slave plantation.

Any of the other C.D.C. Institutions I'd served time at, I'd always be given a title 15 handbook upon arrival there, quoting rules, regulations, and guidelines.

Avenal prevents an inmate from having one, they practice injustices on a daily and regular basis, and do not want an inmate with sense and the knowledge of know how to file claims against them.

The staff instigate acts of in-subordination from an inmate so as to create a situation where an inmate will receive added time onto his sentence, in effect keeping him in the C.D.C. system longer.

Racial injustices and inequalities against Blacks was common practice there in Avenal, and although there are several Black ranking officers there, most all of them are tokens to the white ones, and go along with the mistreatment of the Black inmates.

My release date was to be May of 1997, unless I transferred to another Institution, however, the prospect of being transferred from Avenal was bleak.

Throughout this whole nightmarish ordeal of my cocaine addiction, beginning with the first encounter of freebasing cocaine, over the years, and this last encounter with rock cocaine that led up to this alleged conviction fabricated by the police, I'd missed my calling from the Lord.

Perhaps now because of this incarceration I've been given a clearer understanding of the true cynic and wicked nature of the white man, or maybe GOD has plans for me that I am not yet aware of and this period of imprisonment may serve as a revelation and a character builder for me.

Whatever the reason one thing is for sure, I have earned my edification rights as being reborn in a new light, not only through living by GODS word, but by acting as an anti-rock advocate to help deter people from attempting to commit physical, mental, and spiritual suicide by serving a false lord, the rock cocaine.

From the injustices blacks have endured from the judicial system from their involvement with rock cocaine, Im bent on exposing this wicked substance.

In light of my own Ill fated conviction and unjust imprisonment, I emphatically urge Blacks in this Country to be informed when they are arrested on the governing laws of their charge, and/or to find out for themselves about their charge by going to the law library in that jail.

Ignorance restricts one, the white man already affirms that Blacks are an un-intelligible race of people, which in part is why the system railroads Black men throughout the courtrooms in America.

I'd been studying law books in every prison I've been in, discovering that I was in fact unjustly sentenced, and have begun to put together a Habeas Corpus appeal to reverse my conviction.

I submitted it to the California Third Appellate court district, and am now awaiting a decision.

As I near the end of my term, I am comforted in heart knowing that I will contribute to a cause of enlightening Black America of the deadliness of this rock cocaine.

At the same time I hope that the Appellate court district will rule in my favor and get the Supreme court to reverse the conviction.

This reprisal itself will serve as an act to right a wrong committed by racist authorities of the law against a Black man, and open the doors of justice for Blacks in America's penal system, and pave the way for justice to be administered fairly.

My having ended up in the California's dept. of corrections prison system brought me to the harsh reality of just how suborned Government agencies are in the United States.

From the injustices of the judicial systems lengthy sentences of Black men, to the police brutality practiced on the streets of America, all reaffirms my beliefs of how pragmatic, and austere the courts become towards Black men for the smallest amount of rock cocaine, as opposed to the penalties towards powder cocaine or methamphetamine possession.

These unfair deeds by the system brought to my attention of the unjust tactics that the system enforces to incriminate the Black man in this Country, the message to Black American men is to refrain from any kind of involvement with rock cocaine because it will lead you right onto the modern day slave plantations(prison yards).

Even further, and to the rock addict, whom is a dupe, and a dupe is a non-functional liability in society, meaning that your dispensable, so wake up.

This story serves to illustrate the antipathy portrayed by the power structure in America towards Black American men, thus, in turn, endorsing the efficacy in expunging the Black man from American society, in hopes of deriving at their desired American utopia.

Through the means of rock cocaine their plan of eliminating the Black male is coming to fruition as had been projected by the power structure from the outset.

The disturbing aspect behind this obviation is that the power structures purpose of fulfilling their goal of detracting the Black man from society has become a holistic venture.

Whereby as it may have begun as simply to incarcerate violent or non-conforming Black males in society to long prison terms, however, with the new legislative laws, the system is imprisoning middle class, or otherwise decent minded Black people to prison terms as a norm.

In addition to this deplorable act of injustice, a Black man on parole is both more under surveillance and remanded back into custody on practically any and every suspicion of criminal activity that the parole board reviews as inappropriate behavior.

Moreover, in most instances the boards presiding members are racist white males, whereby a black man hasn't a chance at redeeming himself because he's guilty when he walks through the door of the board hearing session.

Therefore, the only escape from the infractions brought about by governing laws that are enforced upon the black man is that they come to the awareness that rock cocaine was designated for Blacks with the pretense of rendering them susceptible to any and all infringements presented on them by the governing laws and authorities.

Furthermore, acknowledge, rock cocaine for what the power structure designed it for, and are using it to be; a trap, and refrain from any affiliations with the substance either through selling or ingestion.

The escapades of this story are true, real, and furthermore sad, however, these are only a microdot account of the spectrum of Blacks in America whom have suffered on account of their rock cocaine addiction, and/ or distribution.

If it can happen to these individuals, so can it happen to you or anyone, I hope that whom ever sets eyes on the material in this book it will serve to both enlighten and broaden their knowledge to the many downs of the perils of rock cocaine.

I also hope that this revelation will forever prevent any persons Black or otherwise from ever entertaining the idea of smoking rock cocaine.

In closing I'd like to extend this admonishment to the rock cocaine addicts; it goes: I must say good-by now rock, I remember how much love I had for you, you and I were inseparable, I couldn't imagine life without you, I would even take a chance with the greatest miracle on earth, "my life" for you.

You took me for granted though, you misused and abused me so badly, you did not share the same love I had for you, you sent me to prison many times and led me to do wicked things to get you in my body.

You took my self esteem, and left my mind twisted, I had no compassion for anyone, not even myself, you made sure of that.

So this is good by forever rock, I have found a new and nurturing savior, and his name is JESUS, my rock and salvation.

GOD BLESS ALL

AFTERMATH AND THOUGHTS THERE AFTER

Finishing off my term for battery on a peace officer in April of 1997 at Avenal State prison, with 29 days left before paroling, My Father passed away of heart failure.

My family had made arrangements for me to be escorted by two correctional officers to his funeral service, the fee of $2,500.00 would be paid to California's dept. of corrections.

But to my surprise the Warden's subordinates denied the pass required to leave the prison facility.

The loss of my Father, accompanied with being incarcerated and not being allowed to attend the funeral services devastated me.

This again, reaffirmed my philosophy that the system is a ruthless, and wicked an entity where humanity is the issue.

I paroled May 21rst and checked in with my assigned P.O., leaving there I hit the streets.

The mode of street life had worsened, more Black on Black homicides, Tupac Shakur was killed by Alleged rival gang members.

A year later, Heavy D would be killed in retaliation of Tupac'S murder.

Rock cocaine smokers were turning snitch when caught with a lot of rock cocaine to avoid being caught up in California's three strikes and your out law, by turning informant.

Nevertheless, back into the scene I went, mainly behind the indignant feelings I developed while confined within the walls of C.D.C. when my father passed, I, as a result of it became rebellious towards any authority figures.

The following day Kat, the female's address I'd used for my mail when it came, before I went to prison, approaches me in a drug dealing area with her boyfriend.

I'd been unable to pay her for that last month of service because of my spat with the police that sent me off to prison.

In hindsight of my former lifestyle, and their repercussions from past incidents, it was now coming back to haunt me, and that still wasn't enough of a deterrent to keep me from going back into it.

This confrontation might not have come about had I not went back to that area, and changed my ways, however, her boyfriend whom wasn't even with her at the time I was receiving my mail at her place became belligerent and offensive, the situation escalated and seconds later we were fighting.

I was getting the best of the dude, and he pulled out a knife, I was weaponless, continuing to throw punches became futile, I was first stabbed in the elbow, then the forearm and last; sliced on my index finger.

I broke running to find a stick or something with which to use to even up the fight, and the dude chased my every turn of the streets, I wasn't able to locate any defense object, and after a block or so he stopped chasing me.

I stopped also, words between us were exchanged, that's when he realized that he'd come up against a street warrior, he turned and walked off.

After catching a Taxi to the U.C.D. Med center and getting stitched up I resumed my quest of trying to find some rock cocaine to smoke on.

By that weeks end I was back into that way of life again, broke, hustling, and losing that freshness one has when he's released from jail or prison.

Downtown one day a youngster shows up at the 10th and J street block park where drug dealers, prostitutes, rock smokers, alcoholics, and gang- bangers all congregate, the dude had a $900.00 beach cruiser mountain bike.

He was only asking $20.00 for it, I bought it, ride it to the Oak Park area and sell it to another young high roller(rock cocaine dealer) for a half of an ounce of rock.

I am now supplied with enough rock to sustain me for a good little while.

Staying in the mix of things so to speak caused me to neglect staying drug free for the urinal test that I had to take the following month..

Not showing up would be an automatic violation and a warrant for my arrest would issued, so I drank vinegar and a lot of water.

A week afterwards that urinal test came back positive for cocaine, and I was arrested downtown on the K street mall by two bicycle cops whom claimed of being associates with my parole officer.

Murdum, my P.O., to call him a racist would be an understatement, had previously informed these bicycle cops to arrest me on site because I'd given him a dirty urinalysis test for cocaine use.

I was starting out on what would be a total of 14 violations of my parole before finally discharging my C.D.C. number with the State on 06-01-01.

On this violation I was given 3 months with half time, on Thanksgiving day 97, I was released from Susanville State penitentiary.

The wickedness of California's penal system is exemplified by my next violation which occurred on Tuesday the following week after Thanksgiving weekend.

Due to Thanksgiving Holiday I wasn't able to report in on Thursday which was Thanksgiving, or Friday because the parole office was closed.

On Monday I report into the office, my P.O. and two others grab me as I go through the doors and cuff me up, and charged me with failure to report in.

I was taken back to Tracy, Ca, Duel vocational Institution(D.V.I.). and held there for 3 weeks without being screened by the prison board of terms.

I file a 602 form, a document that an inmate can file against wrongful actions of a C.D.C. employee's, to have them reprimanded for any injustices against inmates.

On Dec 23, D.V.I. released me for fear of facing false imprisonment charges.

California's penal system has become pragmatic of covertly and stealthily breaking their own regulations governing their own policies in hopes of slipping injustices pass inmates.

On Dec 23, 97 I was released, in one way this was a blessing because I'd be out for the Christmas Holiday, in another though it would aide in my continued destruction of my life behind my rock cocaine addiction.

My parole agent placed me in the Salvation Army shelter, later that day, and after drinking at an older guys apartment building I'd befriended a decade earlier, I left to make the 11:00 p.m. curfew at the Salvation Army.

Leaving the old mans residence, next door to him was a methamphetamine dealer.

This was an 8 story senior citizens building, I came out of the old guys place which was right in front on the Elevator, next door sitting out front was an old bicycle with a basket on the front of it, and in the basket was a backpack.

I needed a backpack to put all of my possessions in, without any money to buy a bag, I took that one and began my walk back to Sally's.

Along the way something told me to look inside of the bag, upon doing so I discovered mounds of cash, a cell phone, a females diamond ring, two men's watches, and a pouch full of change.

After 30 minutes of tallying up the fortuitous take, not only did I disregard going back to Sally's, but I was $ 1,600.00 wealthier.

Gathering together my small fortune, I hailed a cab, and had him take me to a motel so I could get a room.

The cell phone kept ringing off the hook, not bothering to answer it once, I later included the phone along with $ 100. 00 towards the purchase of an half ounce of rock cocaine.

The female ring I got appraised the next day, it was worth $1,500.00, I sold it for $200.00, the men's watches I traded for rock to the dealers.

I guess GOD was looking down upon me, and decided he'd throw me a gift to see what I'd do with it, however, my degenerate type of lifestyle took control, and after a two week run with fast woman, rock, and alcohol, and the risk of catching a new possession case, I was violated again for not reporting in, this time it was a justified violation, and all that I had came up with from my find was now in the wind so to speak.

On this violation at Solano State prison I ran into T dog, my little panhandling partner from back in the day on Broadway, he didn't fit into prison life, yet he was in there.

The caliber of young men that were being railroaded by the court systems and ending up in prison were all due to the new laws that were being in-acted by the legislative bodies in California and were akin to penal colonization.

The reality of it all made my summarize that, in view of California being exemplified as the Nations trend setter for the Country, that perhaps this form of fascism was pre- empted by this State, only later to become implemented in the Country as the new world order starts taking shape.

The saying in the BIBLE that quotes of the spirit, and the flesh being constantly at war with each other, this was becoming more relevant as a fact.

I could attest to this as it was played out in the behavior I exhibited once I'd paroled back into society again.

This manifestation of negativity and a bad behavioral pattern would come to pass once again after paroling this time.

I'd met a decent, high spirited and good looking Black Woman in her mid 30's named Angel, she was a devout Christian with a nice job, she was attracted to me by my good mannerisms and intelligence.

She was single I'd guessed because of the un-availability of a good viable Black man.

She was wise, yet vulnerable, as I would later discover about her.

Our relationship excelled from the start and remained in tact for about six months.

I moved into her apartment with her and within a month gained employment as a tell-a marketer.

My parole agent visited our place, commended my stability and the violations ceased.

I helped her as best I could financially and kept her in the dark about my past.

Beginning the sixth month of our relationship, rather than being content with this kind of a lifestyle, I opted to give into the lust of the flesh and left out one evening with $50.00 in my pocket in search of a promiscuous female and some rock cocaine.

I indulged myself all-night and into the next morning, getting back to our place the next day and not looking so fresh, I was questioned by her, and with no viable excuse, that was the beginning of our end as a couple.

One incident led to another, and within two weeks she asked me to move out of her place, this is one of the many things that rock cocaine can do to one's life.

Doing what's right can insure happiness, not only did I have something good, but I avoided violations which jeopardized my freedom.

January the 15, 99 brought another violation to me, there are what you would call rogue cops on the beat in America, particularly California.

It's questionable these days as to whether the police are out there to protect the public, or are actually legalized criminals themselves, they falsify reports, plant evidence, manipulate witnesses, among other misdeeds.

On this day I was accosted by two of these rogue cops at 8:00 p.m. downtown, discovering that I was on parole their whole demeanor changed.

I was searched, questioned why I was out at that hour, they put their flashlight beam into my eyes to detect pupil anomalies which in turn indicate drug use.

That night I hadn't smoked any rock cocaine, nevertheless, I was on a mission to smoke some.

The officer fabricated the truth by saying my eyes were dilated, they called my P.O. on his cell phone, got his approval to book me into the County jail, and a code 3056 parole hold was placed on me.

My being booked into the County jail under false pretenses would have ordinarily been followed with a release, but being on parole meant I would stay in jail until my case was heard by the board of prison terms.

With my increasing amount of violations the board would certainly recommend some time spent back behind the walls of a prison.

The board ended up giving me 8 months with half time, I be out again in June.

I began to recognize what the M.O. of the California's prison system was about, it being the monopolization, and/or capitalizing off of the cheap labor of the prisoners, in addition to their receiving federal Aide for each body in prisons.

This greed became so pervasive within the State that the Ideal of rehabilitation of convicts turned into a practice of warehousing bodies for the monetary gain for the State.

It is now become a big business industry for the State of California, whereby a person could be sent off to prison for just about any minor first time felony.

In view of California's new franchise, I started feeling like I was damned if I did right, and damned if I didn't, so my plan was from that point on to just run out my parole with violations, and discharge that number.

In my mind California was pragmatic of Romanism, and all of it's characteristics with it, inflicting atrocities upon it's citizens through, and by it's mandated laws.

This fact is portrayed, and signified by the insignia worn on the Correctional officers uniforms, where there is a Roman female wearing the high helmet on her head, and carrying a spear in her hand while she's overseeing a crowd of subservient workers on the landscape, it's makes an exemplary statement of power over the people, and complete control.

The State of California and it's controlling laws are legislated around falsehood, which is gradually being brought to light.

Doing what was right gave me a promise of stability in life, I'd experienced that kind of a life momentarily with Angel, it felt good, and wholesome, and kept me out of trouble and, prison.

Backsliding cost me the opportunity to prevail in my life and to get out of the furtive predicament I stayed in when I was out in society using rock cocaine.

Yet, in hindsight of how those racist cops fabricated a false statement about my sobriety to my P.O., I felt helpless in both scenarios, and opted to let my fate run it's course.

June came and I was free again, I began my day by riding around town on Regional Transits light rail system as I sat next to a pretty dark skinned young woman.

After making small talk she exclaimed, "Hey my brother I'm out here on these streets, and I'm trying to get high on some rock, do you know where I can turn a date?".

I knew of several old men whom would love to date this woman, so we worked up a plan that we'd both benefit from, and got off of the light rail train at the next stop, and headed towards Oak Park.

One old man I had in mind was out on his porch drinking beer, we walked up and the three of us went inside his place to discuss the issue.

The plan we presented to the old man was that $20.00 was to go to the girl and $10.00 to me, the money was issued out, and I left walking to the store so they could do their thing.

When I returned an hour later the girl was done with the old guy, and was ready to go get her fix of rock, we only needed to walk a couple of blocks to where the young rock dealers were at.

After buying the rock we cut into an alley, she brought out a glass pipe, and commenced to putting a piece of rock unto the apparatus.

The whole Oak Park area is not what you'd call a ghetto per say, however, it is a predominately Black community of Sacramento.

Dilapidated, and boarded up buildings, another remnant of the deprivation, and futilities of the rock cocaine epidemic.

That drug has laid waste to everything, and everyone it has come in contact with.

After we finished smoking the rock the girl began searching the pavement in the alley as if she'd lost something, I noticed that it wasn't a frantic search, but rather a confused state of searching.

I knew this behavior from seeing other rock smokers doing it, as well as other irate disorders when they smoked the rock.

I myself was a little spooked, not just from the side effects of the rock, but because we were smoking the substance out in the open.

I told her she was imagining something that wasn't there, and that she hadn't lost any rock on the ground, but that it was time to leave the area before the law pulled up on us.

No sooner than I'd got the last word out of my mouth the cops passed the alley way, stopped, got out of the car and approached us.

They ask what the problem was, collected our identification cards, ran checks on us, then waited for a response from the dispatcher.

I came back clean, she had a warrant for possession of rock cocaine paraphernalia, so she was hand cuffed and taken off to jail.

I had remembered her name as Tia, she was a hustler, and I liked that about her, so I set my mind on going to visit her at the County jail, her charge was only a misdemeanor, so she'd probably be set free again pending a court date.

Chance, my brother was doing well for himself, he'd gotten another good job at an area hospital, and was preparing to purchase another bigger later model BMW, he was also starting to save his money.

He'd moved into the downtown area, I stopped by his apartment before going downtown to visit Tia in jail.

I'd been grateful this time that the police hadn't harassed me for being with someone they'd arrested since I was on parole and all, and I gave that glory to GOD.

Reaching chances place I knocked on the door, he opened it after the first knock, gave me a hug, invited me in offering offered me a beer.

It was near 3:00 p.m., and time for him to head off to work, he was working the graveyard shift, so he finished his juice, went into his pocket and gave me $10.00, and took off going to catch the light rail system to work.

I walked him to the station which was a couple of blocks away then I headed for the jailhouse to visit Tia.

I didn't spend the $10.00 on rock cocaine but instead bought some alcohol with it.

After about three hours had lapsed I headed towards the jailhouse.

I was not drunk in any sense of the word, yet, when I went to the counter to check in at the visitor's window.

The deputy requested my I.D., after running a check on me he came from behind the glass window and told me to put both my hands behind my back.

While cuffing me he said I was under arrest for trespassing, and took me back to a small booth for the booking procedure.

A few minutes later another deputy arrived with a small pencil flashlight and told me to follow the light with just my eyes.

I was told to count backwards from 30 to see if my seconds were accurate to within that of a quartz clock, lastly I was told to close my eyes, then open them to see if the pupils were dilated.

All of these test I passed, I learned that these test were administered to determine drug influence, so they could charge me of being under the influence in a County facility.

However, shortly after the two young white deputies perjured their statements of my being under the influence of both alcohol and cocaine, they claimed that I was not suppose to be on County premises because I was a parolee.

It had been more than 5 hours since Tia and I had smoked that rock cocaine, the immediate lingering effects of rock cocaine had long been gone, nevertheless, I was booked into the County jail.

Three days later in court the judge dropped the charge of trespassing from a felony to a misdemeanor, and gave me a year in the County, I was also given a year violation from the board of prison terms.

To make the whole situation even worse, while I'd been waiting to see the judge, I ran into Tia in passing and she yelled out to me that she was being let out, and that she'd see me out there somewhere.

The advent of new laws being passed, and enforced by the authorities was not only pervasive, but also a breach of freedom for many, particularly parolees.

In light of the little girl Polly Klaas whom was brutally murdered by a parolee back in the 90's, the legislative law makers of California have become cynics, dogmatic, and have gone overboard with their news laws.

Polly Klaas's father after a while had become indignant behind the States use of his daughter to legislate the 3 strikes your out law, and misuse it.

His anger derived form the State having used his deceased daughter as a stepping stone to implement the 3 strikes your out law, which was supposed to be designed for serious or violent felonies, but the State abused it by sending people to prison for 25 years to life for non violent, and theft cases.

The State cajoled the man into playing host to the initiation of a law that he thought would take brutal and violent people off of the streets, when in all actuality California surreptitiously had it's own agenda at the forefront, and was paving the way to monopolize on locking people up for the smallest felony conviction.

California and it's penal system has become a pathetic travesty of justice, this is reflected every time I entered back into penal system, and observed the type of men coming into the prison system, the lot of them looked frightened, I wondered what they could have done to end up in prison.

I suspect that California is practicing a penal colonization, something akin to what Adolf Hitler was guilty of with the holocaust, only as of yet, without the killing off of masses of inmates.

After serving out my 8 months in the Branch's County jail of Sacramento, I was released again in April of 2000.

Chance had moved out and away from the downtown area, he was doing well working and saving his money, I was proud of him for that.

Holly was doing well and staying away from the rock cocaine as well.

Perhaps my lifestyle of being unemployed, and on parole played a big part of my carefree kind of attitude, and/or personality towards life at the time.

I went on involving myself in drug transactions, and affiliating myself with that sort of activity, I'd given up on trying to collaborate with my parole agent.

Like most all of them, with the exception of a few, their nothing but wolves in sheep skins carrying out their minion duties to the State of California by insuring a high rate of parole recidivism.

In May, I got to the parole office late one day, I was detained in the office and taken down to the jail house, and booked in with a penal code 3056 parole hold under the charge of not following instructions.

At my board hearing they gave my a year eligible for half time, I was sent to Soledad State prison, one of the many I'd come to call penal colonization camps of California.

Soledad wasn't too bad though, compared to many of the other ones I'd been to, while there I'd gotten a job in the diary farm which was the P.I.A., (Prisons Industry Association) is considered the elite positions to have in the workforce of the State prison system.

I was able to save $300.00 over a period of 5 months from my $70.00 a month income from P.I.A., I served 6 and a half months there and was released on Dec the 10th.

Two days later waiting to catch the R. T. bus line at 10:30 p.m. to my mothers house, I was accosted by two racist rogue bicycle officers.

Their claim was that I was loitering in a drug area, so they searched me, found nothing on my person, so, using a cell phone they called my P.O. saying to him that I was hanging around a drug area.

My P.O. told them to take me down to the County jail and book me in.

I was standing by a bus stop awaiting the arrival of a bus, however, in the downtown area youngsters from both the bloods and crips frequent the area to sell their rock cocaine.

This misfortune of being at the right place, but the wrong time was certainly an injustice, though I was guilty of nothing I was on my way back to prison again.

Back in front of the prison board, I was given 10 months illegible for half time, the one thing that my parole agent said to me at the hearing that was sweet to my ears was that I would discharge my number with them upon leaving what ever prison I was sent to this time.

It was a revelation that was a long time coming for me, I had been so eagerly awaiting it to come around, and it finally had.

I was sent back to old Folsom, the very worst prison in the system for many reasons.

I'd passed through Old Folsom in 1995 when I was allegedly accused of battery on a peace officer in Sacramento.

Now I was ending my tenure with the California dept. of corrections in the very same place I'd started it all out at.

Being in Old Folsom again was an affirmation for me of the true savagery, pure disdain, and loathe of heart that the white man feels towards black people.

It was played out everyday there at Folsom in a variety of scenarios, through their mannerisms, and/or the discriminatory actions towards the black men in the different housing units.

Feeling what my ancestors must have endured in the slave era while I was there, my modern day enslavement finally came to an end and I was free from any other imprisonment from the California Dept. of Corrections.

But of course the real test was to come when I would be faced with the temptation to use the rock cocaine ever again while I was out in society.

I suspected, and felt strongly that the U.S Government was culpable, and conspiratorially behind the advent, and administration of rock cocaine.

This transgression committed by the U.S. Government towards Blacks has in effect caused many decent law biding Black people, other minorities, and now many underprivileged Whites, and some yuppies to fall victim to the penal system in this Country simply because of this rock cocaine.

There is, and always has been a double standard in America with regard to Blacks and Whites, and their power of influence or not in America, or whom is entitled to wield it, and of course the differentiation between the have and the have not's.

However, proposition 36 in California opened up a relief door for controlled substance abusers, in hindsight though, this bill is good but was introduced much too late; after the fact, when it could have salvaged many Blacks from being sent off into the penal system for possession.

This rock cocaine is so addictive and destructive, and has now attracted so many White people, the California legislature felt it necessary to provide an outlet for the white rock cocaine abusers as an alternative to prison.

Where was this reprieve for the millions of Black rock cocaine abusers?

In retrospect I felt violated by the U.S. Government to whom is the culprit that has compromised the prospect of myself, as well as the many other Blacks in this Country by means of subjugation to the State, local, and federal authorities: all behind the advent of rock cocaine.

Hindsight has brought me to the acute reality that there never was really a war on drugs, but rather a war against Blacks in this Country.

Deprivation and inequality is not gone, it is a façade with a veneer that renders it more acceptable the way it's being administered now upon Blacks and other minorities.

Rock cocaine was the end to justify the means by which the Black race have become victims of this American society.

In light of this revelation I will now be on guard against the stealthy persona of the White man in this U.S. of America.

I am now free of the clutches of a racist, fascist, dogmatic, and demonic penal system, however, the battle is just beginning over again for me, only on a different front.

I must stay watchful for any and all snares and traps that maybe set for me by the wicked plotting of the power structure in this Country as a whole.

The machinations that accompanies their agenda is a Nationwide and intransigent one, with the sole goal of destroying Black men in America.

There are two quality attributions that the Black race of people have that insures their survival on this earth, but also perturbs the white race.

Them being, one, that Black people are a spiritual being that constantly seeks out GOD in the their quest for overcoming adversities that are put before them, and secondly, their innate ability to adapt in dire circumstantial adversities.

I will pick up the shattered pieces of my life, put back together what is salvageable and build from that, because it's not over for me until the earth I came from reclaims me.

To all rock cocaine addicts or abusers the important thing to remember is to always put GOD first, and to, in prayer, ask him to give you the will to leave this vicious substance of destruction they call rock cocaine alone; because you can not serve and/or walk with the lord, and at the same time run with the devil.

Rock cocaine in it's true form is the devil, and by a person constantly under the influence of it, that drug becomes the tool of their worship to the devil and they are controlled by it.

The end result is deprivation, and subjugation to the wrath of the wicked authorities of the white power structure in the U.S. of America.

EPILOGUE

In conclusion of my story I'd like to elaborate further on the wickedness of this rock cocaine epidemic, and how the substance has evolved over the decades past.

It's evident that our Federal Government does things of importance covertly, I'm reflecting back now when one could smoke rock cocaine and just get a good head rush without that element of paranoia that's associated with it now, as opposed to the rock cocaine that one smokes to date.

Theoretically speaking, our U.S Government may be in the business of experimenting with much of the huge seizures of cocaine from major drug bust, and fabricating that seized cocaine through covert experiments on it to derive from it their desired debilitative concoction, and allow that substance to in turn be redistributed back into the streets of America.

By tampering with I mean that they've experimented with and/or added other ingredients to the cocaine while it's stored in their warehouses.

I remember while in prison I read a book titled the protector, although fiction, the issue I'm going to elaborate on leaves room for imagination about what our government can do without our knowledge and then set their wrath loose upon certain groups in society.

In the book their was a C.I.A. operative whom was assigned as head guardian over a top secret weapon, but the agent defected and harbored the weapon for himself.

The weapon was an air mist, or vapor if you will, that when released into an environment caused intense paranoia upon it's recipients, leading them to act irrational, in a manner that could result in either their own deaths, or the deaths of many.

I'm relating this type of a scenario with the characteristics that develop when one smokes the rock cocaine and becomes paranoid.

This is just my personal speculation of course to the possibility that this type of a scenario could be playing out through the rock cocaine that's in society today.

This type of a mind altering substance is not out of the realm of possibilities that our Government could utilize to destroy the masses of people in secret.

This is just speculation on my part of course, but in light of how the C.I.A was rumored of being behind the big influxes of cocaine coming into the U.S in the Oliver North trial, I wouldn't exclude them as suspect in this.

Freeway rick was a part of the C.I.A's covert operation in the advent of the rock cocaine epidemic in Los Angeles, Ca.

He was a pawn for our power structures purpose of introducing rock cocaine to the Black populace in America, beginning in Los Angeles.

They utilized his worth to them, then laid most all of the Blame to him alone as the main culprit in this scheme of their conspiratorial rock cocaine epidemic.

In the end of it all, he was given a life sentence for his role in their scheme of things, but was later given a commuted sentence of lessor time, with time served and was let out after serving many years in prison.

No other prominent public figure in our Government whom was responsible for the launch of operation rock cocaine was ever indicted or served prison terms.

The long term side effects associated with chronic rock cocaine use, and abuse that I sustained was an enlarged heart artery.

I have run into 2 acquaintances from my past that have spoke on individuals we both knew of, both were rock cocaine addicts of three decades, both, in separate incidents took a hit of rock and died on the spot of a heart attack.

My point and case being, is that catering to this rock cocaine offers it's users a short life full of unusual and precarious predicaments.

So to all people whom reads this book, take to heart the message here and see this rock cocaine for what it truly is, a destructive substance of the devils that is designed to destroy and/or kill you, and either stop using it if you currently are, or never try the substance if you haven't.

GOD BLESS, IM OUT.

Printed in the United States
By Bookmasters